THE UNWANTED QUEEN

THE CARTOGRAPHER'S WAR
BOOK FOUR

ALLISON ANDERSON

OLIVERHEBERBOOKS

For Chase Aiden Manzo
You and Trent were the first boys to ever make me feel like a princess.
You are missed every day.

1
AGONY AND FORTITUDE

PAIN RIPPED THROUGH PENNY—A LIVING, BREATHING MONSTER RAGING inside of her. The magic scraped its scorching claws through Penny's body, and she screamed.

Or at least she thought she screamed. There wasn't noise wherever she was. Only pain.

Always pain.

She bucked against it, hoping, praying, begging the Goddess to make the magic let go of her. It only sank in its roots deeper. The well of plant magic within her broke apart, shredded by the burning, clawing, ravaging monster beating down her defenses. Devouring everything inside her.

But all of this had to be worth it. Something deeply buried underneath the pain and the magic held her resolve. There was a purpose to this suffering, this agony.

A flash of amber streaked through the waves of green and hurt.

There was a reason she had subjected herself to this seemingly endless torment. If only she could remember what it was...

"By the Goddess, I tried to get back to you. I had dreamed up so many adventures..."

. . .

"Do you want to know something funny? There hasn't been a day since we met when I didn't think of you. Did you..."

"I need you to be all right."

"Please, Penelope."

"Just open your eyes."

Penny's limbs lay heavy, not responding to the simplest commands of her clouded mind. This had to be what being stuffed with cotton felt like.

Why did she want to move again? The reason had already been lost in the fog that crowded every particle of her being. Except her skin. It prickled, as if she'd been struck by lightning.

What was wrong with her?

She swallowed, finally finding movement, but the rawness of her throat didn't allow for much saliva to pass. A groan slipped between her lips.

Noise broke through her cotton-stuffed skull. Voices, though none of the words being said registered through the fog. By the Goddess, her head hurt.

"Penelope?"

Penny's heart picked up immediately. She turned in the direction of that deep, warm voice she craved. But there was nothing there. The dark surrounding her didn't allow even a glimpse of his golden eyes or serious face. He was always so serious.

"Open your eyes for me."

Now that he'd said it, all Penny's attention homed in on her outrageously itchy eyelids. When she'd been younger, she played once in the wool cuttings in the sheep barn in Delphine when visiting Paulo and Diana. She'd been itchy from the fine hairs in her clothing for hours afterward, even expelling the stuff from her nose for the entire ride home. It had been nearly as uncomfortable as this.

The brush of fingertips trailed over her forehead. "Please, love." The voice was a haunting whisper in her ear. "Wake up."

Penny reached up to wipe the sheep fluff from her eyes and blinked. The light in the room burned and she shut her eyelids again with a hiss. She rubbed at them with her heels of her hands and pried them open again, finding Aiden's familiar face as she blinked away the itchiness.

A smile stretched at her cheeks. "Hello."

He blew out a breath and rested his head against hers. "Why do you always have to scare the living shadows out of me?"

Penny chuckled, the vibration of it scratching at her throat hard enough to make her cough. "Someone has to keep you on your toes. You can't always be the scariest thing in the room."

A throat cleared from behind Aiden, and he shifted away from her. Penny almost cried out in response. She didn't want him to leave. But he did, revealing the fae standing behind him with vibrant lavender hair. His keen, amber eyes studied her, a laugh swimming in their depths. How long had he been standing there, watching them? By the Goddess, who was this? She blinked up at him a few times.

What on Gaia's—

The revel!

The fog in her brain opened up a sliver.

This was Aiden's—no *High King Aedon of Faerie's* family, the family he'd found since coming to Faerie. Faerie, where he'd been stolen from Olympia, and she'd come looking for him. Where she'd found him at the revel. Where the folk had been celebrating his new title as High King. Where she'd crashed the party and eaten the fruit. The very Faerie fruit the Gray Man had told her not to eat and that would possibly entrap her in the fae kingdom for the rest of her life.

"Oh no," she whispered.

"Indeed, Penelope," said the fae—she tried to recall if she'd learned his name but couldn't. He pulled up a chair beside Aiden's, crossing his boots over the coverlet near her feet.

Oh, she was in a bed. Sweet Gaia, her thoughts were cloudier than Olympia's sky when King Dion was in a foul mood. She pushed up to sit and Aiden immediately jumped forward to help her. The temptation to bat him away so she didn't look like an invalid warred with the desire to allow him to touch her to get her upright. The latter won out, and she gave Aiden a smile before returning her attention to the fae.

"I find myself at a disadvantage," Penny said, "as you know my name, but we have yet to be formally introduced."

He cocked his head to the side. "I am Dair."

Dair. He'd been standing with Aiden's family. He *was* Aiden's family. The family that was trying to replace the one they'd stolen him from, the one left behind in Olympia.

Penny narrowed her eyes. "I would say it's a pleasure to meet you, Dair, but as I have no idea what's going on, I think you and I would both recognize it for the lie it is." Not that she was bitter or anything. These people were just the ones that had made her journey here difficult. If Aiden hadn't been taken, none of this would be happening right now. No, she would be back in Olympia working on squashing Adira's rebellion instead of facing off with a smug fae.

The corner of Aiden's mouth twitched. Penny was probably the only one who would have noticed.

"You were certainly less snarky when you slept." Dair smirked. "I assume those peaceful days are over now."

"*Days?*" Penny's head snapped back toward Aiden. "How long was I asleep?"

"Three days," Aiden said.

"Much shorter than Aiden's little drama moment," Dair chimed in.

"What does that mean?" Had something happened to him? Had they hurt him when he first arrived in Faerie? Perhaps he'd had the same reaction to the fruit as she did.

Aiden waved it off. "It doesn't matter. What matters is why *you* are *here.*"

"Where are we?" she asked.

"We're still in Crann Mór."

Penny glanced around the room. She could see the wooden grain on the walls now that he'd mentioned it. The large, bare space felt empty, even with the humongous bed and the chairs gathered around it. No decorations hung on the walls. No curtains on the windows. She closed her eyes, reaching out with her gift.

A hurricane of magic slammed into her.

Flashes beat against her mind.

Darkness. Light.

Life. Death.

Cold. Heat.

Bliss. Pain.

She cried out, lost in the tumult of it.

That raging monster she'd just released herself from stirred.

The magic went still, though it surrounded her as if she were in the eye of the storm rather than outside of it. She could still feel everything happening around her, the monster pulling at the edges of her consciousness, but a stillness held her in its arms.

Let go, Penelope.

She tried to find a way out of the storm. By the Goddess, it was like wrenching a piece of her soul out from the rest of it, but she pulled the piece that was actually her back into her body. Her chest heaved and she nearly lost the contents of her stomach—whatever was left in there after three days. Stars shimmered on the edges of her vision as the green of her arms flickered.

"Let go, Penelope," Aiden repeated, one of his hands wrapped around one of her green ones. The bright color finally settled into the deep bronze of her skin. Her head fell back against the pillow.

"What was that?" She still sounded breathless.

"*That* was the consequences of your actions," Aiden said, returning to his seat, but not relinquishing her hand. She was glad for it. His hold on her kept her there.

"What did you see?" Dair asked, feet back on the floor and head tipped to the side. "When you tried to connect to your magic, what did you feel?"

"Everything." Penny blinked a few times, trying to wrap her head around it. "I felt so much I couldn't even begin to describe it."

Dair shared a look with Aiden. "Has that happened with your gift before?" he asked her.

Penny shook her head. "And I've connected to the Tree before, but it wasn't anything like what just happened."

Dair's brow turned contemplative as he studied her. "I do not know what to make of it. We have never had a mage eat the *toradh na beatha*."

A new voice entered the conversation. "Or if they have, they did not live to tell the tale."

Penny turned and noticed the hulking shadow blocking the doorway.

The Lòchran.

The assassin stepped fully into the room. His sword peeked out from behind his shoulder, the purple gem on its hilt glittering menacingly.

"Here to finish the job?" Penny quipped. She reached under her pillow but realized she did not have one of her daggers stashed there. In fact, she didn't know where any of her weapons were. Who had taken them? She looked down at the unfamiliar nightdress she wore. Someone had obviously changed her clothing while she slept. Embarrassment creeped up the back of her neck.

"Looking for this?" The Lòchran lifted one of her daggers up for her to see. He tossed it onto the coverlet next to her before she could say anything. "Do not fret, Little Sapling. I would not dream of facing you unarmed."

"Come a little closer and you'll find just how little I need that blade."

"All right!" Aiden stood, coming around the bed to stand between her and the Lòchran. "There is no need to be fighting, Penelope." He turned to the assassin. "Please don't provoke her."

He was blaming *her*? "Excuse me? I'm not the crazy fae assassin that came in here waving a knife around!"

Aiden rolled his eyes. He actually rolled his eyes at her! He never did that, much less at her. "Thaen did no such thing." He glared between the two of them, his levity from the moment before completely gone, and the new High King coming into focus.

"You're defending that cursed blackguard?" She blinked up at him. By the Goddess, this conversation had devolved quickly. Heat spread along her chest. "Even after he tried to kill me? On *multiple* occasions?"

"Penelope, if he'd been sent to kill you, you'd be dead." He rubbed at his temples. "In fact, he was under specific directions *not* to kill you, so we could *send you home*." His voice dripped thick with exasperation.

This conversation had been coming since the moment her mind cleared. She crossed her arms tightly over her chest, doing her best not to grab for the dagger at her feet. "I will not be going home."

His amber eyes flashed. "You blasted saw to *that*, didn't you?" he asked.

Penny almost shrank back, but she couldn't cower from this. She had to own it with her whole being if Aiden was ever going to allow her to stay. "By the Goddess, of course I did! You can't just allow Adira—the very person threatening your kingdom—through the Mist, *King Aedon*. We can't allow her to discover who created it. It's exactly what she wants! We have to keep her cut off from the rest of the rebels until we can find her."

The room quieted, the silence thick and visceral.

Penny studied the three males faces, each a picture of despair. "What happened?"

"It is too late," the Lòchran said quietly.

Her eyes flicked from frown to frown. "What's too late?"

"The Fuath—the *Mist*," said Dair, "it is gone."

The words hit Penny harder than if Adira had punched her in her newly healed ribs. "How? When?" She looked up at Aiden. She told him at the ball Adira was looking for the fae still keeping the border up. "Who created it? When I escaped her camp, she had no idea who it was. There couldn't have been enough time—"

"She saw him," Dair cut in. "She saw him use his magic after you ate the fruit. She must have figured it out then."

Penny's stomach dropped. "Who was it?"

"Fiadh," Aiden answered. He gestured to the other two. "Their father."

The Lòchran and Dair's faces fell further, the fresh anguish wrinkling around their eyes.

"I'm sorry," Penny said. She turned back to Aiden. "I went to the revel knowing Adira planned to be there. She told me she had every intention of killing you at the revel. Once I got there, I realized that likely wasn't her plan at all. She's too conniving to try something she probably wouldn't have survived."

"So, you went to protect me?" Aiden asked, his voice low and simmering with something Penny couldn't name.

"I went to warn you," she replied hurriedly. "I knew she was intent on taking down the Mist. I only knew that if you sent me home, she would strike. All of us would have been in danger if you unlocked the Mist."

"Don't you think I knew that too?" he snapped back. He began pacing next to the bed. "Did you actually think I was going to just pop open the Mist and shove you through without thought? Skies, Penelope, I would have come up with some kind of plan!"

She shook her head, blinking back tears. "It wouldn't have been enough. How much do you want to bet she allowed me to get into that revel for the sole fact that you would send me home? Or that she would get the answers she sought? She knows both of us too well. I had to change the game."

He ran a hand through his hair, a very obvious indication to Penny that he was distressed about more than just her being there. "But your plan failed, and you doomed yourself anyway."

"I didn't know!" With deep breaths, she swallowed back her anger, returning her voice to a normal volume and blinking back her frustrated tears. He was already upset. Yelling wouldn't help the situation and crying certainly wouldn't help her. "Would you have let me stay? All you've ever done is push me away when things get tough. I wasn't about to let you do it again because you thought it was what was best for me. I'd rather die a hundred times than allow Adira Durant—"

"*Don't you ever say that!*" Aiden's voice thundered. The walls of the Tree shook, and shadows billowed over his shoulder. "Don't you *ever* act like your life isn't as important as beating her. We've lost too blasted many to Durant and her cursed schemes. I will not allow any more to die for her revenge against me!"

"Then you can't play into her hands!" Penny pointed toward the door. Her control over her voice obliterated and tears pooled at her lashes. "Do you know how many of *your* people, your fae citizens I watched be dragged into her camp and tortured? Do you know how many left the prison tent she kept me in for weeks and never came back?" She wiped a falling tear off her cheek. "This isn't just about you anymore. It's about everyone and all I did was my best to keep everyone safe. If you'd just listened to me—"

"You have no idea what you were asking of me, Penelope." Aiden's jaw tightened, shadows twining through his hair. "I could never have let you stay. That wasn't an option."

"Neither was going back and letting Adira near the Mist." Penny clenched her flickering hands under her blanket. "She's a *monster* and if you even got within a hundred yards of the border, she would've been on you in a second with the magic she's stolen from those she's tormented."

"You can't say that she would have for sure," Aiden ground out through his teeth. He stopped, staring at her. His eyes followed the traitorous tear that slipped over her cheek. His shoulders fell, and he hung his head. "And now it doesn't even matter. She got exactly what she wanted. The Mist is gone, and you're trapped here."

Penny tried to meet his eyes, but he wouldn't look at her. "You can't say that she wouldn't have anyway. Neither of us can even be sure about what she will do, but I *am* sure I made the right decision to eat that fruit." In fact, it almost felt like fate. Something had pulled her in the direction of the blue beads of fruit on that table. Something had made her swallow each of those six tiny seeds. Intuition sounded so small with how large it felt. Destiny might have been a better word.

But the look in Aiden's eyes when his head snapped up told her that would be the wrong thing to say. "You were wrong, Penelope. It was *not* the right decision."

Penny bit her lips together to keep from screaming. Anger clawed up her throat and it took everything in her not to let it come roaring out. She wouldn't convince him of her choice if he got too angry. That stubborn steel in his eyes attested to it.

A knock sounded at the door. Both fae went to answer.

Penny stared up at Aiden and he stared down at her, locked in a battle Penny didn't know if she would win.

"Cousin," the Lòchran's strained voice rang through the room. "The preparations are completed, and they are waiting for you."

Aiden blew out a deep breath, and the shadows twitched around his arms as he called them back. "We will finish this conversation later, Penelope." He strode toward the door.

"What?" Penny asked indignantly. "You're just going to leave?"

"Maybe if you have some time to yourself, you'll see why your decision was a terrible one." He strode toward the door without looking at her.

Penny balked. "So, you're going to leave me behind in my room like a naughty child, King Aiden?"

Aiden whirled back. "Perhaps you'll stop acting like a child if I treat you like one." He adjusted the waist of his fine jacket and ran shaking fingers through his disheveled hair. "Now, if you'll excuse

me, I have a funeral to conduct and a kingdom to prepare for war."
With those last words, he stomped from the room.

Every bit of anger and frustration sprouting in Penny's heart
withered instantly.

Dair and the Lòchran remained standing where they were, their
shoulders hunched up in obvious discomfort.

"Well, what are you two gawking at?" She hung her head. "The
spoiled child is obviously waiting for you to go so she can throw a
full-blown temper tantrum."

The two fae sped through the door as fast as their increased abili-
ties could take them.

With them went all of Penny's control. A sob shuddered through
her, and she drew her knees up to her cheeks as the rest of the tears
fell.

What had she done?

2

STUBBORN

IT SHOULD BE RAINING.

That was what happened in stories right? Not that Aiden read as much as Penelope, but he felt that was how it went. When the heroes fall and the people mourn, the sky mourns with them. But even with the early spring weather and the storm swirling within the Tree behind him, the sky looked as bright and cheerful as a summer day.

Aiden hated it.

He hated that he would remember this day with fine weather and birds singing. He hated that everyone would walk home in the warm afternoon light, back to their lives without soggy boots and limp hair. He hated that no one would feel a fraction of the hurt he did— aside from the three folk flanking him.

The image of Fiadh falling, bolt sticking out of his back, haunted Aiden's waking and sleeping hours alike.

Aiden stared at Fiadh's body, laid to rest in the soil. There was a sacred place at the base of Crann Mòr where the dead were buried and their spirits returned to the Goddess's loving arms as their bodies decomposed to feed the Tree and give it new life. Fiadh lay there, completely wrapped in black linen and surrounded by fresh blooms and enchanted snowflakes alike.

Shirina stepped forward, a violet freesia in her hand. She marched toward the deep hole where her beloved lay. No words were necessary to express the anguish she felt. It was written in every piece of her being and bled out onto the frozen ground around them. With tears streaming down her face, she used her shadow to lay the single bloom on her husband's chest and stepped away.

The twins each wrapped an arm around their mother when she returned to her place at Aiden's side. All three of them wept silently as Aiden stepped forward.

He didn't know what he would say. The Council had claimed it customary for the High Ruler to speak of the deceased at such things, but nothing about this felt right. Fiadh's death didn't feel right, but he deserved the funeral of a king and Aiden would do his best to give it to him.

Aiden cleared his throat. "I don't think I have the appropriate words to express the sorrow I feel today. This kingdom has lost a great husband, father, and leader. Fiadh cared about everyone he met and strived to do the best he could to help those he felt a responsibility toward. He may have only officially been Winter's King for a handful of hours, but those he watched over and cared for knew him as their king for years prior to that."

He pushed back the lump in his throat. "He taught me what it is to be fae, to feel pride in my family and my heritage. He taught me about the love Danu has for all of Her children and how to be the person She knows I can be. Without Fiadh, many of us would be adrift, for more reasons than one. I am heartbroken that he will no longer guide us from this plane, but I know him to be one of the best of us, and I know the Goddess receives the best of us with open arms."

Aiden shuddered and pushed down the sob he felt building in his chest. There would be time for crying later. His eyes focused on Shirina and the twins for a moment. For them, he could give this. He raised a fist to his heart and the rest of the crowd followed suit. Honoring the fallen was the least he could do. With a nod of his head, four members of the Day Court stepped forward, hands splayed toward the rich soil cradling Fiadh's still form. On cue, the fae's hands pushed forward, sending the dirt tumbling into the hole. Fiadh's black silhouette was lost to the Land in moments.

A soft hand landed on Aiden's shoulder. Shirina's red-rimmed eyes met his. "The Council has asked for your presence in the Council Chamber."

He nodded and set his hand over hers. "I'll go. You should get some rest while it's light out."

Shirina shook her head as a tear slipped out. She wiped it away with the back of her hand.

"Shirina," he said in a quiet voice, "whenever you're ready to speak with him, tell me. I can at least give you that closure, though you can't be with him as you once were." It was the least he could offer. He'd never summoned the spirit of a fae back through to speak with them, but with access to so many of Fiadh's most precious belongings, Aiden would have a tether strong enough to see him, if only in spirit. His gift to commune with the dead could be useful when he wished it to be.

Shirina met his eyes, her own onyx ones glittering with unshed tears and heartbreak. It was obvious his words had sent her to war within herself. She grabbed his hand, her fingers gripping his as if he could keep her from falling to pieces.

"I appreciate your offer, but even though I wish it with every fiber of my being, now is not the time." She took a shuddering breath. "We have work to do, Aiden. Fiadh's killer is still out there somewhere, and our people are dying. We can talk after all of this is over. I will see him on the other side of this battle. He would not be proud of me if I shirked my duties for a few tears. Besides"—she gave him a watery smile—"Fiadh always told me I was stronger than the mountains that held up our beloved city. Let us go see if he was right."

Aiden's thoughts pounded against his skull like a blizzard against the Winter Palace walls. He tried to reign them in. He needed to be clear-headed going into the High Councilors' presence. Proving he could handle a situation in a high emotional state could be crucial. He was High King of Faerie, and he would show his kingdom what he was made of.

He burst through the doors, startling the Councilors gathered around the table. His family followed him in, and he closed the door behind them.

"My Sovereign," Spring's High Councilor—*Deireadh*, Aiden had finally learned—greeted him. "There is much we must discuss."

"I agree," he said, coming to the table. "Our guest has finally awakened and has much to say in regard to the rebels' presence in our kingdom."

"*Guest?*" Rìgh of Summer spat, his face nearly turning the same blue of his robes. "Are we truly going to treat this *mage* as a guest here? She partook of our sacred fruit, desecrated some of our most esteemed traditions, and flaunted her blasphemous power—"

"I would be cautious of your next words, Councilor," Shirina warned, disapproval written clearly across the furrow of her brow. She might not agree with Penelope's presence, but she knew Aiden's feelings well enough to know he wouldn't appreciate the Councilor's barbs.

"Why should we allow such a filthy—"

"*Enough!*" Aiden boomed. "Penelope Barclay is under my protection and will be treated as an *esteemed guest* for as long as she resides within my kingdom. Am I clear?"

Rìgh's jowls quivered in anger, but he bowed his head in acquiescence. Having Penelope there was going to be more difficult than Aiden thought if he had to keep having this conversation with his councilors, let alone the entirety of his kingdom.

"Now," said Aiden, "there's much to do and not much time. First, is there any way to break the bond tied to Penelope so we can return her home?"

Glances were exchanged around the group. Sgiath stepped forward. "There is no account of any mortal breaking the bond or leaving the Land without serious repercussion. The longest anyone lived after attempting such a thing has been no longer than a week. Their entire being is literally bound here, since the magic of the Land must attach to the magic of their life force without the benefit of a gift to hold onto."

"Are we sure the magic even attached to her?" Deireadh of Spring asked. "There has never been an account of a mage eating the *toradh na beatha*. We cannot be sure what it will do to her."

"I have sensed the bond," Aiden said. He had felt it snap into place the moment Penelope had fallen into his arms. She was now as trapped as he was. "I don't know how it works, but I know it's there."

"If the bond has already solidified, there is not much we can do," Sgiath stated. "I can invite my wife to the capital to evaluate Penelope, and perhaps we should call on the Andàn for their guidance as

well. There is much we do not know, and we should use this opportunity to learn what we can."

Shirina nodded her head. "I agree with Sgiath. This should be
viewed as an opportunity to seek the Goddess's will. The Aunties are
an obvious source of knowledge."

"And where should we keep the mage while we conduct our
research?" Rìgh of Summer asked. "We cannot allow it to wander
about."

Aiden ground his teeth together but kept the growl he wanted to
shoot at the fae to himself. "*She* will be treated with the same respect
as anyone else. With the same freedoms and expectations as any
member of our kingdom. Anyone who questions that will find themselves in a very... *uncomfortable* position." Like with his sword in their
stomach.

Deireadh's lips tugged down at the corners. "There are many in
this kingdom who would see her presence here as blasphemy—especially after eating of the *toradh na beatha*. She would not be safe going
off on her own."

"She won't be alone," Aiden said. "She will remain with me for
the entirety of her stay."

"But that is not viable either, Little Shadow." Shirina set a hand
on his arm. "You are High King. There are some places, and some
conversations, Penelope cannot be privy to. Besides, she is a young
woman. You cannot be with her all the time without igniting a bit of
a scandal. Not unless you married her." Shirina gave him a knowing
look. They had discussed it before. No matter how much it hurt, his
marrying Penelope could never truly happen.

"Absolutely not!" Rìgh looked ready to swoon at the very
suggestion.

Sgiath nodded. "It would certainly add more chaos to the situation, which I do not think would be advisable at the moment."
Though, Sgiath's eyes twinkled, as if imagining said chaos. Aiden's
mood lightened a fraction at the Councilor's mirth. Autumn folk
could be absolute terrors when they wanted to be.

"Fine," Aiden grumbled. Faerie might have had some less
demanding societal rules than Olympia, but they would certainly
view his constant attention to Penelope in a bad light. "But as my
guest, and as someone who has insider knowledge of the rebels, I
expect her to be treated with the utmost care."

Deireadh thumped his wooden staff on the solid floor. "We will see it done, My Sovereign. However, there is more that we would discuss with you."

Aiden's spine straightened. "What else?"

The Councilors and Aiden's cousins all settled into chairs as Aiden paced in front of the crescent shaped table. The rest of the meeting went on to discuss what new methods would be implemented to find Durant after her attack at the revel and Fiadh's murder as well as what to do about the border. Messengers would need to be sent to Dion. They had multiple parties of scouts and trackers out searching the forests in Spring as well as patrols guarding the border and the rivers sectioning off each land. With the Aigeans involved, they had to watch every body of water as well as the rebel encampments. Aiden repeated what Penelope said about Durant's captives and the results of Fiadh's death.

That led to the conversation still gnawing at Aiden's insides.

"We simply do not have the fae power to take back Summer," Sgiath said. "Even if we were to muster a force, most of the folk have no training."

"They need to be trained," said Thaen.

Aiden paced the length of the table they gathered around. "Would a draft be necessary?"

Rìgh steepled his fingers. "Perhaps, though I imagine there will be many who volunteer. The Tuatha Dè Dannan are a proud race with a proud heritage."

"Perhaps it would be wise to call more council to our cause," Deireadh suggested. "I know there are a handful of others left from the Faerie Wars that could offer something to our council. All but a few members of the Summer Court left after the revel, but it seems we may need to gather together once again to take down this foe."

"I agree," Aiden said. "Perhaps there's something we're missing, and they could offer some insight." Aiden just prayed they could all gather together without too much trouble. They were already fighting a war against the rebels. The last thing they needed was a war within themselves.

The logistics came together. A fortress stood at the base of Eagallach's peaks, still in residence by one of the Winter nobles. Shirina knew the family and had Dair begin drafting a letter to gain permission to use it as a training ground for fighters. Between himself and

Thaen, Aiden was sure they could get the encampment up and running with drills and weapons training within the week. Sgiath mentioned a similar place in Autumn, a werewolf encampment that would be the ideal place to gather an army together. The werewolf alpha had apparently been a general in the Faerie Wars. Aiden would add him to the list of council members and have him lead the folk gathering in Autumn.

"Speaking of the Courts together, there has been word from Autumn about the Summer refugees." Sgiath crossed his arms and leaned back in his chair. "There have been several skirmishes in the last day or so between the Summer and Autumn fae."

Apparently, peace within the Courts was too much to ask for. "What kind of skirmishes?" Aiden asked.

"The Summer Court is demanding refuge where they should not. They have tromped through sacred grounds and attempted to rouse tumult in the towns they travel through."

Rìgh harrumphed. "These folk have just lost their homes and the Autumn fae are being greedy."

Sgiath scowled. "Greed is not determined by what you hold sacred or the boundaries you are unwilling to cross. Greed is taking that which does not belong to you simply because you think you are entitled to it rather than having to work for what you are given."

"These are *refugees* we are talking about," Rìgh countered. "They have had everything they worked for snatched from them, and you are not willing to help them."

"I never said we were unwilling," Sgiath argued. "I simply said the Summer Court needs to adhere to the rules we have established. Without order, there is only chaos."

Rìgh jutted out his chin. "Everything is already—"

"This squabbling is getting us nowhere," Aiden interrupted. The two Councilors quieted. "While I agree that the Summer fae should have our sympathies, we cannot expect Autumn fae to give them everything they demand. We must meld the two people as best we can for the time being." He turned to Rìgh. "What can we do to help the Summer folk find peace and a semblance of security?"

"Giving them a safe place to land. Brònach is far, and while some are planning on coming to the capital, many wish to stay close to home in the event that the Aigeans leave."

Aiden shook his head. "We must not assume anything at the

moment. While I agree they should have hope, we cannot know what the end of this war will look like. We need to prepare for the event that Flùranach becomes unsalvageable."

He turned to Sgiath. "How can we aid the Autumn folk with such a transition? Is it too much to ask for them to give up a piece of land?"

"We have designated a portion of wood outside Brònach—"

"An uninhabitable wasteland more like!" Rìgh cut in. "My cousin sent word of the conditions of that land. Barren, without good ground or a large enough stream nearby."

"We do not have much above ground water running at this time of year," Sgiath said. "Our water comes from the Winter mountains and will thaw as we get further into the summer months. Where we have the refugees has been scouted for good underground reservoirs. It should be easy to dig wells."

"There is also the subject of provisions," Deireadh added. "The Summer folk are not accustomed to the cold nights."

"That is a good point," Shirina said. "Perhaps Winter can donate clothing and blankets. We have a thriving fur trade throughout the Courts as well and can help equip the refugees for the cooler weather."

Rìgh bowed his head slightly. "That would be appreciated."

"But that will not solve the real problem." Thaen stepped forward. "These folk will be in a precarious place. We have to plan for the rebels coming up the coast."

"You're right," Aiden said, mind whirring with the troubles presented. "We need to make a plan, and the best way to do that is get an idea of what is going on in that camp."

Deireadh grabbed up a pile of missives from the table. "We have plenty of messengers—"

Aiden raised a hand to cut him off and turned to Sgiath. "Ready a portal. I leave for the refugee camp immediately."

3
PRISONS AND POISON

Dearest Penny,

I just heard you've finally awoken, and I can't believe I'm not at the tree to speak with you. Though I did not want to leave, His Majesty asked us to do a little reconnaissance around the city, asking about The Cartographer. I'm sorry I wasn't there to help you when you woke, though Aiden's message assured me you were unharmed.

I will be sure to come see you in the morning.
Your Very Relieved Friend,
Angelica

Outside the window, the sun sank below the snowy horizon of Winter, leaving Penny alone with the night and the Tree she was trapped in. With a huff, she stood from her chair at the quaint table and took up her pacing once again. Her limbs had been wearied after being unconscious for three days, and she'd had to lay about for another two days, but now a boundless energy zipped about her bones.

Aiden hadn't been back to see her.

Penny needed to apologize. She certainly could have handled their last conversation better. If she'd paid more attention, she would have seen his distress in the lines of his face, the sorrow in his eyes. Guilt swirled in her gut, acidic and bubbling. Her heart ached for him, both for the hurt she'd caused and for the pain he dealt with even now.

She tried to find things to occupy her time. The room she found herself trapped in felt like a barren wasteland. The bed sat in the center with a trunk at its foot and a few chairs surrounding it— though if she guessed from the differing styles, they'd likely been brought in while she lay unconscious. A beautiful writing desk cozied up next to the fireplace and a wardrobe stood sentry near the washroom. But that was the extent of the furniture in the expansive room. She'd even checked the wardrobe for a hidden passage, but either she couldn't find it, or it was nonexistent.

At least her cage was pretty if nothing else. The natural wood and the constant light calmed her nerves somewhat. But no matter how much she tried, she couldn't bring herself to try connecting with her magic again. She shuddered just thinking about it.

A small clock on the desk chimed a shrill tune, bragging about the hour. *Stupid clock.* Frustration simmered inside her. She tiptoed to the door and cracked it open enough to see out. Two guards still stood at attention on either side of the doorway.

The door snicked shut, and she slumped against it.

Leaving was the last thing she wanted to do anyway. Aiden needed to see that he could trust her, that she wasn't being impulsive. He needed her to be there to help him. Causing problems within his new kingdom would do little good in regard to that plan. Patience was key here. Patience, and keeping her head on her shoulders— both figuratively and literally.

It had been obvious even before the revel how the folk regarded her. Their expressions had held every range of revulsion she'd ever seen plastered on a person's face. She had more potential enemies here than she did at Adira's camp. It would be wise to avoid stoking the flames of the fae's hatred toward her. She needed to get on their good side, and the best way to do that was to remain in their king's good graces.

A knock sounded against the door Penny still leaned against, and she hurried to open it. Had he come back? Her heart fell at the silver tray of food sitting on the floor waiting for her. A glance to either side told her the guards weren't concerned about the tray or her standing in the open doorway. She sighed and picked up the dishes and kicked the door shut behind her. It was going to be a long night.

The silver clattered as she unceremoniously plopped it onto the table beside the window. She whisked off the lid and steam billowed out along with the tantalizing aroma of food. Rice stuffed tomatoes. At least her prisoner fare was better than what she'd had in Adira's encampment. She could live as a prisoner if they fed her like this every day.

Her borrowed nightdress pooled around her feet as she sat, the same clothing she'd woken up in. The dress the Tree had helped her with was nowhere to be seen, and she didn't feel comfortable asking to borrow anything from any of the folk. She would be indebted to them if she did and, as she hadn't asked for the nightgown in the first place, they really couldn't hold her to anything.

Her fingers trailed over the edge of the wooden plate, small designs grooved into the thin lip. Everything here was delicate and beautiful, just like the people. She lifted her fork and paused, the flakes of what looked like parsley in the rice catching her eye. Using one of her tines, she dug out the little leaf, the soggy grains clinging to the chopped blade of green. She set the leaf aside and dug through another one of the stuffed tomatoes, finding another. With her fork, she cut open the juicy, red flesh and dug through until she reached the bottom and discovered six seeds almost the same size and shape of carrot seeds. She recognized them on the instant, and they definitely weren't carrot seeds.

Curses. She slammed the cover back on the food and shot to her feet. When she reached the door, she opened it with enough force that it slammed against the wall and startled the guards.

"Send for King Aiden."

"Pardon, my lady," one of the guards said, "but High King Aedon is not at Crann Mòr."

Her heart stuttered. He'd left her there. Alone.

She shook her head and straightened her nightdress. "Well, someone has just attempted to poison me, so I suggest you fetch someone."

"Get this out of here," the commanding lady barked. "Now!" Both guards scrambled to take the tray out of the room and the High Councilor of Winter slammed the door behind them with a growl.

"Poison is such a cowardly way to try to off someone," Dair mused as he draped himself over the end of Penny's bed. "And such a horrible way to ruin perfectly good stuffed tomatoes too."

Penny rolled her eyes. It seemed Aiden's cousin held a flare for the dramatic. The fae could probably give Paulo a run for his money.

"Do you know who it was?" Penny asked.

"We will find out soon enough," the High Councilor said. "I have several guards searching the kitchens, and we have blocked the gates. We need to find out who did this." The High Councilor turned to Penny, finally looking at her again after she'd done her initial inspection to make sure she wasn't going to die. "And you're sure you didn't see anyone in the hall?"

"No, my lady." She didn't actually know if that was the proper title the Councilor went by, but it was the best guess she could make. "There was a knock on the door and the tray was on the floor between the guards when I opened it."

"The guards claimed they saw no one," Dair added.

"So, we have a bwbachod who attempted to kill her off," said the lady, turning about as if to look for the little folk in question, "or at least was paid to deliver the food. There are not many brownies that would go against the High King's wishes. If they thought one of us had ordered food brought to her, they would have seen it delivered."

Penny dug her toe into the lush carpet under her bare foot. It really could have been anyone. Fae were not known for letting slights go unpunished, and crashing the revel was more than a simple offense. Finding hemlock in her food had at least been easily dealt with.

"I told the whole staff Aedon expected her to sup with us," Dair drawled, and something alighted in Penny's stomach. Aiden had been planning on allowing her to dine with his family for supper? He hadn't left her in this room with the intention of abandoning her?

The High Councilor set her hands on her hips. "I will find who delivered the food and have them tell me—"

"King Comhachag's servant ordered the food," a voice peeped out from next to Penny.

Penny jumped and she squeaked in surprise. Her mouth fell open as she saw the little brownie standing no taller than her knee beside her. She'd never seen one of the elusive creatures outside of drawings before. Thick, black hair poofed from its head in tiny spirals, held back by a red kerchief. The tips of its wide ears drooped down to its twiggy shoulders. Its wide eyes flicked from face to face. A nervous smile quivered on the creature's lips.

"What proof do you have?" the High Councilor asked, eyes darting from Penny down to the brownie beside her with curiosity.

The brownie dug in its pocket and held out a piece of paper to Penny. She took it slowly from the brownie, afraid of accidentally spooking it. She opened the note and read it aloud to the room.

Euan,

Prepare a tray to have sent to the mage scum. I have left a packet on the bedside table in your room to include within it. Once it's prepared, have one of the brownies deliver it before HC of Winter wakens to avoid suspicion.

-C

She refolded the paper. "Your help is greatly..." Penny's words trailed off. The brownie had already disappeared.

The Councilor turned to her son. "Send for Aedon. He will want to know about this."

"I always knew King Comhachag would be trouble," Dair mumbled as he pushed himself up off the end of the bed.

Penny sank into a chair. "What will be done?"

"I do not know," the High Councilor admitted. "We will have to speak with the rest of the Council about this. We will question this Euan first and go from there."

"And what would you like me to do?" Penny asked. She could help with the interrogation or run patrols in the evenings.

The fae quirked an eyebrow. "You? We need to keep you here until we can figure out if anyone else is going to target you."

"Wait, what?" Penny straightened. "I'm no use lying around while someone is trying to kill me. I can help."

She sat at the table across from Penny. "I know the folk we are dealing with. Aedon has told me a bit of your history. You may come from a world of spies and assassins, but the spies and assassins of this kingdom can read your thoughts and kill you without laying a finger on you. It would be best to keep you as out of the picture as much as we possibly can."

Penny shook her head. "You can't expect me to sit around until this whole thing blows over."

"You have been through quite an ordeal recently and we do not know how that is going to affect you," the Councilor said. "With the way Aedon said your magic reacted this morning, I worry about what would happen if you got into a fight. The best warriors know when to forfeit a battle and when to wage one. Going into a fight without knowing your own strengths and weaknesses can kill you just as swiftly as an enemy's blade can."

"But you can't just leave me in this room."

"And we do not plan to," she said. She stood and walked toward the door. "Because you will be in a different room while you recover, and we root out who else has plans to kill you while under our care."

Penny groaned. First Aiden cut her off, and now the High Councilor was ready to put her on house arrest. The door shut behind the fae and Penny sank into a chair, the smell of poisoned tomatoes lingering in the air.

Tonight was going to be a long one.

4
STEALTH

Aiden grabbed the mud-covered ellyllon fae by the collar and yanked him back into his chair. On the other side of the table, Thaen held another ellyllon down at the shoulders.

"Let's keep our seats lest we lose our heads, hm?" Aiden admonished.

Aiden and Thaen had been holding court in a farmhouse just outside the refugee camp for nearly three days. The sun had gone down ages ago, and Aiden's patience grew thinner by the minute. There had been every number of complaints coming through the door since he arrived, and he was sick to death of playing nursemaid to squabbling children.

But no one else was willing to do it.

The Summer fae across from him scoffed. "If anyone is losing their mind here, it is him." He pointed at the fae in the chair beside Aiden. "Cursed Unseelie tried to kill me."

"Do I really look like the one who was out to kill? I nearly suffocated in your cursed mud pit!" the other bit back, dried mud sloughing from his clothing. "You are the one who tried to put your filthy Seelie hands on my *taghadh*! I was justified in coming after you."

Aiden looked to Thaen. "*Taghadh*?" he mouthed.

"It is complicated. Like a soul mate, but since we believe the

Goddess allows free will and all, having someone that is soul bound to love you does not make any sense."

Aiden touched the pocket of his jacket with his fingers, the tiny pouch he'd carried around since the revel pulling at his thoughts. He'd continued to carry it with him, not wanting anyone to find it in his things. At least, that was what he told himself.

The fae in front of Aiden glanced back at him. "What kind of king are you if you do not even know what a *taghadh* is?"

Aiden refrained from rolling his eyes. "The kind who has a war to prepare for and despises wasting his time on *petty squabbles*." He glared between the two males, allowing his shadows to drip to the floor and the black veins to sprout along his arms.

Thaen released the Summer male and came to stand beside Aiden. "We understand the strain you are under, but we must work together—"

"I refuse to work with Unseelie sc—"

Thaen's hand wrapped around the male's throat. "If I hear you utter that term one more time in my presence, I am going to skin you alive and feed your flesh to the yumboes under Autumn's forest while you scream. And then, Goddess willing, I will end your pathetic little life and bury you so deep in the ground neither kobold nor Goddess will find your measly little bones."

The male quivered, his abalone skin paling further.

The door to the farmhouse swung open and a familiar head of purple hair popped in.

"Hope I am not interrupting anything important," Dair said.

Aiden glared down at the two males, their heads hung, but tempers simmering. "You didn't. In fact, we're basically done." He pointed at the Summer fae. "You will promise this male to never go near his family again and you"—he pointed at the Autumn fae—"will take the promise and leave."

"I would never—"

"That is hardly enou—"

"*Now!*" Aiden bellowed.

The two males quickly crossed the floor and shook on the promise before vacating the room as fast as their immortal legs could carry them.

"Bravo," Dair muttered. He visibly shook himself and turned to

Aiden. "Sorry to disappoint, but I have come with another problem that requires your immediate attention."

Aiden slumped into a chair, realizing too late it was the one the mud-caked ellyllon had sat in. He jumped up out of the seat. "What now?" he grumbled as he swiped the dirt from his sleeves.

"Well..." Dair cleared his throat. "The Summer King tried to kill Penelope."

Shadows burst from Aiden. "*He did what?*" The walls shook with his words, and Dair stepped aside as a decorative plate smashed to the ground. "Where is he now? By the Goddess, I will fillet the blackguard with his own blasted crown!"

Thaen stepped forward. "Easy, cousin. King Comhachag is not someone to trifle with."

"You think *he's* someone not to trifle with? Aiden stepped right into Thaen's space and lowered his voice. "If he so much as touches a hair on her head—"

"You will what?" Thaen didn't look so much as mildly bothered at Aiden's proximity, which made Aiden angrier. "Kill a fae king to protect a mage girl?"

"She's more than just a mage girl," Aiden ground out.

"You are right. She is a problem and one you need to fix quickly."

"How dare—"

"This posturing is great and all," Dair interrupted, "but can we please go back to Crann Mòr to finish up? I have not eaten supper yet and the stuffed tomatoes Penelope was nearly poisoned with are sounding better by the second."

Thaen quirked an eyebrow at Aiden.

Aiden had to consciously unclench the fists at his side. "Fine. There's not much more we can do here anyway."

The three of them left the farmhouse without a backward glance. Thaen mentioned something about tracking down Sgiath for a portal and left without another word.

Dair skipped up beside Aiden. "How did it go?"

"Probably as bad as you could guess but multiply it by the fact that no one wants a half-mage fae as High King." He took the handkerchief out from his pocket and wiped his hands. Too many handshakes had left what felt like a film over his palm.

"Well, no one ever said being a ruler was going to be easy."

Aiden sighed. No, they hadn't.

Aiden slumped in his chair next to the door, exhaustion pulling at his eyelids. After rushing back to Crann Mór the night before, the only thing he'd actually been able to do was find a new room for Penelope that shared a door with the one next to it. He'd had all his essentials removed from the High Ruler's still-unfurnished suite, much to the staff's dismay. With this new room, he was only a door away and didn't have to worry about anyone suspecting anything abnormal was going on besides him wanting to be next door to his guest.

Aiden blew out a breath. Who was he kidding? All of this sounded abnormal no matter which way he spun it.

They'd been unable to find the poisoner. The Summer King refused to allow the guards to question any of his people, even going so far as to threaten Aiden with open rebellion if they tried. And he would keep that promise. Aiden had learned at least that much about the ruler. When Thaen had asked King Comhachag if he'd ordered it, the king openly admitted to it, stating Penny had broken sacred law by eating the *toradh na beatha*. It had been a good thing Aiden hadn't been the one to speak with him. He probably would have ripped off King Comhachag's head, crown and all. But that would have only broken the fragile alliances he'd made with the Day Court. No, he would have to speak to the High Council tomorrow to come up with a plan to track down the servant. While he couldn't go after the Summer King—at least, not yet—he could show the rest of their people that meting out punishment in the name of the Goddess without proper authority would not be tolerated. This kind of thing would not go unpunished, not under Aiden's rule.

And especially not with Penelope being victim to the attack.

Aiden scrubbed a palm over his face. Wind and snow, what was he going to do with her? He knew better than to keep her locked up in a room for the foreseeable future, but she couldn't go parading about Faerie. After the revel, she would be too recognizable. Everyone with a grudge against mages would be on the lookout for her. There were only so many things he could do to protect her without causing a stir within the Courts too. After speaking with Rìgh and, in light of the King Comhachag's attack, it was obvious Summer would likely continue to cause problems.

But he also couldn't send Penelope away. His heart shrank away from even the thought of taking her back to Olympia. Just knowing she was here, where he could see her, sent his blood racing. She'd come for him again and again and each time it was harder to pull away. Skies, he didn't *want* to pull away. He thought he knew what pain was when he believed he'd never see her again. This, knowing she was here but knowing it would seriously endanger her to pay her any more special attention, was agony. After holding her again, after watching and waiting for her to die after eating the fruit, he couldn't let her go. But he didn't know how he was going to save either of them if he didn't.

The doorknob next to his shoulder turned, catching his eye. The door opened a fraction, and a pair of serious, emerald eyes peered through the gap. He could only see her face because of his better eyesight, both of their rooms cast in nearly complete darkness.

With a frown, she flicked her fingers in the language he'd taught her as an Underworld operative—similar to the sign language Evan used to speak in Olympia.

Window.

Invader.

One.

Aiden leaped from his chair on silent feet and crept into the room after her. Sure enough, a shadow hunched on the windowsill, using a thin beam of light to silently cut through the glass. It looked as if the process took quite a bit of magic. The beam moved slowly and only made a hole big enough for the shadow to stick their hand through.

Aiden stepped over the small pile of blankets next to the door. Penelope must have had close to the same idea he had and stayed near.

Penelope gestured for him to go left around the room while she went right and put the bed between her and the invader. She was wise enough to realize she would not do well facing off against this opponent. Aiden wrapped himself in more shadow and crept across the room.

The invader had unlocked the window and pulled one of the hinged panes outward. They crept through quietly and closed the pane, allowing the lock to click into place. Obviously this Tuatha was not very well trained. Aiden would never close off an avenue of escape, but he wasn't going to complain about this fae making the mistake. Their lack of training was a point in Aiden's favor.

Aiden sprang from the shadows, running straight into the invader and knocking them to the ground. A feminine cry of alarm shouted out. The large cloak had hidden the lithe form of the fae, and she shed the cloak and brought her hands together. The air in the room spun out of control, ripping Aiden away from her.

The outer door burst open. Thaen's hulking form stood firm against the onslaught of the wind tearing through the room. He held his sword in front of him and hollered at the assailant, though his words were lost to the wind.

Aiden pushed against the bluster, using his shadows to create a shield for him to walk behind. As he got closer to the bed, he checked for Penelope.

She wasn't there.

He searched frantically about the room but didn't see her anywhere. He peered around his shadow wall at the invader, whose sole focus was on Thaen as he pushed closer to her, using a shadow shield of his own. She cast bursts of wind in his direction strong enough to cut through his shadows.

Aiden kept searching for Penelope, but she was nowhere in sight. Had something happened to her? Had she gone to get help? His boots slid over the slick floor. He shoved his shield against the wind.

A shadow shifted at the feet of the invader and steel glinted for only a moment before plunging straight into the invader's boot. The fae roared, her voice carried on the winds of the room and shaking the walls. Light burst from her, blinding Aiden and disrupting his shadows.

Aiden blinked away the lingering afterimage, finding Penelope laying on the ground near the raging assassin. She removed the dagger and rolled away as the invader turned to attack. Before Aiden could send a shield that way, the ground where Penelope had been exploded in slivers of wood as the air punched the floor. Thaen barreled forward immediately and tackled the fae to the ground. With a single blow to the head, he knocked her unconscious.

Aiden's shadows dissipated, and he wrapped Penelope up in his arms. First the poisoned food and now this? His hands trembled as he tightened his hold on her. "You've managed to thwart your assassination twice in one night."

She kept her arms firmly around him but looked up from the circle of his arms. "All in a day's work, I suppose. Though, there weren't nearly as many people trying to kill me in Olympia." She smiled, though it didn't quite reach her eyes, an obvious sign of how serious she knew her situation was. "It seems I've come up in the world," she joked.

"Or gone down," he mumbled. He tried to fight the smile, but something must have shown on his face because even in the darkness of the room her eyes lit up. Why could she always get a smile from him, even after they'd just had their very lives threatened? There was something wrong with him.

He lightly kissed her temple, not even able to withstand the temptation by a fraction. His attention turned to where Thaen had created shadowed cuffs to hold the invader. Aiden had learned to create those under Durant's tutelage. It wouldn't be too far-fetched to assume she'd learned it from other members of the Night Court. Now that he knew she'd retrieved knowledge from Faerie, many of her practices made more sense to him.

"I cannot believe they would make another attempt so soon," Thaen growled, depositing the invader in a chair and dragging it across the room and into the hall. A trio of guards crowded the doorway and Thaen thrust the captive at them, ordering her imprisonment in the holding cells until she could be interrogated.

"You're assuming Comhachag was behind this as well?" Aiden asked.

Thaen lifted a hand and dangled a golden medallion from a leather string. The round medallion showed a four-leafed clover surrounded by twelve turquoise stones. Summer's insignia. "She is a member of Comhachag's guard."

Aiden ran a palm over his face. "This is ridiculous. Why would he want her dead?"

"She is a mage, and he is Tuatha. It could not be simpler." Thaen stuck the medallion in a pocket at his chest. He would be better suited approaching the Council with this than Aiden at the moment, who still couldn't get his heart to stop thumping against his ribcage.

"Well, I don't exactly view my death and the reasons behind it simple at all," Penelope snapped. Defiance sparked in her eyes. "You claim it's merely my existence that offends him, but that makes absolutely no sense."

"You are a *mage*. To fae like Comhachag, that is all the sense he needs."

"That's utterly ridiculous."

Thaen grunted, not agreeing or disagreeing.

Aiden squeezed Penelope's hand, but he kept his eyes on Thaen's face. "What are we going to do?"

Thaen's gaze remained on Penelope for a few moments before he turned toward the door. "We call a family council."

"I do not think it wise to challenge Comhachag at this time, Little Shadow," Shirina admonished, her hands cradling a teacup Penelope passed to her. "While I agree there should be repercussions to his actions, we need to think of the long term rather than instant gratification. If you go after them too soon, he will drag Penelope through the mud and up to an execution stand for her actions. Let the dust settle a bit. I'm sure the Goddess has a plan and will execute judgement in due time."

A grumble pushed against Aiden's lips, but he withheld the urge to murmur. Instead, he slouched back in the rocking chair he sat on in the small nursery Thaen had gathered the family in. Aiden had wanted this conversation private and somewhere no one would think to look for them. Thaen had led him and Penelope to the quaint nursery, saying no one would even dream of their High King tucked away amongst the young ones' toys and tiny beds.

Aiden reached up to run a hand through his hair for what had to be the fiftieth time since he'd watched Penelope stab the assassin in the foot. Before his fingers could rake the top of his head, Penelope grabbed his wrist and brought the hand down to cradle in her lap on the stool next to him. She picked up one of the teacups from the miniature table in the middle of their group and placed the warm drink in his palm.

"I can understand thinking long term," Aiden begrudgingly admitted, "and I don't wish to go to war with the king, but how are we to dissuade him from attacking again? After what happened tonight, I don't see this problem going away quietly."

"Nor I," said Shirina. "Comhachag does not do *quietly* if it does not suit him."

"Perhaps we could poison his drink and see how he likes it," Dair suggested from his perch on the rocking horse. His gangly knees stuck out on either side as the wooden stallion rocked back and forth over the floor.

"We cannot poison a king," Thaen snapped and Dair rolled his eyes.

Shirina stood. "I think the best course of action is to take Penelope out of the equation."

Aiden felt more than saw Penelope tense beside him. He could feel his own hackles rising. "What are you suggesting?"

"We need to remove her from Crann Mór. Dair and I are already discussing departing for Winter. Allow us to take her with us. She can come to Eagallach where there will not be nearly as many folk looking to murder her in her sleep and she will be safe on the mountain."

Cold pierced Aiden where he'd just begun to thaw after Penelope's arrival. His head shook of its own volition, his body coming to a conclusion before his mind could. "I can't just let you take her." *Not after I only just got her back.*

Penelope placed a hand on his arm. "I don't want to leave either, but maybe they're right. I should go."

Dair straightened on top of the horse, nearly toppling it over backward. "Finally, someone with some sense around here. Penelope can go hide away in Eagallach while you and Thaen stay to schmooze the Courts. Once they like our half-mage king, they are sure to change their minds about the full mage girl that ate our sacred fruit and spat on all of our traditions."

A purple, streaked shadow sped across the floor and sent Dair all the way backward on his horse, toppling it. A twitch curled Thaen's lips for a moment before Shirina whipped around to glare at him. Aiden sent Thaen a grateful look, having been half tempted to do the same thing.

Penelope *should* be out of reach from the rest of the Court's machinations. If Summer was already making moves against her, it wouldn't be long until Spring joined the game. Aiden didn't have time to combat his Courts as well as the rebels. There was enough division within them already, and he needed to gain his kingdom's trust. Faerie had so much potential for good, and if he didn't play the game correctly, they would lose the chance to ever accomplish anything great. Aiden loved this kingdom, even if they were still warming up to him.

He looked over at Thaen. "If she goes, I need you to go too."

Penelope looked at him sharply. "Excuse me? He's not coming."

Aiden turned to Thaen, knowing his cousin couldn't see the pleading expression on his face, but hoping he could feel it all the same. They had plans to visit the training grounds that were even now being put to order at the base of the mountains every other day for the next few weeks. It would be easier for Thaen if he was already in Eagallach to take care of things rather than stuck here with him and going back and forth. It would ease Aiden's mind immensely to have him there to watch for attackers even if Penelope and him didn't get along.

But instead, Thaen shook his head. "No."

Penelope sat back down, pacified by the answer.

"Why not?" Aiden asked. "I need to ensure her safety and you're the only one I can trust to do that."

"Oh, my aching heart," Dair said dramatically.

Aiden ignored him. "Seriously, Thaen. It'll be easier for you to be there anyway. I need more eyes on the training grounds. With you there every day, it will ensure things are getting done properly."

"But if I am there every day, who will be watching your back?"

Aiden gestured to the door, where he knew two of the Tree's guards stood outside. "I have an entire Tree swarming with guards."

Thaen leaned back. "Yes, guards that let The Cartographer herself inside to kill my *athair* and allowed Penelope to almost be poisoned." He shook his head, dark dreads swinging. "No, I will not leave you in this viper's nest alone."

"So, what would you have me do?"

Dair snorted. "Come with us of course."

Aiden glanced over at Penelope. He couldn't, could he? How would he keep her safe if he was there too? He shook his head. "I can't gain footing with the Courts from Winter. It would look like I was playing preference."

Shirina stood, gliding through the toys to settle at the window. "High Queen Rìanoch regularly took sojourn with her consort to Spring before he died. It is only natural for folk to gravitate to their home Court. Yes, it would make things a little harder, but it would comfort me to have you close, to know that demon woman would have a harder time getting to you on the mountain than in the Tree."

Aiden opened his mouth to argue, his mind and his heart tearing him in two, but Shirina turned to meet his gaze, and all of the words melted away. Shirina's grief opened up just enough for him to truly see its depth, and he felt a sliver of it in his own heart. They'd already had someone taken from them, and Aiden would do whatever it took to make sure that they didn't lose anyone else.

And that included Penelope.

As he looked down at the pair of intelligent, emerald eyes, he knew he couldn't give her up. He couldn't protect her if he was here and she was there. If he would never truly be allowed to have her, at least he could torture himself by being closer to her.

"All right, we will go to Eagallach."

5
KINGS AND PALACES

Dearest Penny,

I know I said I'd be there today to go with you to Eagallach, but Devan and I will be arriving later tomorrow. Make sure to save a spot for me at supper, and I will catch you up on all the Winter Court gossip. By the Goddess, I'm going to need at least a moment to put my feet up.

Your Very Pregnant and Tired Friend,
Angelica

PENNY HAD THOUGHT THE PREPARATIONS FOR TRAVEL DURING HER YOUTH HAD been chaotic. Mother had always made sure to pack every single thing they could possibly have need of—going so far as to supply extra clothing on every half day journey they made. When she'd travelled to Olympia for her debut, Mother had packed two whole carriages worth of things from Barclay Manor even though Barclay House in Olympia had been fully furnished and most of Penny's ball necessities had been awaiting them there.

But nothing could have prepared her for moving a king, let alone a *High King*.

It took three entire days. Servants bustled about the space—trow, satyrs, darklings, dwarves, trolls—the entire Tree in an uproar over the impromptu departure. Trunks were packed, furniture covered, and all of Aiden's necessary materials needed for ruling and regulating bundled up and sealed until they could be delivered to Eagallach. Not to mention all the gifts that had been pouring in during Aiden's stay in the great Tree. While portalling everything would be efficient, Sgiath and Farrah could not make more than two or three trips in a single day without getting overly tired. With the amount of things piled in the hallway between Penny's and Aiden's rooms, it would take at least a dozen. Perhaps a few flying carpets would need to be acquired, though Penny had no idea what the protocol for that would look like.

"You'd think I was relocating the entire capital with how much stuff is here."

Penny turned as Aiden deftly wove through the piles. She smiled at his scowl. "Considering where you reside will be the most important place in the kingdom, I can understand the hubbub." She toyed with the end of her braid. "A king should not have to move from his home." This was not helping Aiden. This was making his life more difficult. She wasn't worth this kind of effort, especially as she had no idea where they stood now.

The divide between them seemed to stretch further and further every minute. He had an entire kingdom of people that needed him. Who was she to take him away from that? By the Goddess, they'd both changed so much she didn't even know if they were the same people they'd been when she'd agreed to marry him. Did he feel like he had some kind of obligation to that? After everything that had happened?

His scowl softened into a frown. "Do you think that's what's happening? That I'm uprooting myself from my home to follow you to Eagallach?"

Penny grimaced as he said it aloud, but a small piece of her—a very small piece that she wasn't going to even acknowledge—was pleased. He had always been the one to do what was right, even if it hadn't always been the correct thing to do. He'd abandoned her in Eleusion before the rebels had burned down her home and had distanced himself in Olympia for her safety. While she understood why he'd done those things, it also made her wary. "Isn't that what you're doing?"

Aiden studied her for a moment, his eyes capturing hers, before softly shaking his head. "You know it's not." He took a step closer. "Though, I can't help but be somewhat glad all the same." His fingers lightly brushed the back of her hand.

Penny's heart jumped in her chest. She kept his gaze as she lifted her fingers to entwine them with his. It almost felt like a dare. As if she was daring him to admit he still felt as deeply about her as she did him. She knew he had his own reasons for following her to Eagallach. It would have riddled her with guilt if she was ripping him from where he wanted to be. Duty was important to him. It was what made him a good leader both here and back in Olympia. It would cause him grief to feel conflicted because of her. She'd caused enough problems as it was.

But knowing his words in the nursery didn't fully reflect what he was feeling inside, didn't articulate what this small touch of their fingers truly meant, had her blood singing.

"Are you love birds done twittering sweet nothings in each other's ears," Dair called, "or can we go now?"

Penny spun, mortification blazing into her cheeks, and saw Dair and the Lòchran standing a short distance down the hallway. Dair's smirk deepened enough to flash a pair of dimples as he looked over her face, and she ducked as the heat went straight to her hairline. Sweet Gaia, she probably looked like a tomato.

"Is everything ready?" Aiden asked in a calm voice. Penny glanced up in surprise at his collected tone, but she bit her lip when she saw the tinge of pink at the point of his ear.

"Yes, cousin," the Lòchran replied. "We are all assembled in the Receiving Hall."

"Excellent." Aiden offered Penny his arm. "Shall we?"

The Lòchran frowned in the general direction of Aiden's elbow, but Penny took it. Aiden gestured for the brothers to proceed them down the winding halls. Penny did her best not to openly stare at their surroundings, but she couldn't help taking in all of the insides of the Tree as they descended its many staircases. While she'd been there for several days and had to traverse the structure to get to Aiden the night of the revel, there hadn't actually been time to *see* very much of it.

Their rooms had been located near the midpoint of the towering Tree, the views on the outside of the Tree allowing them to see over the city structures and out towards the four seasonal lands. Balconies opened up along the Summer and Spring sides, catering to the flying folk and allowing the cool breezes into the Tree. The other side also had wide openings, but most were closed due to the colder weather during the colder months. Snow swirled outside the windows as they walked around the Winter quarter.

The entire Tree fascinated Penny. If her gift wasn't acting out, she would have connected to the structure to simply study it. But a shudder ran through her as she recalled attempting to connect with the Tree. After the first incident after she woke, she'd tried again only to induce the same soul-ripping result. Aiden looked down at her in concern, but she waved a hand to say nothing was the matter. She would need to look more into what was going on with her magic once she was in a safer place to do so.

Their group turned down a hallway that widened into an expansive hall. Shirina stood in the middle, directing servants as they passed.

"There you are." Shirina turned in their direction. Penny had finally learned the Councilor's name during the manhunt—or rather *fae*-hunt—for her would-be poisoner. Not that the search had been fruitful or mattered much in keeping Penny safe. There were more fair folk looking to kill her than just the Summer King, if Penny guessed right.

Dair frowned at his mother. "How did you beat us down here?"

Shirina shifted a box in her hands and pointed at the wall were a gate closed off an alcove. "The lift."

Before Penny could take in the contraption, Aiden stepped forward and blocked her view. "You mean I haven't had to traverse every cursed stair in this Tree to get from place to place?" He glared at the Lòchran who smirked in response.

Shirina blinked before also turning a glare on her son. "Wind and snow, have you really made your cousin take the stairs for everything? No wonder Our Sovereign is regularly the last to arrive to things."

Dair snickered from beside the Lòchran. "He never asked."

Penny narrowed her eyes in his direction. While he'd been the most welcoming of his family members, Penny guessed he was only fine with her being there because she gave him something to laugh about.

He deserves a good smack upside the head.

As Penny continued to glare at him, she caught the faint tendril of green near his feet. A sapling burst out from the ground behind him and used a trio of leaves to swat at his head. His purple hair whipped into his face. It disappeared before he turned to see what had hit him.

Penny's mouth fell open, and she looked up to Aiden, but he had gone to speak with the others congregating in the middle. She turned back and saw the Lòchran appraising her. The Lòchran's pale eyes took her in and then glanced down to where the sapling had burst out of the wood.

Penny looked about for any excuse to escape his questions and held out her arms. "Lady Shirina, let me take that box for you. It looks rather cumbersome."

"Oh, it is fine. I was just about to put it with the others before—"

Penny grabbed the box and beat a hasty retreat to Aiden's side.

What on Gaia's green earth just happened?

"... agree that we should prepare for the worst," Aiden was saying. "We need to have a system in place to receive messages quickly while on the mountain since the spring storms won't allow for the pixies to travel safely."

"We have a few enchanted items back at the Palace that might be able to help with that," Shirina said. "Perhaps it would be wise to commission more from some of the gifted in Eagallach."

Dair clapped his hands. "Let us depart then. I am eager to get back and continue my dreamless nights in the comfort of my own bed."

Shirina bowed her head, a sad smile pulling at the corners of her mouth. Penny couldn't imagine how it must hurt her, returning to the home she'd shared with her husband. Shirina gestured toward where Aiden's attention remained riveted. "Sgiath and his daughter are coming down the lift as we speak."

Penny looked over at where the gated box had been minutes before to see the thing descending from above them. The contraption halted at the bottom and a familiar head of white hair zipped across the room.

"Penny!" Farrah grabbed Penny up in a hug. "Oh good, gracious gourds, I'm so glad you're all right."

Farrah set her down and Penny pulled back far enough to look in her dark eyes. "I'm happy to see you too, Farrah."

A hand settled on Penny's shoulder. "Time to go," said Aiden. "I'm sure the two of you will be able to catch up later."

"Of course, My Sovereign," Farrah said with a bow of her head. "I'm looking forward to it."

Aiden pulled Penny in the direction of the rest of his family as Sgiath wove the portal in the open air of the Receiving Hall. Orange glittered within the black mass, similar to Farrah's red. The portal was larger than one Penny had seen Farrah make, but with the undulating shadows beckoning them, she couldn't decide if that was a good thing or a bad thing.

Shirina stepped through first, followed closely by the twins. Penny's steps faltered as she got closer. There was so much unknown on the other side of that portal. Yes, she had traversed an entire kingdom, faced rebels and bloodthirsty fae, but she'd had a mission then. Now that she'd found Aiden and delivered her news, what was her purpose?

Aiden's fingers slid between hers. "I'll be with you the whole time."

His touch sent her stomach aflutter. She took a deep breath and allowed the shadows to sweep her up into the unknown. The darkness swallowed her, the silence ringing in her ears until she felt the opening. With Aiden's hand still in hers, she stepped through the other side.

She opened her eyes and tried not to gasp at the arched ceiling soaring above them. Multiple chandeliers dripped down like icicles, sparkling like nothing Penny had ever seen. A set of staircases curved up near the back of the hall where a tall set of doors stood sentry, and other staircases went off to other sections of the palace. *Why does everything in Faerie have to be so much grander? So much prettier?* Penny stared at her reflection in the black granite floor. Veins of gold and white quartz shined through, adding color and light to the onyx expanse.

Aiden's reflection joined hers. "You handled the portal well."

Penny straightened and looked up at him. "They certainly

haven't had the same effect on me as they have in the past. I suppose facing scarier beasts puts things into perspective."

His expression turned thoughtful and somewhat melancholy. "I suppose you're right."

A clap rang out, cutting off their conversation. Penny pulled her hand from Aiden's and found Shirina sending an uncertain expression her way. The rest of the group encircled them, Sgiath having left Farrah behind as a temporary messenger for Aiden.

"Welcome, Penelope," Shirina said, "to the Winter Palace."

Remembering the rules about saying *thank you*, Penny said, "It is very gracious of you to invite me to your home. It's beautiful." And beautiful wasn't even a good descriptor. If Queen Shaunie ever visited, she would be racing home to demand King Dion begin renovations on Olympia's palace at once.

Shirina glided over to Penny, though her expression remained uncertain. "How about a tour?"

"You may want to forgo the fountain this time though." Dair chuckled, flashing a smile in Aiden's direction.

A blush creeped into Aiden's ears, and he rubbed the back of his neck. "I think Penelope will be much better behaved than I was."

"She better be," the Lòchran grumbled as he strode past them toward the stairs. "I will be in my rooms."

"I would like if you joined us for the tour," Shirina called after him.

The Lòchran waved a hand. "I have a book I need to read."

Penny glanced at Aiden. "He can read?" While the Lòchran's blindness hadn't been discussed outright with her, she'd gathered enough information from interacting with him and from things the family said to understand that reading would be quite a feat.

Aiden shook his head.

So, it wasn't even a good excuse. Heat prickled at Penny's chest.

Dair skipped behind his twin, his lavender hair flicking behind him like a flag. "I will also be in my room. Call us when it is time for breakfast."

Penny looked about for a window to see what time it was, but there wasn't a single one in sight. She could not even begin to guess what hour it was.

"Oh, how I would trade my magic for a pair of obedient sons," Shirina groaned. She looked back at Penny, hesitant. "I would be happy to show you around, though Dair would likely be much better at it than I." The words were sincere, but the weariness around her eyes spoke volumes about how she would like to avoid it.

Penny understood. It was partly because of her that Shirina's husband was dead. If she hadn't shown up and caused a spectacle, Fiadh might still be alive, and Aiden's life would be so much simpler. She was the mage girl none of this family wanted for Aiden, the girl he wouldn't let go. Well, she wasn't keen to let go of him either but demanding a place in his family would not be the way to go about it. Aiden needed to charm the rest of Faerie into liking him. She had a much smaller, though no less intimidating group, to woo.

Aiden took Penny's hand. "We don't have to do a tour now," he said, giving her an out if she desired it.

"A tour sounds lovely, but let's put it off until tomorrow. If it's not too much trouble, I'll just retire." Penny pulled her brightest smile onto her face through sheer force of will. "Though, I will request we see this infamous fountain first thing, if its amenable to you."

6

STRIKE

Sitting across the table from Penelope at breakfast felt like the remnants of a nightmare fast turning into a dream. He kept having to remind himself that he shouldn't want her there, that even breathing the same air as him put her in danger.

But he couldn't help it.

Dair said something snarky across the table at her and she gave it to him right back as she passed a bowl of some kind of melon to Shirina. Thaen smirked, even though he tried to hide it. Skies, watching her interact with his family was one of his most hidden wishes come to life. Could this be the start of something? Penelope here, laughing and joking with his family? It was like seeing his dream play out in front of him.

But it couldn't last.

Even as she laughed, the dream slid sideways. Aiden saw the way Thaen's eyes watched her every movement, the way the staff around them kept flicking their eyes in her direction. He saw how Dair sized her up, needling her with intrusive questions. Even Shirina acted strangely, not saying anything and simply watching how Penelope responded to every challenge.

Aiden put his fork down next to his plate, the rich food having lost its flavor. He needed to come up with a solution. Her safety was at risk the longer she remained there. She should have never been put in the situations she had been back in Crann Mòr. Just the possibility of her being hurt sent all sorts of emotions zipping about in his blood.

Penelope needed to get to safety, and Aiden needed to make a plan to get her there.

He turned to Shirina on his left. "Any word from the Aunties?" he whispered.

"Not since you asked two hours ago." She gave him a soft smile, though it didn't reach as far as it would have only a week ago. The seat across from her had remained empty since their return to the Winter Palace the week before. "I am sorry I cannot give you an approximate time for their reply either. With them having visited so recently, I do not know when they will get home to receive the message."

Aiden straightened the fork he'd set down. "It's fine."

It *would* be fine. Now that they were in Winter, Aiden didn't feel as worried about Penelope's safety. His family would do their best to take care of her, and Aiden could give more attention to, well, everything else.

He'd spent most of the last few days down at the fortress. More than a thousand fae had already arrived to train, and they expected another three thousand more by the end of the week. The numbers from the training grounds in Autumn were well within five thousand, their numbers swelling rapidly with the influx of refugees. The Summer Court was angry and having the structure of the training to pour their fury out was helping them get along with the Autumn fae. At least that was going as well as it could.

Shirina set a hand on his arm and gave it a squeeze. "I am sure the Goddess has a plan. For both of you."

Aiden tried to smile back but felt it cross his lips as limp as Shirina's had been.

Penelope's enchanting laugh rang out over the table, her eyes sparkling as they met his. He sent up a silent prayer. If Danu did have a plan, he prayed it would reveal itself soon.

The door of the family dining room swung open for the palace's housekeeper. The trow female took up the entirety of the doorframe, her chatelaine jingling at her waist. "I apologize for interrupting, My Sovereign."

Aiden waved off her apology. "No need. What do you need?"

"The Andàn have just arrived, My Sovereign."

"Quick!" Dair leapt up from his seat. "Everyone, hide your coin purses."

Praise the Goddess. It seemed the morning would be taking a turn for the better. Aiden stood. His stomach dropped as his mind cleared. The Aunties would know just what to do.

"Interesting," Auntie Niomi said, pinching a curl of Penelope's hair between two skeletal fingers. It was brown in the candlelight, but some of the strands shimmered red as they were lifted up. Auntie Niomi sniffed at the ends. "We have never seen a bond quite like this."

"Of course not," snapped Auntie Taddie, smacking Auntie Niomi's hand away from Penelope. "She is a mage. She has magic, but her magic is so like Mother's, there is no differentiating the two."

"What is your magic, dearie?" Auntie Niomi asked.

"I have power over plants."

The Aunties all sucked in a breath. "Creation," Auntie Taddie said.

"It all makes sense now that you mention it," Thaen said. "That is why I cannot see you and why Aedon could not separate your gift from Hers."

Auntie Tori grunted, sniffing the top of Penelope's head and making her flinch. Aiden knew what Auntie Tori smelled. That rich spice of cinnamon and citrus. And the new scent of her bond. He'd noticed it when he'd held her. She smelled like springtime and freshly tilled earth. Like the orchards back in Eleusion. It wasn't a bad thing. The scent fit Penelope perfectly. It was just different. New. Unusual.

Penelope snatched her hair from Auntie Niomi's claw-like fingers. "But what does all of that mean? Is there even a way to separate them?"

Aiden couldn't tell if her question held hope that they could find a solution or hope that they wouldn't. He prayed it was the former. He really didn't want to fight her on this. Getting her home was still the best solution. For everyone.

"It means we cannot figure it out quite yet," Auntie Niomi said.

"With your magic linking you to the Land and your status as mage, there is much we do not know. Will your magic react the same way it used to? What does this mean for the High Crown? If you are irrevocably linked, what will that do to the folk? Does this mean Danu has accepted you as a part of the Land or that the Land is holding you captive?"

"Many things to look into," Auntie Taddie said.

"Is she able to return to Olympia?" Thaen asked.

"Perhaps," Auntie Taddie replied. "Or it could do even more harm than it would to a regular mortal. With the magics being so inseparably linked, she could simply turn to dust the moment she stepped foot out of Faerie."

Aiden's shoulders tightened. He met Penelope's eyes and saw the flash of fear before she stowed it behind a facade of calm. Did she think he might test the theory? Or that someone else might consider it? He got to his feet, no longer able to sit still.

"Best not try out that possibility, dearies." Auntie Niomi took Penelope's hand and patted it. "Would not want this fine skin drying out like that."

Penelope withdrew her hand. "Is there any way we can know for certain?"

Auntie Taddie sagged into a chair, her patchwork of skirts bunching up around her like another layer of her cragged skin. "This is certainly something we can ask about, but I cannot tell you if we will get an answer."

Shirina stepped forward. "Will you be leaving us then?" Aiden could see the wish for them to remain written plainly on her face. *Stars.* He needed to be better about reaching out to her. She'd just lost her soulmate if he understood what Thaen had said correctly.

Auntie Niomi gave her a sympathetic look. "We will take up residence in the temple for now and council together about what to do."

"So, you'll stay?" Aiden asked.

Auntie Tori nodded for all of them.

"What will you do in the interim?" Auntie Niomi asked. "Cannot exactly let the little thing run about, you know?"

"The *little thing* is sitting right here," Penelope grumbled.

"Pardon us, child," Auntie Taddie said. "It has been a while since we have been in mortal company. We forget how fragile your feelings are."

Penelope rolled her eyes. "It's not about my feelings so much as it is about you discussing what to do with me. I'd like to be part of the conversation rather than just the subject of it."

"What would you suggest, Penelope?" Shirina asked.

"You could come to the temple with us," Auntie Niomi offered.

Auntie Taddie chimed in with "We have a remote tower not far from here."

"Locking her in her room did not go well the first time," Dair said.

"Dungeons might work," mused Thaen.

Penelope stood abruptly. "*None* of those options will go well." She clenched her fists at her side and green eyes sparking. Something within Aiden jumped to attention and readied to back her in whatever battle she was about to instigate. He rubbed his fingers along the upper ribs of his chest. His heart beating hard as he watched her. A flash of green at her skirts caught his attention, but when he looked, she'd moved them behind her back. He shook his head. The last time she'd connected with her magic, it had practically incapacitated her. She wouldn't be standing if she had accessed her magic again just then.

Penelope tilted her chin, her upbringing as a future duchess on full display. "I'm here to help win this war and take down Adira Durant in whatever capacity I can. Locking me away won't solve any of your problems, and I promise if you attempt it, I will become more of a problem than I already am. Of that you can be certain."

Aiden never knew whether to be terrified or impressed when she struck that way. She was a fearsome, beautiful thing to behold. It was tempting to simply stride over to her and kiss her senseless.

He shook himself. "Penelope's right. Hiding her away won't fix anything. We need her help if we are going to have any chance against Durant. She knows her. Knows the inner workings of her command chain. She'll be invaluable in the coming confrontation."

Penelope looked at him with what he would have described as gratitude, but he felt anything but gratified. More like terrified.

"So, she stays in the palace and works from here," Dair said. He quirked an eyebrow in her direction. "I do hope she is house trained." Penelope glared, but Aiden saw the teasing glint in Dair's eye. *Always one to rile folk up.*

"Shame on you, Bruadair," Shirina admonished. "Penelope has been nothing but reasonable in the few days she has been here."

"Stars, *Màthair*, not you too," Thaen groaned. He glowered at Penelope. "Stop trying to win everyone over, *mage*. I have seen what you can do with a blade, and it is nothing kind."

Penelope gave him her most dazzling, innocent smile. Aiden clenched his teeth. He nearly pummeled Thaen for being the recipient. By the Goddess, he needed to get ahold of himself. Beating his cousin to a pulp simply because she looked at him...

"Then it's settled," Aiden cut in. "Penelope stays and helps us gather intel while the rest of us look into breaking her bond with the Land and work on thwarting whatever plans Durant is brewing."

"Do not forget about the assassinations attempts," Dair piped in.

"Right." The word came out simple and clean, but Aiden knew it would be anything but. "We should all get some rest. We have a lot to do tomorrow."

Everyone filed out of the room except Penelope, who walked over to a vase of flowers on one of the decorative tables behind him. Aiden saw the white daffodils there as well. Where had Shirina found them? He hadn't seen the blooms since Olympia. Actually, that wasn't true. He'd seen them in that oasis in the Farraige Gaineamh, but the Land had taken credit for those.

"I'm sorry," Penelope said quietly, running a finger along one of the white petals.

Aiden stepped closer, drawn to the quiet in her voice. "What are you sorry for?"

She gave him an exasperated look. "Oh, I don't know. For ruining your first official weeks as High King? For sewing contention into your newfound family? For separating you from your folk, your kingdom?"

"Stop." Aiden took the hand she had been using to peruse the flowers. "You haven't done anything wrong."

Penelope looked up, tears lining her lashes. "You're right, but everyone will always believe I did."

Aiden opened his mouth to reply, but the door opened.

"Aedon," Thaen called from the open doorway, "the High Councilors have arrived to go over the patrol reports."

Wind and snow, he was never going to have a chance to speak with her without being interrupted by something. A part of him was grateful, having his heart cut off from what it wanted. But with the gratitude came a bit of bitterness. A bit of rebellion. He *wanted* to talk to her. He nearly said it could wait, but she rested a gentle hand on his arm. Electricity zinged all the way up to his chest.

"You should go," Penelope whispered. "There are more important things to do." She swept past him and Thaen into the hallway.

Aiden let out a long sigh as she left, making the decision for him. "All right. I'm coming." He followed Thaen out into the hallway, Penelope nowhere in sight.

7
HOUNDS AND HISTORIES

Dearest Penny,
Of course I'll take a walk in the garden with you.
Say after tea? I could use the distraction in this palace
of tension, even if it is cursed cold outside.
Your Fidgety Friend,
Angelica

PENNY GRABBED THE THICKEST CLOAK SHE COULD FIND IN HER BORROWED things and opened the door to her rooms, ones located near the family wing. It still made her cringe. Aiden worried about having any visitors attack her in the guest wing, but she felt as if she was crossing some kind of boundary. She wasn't family, royalty, or anything in between. And being only a sitting room away from Aiden? She closed the door and let out a weary breath. A walk outside was just what she needed. Hopefully, the fresh air would help her clear her mind of all that had happened in the last few days. After the Andáns' arrival two days ago, she couldn't help feeling like the palace was nothing more than a gilded cage. She'd done her best to stay out of the way, but she needed to get out or she was going to go absolutely insane.

Getting from her new rooms to the Great Hall wasn't too challenging of a feat. Shirina had been kind enough to tolerate Penny's presence long enough to show her around. Dair had accompanied them for the last half of the tour, but the air had still been thick with tension. How was she going to win over Aiden's family? While being polite had its uses, she was going to have to work harder to break through the frost of the Winter royal family.

Penny found the front door to the palace and opened it. The cold nipped almost pleasantly at her nose as she stepped out into the cold. The sun hung high in the sky, not a cloud in sight. The walls around the palace didn't let her see much of the other peaks, but the gardens within were distracting enough. Blue holly, wintercreeper, and juniper added splashes of color under the dusting of snow from the night before.

Penny turned down one of the pebbled paths, cleared of snow. A trio of barks rang out ahead.

A grin pulled at Penny's lips, and she ran toward the sound. Just as she rounded a corner, a mass of spotted fur jumped into view, nearly plowing into her.

She fell back into a pile of snow that had been pushed off the path, but she laughed.

"Spot! By the Goddess, am I happy to see you!"

Before she could stand back up, all three of Spot's muzzles were in her face, sniffing her over and licking her cheeks with his cow-sized tongues. She shoved him away with a giggle and stood. He sat back on his haunches, all three tongues lolling and his thick tail thumping against the ground. He hadn't grown any larger since she had seen him last, his shoulders about the height of one of Lord Hermen's oxen. Odd for a dog, but Spot had never been normal. His trio of heads turned this way and that, catching whiffs of things Penny could never smell with her own nose.

"Sweet Gaia, what is that thing?" Angelica stood at the end of the path, a hand to her chest.

Penny walked over to Spot and slung an arm around one of his necks. "Angelica, meet my good friend, Spot." She scratched at each of his ears, right where she knew he loved it. "He's the goodest boy I know. Yes, he is."

Angelica took a few tentative steps toward them, though she didn't come close enough to touch or be touched. "This is King

Aiden's dog? From Olympia?" She gave him a thorough once over. "I thought he was supposed to be, you know, *normal size.*"

"He was when I first brought him through the Mist, but the magic of Faerie must have done something to the magic in him. And he's not the only one. Mine's been acting strangely as well." She took a step toward Angelica and lowered her voice. "It's one of the reasons I wanted to talk out here." She had been more than elated when Aiden asked Devan and Angelica to join them in the Winter Palace before they were ready to return to Olympia. Aiden needed access to Devan's small network here in Faerie and Penny needed her friend more than ever.

"All right, tell me what happened," Angelica said.

Penny gestured toward the window only a dozen feet from where they stood. "Let's get a little farther from prying eyes."

She tried her best to map out the palace in her mind from the outside as she followed behind the dog. Shirina's tour earlier that morning had covered most of it, but she'd have liked to have a more solid idea of where she would be staying for the foreseeable future.

Penny recalled the moments of her magic acting out of sort to Angelica as they walked. "I had an inkling of a thought that I should smack Dair upside the head, and a sapling sprang out from the floor of Crann Mòr and did exactly that. Then, two days ago, we were meeting with the Andàn—"

"You met with *the Andàn?*" Angelica squealed and then looked around sheepishly. "Sorry, continue."

"When they were talking about what to do with me, I got so angry. A pot of flowers sat on a table behind Aiden and nearly a dozen white daffodils sprang up between the blooms. I don't think anyone saw, but I can't be certain."

"Were you connected to your magic?"

"Not consciously." She hadn't even thought to check if her hands had been glowing. "But I know I did it, or that I influenced it. I just don't know how."

"Have you confided in King Aiden?"

Penelope sighed. She'd thought about it almost constantly for the last two days but hadn't worked up the courage to seek him out to talk about it. In fact, she hadn't had the courage to seek him out at all. Keeping out of the way seemed like the best thing for everyone at the moment.

While she was somewhat of a decent spy, she had no history in the war room. She would be as unwelcome as a cabbage in a tomato garden. As it stood, her cabbage-ness was enough of an issue for Aiden and his family. "I've been problem enough for him. I don't want to add to his troubles."

"But love is about sharing burdens—"

"But what if he's not in love with me anymore?" The words flew out before Penny could trap them behind her teeth. Tears gathered at the corners of her eyes. Aiden hadn't said as much, but the fears she'd been pushing down came bubbling up.

Angelica stopped her in the middle of the walkway. "What is that supposed to mean?"

Penny looked around the empty gardens before lowering her voice. "He's a king. A *High King*. He has so many more paths he could take now." She didn't mention everything else. He'd become a new person with his new title, more open, more lively. While she still caught him straightening his cuffs when he grew anxious and keeping quietly to himself after a long day, this new family of his had helped him out of his shell—a shell he'd only allowed Penny to glimpse into.

"And has he changed too much? Have *you* fallen out of love?"

If anything, she'd fallen more in love with him. He'd blossomed into this wonderful man; the man she knew he'd always become. He'd just done it without her. Penny played with a stray curl. "I can't imagine how much he's been through in the last several months. I love him. I want to be here for him, help him, but I don't know how I can when everyone is telling us to stay apart."

"I'm not telling you to stay apart," Angelica teased.

Penelope nudged her with an elbow and pulled her back into their walk. "You know what I mean."

"Well, I think the two of you need to hash it all out. He's changed, but so have you, Penny. By the Goddess, you're an entirely different woman than the one I left behind in Olympia over a year ago. Look at where we are!" She gestured to the lofty hallway. "You're in *Faerie*. The Penny Barclay I knew would have never stepped foot in this kingdom, but this Penelope Barclay did."

"And look where it's gotten me," Penny grumbled. "I've been nearly killed twice, and my magic is going mad."

"Yes, but at least you got out and saw the world."

"But what if I can't ever go back?"

Angelica ushered her toward a small gazebo with a table and chairs. "Are they so sure you can't?"

"It's certainly not looking good." Penny groaned when they stepped into the enchanted space. Warmth seeped into her boots from the enchanted rocks making up the floor. They needed some of these in Olympia's palace for the garden paths in the winter months.

Angelica gracefully perched herself on the bench and patted the seat beside her. "But I thought they were looking into it."

Penny slumped into the proffered seat. "Angelica, when I ate that fruit, I knew what the consequences would be. I don't know how, but something inside of me told me if I ate it, I would never return to the life I once had. I would never become Duchess of Eleusion. I would never get to grow old in Barclay Manor like my ancestors before me —not that it matters much anymore. With Mother off possibly gallivanting with the rebels, I don't know that there will be an Eleusion to return to."

She didn't even mention any of the other lands under attack. Would there even be an Olympia to return to? The rebels had only grown bolder since the Mist had come down, which had to mean the battle was still raging in Olympia as well. What were Dion and Shaunie doing now? What about Paulo and Diana?

There were so many other things that Penny didn't have answers to.

"So, you don't want to go back?" Angelica asked, carefully.

Penny covered her eyes with her hands. "I don't know what I want. I thought I did. I thought I knew what I was getting into, but now? Now I have no idea what I'm going to do, and I'm *scared*. I'm scared of losing Aiden. I'm scared of what my mother is doing. I'm scared of losing this war and the little bit of freedom I've carved out for myself. I don't know how I'm going to survive a place with so many immortal beings who wish to see me dead, and I can't even use the one tool in my arsenal that could even the fight." She looked down at her bronze hands, not a fleck of green on them.

"I think you should figure out what you want," Angelica said. "If you want to go back to Olympia, then you should do everything in your power to figure out a way back. But"—she grabbed Penny's face between her hands—"if you want to stay, you need to prove to every single fae here that this is where you belong and you're not going anywhere."

Penny took a deep breath. "You're right. I just need to figure out where I'm going from here."

Angelica swung an arm around her. "You've got this, Penny."

A laugh bubbled up in Penny's chest, but she swallowed it back. She had no idea what she wanted, but hopefully, she'd figure it out soon.

Penny stared up at the portrait of Queen Morana hanging on the wall.

It really was remarkable how much Aiden looked like her. The only similarities he had to his brothers were his deep brow and the very straight nose. Everything else came from this woman—this female. A fae. A queen.

"I feel like I'm having déjà vu."

Penny spun and found Aiden leaning against a pillar just inside the door. The finely tailored jacket he wore accentuated his lean form. His shoulders were broader than they had been in Olympia, and he seemed to fit into this version of himself much better than he had as Lord of the Underworld. The mix of smart clothing and confidence had her palms sweating.

She took a step toward him. "I thought you were in meetings all day."

Aiden watched her under dark lashes, amber eyes gleaming with something she couldn't quite catch at that distance. "We ended for lunch a bit early. Apparently, it doesn't take long to draft letters to all the Court nobles asking for advisors when only a handful have any combat experience." He looked up at the pictures. "I wonder how many of them had training."

Penny followed his gaze to the pictures around the room. "They all look so young."

"I think many of them were." His voice drew closer, but Penny didn't want to be distracted from what he was saying by whatever he held in his eyes. "Fiadh told me that many of them died in the Faerie Wars and in the wars before that. Apparently, Faerie was not as peaceful a place before my aunt came to power."

Penny looked over at the portrait of the woman next to Queen Morana's. "I'm sorry you never had the chance to meet them."

Aiden stepped in front of her and grabbed her hand. "I'm not."

Penny looked up then. His amber eyes bore into her, something warm and fierce swirling in their depths. That gleam revealing itself.

"Why not?" she whispered.

Aiden lifted her hand to his mouth and pressed a featherlight kiss against her knuckles before using his grip to pull her a step closer. "You know, I've been trying to find a moment to talk to you about everything."

She bit her bottom lip. "You have?"

He ducked his head, getting close to her ear. "Why are you whispering?" he whispered.

She jumped back from him. "I don't know!" she yelled much too loudly. She cringed and cleared her throat. "Was there something specific you wanted to talk about?"

He still hadn't relinquished her hand. "Yes. Us."

"*Us?*" she squeaked. Great Goddess above, she couldn't get a handle on her vocal cords. How did he always cause her to lose control of herself?

Aiden laughed. "Yes. A lot has happened since I saw you in Olympia."

"You could definitely say that. You became a High King."

"And you became a seasoned explorer of Faerie." He shook his head. "I still can't believe you did that."

"Why wouldn't I have?" Penny asked. "You know how I feel. I would have done anything to get you back."

Aiden pulled her hand to his chest. "And I you. I tried, Penelope. I tried for weeks to figure out how to get back to you. I can't tell you how many fights Thaen and I got into."

Penny quirked an eyebrow. "Why doesn't that surprise me? He seems to want to get into fights with everyone."

"He's really not so bad. We had a rough start, but I would trust him with my life now. It's been a trying few months, Penelope. For all of us."

She blew out a breath and closed the distance between them, her dark-blue skirt brushing the tops of his boots. "I know. But I'm glad we're together now."

He leaned his forehead against hers. "And I'll take whatever time with you the Goddess will give me."

Penny closed her eyes. But how long would that be? Would she return to Olympia, or would she decide to throw caution to the wind and stay with him?

She leaned forward, her nose brushing against his. "I—"

His lips crashed against hers, cutting off every word and every thought crossing through her mind.

Warmth spread through every inch of her body.

His hands wrapped around her back, drawing her closer to him until she was crushed against him.

By the Goddess, it was like they never left that blanket under the oak tree. Like they hadn't been separated for months, like that chasm between them wasn't miles wide. Nothing had changed between them. His soft lips against hers were like coming home after being away for so long. The thought of this, of loving him, had carried her through all of Faerie and straight into that revel.

This was what she was here for.

He pulled away.

Penny stumbled and he held her shoulders. She blinked up at him, her thoughts still wrapped up in that kiss.

But her mind cleared when she found the agony in his amber eyes.

"Aiden—"

He shook his head. "I'm sorry. I didn't mean to—" He stopped abruptly. "I need to go."

He ran from the room.

Tears gathered at the corners of her eyes. Perhaps none of this had anything to do with what she wanted. Perhaps her opinions and her wishes didn't matter if he was the one who was going to simply run away no matter what.

8

SNEAK

AIDEN GRITTED HIS TEETH AS HE PUSHED HIS AWARENESS OUT AS FAR AS HE could. The magic tying him to the Land had become steadier during his waking hours since his anointing, but he still couldn't grasp everything he saw. Trying to push his consciousness into Flùranach was like standing too close to a painting. He couldn't see the full picture. It was like watching millions of lights and colors and shadows and shapes all clashing against one another. He understood *something* was happening, he just couldn't grasp what.

His consciousness returned to the Winter Palace and the family sitting room. He slumped back in his chair and let out a sigh. "There's nothing. I can't concentrate well enough to even grasp what I'm seeing."

Dair passed him a glass of water. "Do not fret too much, cousin."

He downed the water gratefully. "We need eyes on Flùranach." It had been over a month since Durant had taken the city with help from the Aigeans. He had no idea what was happening within the city walls, but he knew whatever it was wasn't good.

"I am with you," Thaen agreed. "I could easily infiltrate their ranks and gather intel. I would just need Sgiath or his daughter to portal me in."

"I've already told you, that's too risky," Aiden said. "We don't even know what kind of security they have set up. Without knowing where Durant is, I can't send you alone in good conscience."

"At least allow me to gather a team," he argued. "I can collect a few of the guard here that I trust and scout out the surrounding area."

"If I could just figure out my sight with the Land, we wouldn't need to send anyone."

Thaen made more suggestions, but none of them felt right to Aiden. Without being able to see what awaited them there, he feared sending anyone. If he could just see for himself, perhaps then he would know how to handle it better.

"Instead of bickering, why not the both of you just go?" Dair said from where he was sprawled on the floor, fiddling with the spare figurines used on the table to mark where the opposing forces were. He lined them up in pairs like dancers rather than soldiers.

"I will not take our High King into danger of such a nature," Thaen said. "We do not know what may wait for us on the other side."

But Aiden's thoughts were already spinning with possibilities. "Which is why you should take me. If I get closer, I may be able to more clearly see what's going on." Not only that, but over the last week, his mind continued to stray to a certain green-eyed maiden with the softest hair his fingers had ever—

No. He wasn't taking another stroll down that path of thought. He needed to get out of the palace, and this was the perfect way to do it. He studied the map, figuring out where Sgiath would need to portal to not alert the rebels in the city. "We wouldn't have to get as close to the city or risk anyone getting caught."

Thaen growled and began pacing in front of the fireplace. "I cannot take you. It would go against what I have sworn to do."

Aiden looked up. "And what exactly have you sworn to do?" Thaen shook his head, but Aiden couldn't tell if it was out of unwillingness to divulge or simply frustration.

Dair gave out a dramatic sigh. "It is because he wants you to accept him as your *sgàile*."

"My what?"

"Shut up, Dair," Thaen bit out.

"Do not snap at me because you were too cowardly to ask him."

"I am *not* a coward." Thaen strode in Dair's direction.

Aiden caught Thaen before he could lunge for his twin. "What is he talking about? What is a *sgàile*?"

"It is like your own personal bodyguard," Dair supplied.

Thaen's furrowed brow deepened. "It is a sacred guardian. Someone whose sole purpose is to protect those whom they have sworn themselves to. They take a magical oath that binds them to the one they are guarding."

Aiden shook his head. "I can't let you do that. You have a duty to Winter until the High Council meets again to decide who will be king, and you're technically my heir at the moment, though the Land has not actually named you. I can't allow you to put yourself in danger by protecting me all the time."

"And I can still be those things as well. The only thing that would change is that the Land would also recognize me as your guardian and may give me better ability to protect you than I can now. Some *sgàile* have been known to have even been able to sense where their charges were."

"And you want to swear yourself to my protection and all that?"

Thaen placed a fist over his heart and bowed low. "It is my greatest wish."

Aiden watched Thaen. He already had an inkling about how the role of Winter King would play out, though he didn't want to give much thought to it. Fiadh's death was still a fresh wound, but the Land nudged him about it more often as the days went on. It would need to be settled with the High Council sooner rather than later.

And Thaen was certainly the only fae Aiden could see taking on the role of bodyguard. Aiden trusted him more than he trusted his brothers, perhaps more than he had ever trusted anyone in the Underworld—besides Hart, who had been more like a brother than anything else. But he was gone now, and Thaen had shown Aiden time and again he only had his best interests at heart, even when those interests weren't what Aiden believed he wanted.

Thaen remained still as he waited for Aiden's answer, but Dair began to squirm. "Just put him out of his misery."

"Are you sure this is what you truly want?" Aiden smirked. "You know I won't make it easy on you."

Thaen looked up at him, hopeful. "I would never suggest you do."

Aiden slapped him on the shoulder. "Then wish granted, cousin. I will never deny you such a thing if it is in my power to give it."

"I cannot tell you how grateful I am."

"You may want to hold back on the praise." A grin stretched

across Aiden's cheeks. "We'll do all of the swearing and binding after we get back from Summer."

Thaen grumbled for the hundredth time as Aiden crouched low in the sand. The shadow on that side of the dune concealed them as they peered out across the mile of moonlit sand where they'd had Sgiath deposit them. They had two hours to get in and get out before Sgiath returned with an entire contingent of guards.

"I see the barrier," said Thaen. "They have cast a rather extensive glamour over the city."

"How can they block us so easily?"

"Death," answered Thaen gravely. "A lot of it."

This must be what Penny had spoken about when she mentioned the device Durant had. The way they had hidden their camps from the Land's sight. How much magic would it take to create something like this? How many fae had been stripped of their lives and their magic to accomplish it?

Thaen held up a hand and took a few silent steps forward. Aiden followed behind, disregarding Thaen's obvious command to stay behind.

"I wasn't always a High King, you know," Aiden said.

"Yes, I saw skills that were passable as mortal spymaster. After learning you had been trained by the demon woman herself, I had expected something much more challenging. It is a wonder we have not caught her already considering her paltry tutelage."

Aiden frowned. *Paltry?* He'd been named Lord of the Underworld! The title had been infamous in Olympia, more so even than his actual name. His spies had been some of the best. He'd been an excellent trainer. "I trained Penelope, and she got the upper hand on you at the revel," Aiden mentioned.

"You do not get to take credit for the fact that I could not see Penelope."

"I suppose you're right. I can't take credit for that." In all honesty, he couldn't take credit for her at all. She was her own force to be reckoned, with and it had nothing to do with the training he'd given her with a blade. Aiden frowned. "Can you see her now?"

Thaen shrugged his shoulders. "Not in so many words. I can see the magic move when she does, but I cannot actually *see* her. I have adapted my other senses to her. I can smell her, hear her heartbeat. Her being human makes it easier, and I can distinguish her from the fae in the palace."

Aiden's thoughts strayed to their moment in the gallery again, the wide-open sky above them breaking down his resolve not to dwell on the moment. He could still feel her lips pressed against his, her heart beating against his chest. He'd been a blasted idiot to let himself kiss her. It would be difficult enough as it was to let her go when the Aunties came back from their sojourn with a solution. After kissing her? He'd be tearing his own heart out when she went back across the border. Running out of the gallery had been a coward's exit, but his mind had caught up with his heart, and he'd needed to remove himself before he'd done something foolish. He hadn't allowed himself to be alone with her after that. He'd kept their conversations short and didn't linger in her presence for longer than necessary, even if all he wanted to do was kiss her again.

He followed Thaen through the dunes, the lights of Flùranach beckoning them forward—along with the trepidation of what they would find. Aiden had seen Flùranach in his walkings with the Land. It was beautiful, the sandstone buildings and desert plants bright along the dark, blue sea. The city spread across the coast, lining the water rather than venturing further into the hot, sweltering sand. The devastation the water folk must have wrought...

Thaen tucked himself into the shadow of Flùranach's wall. The large barricade guarded the city from the winds and storms off the desert rather than an invading army but was just as effective for both. Aiden hugged the wall, wrapping the shadows tightly around him. He skimmed the surface of his connection with the Land, allowing only a slight awareness to overtake his senses. If he allowed too much, the magic could overtake him, and he'd be unaware of his physical surroundings.

Thaen signaled up ahead and Aiden slowed his steps. A large door stood sentry along the wall. Aiden took a step closer, but Thaen held out an arm and shook his head. Aiden allowed more of the Land to take over his mind and he saw what Thaen did. A handful of humans stood on the other side, one holding some kind of enchanted object. But that was as far as he could see and even that was a murky sense rather than the sharp picture he could usually conjure even in such a state.

"Looks like some kind of light magic," Thaen whispered. "It would not be wise to tempt a forced entry. Is this close enough?"

Aiden looked about with his physical eyes. Nothing moved over the dunes. Even the ifrits that were known for terrorizing those on the dunes at night knew better than to come near this place.

He closed his eyes.

The barrier over the city swept down the walls, giving less than an inch for Aiden to squeeze his consciousness through. He shook his head. "We need to get inside or at least on top of the wall."

Thaen made a frustrated noise—something between a grunt and a growl—and nodded toward the other end of the wall. "It would be foolish to scale the wall here."

They continued down the wall for another fifteen minutes, Thaen's eyes continually scanning the rough stone like he could see through it. He probably could. His sight was similar to Aiden's connection with the Land, but different enough that he could take apart the pieces of the glamour and the wall to get a semblance of a picture on the other side. Several times, they had to tuck themselves against the wall to hide from the patrol on the wall above. Praise the Goddess they were part of the Night Court and wielded shadow.

The babble of water sang ahead of them. Thaen pulled up short at the bank of a river. The waterway wove through the dunes below. The water rushed under the wall through a tunnel and likely ran through the city out into the ocean.

"Do you think we can dam the water?"

Aiden blinked at Thaen next to him. "Do I think what?"

Thaen stared down at the water. "I bet we could if we had the *sgàile* bond, we could do it," he mumbled.

Aiden's brows furrowed. "What exactly does this bond require? Is there some kind of ceremony?"

Thaen rubbed the back of his neck. "It is a simple thing. Clasped hands and a few words."

Aiden grabbed his hand. "Like this?"

Thaen jerked back. "You want to do this here? Usually there is a bit more thought put into it. The families gather. There is a banquet after."

"You know I'm not one to do things the usual way." Aiden

gripped his hand tighter. "If we're going to get back to Sgiath, I recommend you hurry."

Thaen squared his shoulders. "Are you sure about this, cousin? This is not a small thing you are agreeing to. Your very life will be linked to mine in a way that makes it so I can protect you. I will know when you are in danger. I will know where you are at all times so that I might find you in peril. But with those things comes a transparency that most people do not share between each other."

Aiden clasped Thaen's shoulder with his free hand. "What do I need to say?"

The magic under Aiden's feet stirred, as if acting as witness to what Thaen would share.

"All you have to say is, 'I give this Tuatha my word and my bond, that he may protect me in times of peril and hardship.'"

Aiden repeated the words immediately.

Shadows gathered around their hands, the inky black of Aiden's magic summoned by the words.

Thaen looked at their clasped hands, eyes wide.

"I think it's your turn," Aiden whispered.

Thaen let out a deep breath. "All right. I give this Tuatha my word and my bond, that I will protect him in times of peril and hardship."

Aiden's shadows were joined by Thaen's, the purple streaked magic swirling with his over their hands. The Land under them practically purred as the shadows sank back into their skin.

Aiden blinked up at Thaen. "That's it?"

But Thaen's eyes were wide. "Stars, I did not think it would be like this."

Aiden pulled his cousin closer, looking into his pale eyes. "What's wrong?"

"Nothing is wrong. The bond is strong. I can sense magic, but this... Cousin, I can practically see every strand of your hair, it's so strong. My heart is so full. I just... Thank you, Aiden," Thaen said reverently. "I know it was much to ask of you, to give your trust in such a way. I will not let you down."

"I don't know what you're thanking me for. You just locked yourself into the toughest job in the kingdom." Aiden let go of Thaen's hand. "Now, let's see if we can use this to our advantage."

As if they were working off the same cue, both Aiden and Thaen thrust their hands out toward the water. It was as if Thaen had been working with him since he was a child, they moved so flawlessly together. It was almost eerie how well Thaen mimicked his movements, but if anyone could be trusted with such insight, it was Thaen. A wall of shadow grew, giving them six feet between the dam and the now-empty tunnel leading into the city.

"Let us move," said Thaen. "We only have an hour to get back to the rendezvous."

Aiden followed after Thaen as he slid down into the bed of the nearly empty river. An ankle-deep trickle of water still surrounded them, but Aiden didn't mind overly much except for the now-soggy boots he sported.

Thaen reached the other end ahead of Aiden, checking the perimeter before hoisting himself up onto the bank. The ground within the city was more compact than the dunes without the walls. Aiden followed him up.

When Aiden reached the top, he froze.

"It is worse than I imagined," Thaen breathed.

A few buildings crumbled to the ground along the bank, some scorch-marked and others crushed by waves or large rocks. One of the houses looked as if its entire roof had been sliced through by a sword, the flat top sliding onto the ground to the side of it. The bridge spanning the river stood completely ruined, the edges reaching for one another and the stones making up the middle resting in the water beneath.

How much of the damage came from the rebels? How much from the fae that tried to fight them off? If the rebels had done the damage, they had more magic than Aiden could even begin to guess at.

And then there were the rebels themselves.

Fires burned in the streets, casting shadows over the sea of tents and faces. A group of men burst out from one of the buildings on the waterway, drinks in hand and cheers on their lips. A pair of rebels dragged an ellyllon female behind them in chains, her eyes vacant as she listed after them. Iron cages hung above the street; sylphs, basilisk, and even brownies hung in the air above open flames and jeering humans.

This was the future Durant so desperately fought for? One of pain and anguish and horror? It made no sense. Durant had always been a leader of order, of justice—however skewed. Even she could not have stooped so low as all this. Yes, she could be brutal, she could be monstrous, but for some reason he couldn't reconcile the woman who had raised him with the leader of such abhorrent actions.

Thaen pulled him back down into the water way. "Breathe, Aiden. You need to focus on why we are here."

Aiden nodded, only half understanding what Thaen said. He reached for the connection within him once again and pushed it out into the city.

What he felt in that one moment was much worse than what he could see on his own.

His senses were compounded by cries of the fae within the city. Children taken from their mothers and shackled to each other as they were paraded along a balcony to humans below waiting to buy them. The girls went faster than the boys.

Bodies—bwbachod and ellyllon alike—hung in long lines above the main street of Flùranach, limbs askew or even missing. The wails of widowed wives and fatherless children rang in Aiden's ears. He saw folk dragged, beaten, spit upon, flogged, violated, all while the humans sat back, watching and laughing.

He couldn't take anymore. He broke the connection and raced to the bank to be sick onto the sand.

Thaen came up beside him, guarding his back as he washed his face with the water swirling at their legs. "That bad?"

"Worse," Aiden said hoarsely. He took a deep breath. The depravity knew no bounds. He heaved again just thinking about it.

"Did you find her?"

Aiden shook his head. "I'll try again."

Thaen nodded, but Aiden could see the worry in his eyes.

Aiden pulled himself from the bank and took a deep breath. He closed his eyes once again, taking a page from Penelope's book, and reached down into the soil beside him.

At least he was prepared this time.

He pushed through the torment of his folk and found the center of the city, the center of the anguish crying out around them. He pushed his consciousness out of his body, as he did within his dreams, and transported himself to Durant's center of operations. A large inn squatted in the middle of the city, messengers and fighters streaming in and out of it. Aiden walked past them all, even walking through a few of them on his way to the closed meeting room in the back. He walked straight through the door.

"... coming up from Olympia," said one of the men on the other side. Aiden didn't recognize him, but he did spot a few in the crowd he did. "If we gather our troops and take Brònach—"

"Except we don't have the manpower for such an excursion," cut in one of the few women in the group. She stood next to the one with salt-and-pepper hair Aiden recognized from Olympia.

Aiden leaned over the table, trying to figure out where the troops were and what their next moves were. From what he heard as he watched, not even the rebel generals knew what their next step was. They fought back and forth, throwing this idea out as fast as they shut down that other one. It was worse than sitting with his Councilors.

"We need more gifts," said another, "and we need Olympia's throne for ourselves."

So, they hadn't seized Dion's throne. A pressure he'd been carrying lifted from his chest. At least his brother was still alive. Even if Aiden hadn't cared about Dion as his brother, he would have as a king. If Durant managed to take Dion's throne, Faerie would be in a world of hurt. They needed an alliance with Olympia. The sooner the better. The few messengers that had made it past the rebels at the border hadn't been able to breach the palace's defenses to get inside. The Council had insisted they wait to send word until they had a better idea what was going on. Aiden would have to find a way to get word to Dion. He might even have to send Devan and Angelica back before they finished the intelligence network they were building. Both kingdoms stood a much better chance taking down this rebellion together than they did on their own.

Durant sat at the head of the table, green eyes flicking back and forth with the conversation. Aiden took the moment to truly look at her. Besides the few added wrinkles on the sides of her mouth, she looked exactly the same as the night he had killed Father. He'd sent her on a wild goose chase, claiming there were insurrectionists in Calypso. She'd had no reason to doubt his claim. He'd given her none. Not until he'd sunk the sword through Father's cold heart.

Where had she been all that time? The slight darkening of her skin suggested she'd spent time in the sun. She'd either traveled a lot or she'd been somewhere she had to be outside. He'd guess the continent, since he hadn't been able to find her anywhere within Olympia. How had she gotten past him? Looking at her now, with the predatory gleam in her eye as she watched her men bicker, how had he let her escape all those years ago?

Something in Aiden's stomach tugged. *Curses.* He needed to leave. But if he left now, he would go away empty handed. The maps on the table gave him very little. He felt his body move, but he did his best to stay in the moment. They only had this one window. This one chance.

Durant lifted a hand, nonchalantly, but everyone in the room knew to go silent.

"I've already set things into motion," she said, her voice calm and commanding in the silent room. "We don't have the ability to take Autumn at this time. They would see that coming and we cannot lose the element of surprise." She stood over the table, a large, detailed map of Faerie and Olympia stretched out before her. She settled two fingers on the border. "We have men coming up from Olympia within a fortnight."

"And what do you plan to do with them?" asked a gruff man in the corner. Icy-blue eyes flashed over the maps on the table, sharp with keen intelligence. He leaned against the back wall, looking nonchalant, but his ease only added to his air of danger. His clothing and the short blades strapped to his chest told Aiden he was from the continent. Penelope had said Durant was working with them as well, though she hadn't mentioned anyone in particular.

Durant pursed her lips, more at being questioned than having to think, Aiden knew.

"If we're quick,"—Aiden recognized Father's old court advisor that spoke—"we could avoid the worst of the heat coming in the summer months. It would be best to take the Night Court when their weather is less temperamental."

"But we aren't taking the Night Court yet."

Everyone else followed Durant's gaze toward the west side of the map.

Sona.

The capital of Spring stood in the middle of the dense forests of the land. Aiden had used his connection with the Land to visit a few times, wandering through the houses hanging from giant branches and walking along the limbs as wide as roads. It was a beautiful place.

And now it was Durant's next target.

"Then I'll pay half of what you've asked before you take Sona," said the foreign man, "and the rest after the battle is finished."

Who is this man? Aiden had never seen anyone speak to Durant in such a way, much less make demands. Aiden would have been impressed if he hadn't been part of the very rebellion ripping his kingdom apart.

Durant glowered. "That's not what we agreed."

"We also didn't agree on sending another one of my best operatives to Olympia to deal with your little king problem." He shrugged, not at all affected by Durant's obvious disapproval. "Plans change and we must be flexible."

The door to the room burst open, and a boy nearly sprawled on the floor at Durant's feet. "Your Grace, there's word of intruders at the wall."

Durant came around the table. "What kind?"

The boy paled. "The Lòchran, Your Grace, and the High King is with him."

Aiden fled before he could see Durant's reaction. His consciousness flew back into his body, and he came to with a gasp, Thaen's bulky shoulder digging into his stomach. Thaen ran through the water, the level reaching above his navel now.

"Put me down!" Aiden urged and Thaen was quick to oblige.

The sound of yelling and splashing rang from behind, and Aiden glanced back to see a dozen men on their tail. He pushed off the riverbed with his feet and began swimming, his arms cutting through the water faster than trudging through the silty bottom was. He kept pace with Thaen, and they made it out of the wall. Thaen cast a shield and a dozen arrows rained down on them the moment they breached the opening. Aiden reached for his connection with Thaen as they scrambled up the embankment.

"Take out the dam!" Thaen shouted, his sword out as he turned to face the oncoming rebels as he tugged his magic out from within the dam.

Aiden pulled his magic, and the blockade broke apart, sending a wall of water toward their pursuers still trapped in the tunnel. He raced out toward the sand, Thaen's shield still taking hits until they were out of range. Aiden looked back to see the outer doors open, and a crowd of horsemen charge out onto the sand. Thaen let his shield drop, and they sprinted across the sand until they reached the meeting point.

Aiden looked up at the stars above them. Sgiath had agreed to be there within moments. "Where is he?"

Thaen shook his head, watching the approaching host with determination. "He'll be here."

Aiden could hear the stomp of hooves against the sand. He drew his sword and spread his feet.

Another second and he could hear the huff of the horses' breaths.

Another, and there were the glinting leers of the rebels' teeth.

Another and he felt the spray of sand from the horses surrounding him.

He swung his blade.

The cry of the horse told Aiden of its fall before he saw it tumble down the side of the dune. The next horse came, and its rider held a lance at Aiden's eye level. Aiden ducked the iron tip and used his sword to cut off a large chunk of the wooden shaft. They came, one after the other, surrounding him.

Black flashed in the corner of Aiden's vision and rough hands grabbed him by the back of his coat. Shadows stole all sight from him, and he heard nothing for a few heartbeats until he was spit out onto a lush carpet and the smell of a fire.

Sgiath closed the portal, severing an arm reaching out through the black mass. Before the severed limb could hit the ground, he'd summoned another portal, and it disappeared. Only a smattering of blood on the hardwood floor remained.

Aiden scrambled to his feet. "Your timing was impeccable."

Sgiath quirked an eyebrow. "I thought you said you would be able to get out without notice."

Aiden shrugged and sheathed his sword. He turned to Thaen. "Why didn't you wake me?" Thaen knew how to get Aiden back into his body. If Aiden got sucked too far into his connection, Dair had shown Thaen the pressure points on Aiden's body to wake him even if he was completely asleep.

"Did you get what we went to get?" Thaen asked.

Aiden nodded. "More." With their knowledge of Durant's plans to attack Spring, they'd gained the upper hand.

Thaen grinned. "Then nothing else matters."

9
SPRING AND THREATS

Dearest Penny,

I can't meet this afternoon for tea. I have a teatime set up with some of my contacts in the city regarding the attack on Spring. Can we meet after dinner?

If you're looking for something to occupy your time, I suggest taking a stroll through the palace library. I think you'll find it somewhat remarkable. Even I can say it was rather impressive, and you know I've never been the scholarly type.

Your Apologetic Friend,
Angelica

PENNY QUIETLY SHUT THE LIBRARY DOOR BEHIND HER. SHE'D MADE IT PART OF her schedule to visit there every other day, collecting Faerie tales and history she'd had no access to in Olympia. Her first foray into the library had been somewhat awkward, the few librarians in charge of the space giving her looks as if they believed she were a barbarian come to tear the books from their shelves and shred them to bits. But after the first few days of her coming and going, they'd seem to notice the books that she took came back in the same condition they left in and that was all that mattered.

She glanced down at her newest found treasure.

The Battle of Mastery: Redefining Your Gifts and Discovering Your Inner Strength

It had sounded like just what she needed to figure out her magic. She'd tried again to connect with her gift, and while it had gone far better than the first time, it had been so overwhelming she'd had to stop. It was worse than when she'd first arrived in Faerie. Her gift wouldn't even do anything because she had absolutely no control of what was happening inside of her. The sapling and the daffodils had been flukes, and she couldn't figure out how to recreate them.

The door to her room called to her. The last rays of sunlight painted the horizon, reds, pinks, and purples in large strokes across the sky. The Winter Palace always seemed to be sleeping during the day, likely due to Shirina's odd hours. The price of fae gifts hadn't completely sunk in for Penny. She didn't know whether it was better to have a permanent price, or one she could recover from.

Would she end up with a permanent price? She shuffled the book from one hand to the other. Was her magic changing so much she would eventually have to pay the way the fair folk did?

As she turned to the corner to the family wing, she ran straight into a row of very shiny buttons.

Dair jumped back, eyes wide and hair tousled. He took her by the shoulders and looked around them. When he found no one else in the hallway, he looked down at her.

"You did not see me," he said quietly. "If *Màthair* finds out I was up here, she will suspect me of putting a snake in Thaen's bed."

Penny looked past him to the door of Thaen's rooms, the one across from Aiden's door. "Did you put a snake in Thaen's bed?"

Dair put a finger to her lips. "If the brownies hear, they will get rid of it before Thaen gets back." He slid past her down the hall. "Do not tell a soul!" he whispered over his shoulder.

She watched him slink away, disappearing down one of the many hallways. When no one else came rushing after him, she turned back toward her room.

"All right then."

With the images of snakes slithering about the palace, she slipped into her room, watching the floor for any sign of scales. She'd made it halfway across the small sitting area she shared with Aiden when a throat cleared. Penny jumped and drew her dagger from her waist. She sagged in relief when she saw Shirina sitting on the white divan next to the fire, silver dress glittering.

"Sweet Gaia, you scared me half to death." Penny tucked her knife back into her sheath, though the shock at finding Shirina in her rooms did not abate. Had she witnessed the exchange between her and Dair? If that had been the case, Shirina likely would have gone after him herself. Him or the snake.

No, she'd keep the snake business to herself. It would be a point in her favor in Dair's mind, and Thaen could do with a little bit of discomfort.

Shirina smirked. "You came in, mind spinning. A copper for your troubles?"

Penny cut off her nervous laugh. "Oh, it's nothing. Besides, with such a beautiful dress as that, I should charge more than a copper." Shirina chuckled and Penny set the book down on the table next to her bedroom door. Daylight had finally made its grand exit out the window. She turned back to Shirina. "Is something the matter?"

"Not at the moment." Shirina settled back down into the cushions of the divan. "I think these last several days have been enough of a worry for all of us."

Penny silently agreed. Aiden had returned from Summer almost two weeks ago—without her knowing he'd gone in the first place—with reports that Adira was readying to attack. Penny had been in a near panic when she'd found out and had been ready to give him the verbal lashing of a lifetime, but when she'd gone looking for him, he'd already trekked down the mountain to the training grounds. By the time he'd returned, the anger had dissolved into a puddle of worry and sorrow. The days following had been filled with meetings and trips back and forth from Spring. She'd barely seen him in the last week, but she knew when he returned from his daily trip down the mountain and always made sure to greet him at the door, no matter that they didn't have more than a few moments before someone else came looking for him.

But perhaps it was better they didn't see one another.

There were so many questions she wasn't sure she wanted the answer to. She needed to focus on her magic and on winning over Aiden's family so she wouldn't have to worry about being welcome if she did have to stay in Faerie. After that kiss nearly three weeks ago, she knew she couldn't give Aiden up so easily. Not without trying her best to figure out what was going on between them first.

She settled onto a chair farther from the fireplace, but near enough not to make Shirina throw out her neck trying to speak with her. "I'm glad to hear nothing's amiss, but I'm still curious as to why you're visiting me." It wasn't like no one came to speak with Penny, but it was the first time Shirina had crossed the threshold into her rooms.

"I wanted to know if you would like to go on an outing."

Penny's interest piqued. "What kind of outing?" she asked, maintaining her calm. She'd sell all her hair to get off the palace grounds for even a moment. While it was a wonderful place and there was plenty to explore, the fact that she couldn't simply walk out rankled her.

Shirina clasped her hands in her lap. "I am preparing to portal to Spring this evening to attend to some of the evacuation and bring Aiden a report on how everything over there is going. The Eiles are also joining me, and I thought you might enjoy seeing the folk Aiden is king over as well as try to get everyone more used to your face if you are to remain here. Would you like to accompany us?"

More than anything. But Penny wouldn't speak the words aloud. She couldn't let anyone know how cooped up she felt. How she almost missed being out in the wilds of Faerie like she had only a few weeks ago. If she wanted to prove she belonged here, she needed to act like she wanted to be there.

"If you don't think it would cause too many problems, I would love to go." Who knew what the folk would think if she showed up. Being in Spring would likely be worse. It could make Aiden's work with the refugees harder on top of dealing with the Spring evacuation.

Shirina shrugged. "Even if it does, we are in a blizzard of trouble, and no one will notice one more snowflake. Folk will talk, of course, but it may be better to get you out in the public eye and at least get a feel for what your future will look like. We will mostly be helping load wagons and attending to a few of the Spring Court noble families. A handful have requested to come to the Winter Palace, so they can be more involved in the war effort."

This was an olive branch, just as her encounter with Dair in the hall had been. Shirina had certainly been feeling Penny out the last few days, but Penny still felt like she was walking through freshly planted rows of seedlings around Aiden's family. She'd done her best to be present at every meal and engage in at least one conversation with every member of the royal family daily.

Except the Lòchran. He could jump in the Mist for all she cared.

But this invitation was exactly what she had been waiting for, a chance to prove herself to them. To show them that they could trust her.

Penny tried not to look too eager. "Then yes, I'd love to join you."

Penny twisted the end of her braid with her fingers as she sat in a wingback chair in a corner of the family sitting room. She could tell this room was treasured. The furniture looked comfortable rather than elegant; the floor covered in mismatched rugs; the paintings hanging from the walls whimsical rather than stately. It felt like walking into someone's home rather than a room in a palace.

Shirina had left to find Farrah. Angelica and Devan were finishing up whatever business they'd been up to. Aiden had told them they would be going back to Olympia by the end of the week. They were needed to establish communication with King Dion and Prince Evan.

Her heart sank just thinking about them leaving. The last week had only been survivable because she'd had Angelica to help keep her sane. But with Angelica's baby due to arrive in a few short months, it was expected they leave in a week or two. Her family deserved to be a part of that child's life, and that child deserved to be in a place that could keep her or him safe rather than a war front—though, who could say how Olympia was faring?

The door swung open, and Shirina glided into the room with Farrah on her arm, followed by Angelica and Devan. Penny tried to pull on her most serene, courtly mask, but it must have faltered because Angelica frowned and crossed the room to her.

"What's wrong?"

Penny waved her off. "Nothing at all. I'm only a little nervous about our adventure."

Angelica wrapped an arm around her. "I'm so looking forward to getting you out into more of Faerie."

Shirina turned back. "Penelope, it is probably best we leave the blades behind. While I do not like the idea of you being unarmed, I worry a fight would definitely break out if you walked in with a blade strapped to your hip."

Penny bit her lip but did as Shirina asked. It almost felt like she was disrobing with how vulnerable the loss of them made her, but there was nothing for it. She hesitated when she bent down to reach for the dagger, but Shirina must have seen.

"We will take a few guards with us," she said. "There should be nothing to fear."

By the time she set her last blade on the table, Shirina and Farrah had disappeared through the swirling portal.

Penny looked to Angelica. Her friend already looked a little green in the cheeks. "Are you going to be all right?"

Angelica took a deep breath. "It will be worth all the vomiting to get out of this weather."

Devan offered his wife a hand and she took it, still holding onto Penny as they neared the shadows. Angelica looked to both of them. "I'm sorry for what you will see next." She pulled them into the portal.

Even through the dark, Penny was more concerned about Angelica than she was about the complete darkness pressing against her. She could feel Angelica shake as they traveled through the magic. They came out the other side, all three of them staggering into the Spring forest. Angelica stumbled ahead of them, finding a wide, lush shrub to be sick into. Devan followed after her quickly.

Penny straightened, taking in the wide, red trunks surrounding the crystalline lake in front of them, and the portal dissipated.

Farrah came up beside her, eyes on whatever was above them. "Welcome to Sona, Penny."

Penny followed Farrah's gaze and gasped.

The trunks stretched into the sky for what felt like miles, holding aloft an entire city surrounding the water. She couldn't even view where it ended, it was so large. Swinging bridges spanned the empty spaces, connecting trunks and wide branches. Buildings hung in open air or attached themselves to the outer ring of the trunks themselves.

"Isn't it marvelous?" Angelica said, seeming to have once again gained her equilibrium.

"Come along," Shirina called. "We had best get to the city center before dark."

Penny followed behind the group. At the base of one of the trunks, a lift awaited them. The entire group piled into the contraption. Shirina pressed a brass key, and the basket flew up into the air. Penny latched onto Farrah's arm, and the fae let out a lighthearted laugh. In moments, they were at the lowest branches of the giant trees. Up close, the city was even more spectacular. Fine fabrics in different hues snapped in the evening breeze. The sound of people had Penny near smiling. The smell of roasting meats and baking bread circled them, making her stomach grumble.

And the folk.

There were flying folk, were-creatures, and others that leapt from place to place. Ellyllon, yaksha, goblins, xana, and even a number of banshees all walked in the branches above Penny's head. But the undercurrent of the place drowned out the excitement. As Penny caught the eyes of the faces around her, she saw the fear and weariness plain in their expressions. These people had to leave behind their homes, their livelihoods. Just as she had when the rebels took Eleusion.

Despair and empathy cut her to the quick. She hurried her steps and caught up to Shirina. "What's the plan?"

"We are headed to the Spring Palace to speak with the Spring Court. There, we will deliver the plans for the refugees at the Winter border." She patted the satchel swinging at her hip. "I brought maps with the best routes into the mountains as there is still a bit of snow until the end of next month. These will be distributed to the Court's noble houses who have been charged with leading groups of fae in different directions. We have also come to see what supplies they may need before they travel. It is still rather cold and while the fae are hearty, it does not mean we cannot be killed by unpreparedness."

Penny nodded. It seemed everything had been planned out with precision and forethought. "Anything you would like me to do? I feel somewhat useless without a job." At least Angelica and Devan had already treated with these folk and would be working on strengthening those ties. Penny could only describe herself as a spectacle at this point.

"I think it will be good to simply have you walk with us, though if you must do something I suppose you can carry the maps." Shirina swung the satchel's strap over her head of tight, black curls and passed it to Penny. "That should be safe enough. We need to show the folk you are not a threat and encourage their acceptance of your being here. We do not know if you will ever be able to leave, and it is best to plan for every eventuality."

Penny bit her lips together and took the bag. *That sounds a lot like they don't actually need my help.* If anything, they were trying to help *her*.

As if reading Penny's mind, Farrah said, "Don't fret, Penny. There will be plenty to do."

The group made it to the Spring Palace. Like Crann Mòr, the biggest tree in the forest was carved out, allowing fae in and out like it was a tall building rather than an actual tree. Lights beamed out of windows, and fae zipped in and out, messages or supplies in hand. It seemed as if most of the city went in and out before Penny followed Shirina through the large open doors. The entry hall was made up entirely of intricate friezes carved—or possibly even molded—into the trunk. An entire forest stretched across the walls, many of Faerie's inhabitants dancing through the crafted trunks.

"Leaves above, you have finally made it," called a voice from ahead.

Penny turned from the masterpiece to where a group of elegantly dressed ellyllon stood at the top of a set of stairs. One, likely the Spring King, stood at the forefront of the group, his long, lemon-yellow hair woven with early spring blooms and a crown of purple thistles around his head.

"Good evening, Falaichte." Shirina gave a slight nod of her head. "Of course we came."

The woman beside him gave a slight sniff. Turquoise hair fell in a straight sheet down her back and her eyes flashed when they landed on Penny. She stepped in front of the king. "What is the *mage* doing here?" she sneered.

Shirina gestured for Penny to step up beside her. "I brought Penelope with me to show her the other Courts. If she is going to be staying—"

"*Staying?*" another fae scoffed. "That thing should have been disposed of the moment it stepped foot on our land."

"Indeed," added another. "Parading it about like a pet may be fun for Night Court folk, but there should at least be some kind of leash on the thing."

Angelica took a step forward, but Devan held her back. Penny gave him a grateful half smile. She could take the insults as long as no one got hurt.

One of the fae broke away from the others. "I think it an excellent idea to have her walk around." He pushed a pair of darkened spectacles up his nose. "We have never been able to truly study the mages, and what an opportunity, considering she is the only one who has eaten our sacred fruit."

Shirina gave the spectacled fae a nod of thanks. "Penelope Barclay is a *guest* in our household and has the favor of our High King."

"Ah, yes, the *mage* king," spat the Spring King. He stepped down the stairs. "It seems there is to be an outbreak of mages in our future."

"I fail to see what this has to do with the evacuation, Falaichte," Shirina said, eyes cold. "We have brought the maps for the routes as requested." She held out her hand to Penny, who placed the satchel in her palm.

The crowd behind the king drew back. "You let it have access to the maps?"

Shirina's brows furrowed. "Yes. She is fully capable of holding a bag."

"What if it tampered with them?" asked the turquoise-haired beauty. "It could have sabotaged the entire evacuation."

"Paranoid much?" Angelica muttered.

Apparently, Shirina had been wrong, and Penny carrying the maps was, indeed, not a safe job for her to do. She folded her arms over her stomach. They acted as if she were some kind of diseased animal rather than the girl who had risked her life—multiple times —to try to help them. Would she ever catch a break?

Shirina raised her hands placatingly. "I have had Penelope in my house for weeks. She is as honest and kindhearted as the best of us. Shedding prejudices on her just because of who she is—"

"You mean *what* she is," snapped the king. "She could be the paragon of flowering virtue, but that does not change the fact that she is also an *abomination*." His face morphed from elegant serenity to mottled rage.

Devan took a step forward, leaving Angelica to stand next to Penny and positioning himself in front of them. Angelica took Penny's hand and gave it a light squeeze.

"Listen to yourselves," Shirina admonished. "You are spouting the same vitriol The Cartographer and her rebels are poisoning the humans with. Do you honestly believe this girl to be such a threat to you?"

"Yes," several of them barked.

"Perhaps the humans would like to accompany me elsewhere?" the fae with the dark glasses asked. He skipped down the steps and approached Devan. "We can let the higher ups work without so many distractions," he whispered.

Devan looked back to Penny, obviously waiting for her permission. She watched the fae, looking for any malintent, but found none on his face. Her gaze flicked over his shoulder to the rest of the Court members, all watching their group with trepidation. But did they want her to take the offer to get out of their sight or for something more sinister?

Shirina stepped closer. "Go with Dìomhair." She turned to Farrah. "Accompany them, would you? Then we can be sure they have an avenue of escape if anything bad happens."

Farrah nodded and took Penny's arm. "Come, Penny. Let's get you away from such disgusting creatures."

The Spring Court balked at Farrah's tone, but a small smile pulled at Penny's lips. "Thank you," she whispered.

Dìomhair led them out of the entry hall by a side door. He shook himself when the door closed behind him. "Blossoms and blooms, that tension was sickening. Are you all right, Lady Penelope? Their words were a bit harsh if I do say so myself. You look like such a lovely little thing."

Penelope wrapped her hand around her left wrist. "I'm fine." It wasn't the first time she'd been subject to public scrutiny, and it sure wouldn't be the last. Angelica wrapped an arm around Penny's shoulder. Penny squeezed her arm, trying to communicate confidence, though she didn't feel it. She might be tough but being so rejected by those she'd wanted so badly to meet growing up... A small part of her naive heart broke. She pushed down the uncomfortable feeling. "So, *Dìomhair* was it?"

"Yes, my lady."

"What makes you so different from the rest of your Court? Why don't you care about being in the company of a mage?"

Dìomhair shrugged. "I suppose I have simply seen more of the world than my peers. I am originally from Flùranach, but my *tiodhlacan an spioraid* ended up being better suited for Sona's ecosystem. I have not always lived the way my fellow Court members have."

Penny watched him carefully. "It certainly shows." Though if he was also from Flùranach, wouldn't that Court's prejudices also bleed into his upbringing?

He must have seen the skepticism on her face, because he continued, "I was raised by a family who worked for the Summer King, but we were not members of the nobility. Once I left, I made good friends in high places, but my upbringing was that of the lower class. I will never forget the principles I was raised by."

"And what were those?" Angelica asked.

He pushed open the front doors to the palace. "Never judge a tree by its bark."

"This is the city center," Dìomhair explained. "The whole city has scrapped together supplies and donated extra items for our trek within the next few days."

Devan gave a low whistle, and Penny couldn't help but agree with his assessment. The entire market square was divided up into a wagon assembly machine. Ellyllon and bwbachod stood in lines around the square, stuffing sacks and boxes full of supplies and loading them into the backs of wagons.

"How do you get the wagons to the ground?" Penny asked.

Angelica pointed to the west, where a line of wagons jostled over a bridge. "There are ramps leading down to the ground, and the lifts can transfer things as well."

"Yes," beamed Dìomhair. "And thanks to the High King's warning, we have plenty of time to vacate before the rebels arrive." He stepped out into the street, turning heads in his direction.

Penny's direction.

Her stomach churned. Apparently, word of her had spread even to this city, though she wasn't surprised. From what Angelica said, the fae were ruthless gossips. Of course, what happened at the revel would have reached even these parts. And since not many humans came to this kingdom, it was likely obvious to everyone who she was.

Angelica and Devan strode behind Dìomhair, but Penny grabbed Farrah's arm and pulled her back. "I shouldn't go in there."

Farrah's eyes widened and she looked back over the crowd. "Perhaps you're right."

Whispers morphed into hisses.

"Mage scum."

"Blasphemous."

"Filthy abomination."

Penny dragged Farrah back the way they'd come, but a few of the fae broke away from the assembly lines and followed. A centaur and two ellyllon neared them before they could escape the square.

"Are you the mage that crashed the High King's revel and ate our fruit?" one called from behind.

Farrah straightened to her full height. "This is a guest of the High King. We are here to check on preparations for the evacuation and see what aid we can provide."

Penny had never heard her friend speak so eloquently. A rustle behind Penny had her spinning a moment later. A pair of satyrs boxed them in from the other side.

"*Farrah*," Penny whispered. She searched for Angelica and Devan in the crowd but couldn't see them.

Farrah's eyes flicked over the faces. "Is there a problem here?"

The centaur spit on the ground near Penny's feet. "We do not want such filth coming into our lands and casting its black magic near us."

"The rebels only attacked after this creature intruded on our borders," said a satyr. "It is bringing them down on our heads."

Farrah held up a hand, shadow swirling in her palm. "Let us pass. I do not wish to cause a fight."

An ellyllon spread open his arms. "The fight is already here."

The five fae lunged forward, and Farrah's shadows pooled onto the ground, catching the centaur and sending the fae—only Farrah and the Goddess knew where. The other four evaded the traps and reached for Penny.

Penny reached for her daggers, but belatedly remembered she'd left them in Eagallach.

"Run, Penny!" Farrah called out, one of the satyrs caging her in his arms.

Penny turned and ran.

She tried to remember the path she'd taken from the palace. She made it past a single intersection before she was tackled to the ground. Her face hit the rough wood under her, making her see stars for a moment. She rolled with her attacker, hitting at tender parts with her knees as he clawed at her. He grabbed one arm, pulling until she heard something snap. She cried out and hit him in the face with her other elbow, bloodying his nose. Pain radiated through her other arm but was dampened by the adrenaline rushing through her veins.

With a few well-timed twists, she was able to get out from under him and back to her feet. He followed and sent a fist straight to her face. Stars speckled her vision, but her training kicked in. A solid hit landed between his legs, and he doubled over in pain. Penny barely took two steps when the other satyr leapt over them, landing nimbly on the walkway behind her. The other ellyllon followed close after, stopping beside her friend. Penny got to her feet, keeping the attackers in sight.

"Did you really think you would be allowed to walk these streets unharmed, mage?" the satyr sneered. "Every fae in this kingdom wants your head on a pike outside of Crann Mòr."

That definitely wasn't true, but Penny wasn't going to argue the point. "I mean you no harm." Her lip stung. She prodded it with her tongue and tasted blood.

"Do not speak to us, you pile of filth," sneered the ellyllon female. "You have done nothing but bring misfortune to our kingdom, and we will see to it that you stop."

Penny held up her uninjured hand to ward them off. A faint flicker started up around her fingers.

The three Fae stepped back. "Even now, it summons its dark powers."

"No, I—"

The three lunged toward her.

Penny ducked, tucking into herself as much as she could to escape whatever punishment they were about to subject her to. She closed her eyes, waiting for the fresh bite of pain.

Goddess, save me.

The ground by her feet shuddered.

She opened her eyes and watched the wood under her boots explode.

Branches surged upward, locking tight around her and pushing back her attackers until a solid wall of wood stood between her and them. Their cries sounded until they were cut off suddenly.

Penny stood in the center, still hunched over and breathing heavily. Her whole body ached, and she fell back to sit on the rough ground, cradling her broken arm. Instead, she landed on a lump of soft moss. A few posies popped up around her.

Tears caught the corners of her lashes. A small sob broke free, and the drops fell onto her cheeks. She wrapped her unbroken arm around her knees and buried her head in her skirts. By the Goddess, what was she going to do? All of these folk wanted to kill her simply for existing. Her heart ached in her chest and another sob broke free. It wasn't fair in the least. It wasn't right. Was there no one in this blasted kingdom that would give her a chance?

She sat in the middle of her newly rendered cage, allowing the adrenaline rush to slip away. Hopefully Farrah got away, though the attackers probably wouldn't want to hurt her since she was one of them.

"Penny!" Angelica yelled from the other side of the wall of branches.

Penny gave herself a moment to swipe the tears from her eyes and winced when she felt the swelling around her eye and the split in her lip. Aiden would be furious when he saw her. She tucked her head back between her knees. *Perhaps I should just stay here, out of everyone's way.*

"Penelope?" called Shirina. "Are you all right in there? Can you hear us?"

Before Penny could respond, the walls to the left of her separated into an arch of their own volition, revealing the company she'd arrived with as well as the Spring Court.

Penny let out a deep sigh. "Yes, I'm all right." A blanket of moss she hadn't noticed wrap around her shoulders fell away as she got to her feet.

10
SEETHING

AIDEN STRODE THROUGH THE HALLS OF THE WINTER PALACE, ANGER OOZING from every pore and dripping onto the floor in black, frothing shadows. The moment Dair had come to the training grounds with word of Penelope's arrival and the state she'd been in, Aiden had ended the training session he'd been in the middle of and followed Dair back through the portal.

If he'd known Shirina had planned on taking Penelope to Sona, he'd have never allowed it. At least, he'd never allowed Penelope to go without him or Thaen. She wasn't trapped here. She wasn't a prisoner. But she'd needed protecting, and he hadn't been there.

A low rumble started up in his throat.

"Blizzards, you have got to quit growling. It is unbecoming of a king."

Aiden glared at Dair beside him but didn't respond. If he did, it might have come out as another growl. It was the only thing he could do. His chest ached and fear buzzed through his bones. Dair said she'd been injured, but how injured? He couldn't bring himself to ask. He wouldn't be anywhere near reassured until he saw her with his own eyes.

Aiden turned down the hallway to her room, and Thaen intercepted them, holding aloft a beheaded snake. He tossed the carcass at Dair. "Yours, I believe." Dair fumbled to catch the still twitching reptile as Thaen stopped Aiden at the door.

"Cousin, perhaps we should calm down before rushing in there."

"I am perfectly calm," Aiden said through gritted teeth. Blasted guardian bond. Anytime Aiden's heart kicked up, Thaen arrived with that crease between his brows. That crease wrinkled as Thaen raised a dark eyebrow but said nothing. Aiden pushed past him, not willing to let one more moment separate him from the girl he had told himself he would love from a distance.

He burst through the door, slamming it against the wall much more forcefully than was probably necessary. He ignored the thought and pushed further into the room, bypassing the small sitting area and walking straight into Penny's bedchamber, to the Mist with propriety.

The Eiles and Farrah stood by her while Shirina spoke with Farrah's mother in the corner. Annalysa had arrived while Penelope had been gone. When Aiden had learned about her trip.

The room quieted as each person turned to him. He finally found Penny hunkered down under her sheets, her small body turned away from him.

"I'm fine, Aiden."

Penelope's voice sounded scratchy, as if she'd been crying. And he knew her well enough to know if she was in bed, she was far from *fine*.

"I don't believe you." He took a few steps and rounded the bed.

Penelope tucked her head under the coverlet. "It's improper for a man to see a woman in her bedclothes."

His self-consciousness stopped him for only a second before he crouched down by her head and lifted the edge of the blankets. Penelope's eyes were closed, but her eyelids couldn't hide the injuries on her face or the wrapped arm she had tucked to her chest.

That frothing anger turned to a roar in his ears. He took a few, deep breaths before speaking. "Who did this to you?"

Penelope shook her head, hiding her face in her pillows as a single tear leaked out and dripped from the tip of her nose.

He turned to Shirina. "Who. Did. This."

She swallowed. "It was a group in Sona, though we do not know exactly who all was involved. The Spring Court was in an uproar before we left. We decided to handle the matter later, since we had more pressing concerns."

"More pressing..." He stopped. "You think I wouldn't want to know exactly who harmed her? How did they even get close enough to touch her, let alone leave those marks on her body? Did you not think—"

"I *thought*," Shirina interrupted, "that keeping the peace at the moment was more important. I was not in a position to threaten anyone and, after what she did to the folk that attacked her, I figured bringing her back here and getting the Spring Court out of Sona was priority."

He glanced back at the bed. Penelope still hadn't come out. "What do you mean 'what she did?'"

"She crushed a few of them," Devan answered. "Created a wall around her, and the wood grew so thick it smashed the fae attacking her between the building fast enough it killed one of them and seriously injured the other two."

Penelope's shoulders quivered under the blankets.

Stars. How had he let this happen? If he hadn't let his emotions get the better of him, if he'd been at the palace instead of trying to get out of it at every opportunity, maybe he could have prevented this. He would have been around to learn about the trip instead of avoiding any hallway Penelope might have been walking down. He might have had the opportunity to go with her.

Penelope wanted to prove something to him, that was obvious, but he couldn't watch her get hurt, not when he'd worked so hard for so long to keep her safe.

And now, not only was she hurt, but he hadn't been there to help her.

"Everyone out," Aiden said quietly. The rest of the room stilled for a moment before he said it again, louder.

Shirina ushered everyone from the room before turning back to Aiden. "Little Shadow, I—"

He didn't look up from where Penelope lay. "I don't have the strength to deal with whatever warning you are about to deliver, Shirina. I just need everyone to give us some space. Right now."

"All I wanted to say was I am sorry. She did not deserve what happened in Sona, and I deeply regret my part in it." Shirina closed the door quietly behind her.

Aiden let out a breath and slowly lifted the blanket, revealing Penelope's face once more. Her eyes remained scrunched shut.

"Are there any other major injuries besides your arm?"

Penelope shook her head.

Aiden lifted the blanket higher and kicked off his boots.

Penelope opened her eyes, one squinting due to the purple swelling around it. "What are you doing?"

"You were just attacked, your face bruised and arm broken. I'm going to hold you until I can convince myself not to leave this room and murder every single member of the Spring Court."

Penelope didn't move to give him space to lay next to her, but she didn't protest when he wrapped his arms around her and tucked her head under his chin. Even now, the faint smell of cinnamon and earth met his nose.

"I'm so sorry," Penelope whispered.

Aiden shook his head. "You have nothing to be sorry for."

Holding her like this brought on so many emotions inside of him, he had to remind himself not to pull her closer and squash her against him. There wasn't the shocking spark of electricity that ran between them when they touched, but there was something warm, soft. He wanted to bury his face in her hair and breathe in the scent until he was dizzy with relief that she was all right.

But he didn't. Instead, he held her as she cried. He held her as she let out the pent-up emotions he knew she'd held back in front of everyone else for the last month. He held her until her breaths evened out and the sun peeked through the curtains.

"I swear, I never wanted any of this to happen," he whispered into her hair. "If anyone has something to be sorry for, it's me."

"You called, Your Majesty?"

Aiden flung the large leather ball as far as he could across the open courtyard. Spot chased after it with as much gusto as he had Aiden's first throw, which had been at least two dozen throws before. Spot made it halfway across the courtyard before Aiden turned.

Devan stood at the top of the stairs leading to the front entrance. His breaths puffed out in clouds in front of his face, but Aiden couldn't feel the cold, only this burning in his blood. After seeing Penelope injured, Aiden hadn't been able to leave the palace for three days, worried something else would happen while he was gone.

After a full week, Penelope had fully recovered, even returning to her regular haunting of the halls. By the Goddess, he didn't know what to do with her. He was nearly ready to charge into the temple and beg the Aunties to tell him what to do. But he couldn't do that, so he had to focus on things that he could do.

"Hello, Devan. Do you and your wife have a minute to speak with me?"

"Of course. We're at your beck and call."

Spot returned, his left head holding the ball between his dripping jaws.

"Off you go, Spot," Aiden said, pointing in the direction of the stables the dog had taken over. All the horses had been moved to the fortress, much to Spot's distress. The poor dog had grown lonely since their departure.

"I'll be back," Aiden reassured him.

Spot loped away and Aiden joined Devan at the stairs. "Should we collect Angelica and meet in the study?"

Devan led Aiden through the palace toward the guest wing. Before they reached the Eiles' rooms, Angelica burst from one of the washrooms halfway to their own quarters in the guest wing.

"Sorry for the delay," she said. "I meant to meet you out front."

Devan chuckled and took his wife's hand. "His Majesty has asked we meet with him in his study."

"Oh, sounds ominous," she teased.

Aiden led the way toward the dubbed "ominous study". When they reached the door, he pulled a key from his pocket and unlocked the handle as well as the charm he'd had put on the lock. He couldn't risk someone going through important information. He gestured for Angelica and Devan to proceed him into the room.

"Is she going to be all right?" Angelica asked.

It was obvious who Angelica referred to. Aiden sighed and sank into the chair behind his desk. "Annalysa is said to be the greatest healer on this continent. Penelope told me of the care she received before she arrived here. She should be completely healed by sundown tomorrow."

Angelica plopped into the chair across from him. "You know that's not what I meant, Your Majesty."

Aiden waved a hand. "Please, just call me Aiden."

"Fine, Aiden, but you know I'm talking about Penelope's future in

Faerie. If she's to expect that kind of treatment for the rest of her life, she'll never find happiness here. She needs people. Needs to feel valued." Tears gathered at the corners of Angelica's deep, brown eyes. "How can she be happy when everyone is calling her horrible names and trying to murder her on the street?"

Devan set a hand on Angelica's arm to comfort her.

"I have the same feelings you do, Angelica," Aiden admitted.

"Then what are we going to do about it?" She wiped away her tears. "If she can't be safe here, we need to figure out how to get her somewhere she will be."

"I completely agree," Aiden said. "I've been searching for another way, either to break the bond she has with the Land or find a way for her to at least live in Olympia as the fae can. We haven't found anything of use yet, but I'm hoping—*praying* we find a solution."

"What can we do to help?" Devan asked.

Aiden straightened one of the papers on his desk. "Actually, I need you both to return to Olympia as soon as possible."

Angelica straightened. "What? Right after Penny was attacked? You can't expect me to just up and leave her."

"You two always knew you would have to return to Olympia eventually." He glanced between the married couple. "With the threat to Penelope, the dissonance within the Courts, and the rebels' alliance with the Isles, we need to collect allies. Faerie does not have the numbers to fight off the rebels' growing horde."

The scouts Aiden had sent were reporting numbers double and triple what Faerie had between the two training encampments. While fair folk were more powerful than humans, the fight was tilted in their favor by the stolen magic and the Aigeans. If Aiden didn't get help, and soon, Durant would take them before winter even kissed the air.

He leaned over the desk. "I need to speak with my brothers as soon as possible. I need someone I trust to relay information back to me. I need someone who knows Faerie and can help them understand where things are on this side of the continent. I need both of you to help me."

Angelica set a hand over her heart. "But Penny..."

"I know." *Skies, do I know.* This would hurt Penelope. Angelica was her best friend, her one confidante in this foreign place. Sending the Eiles back to Olympia would leave Penelope without anyone to rely on—besides him, but he'd been doing a poor job of being reliable lately. Something he hoped to remedy immediately.

Angelica thrust her finger into his face. "You listen here, Aiden. I will do this because I know it's what's best for our kingdoms, but if anything—and I mean *anything* happens to Penny before I return, by the Goddess, I will hold you accountable. She deserves all the happiness in this world and more. She's one of the best people I know, and I refuse to see her hurt."

Aiden tucked back his smile. "Do you think so little of me, Angelica?"

Angelica sniffed, blinking back fresh tears. "No, or I would take her from you this very instant. I'm just making sure I'm being clear with you. You will give her whatever she needs, and you will find a solution to this mess she's been put in, or Goddess help me, I will reign fire and vengeance upon your entire kingdom and the blasted Cartographer, and her band of jolly rebels will be the least of your concerns. Do you understand?"

Aiden stood and took Angelica's hand in his. "I would do nothing less."

Devan shifted in his chair. "What do you need us to do?"

Aiden's eyes opened. He lay in the middle of a clearing in what looked like Spring, the thick vegetation and the map within him attesting to the location as his consciousness slowly caught up with what he was seeing.

Had he finally fallen asleep? He'd tossed and turned in his bed, the first inklings of dawn reaching its fingers across the sky out his window. The gray of early morning was just giving way to the blue of full day through the leaves above. The dreams had alluded him for days, and a small part of him had wondered if he'd done something wrong.

A glimmer of awareness pressed against him, and he opened up to the magical bond tying him to the Land.

Patience.

He nearly sighed. He was oh so tired of being patient.

A nudge pulled him in a westward direction, and he allowed the magic to pull him along, the forest zipping by him in a blur of colors and sounds. He stopped on the outskirts of Sona and saw the first wave of rebels reach the trunks of the trees.

"They're early," Aiden gasped. The war council had planned for another three days. The evacuation had only finished hours ago, the last of the city guard having fled in the middle of the night after making sure no one was left behind.

The men surged forward, climbing the trunks and using enchanted armor to move with the agility of the most athletic fae. A head of silver hair came out of the crowd, a glorious frown on her face.

Aiden crept closer.

"What do you mean no one is there?" Durant looked up into the trees, listening as a scout rambled in her ear.

"I'm sorry, Your Grace." He pulled a chain and a young fae female staggered forward, eyes glazed. "My fae didn't give an accurate report. I don't know how she didn't realize the city had been abandoned."

Aiden's blood boiled. How dare he? How dare he treat this Tuatha as if she were nothing but a tool to be used at his disposal. She was not his plaything. She was not his tool. She was Tuatha Dé Dannan, a child of Danu and a fae. This rebel had no claim on her, and the very idea that he thought he did had Aiden's entire soul raging.

"You mean to tell me the entire city has up and left?" She practically screeched the words. Steel flashed in her hand.

The fae staggered back, the blood pouring through her fingers wrapped around her throat. The scout jumped back as she slumped to the ground, too weak to even heal herself before her life dripped out between her fingers. Aiden reached out to catch her, but she went right through him. He felt his entire soul go cold.

Durant had never tolerated bad news well. He knew this, and yet, as he watched this fae's blood pour out and the light leave her eyes, he could do nothing but stare in shock.

"Nedra!" Durant snapped, wiping the blade of her dagger on the now-dead female's skirt.

The rebel woman with the salt-and-pepper hair jogged out of the crowd. "Yes, Your Grace?"

"How did they find out? No one was supposed to know our plans until we were already on the move. An evacuation of this scale would have taken weeks."

Nedra—finally a name for the woman at Durant's right hand—nodded. "I agree. I'll reevaluate the wards while you're away."

Away? Did Durant plan on leaving the rest of the group?

Listen, the Land insisted.

"We need those charms to be strong enough to last until the siege in Winter," Durant said, pointing her dagger at her general as if hoping to make a point. "We can't have the cursed fae learning our plans. They must not see us coming."

"I'll get working on them at once. I should have the glamour recharged within the hour."

Durant sheathed her blade. "See to it. And I want my glamour before I leave this afternoon. I can't go running about Faerie looking like a blasted warlord."

Aiden's ears perked. Where was Durant planning on going?

The two separated and Aiden was tempted to chase after Durant, but Nedra was the one in charge of the wards protecting the rebel army. If he could learn more about that, he might be able to find a way to work around the glamours in the future. He followed her as Durant marched in the opposite direction toward the city.

The pillaging had already begun. Rebels ran past with enchanted objects in hand. Soldiers tore through homes like rampaging bulls, leaving only destruction in their wake. It wasn't an army occupation so much as it was an invader's pillage. Praise the Goddess the Spring Court had already gotten out.

Nedra glided through the soldiers and jumped into the back of a large wagon. Aiden pushed through the walls, hoping to gain access inside, but something kept him out.

The Land bristled. *Secrets.*

Yes, this woman had plenty of secrets.

Aiden turned to find Durant once again, but Nedra jumped out. A bracelet hung from her fingers, and she clasped it around her wrist. The magic set over her and Aiden found himself looking at a satyr. Nedra looked over the glamour, likely memorizing it as much as Aiden did in that moment. The fur of her legs was a deep brown. A pair of horns curled around her ears and through her now-brunette hair hanging down to her waist. Her hooves clopped over the ground, making all the right sounds and seeming like a real glamour.

Nedra shrugged the bracelet off and raced back toward where Durant had disappeared.

Aiden followed behind her.

He found Durant holding court at the base of one of the trees, generals and scouts running back and forth with orders and reports. Her scowl had deepened. Aiden could have jumped for joy.

Nedra unclasped the bracelet and handed it to Durant.

"I trust everything is in order?" Durant asked.

Nedra nodded. "This glamour is even better than the one you wore to the revel."

With a smile, Durant tucked it into one of the pouches attached to her belt.

"Are you quite sure you must leave?" one of the generals asked.

Durant gave a sharp nod. "With the High King out of Crann Mòr and our attack here, it seems the perfect time to break into the Tree and gather information. I'll be in and out within the week, and we'll have a better idea of what kind of force we'll be up against."

"Can't you send one of the other men?"

Durant narrowed her eyes in the general's direction. "Are you suggesting I'm not the best one for the task?"

"Not at all," he said, hands out placatingly. "Only that I wish you wouldn't put yourself in unnecessary danger."

Durant snorted. "Please. The only way anyone will know I'm there is if they hear me having this conversation with you right now." She gestured to the busy space, a smirk pulling at her lips. "Does it look like we have any traitors in our midst?"

Aiden could only smile.

11

PROBLEMS AND GOODBYES

Dearest Penny,
Can Devan and I meet in your rooms within the hour? I have something I'd like to discuss with you.
Your Clingy Friend,
Angelica

"You're really leaving?" Penny asked. She scooted closer to Angelica on the sofa. Penny had received her note that morning, a week after their return from Sona. Her arm felt much better since Annalysa visited. She reached for Angelica's hand. "When?"

"We have to get the house packed, so His Majesty has given us a week to prepare."

One week. The world wasn't actually crumbling, but something inside of her felt like it was. She'd lost her home, her magic, her family. And now she would lose her friend.

"Dearest Penny, I'm so sorry." Angelica set a hand atop her growing abdomen. "We have to go. I know it's selfish, but a large part of me has been hoping we would be able to go earlier. I miss my mother, my siblings, sweet Gaia, even *my father*. If I was in any other situation, if I wasn't carrying this very wiggly babe—"

"You're not being selfish. You're doing what's best for your family and your kingdom." Penny set her hands over Angelica's, blinking back tears. "I'm not the most important person here. This baby will come into the world surrounded by loved ones."

Angelica shook her head. "But you *are* important, Penny. Don't you forget that. Just because everyone is busy or has to focus on other things doesn't make you any less important to them. You are the sister of my soul, Dearest Penny, and I love you probably close to as much as I love Devan."

Devan turned in his chair. "Say what now?"

"Hush, Devan, I said *close*." She shook her head, but a smile twitched at the corner of her mouth. "We're going to go to Olympia, get King Dion and Aiden in communication with one another, and make sure Adira Durant is finally taken down."

Penny let out a long breath and tried to push a smirk onto her face. "You're doing what any good spy would."

"Of course I am. And," she said with a smile, "I did make sure to get you a present."

She turned to Devan who was already fishing a small bundle out of his jacket. He passed it to her, and she opened it to reveal a leather cuff. "With everyone here trying to kill you, I figured you could at least have something to defend yourself with. Father gave it to me before I left, but I think you should have it."

The small cuff held the dark blade, and Penny wrapped it around her wrist before tucking it under the sleeve of her borrowed lavender dress. "You always give the best gifts."

"And I will continue to give more," she decreed. "I'll have every kind of weapon commissioned to send to you and an entire wardrobe of Olympian fashions so respectable even your mother would be jealous."

"Will you try to find my mother?" Penny practically whispered. "We need to figure out where her allegiances truly lie."

"Of course," Angelica answered. She gave a dramatic shudder. "I can't imagine what havoc she's been wreaking since you left, rebel or not. Perhaps, if I tell her you're fighting rebels here, she may turn that fury back on them and take them all out herself just to get to you."

Oh, Mother. Penny would likely receive the verbal lashing of a lifetime when she saw her again. Penny swallowed back a lump in her throat. Would this war be the thing that finally tore them apart?

There might not be a future for them at all, even if a small part of Penny's heart still ached for Mother's respect.

Angelica groaned and put her feet up on the ottoman across from them. "By the Goddess, my feet will be so grateful we're portalling, but my stomach will not. I'll probably only eat a bit of bread and water for supper with Aiden's family and eat more after I get to Olympia."

Devan winced and Penny tried to give him a sympathetic smile. "You'll finally be able to see your mother though, and you know she'll be nothing but the most attentive grandmother."

"I'm not worried about her at all. Father on the other hand, well, he will not be permitted to leave the room with the baby on my watch. I watched him enact some of the most ridiculous pranks on my mother with my younger siblings. I won't allow him to pull one over on me!"

Penny laughed, some of the tightness in her chest loosening. How long had it been since she'd laughed last? Days? Weeks? Sweet Gaia, it was nice to talk about pranks and ridiculous parents. Life had become so dark; it was hard to remember that there were things to laugh about.

"I'm going to miss you," Angelica said.

Penny grasped her hand tightly. "I'm going to miss you too."

Penny fiddled with the new weight of Angelica's present at her wrist as Aiden paced across the black granite floor of the Grand Hall.

"You have the letter in your bag."

Devan nodded. "Yes, Your Majesty."

"You're going straight to the palace after taking Angelica to her parents."

"Of course, Your Majesty."

"You will deliver the letter straight into Dion's hands and no one else. Not even Evan."

"Absolutely, Your Majesty."

"And you're going to stop calling me 'Your Majesty.'"

"Not a chance, Your Majesty."

The two of them grinned at one another. Penny often forgot that

Devan had been Aiden's operative before he became Angelica's husband. She hadn't seen the two of them work together before, but there was an obvious camaraderie.

"If you're quite done teasing one another," said Angelica, "I'd like to get this journey over with sooner rather than later."

The Eiles would be accompanied by Farrah into Olympia. Farrah would go with Devan to speak with the king and return to Faerie with news. Devan bounced on the tips of his toes. Penny held her breath as Farrah summoned the doorway to Olympia. A doorway she herself would have gone through if she hadn't eaten the fruit.

Angelica marched forward and wrapped Penny in her arms. "I wish you could come with me."

Penny squeezed her back. "My heart goes with you even as I stay behind."

Angelica wiped tears from her eyes and held Penny by the shoulders. "I'll send word as quick as I can."

Penny nodded, not able to voice her feelings without losing her composure. Devan came up beside Angelica and took her arm. The two of them disappeared into the shadows.

Farrah waited at the edge of the portal. She met Penny's eye and then turned to Aiden, a fist over her heart. "I will be back in one week with news."

Aiden came up beside Penny and gave a quick nod.

Farrah disappeared as well.

A lump grew in Penny's throat. In a kingdom with few allies and more enemies than she could count, it was more than a little difficult to watch her friends disappear one after the other. Her fingers encircled her wrist, wrapping around the skin above her knew cuff. She looked up at Aiden, who was already watching her, a concerned frown on his face. He reached over and grabbed her left hand, pulling it up close to his face. He found the small knife hidden in the cuff and returned it to its home with a smirk.

He tapped the skin where she had held her wrist. "I've been meaning to ask, what happened to your ribbon?"

Penny heart squeezed in her chest. Of course he had noticed. "I lost it." It wasn't technically a lie, but she didn't have the willpower at that moment to go into it more.

Aiden's expression turned sad. He knew what that ribbon meant. "I'm sorry."

"I think I'm going to take a walk," she said, pulling her hand from his and stepping away.

He took a step to follow. "I can come with you." Though it came out more as a question than a suggestion. "I have to leave for Crann Mòr soon, but I'd like to be with you if you need it."

She considered it for a moment. The mission to Crann Mòr was the break they'd been waiting for. There would be preparations to make. He didn't truly have time for her, but it touched her heart that he was willing. "I think I'd like to go alone this time." She chewed on her bottom lip. "Perhaps we could do something when you get back?"

Aiden nodded. He lifted a hand and gently tucked a stray curl behind her ear. "I'm here for you. You know that, right? If you want to be alone, I understand, and I won't deny you your space, but if you need someone, I'll follow you anywhere."

His words warmed the coldness seeping through her chest. She stood up on tiptoe and pressed a small kiss to his cheek. "Thank you."

He took a deep breath. Long, black lashes covered the darkening of his amber eyes. He used their joined hands to pull her to him. "How can both being apart from you and being close enough to touch you torture me?"

Heat spread into Penny's cheeks, and she ducked her head. "I understand what you mean. It's certainly a problem."

Gentle fingers lifted her chin. Her gaze caught in his honeyed one. "Penelope, you have never been, nor ever will be, a *problem*. You've been an answer to prayers I've whispered for years and a blessing I'll work every day of my long life to deserve. Even if staying together seems impossible—if my being near you puts you in more danger—every second I've been with you will have been worth the pain I will feel at not being able to call you mine."

Penny pulled away from him, heart pounding in her chest. "So, you've given up then?"

Aiden's brows furrowed. "What do you mean?"

"You just said it seems impossible."

"That's not..." He took a deep breath. "Penelope, it would kill me if something happened to you. I'm going to do everything I can to protect you, even if that includes from the wishes of my heart."

She crossed her arms over her chest. "What, do you think I'm not strong enough? That I can't protect myself?"

"I would never say that, nor do I think it *at all*. You're one of the strongest people I know."

"Then *why*?" she begged. She felt the tears gather behind her eyes. "Why do you keep saying you have to let me go? Why is it so easy for you to push me aside when all I've ever wanted was the future I dreamed up with you?"

Aiden stilled. "You think it's easy?"

Penny threw up her hands. "Considering how many times you've left me in the dust, yes! Even before Barclay Manor—at the *blasted* debut ball where we met—you've always been the one to disappear, and I've always been the one who had to go after you."

"And you never thought to ask why I left?"

Penny blinked, but the hurt was too raw. "You left because it was the easiest thing to do."

"I left because it's what I thought was best for *you*!" He combed a hand through his mussed hair. "I left you in that garden the first night I met you because if your mother saw us together it would've raised too many questions, and your reputation would have been at stake. I left you in that alleyway in Eleusia a year later because the man you'd captured had escaped, and I wanted to make sure he wasn't gathering more of his friends to come back for you. I left Eleusion because folk were being murdered, and I needed to keep the kingdom we lived in safe. I left you alone in Olympia because the rebels were gathering, and I didn't know how I would keep you safe while also trying to figure out who was a traitor and who wasn't."

Every word hit like a physical blow, but it only enraged her further. How dare he! How dare he throw everything back in her face.

He crossed the remaining steps between them, shadows flicking around his limbs. "The only time I haven't left of my own free will was when I was brought here, but apparently that's a strike against me as well."

She gritted her teeth. "But even when I went after you, you still chose to run from me. When I went to Olympia to find you, you ignored me for weeks. Even here! I came across an entirely new world to find you and all I get is your censure for it? How am I supposed to know you're trying to protect me when all you've done is leave me behind every time it's grown too hard for you?"

He stared at her, his amber eyes dark. "Is that what you think of me? That I would desert you because I was *uncomfortable*?"

"What evidence do I have contrary to that?" She folded her arms across her chest. "How am I supposed to trust that you won't run away the next time I need you?"

His entire body had become a statue, his mask having spread from his face to cover his entire body. She couldn't read anything but the shadows of fury in his eyes.

He took a single step back.

"I would think everything that has happened—Sissy's death, Hart's death, Fiadh's death—would be proof enough of the danger that surrounds me at every turn. That you should be the one running from me. All I've done is try to shield you from that as best as I know how. Have I made mistakes? Yes, but I also am not the one who goes running into danger whenever it pleases me. That falls squarely on your shoulders."

The heat in her chest ebbed slightly, allowing exhaustion to flood into her limbs. She took a deep breath. He had done all those things for her, but she was so tired of running.

"Aiden, I—"

He held up a hand. "If you want to condemn me for trying to keep you alive, fine, but don't expect me to stand by and say nothing while you put your life in danger. I refuse to be bullied and beaten into staying silent on things I don't agree with. I've had enough of that to last a lifetime." He passed by her, the sleeve of his jacket barely brushing her arm.

A door clicked shut behind her.

Her heart pounded against her ribcage, the fire fully snuffed out.

He left. *Again.*

But this time, she'd been the one to actually drive him away.

What had she done?

After all the trouble she'd already put him and everyone else through, she had to go and ruin everything. She knew Aiden was a good man. He was the love of her life, and she'd just told him she didn't trust him. Why? Why had she let her frustrations get the best of her? Why had she let being stuck in this kingdom, this situation, this cursed palace become a raging beast inside of her?

Her eyes found her perfectly polished reflection in the floor. *I have to get out. I have to get out right now.*

She ran.

Her slippered feet beat against the black granite floor. She ran through the entry hall and out into the cold, evening air. Tears blurred everything, but it didn't matter. Everything was covered in snow, white and suffocating. The tears began falling and she turned away from the path, crashing through the thick blanket that froze her toes and clung to her skirts. Her toe found a rock and she stumbled, but was up a moment later, dragging more of the white with her gown.

Sweet Gaia, she hated snow. She hated it so much she wanted to bury it so far in the ground no one would ever remember its existence.

Green flashed at the edge of her vision, and she allowed her gift to surface.

The pain ripped through her, but she clung to it. Pain meant she could still feel something besides the crushing despair she felt taking over. She crashed to her knees in the snow.

"Penelope?"

A vaguely familiar voice cut through the shallow connection. Goddess above, it was like fae just popped up anytime she was feeling weak. She wouldn't have been surprised if they could smell the vulnerability on her.

Penny opened her eyes and found the kind, Spring fae she'd met in Sona in front of her. Her glowing arms reflected off the dark tint of his spectacles. The Spring Court had decided to stay in the Winter Palace until their evacuation had finished. Penny had done a good job avoiding them thus far, but at least she'd ran into the least threatening member in her moment of irrationality.

She stood and tried to brush away the snow hanging from her dress. "I'm sorry. I didn't know anyone else was out here." She tried to summon a pleasant expression, Mother's insistent tutelage about not allowing emotions to show whispering in the back of her mind. "Dìomhair, wasn't it?"

He nodded and looked around. His eyebrows raised a fraction. "Are you out here on your own?"

"Very much so," she whispered. By the Goddess, she'd never felt so alone. Aiden was probably on his way to Crann Mòr already. She ran, so why shouldn't he?

Dìomhair took another step toward her, his head tilted to the side. "The weather is quite cold. Does anyone know you are out here?"

Penny shook her head, trying to brush more of the snow off her skirts. "I came out to be alone for a moment." But even with the intent to be alone, she couldn't be inside the palace. Even the blasted courtyard had to be occupied.

"Well," said the fae, "it seems the Goddess has smiled upon me today."

She looked up at him.

A feral grin stretched over the male's face. "This will be much easier than I anticipated."

In a flash, he was on her.

His hand flicked and a blade shot out of his sleeve. He buried it in her stomach.

Penny gasped, more surprised than pained. It had taken him less than a second to reach her. She hadn't even had a chance to block him.

Dìomhair leaned into her ear. "Poor little mage. Did you really think any of us would ever truly be your friend? Did you honestly believe you would get away with what you have done? You are a stain on this land, one I fully intend to clean up with or without My Sovereign's permission."

Her fingers twitched at her wrist and her legs fell out from under her. The pain hit her then, searing through her abdomen.

The fae knelt with her. "I knew I would have a better chance of killing you if you trusted me. I was disappointed my friends in Sona could not accomplish the task. I thought it would take much more effort to do the deed myself, but then you walked right into my arms today. Thank you for making it so easy for me."

"Next time"—Penny gasped—"you try to kill someone... make sure you actually kill them... before they have a chance to return the favor." She drew the small blade from her wrist and stabbed it into the side of his neck.

He jerked back, reaching for the iron embedded in his throat as it burned the skin around it and poisoned his blood. She'd made sure to hit the artery.

Penny couldn't hold herself up and fell to her side, though she tried to drag herself as far as she could from him. She couldn't jostle the blade still sticking out of her stomach. It would cause worse damage and possibly hit something more vital than her liver. Her fingers went completely numb. Bright red blood dripped onto the clean snow. Great Goddess, if she didn't get up, she was going to die.

She looked around. *Please, just something. I just need to get out of here.*

The fae had stopped struggling on the ground.

Penny swallowed back a sob and tried to push herself up onto her elbows. Pain seared through her, and she gritted her teeth against the scream pushing itself against her teeth. She couldn't let anyone randomly come upon them. She needed to get to someone who would help her.

"Hello?" someone called out.

Penny recognized that voice. Relief surged through her. Dair. Dair would help her. If for nothing else, just to make sure his cousin wouldn't be blamed for the death of a Spring Court member.

Dair walked around the corner, followed by the rest of the Spring Court. All warmth fled Penny's body at the sight of King Falaichte coming up beside him.

Dair's eyes widened, and he was at her side before she could blink. He took her hand in his and looked at the blade protruding from her abdomen. The color leached from his face.

"Penelope, what—"

One of the females let out a bloodcurdling scream. "She killed him! She killed him!"

12

SOVEREIGN

Aiden strode from the Council Hall at Crann Mòr, sword out and shadows billowing at his feet. The connection within him was stronger in the capital and the magic tried to sooth his aching heart. He wanted to shove it away. He wanted to feel the throbbing pain in his chest.

"What has you in such a mood?" Thaen asked from beside him, the picture of ease.

Penelope. Great Goddess, she was such a hypocrite. She claimed that everything she'd done had been for him, but he knew better. She wanted all of this for herself too. She felt repressed back home, her mother having protected her from so many things growing up. But at least she'd been loved, safe, until the rebellion began. Aiden had never had any of that. By the Goddess, he'd been thrown into a pit of trained fighters when he was ten just to see if he could make it out alive. He hadn't been cared for except by his brothers, who were never in a position to truly help him until Father died.

Penelope couldn't say that what he'd done had truly hurt her. It may have seemed unkind, but he'd done it to save her from his life. He'd done everything in his power to give her the chance to make her own decisions. He'd treated her as an equal. But apparently, *he'd* have to pay for the times he'd tried to protect her from harm.

"Glaciers, cousin, your shadows are biting."

Aiden looked over to see Thaen frowning at him. He reined his magic back in. If he let them get too out of control, sometimes the shadows really could sting, though he hadn't the faintest idea how. They'd never been able to do that until he came to Faerie.

"My apologies," Aiden mumbled.

"Do you want to talk about it?"

Aiden looked over and could see the concern on Thaen's face, though his cousin looked as if the last thing he wanted to do was talk about feelings.

"No. I want to catch Durant."

Thaen gave him a savage grin. "That is what I like to hear."

Aiden pushed aside the feelings his conversation with Penelope had wrought. He would deal with them later. Durant needed all his focus right now.

He led the way to the guard barracks at the base of the tree, watching for any sign of the satyr created by the charmed bracelet as they strode through the endless number of hallways. He had searched with his connection the moment he'd arrived, but with so many fae within the tree and so many glamours coming in and out— not to mention his cursed emotions—he'd given up trying to find her that way. He had a few contacts, vetted by Devan and Thaen alike, within the Tree. They were also on the hunt, though none of them had found her yet either. But she would be there, somewhere.

They reached the barracks, having used the lift this time to traverse the height of Crann Mòr. More than half of the Tree guard had already been sent to Eagallach to train for real battle. The empty rooms felt like a bad omen when it would be important to have fae scouring the Tree. The rebels had been able to exploit every single weakness Faerie had. Aiden held back curses he wished to throw Durant's way. They needed to find her. They needed this win.

The darkling captain sat at his desk and jumped to his feet when Aiden crossed the threshold into his office.

"My Sovereign," Captain Sealgair stammered between fanged teeth. He stood and performed a bow, his black wings on display. Some darklings had wings, though Aiden hadn't seen many with them because they only flew at night. He straightened, standing a head shorter than Aiden, though his wings made him seem taller. "I was not aware you were in the capital."

The only light in the room was a glowing orb hanging from the ceiling by a cord, which the darkling somehow made brighter in order to give Aiden a view of the room. No windows to cast harsh light on the darkling's membranous wings as he worked. No outside access to allow for listening ears. The darklings' nocturnal tendences worked in Aiden's favor.

"I apologize that we could not send word, but I did not wish to give our intruder any notice." Aiden went on to explain why he and Thaen had come, sharing his account of Durant getting hold of the glamour and planning to use it to sneak her way into the Tree.

"I understand," the captain said. "I will send my men to search the tree for this satyr. We should have reports soon if the brownies will be at all amicable to helping us."

Aiden nodded. "Excellent. The Lòchran and I will join in the search."

The captain nodded and led them out the door.

Aiden and Thaen started in the kitchens. Aiden learned there were five separate kitchens in Crann Mòr. One for the barracks, one for the servants' quarters, two for the main part of the Tree, and one for the soup kitchen where the poorer families could come for meals. There wasn't much in the way of poverty in Faerie, but there were still those that fell on hard times every once in a while. High Queen Rìanoch had been the one to install such a place into the Tree.

They reached the soup kitchen first, walking past the hot ovens and boiling cauldrons. One of the fires even had a wild hog native to the Autumn Court on the spit. But Durant wasn't in those kitchens.

Aiden and Thaen swept through two more before they were accosted by a band of brownies in the hall. A half dozen of the small bwbachod jumped out of nowhere, waving their small hands.

"Our Sovereign, we found the intruder."

"Where?" Aiden asked.

The tallest brownie pointed down to the floor. "The good captain is hauling her to the dungeons, though they have had a rough go of it."

Thaen bounded toward the stairs, and Aiden followed right on his heels. When they reached the large staircase, Thaen didn't turn and simply ran off the edge. Aiden followed immediately after, only holding his breath as his feet wheeled under him. He could easily survive a three-story jump; he'd even managed five when he was a boy without breaking limbs. But this staircase was dozens of stories, taking up the core of the tree. The air screamed past him as he fell.

The magic of the Tree called out to him. Spots of light bounced against the walls around him, following his decent. As Thaen got closer to the ground, sparks of violet and black burst from his hands, slowing him. Aiden followed his lead, his jet-black shadows pushing against the fall. Thaen landed on his feet below him. Aiden touched down and stumbled a few steps, but he kept his boots under him.

Thaen didn't offer any kind of remark, but his self-satisfied smirk said enough.

They raced toward the dungeons. Aiden only knew the general direction, so he allowed Thaen to take lead until he could hear the clash of a fight beyond a thick, wooden door. Aiden shoved it open. The door crashed against the wall, making the inhabitants—all except one—jump.

Durant sprang out of the darklings' grips with the distraction, lunging for the door at the other end of the hall. Captain Sealgair barked out orders, and his soldiers leapt after her, their speed cutting her off before she could reach the door. One got too close, and she grabbed the bone knife they had strapped to their thigh. It was out of the sheath and in the darkling's gut before the fae even noticed she'd grabbed it.

Two more darkling's reached them and were able to subdue her. They grappled her to the ground, cuffing her hands behind her back with thick manacles. She grinned up from the floor, teeth bloodied.

"There he is! The boy king himself! What an honor it is, Your Majesty." Durant called to him from the ground.

Captain Sealgair gnashed his fangs at her. "Do not speak to Our Sovereign, rebel filth." He hauled her up and practically threw her into the closest cell.

She jumped at the bars, trying to keep the darkling from locking the cell, but he turned the key right as she hit the cold iron. The other darklings jumped back in fright.

Durant laughed at them, green eyes glittering, then turned to Aiden. "My, what loyalty you have instilled in your minions, Aiden. Or rather 'Aedon.'" She turned and spat a glob of blood onto the floor. The manacles fell from her wrist next, and she pulled a hand-kerchief from her jacket pocket to wipe at her mouth like a proper lady. "I, of course, had to change the name to make it more Olympian after your mother died. Sweet Gaia, we couldn't have King Horace's son have a Faerie name."

Aiden's step faltered for a moment, but it was enough to make her bloody smile widen. She'd always done that, tossed bits of information at him to throw him off and make him falter. He chastised himself for allowing it this time.

Aiden came to the gate of her cell. "Hello, Durant. Fancy meeting you here."

Durant sat primly on the thin pallet in the cell. "I must admit, I'm rather impressed. I thought I'd done a rather good job of hiding where I was going. Only a handful of my most loyal generals and advisors knew. Which one of them ratted me out?"

Aiden kept his face completely blank. "I suppose you will have to ask them when they join you in here."

Durant pursed her lips, plucking a piece of straw from her trousers. "I suppose it was bound to happen. These kinds of things come with so many risks, and I'd had so much success recently I was practically daring the Goddess to give me some bad luck." She rested her elbows on her knees and set her face in her hands. "Tell me, how was your cousin's funeral?"

Thaen lunged at the bars before Aiden could catch him. "You will pay for my *athair's* death."

Durant's eyebrow quirked. "This is all you have for me, Aiden? Darklings with no bite and a child that misses his daddy? I expected more from the boy I raised."

For some reason, Aiden could just imagine Penelope rolling her eyes.

Why did he think of her in that moment?

He shook his head, dispelling the image. "Why are you here, Durant?"

"I came to see how you were doing, of course. I've been feeling so out of the loop lately, I just had to check in for myself. I'd heard you went to Eagallach, but I didn't know where our other friend had gotten to."

She was talking about Penelope. Aiden kept his face blank with all the strength he could muster. Durant was certainly playing games which meant she was also trying to gage what was going on and get reactions from him. He refused to give them to her. "If you're asking after Spot, he's doing very well in Eagallach. The snow seems to suit him."

"Ah, so he made it to you after all. I do owe him for bringing that troll into my camp. The beast gave us so many ingredients for our enchantments after we killed it. Paid off a quarter of my debts to my sponsors on the continent."

The fae around him hissed.

"But no. I was actually referring to Penny." She set her hand to her heart, wistful. "The two of us had such a wonderful bonding experience while she was with me. I was so frightened after watching her collapse at the revel. I do hope nothing bad has happened to her. This is such a horrible place to be a mage, after all."

Aiden kept his jaw from tightening. "Penelope is in the best of health, I assure you."

Durant grinned. "Oh, I imagine that won't last long, will it, Lòchran?" She turned to Thaen. "It must be so difficult having a mage around, what with your conviction to the Goddess and all. How it must rankle you to have a mage so close to your king." She pursed her lips. "Though, he's a mage himself, isn't he?"

Thaen kept his arms folded over his chest. "You forget yourself, mortal. The Night Court does not hold the mages in the same light as those in the Day Court. Besides, Penelope has been quite the breath of fresh air. Our entire family has quickly found themselves besotted with her."

Aiden nearly looked over at Thaen with surprise. Had his family really found themselves under Penelope's spell, or was Thaen only pretending for Durant's sake? He would have to talk to them about it later.

Durant clucked her tongue. "Yes, Penelope certainly has a way of making friends." It seemed as though the thought almost rankled Durant. Why? Did she hope Penelope would have a hard time here? Aiden almost frowned. *Probably.*

He leaned against the bars, making sure his clothing kept him separated from the pure iron that made him itch slightly just standing near it. It was time to get some information. "How goes the war in Olympia? I can't imagine it has been much fun not being able to take Dion off his throne."

Durant's smirk only deepened. "Well, I wouldn't say that." Something Aiden couldn't quite decipher flashed in her eyes, but she hid it behind a contemplative expression before he could translate it. "He had quite the gall to get that young queen of his pregnant. After so many years of dalliances and not a single illegitimate child, I must admit I didn't think the boy had it in him. But I suppose it's always a delight to be surprised."

Dion was going to be a father? Aiden wanted to smile. Penelope would be overjoyed to—No. He needed to stay on task. He couldn't break his focus.

"Yes, I hadn't quite decided what to send as a gift," he said. She didn't need to know there hadn't been communication between the two of them. "Dion's convinced he'll have a male heir, though I think Shaunie will be able to will a daughter into being."

"I always did admire that girl's grit," Durant admitted. "Though I'm sad she hasn't killed the boy off and taken his crown yet. My spies in the palace say she's still as smitten with him as she was as a child. Weak."

Aiden soaked up every piece of information. "I'm sorry we've all turned out as such disappointments in your eyes." He slid his hands in the pockets of his jacket. "Perhaps you'll be happier with the Aigeans then, since the Olympian royal family didn't work out the way you hoped."

"Did you like my little surprise in Flùranach? I so wish I could have been there to see it. The admiral I work with said it was as easy as skinning a fish. No one even saw it coming, though you did foresee our attack on Spring. How did you manage that one?"

"You know I'm not one to brag, Durant. However, with you on that side of the bars and me on the other, I'm finding the urge most tempting."

Durant leaned back on her pallet. "Enjoy it while you can. I'm sure I'll be out as soon as it pleases me to be."

Captain Sealgair hissed. "Do not count on it, mortal." He barked orders, directing two darklings to remain with her near the cell and two more on either door before turning to leave.

Thaen glared at Durant between the bars, but Aiden dragged him toward the door after the captain. They would need to discuss her imprisonment but not within her hearing.

"My Sovereign, I would like to discuss plans for the rebel's long-term imprisonment."

"Why not kill the demon now?" Thaen asked.

Captain Sealgair turned back to him. "Was she marked for death?"

Thaen growled. "No."

Aiden stopped mid-stride. Why hadn't he thought of that? If Durant had been marked, would Thaen have risked himself to kill her, no matter the consequences? A shudder ran through him. Praise the Goddess Durant hadn't been marked. Aiden didn't think he could have allowed his cousin in that cell. He resumed his steps, returning to Thaen's side.

"Without a mark for death," the captain continued, "I would advise against killing her."

"Why?" asked Aiden.

Captain Sealgair clicked his teeth together, likely in agitation. "If we kill her, we create a martyr. The rebels do not need any more motivation to attack us. If we were to ignite not only their prejudice but also their wrath, we would find our enemies at our door sooner than we would be prepared for."

"But holding her here isn't viable for long," Aiden said. "She's probably one of the greatest strategists on this isle. She'll have already planned an escape."

Thaen tapped the blade over his heart with his finger. "What is the likelihood that we can keep her here?"

Aiden blew a breath out between his lips reaching for the door to the Council Chamber. "I—"

The door under Aiden's hand opened, and a flash of purple streaked across the doorway.

"Dair?"

"Praise all the stars in the sky." Dair grabbed Aiden by the arm and pulled him toward the already open portal in the middle of the hall.

Thaen pulled ahead of them. "What is the meaning of this?"

"You both need to get home. Now."

Aiden felt his stomach drop. "Why? What's happened?"

"Something happened to Penelope."

13

BROWNIES AND DREAMSCAPES

Penny stared at the canopy above her bed. Annalysa had already healed the worst of the wound, making sure there wouldn't be infection to battle later and healing most of the damage to her liver. Annalysa had put her on bedrest for the next three days to allow the muscles to return to their proper place. The bandage around Penny's stomach sported a bit of blood, but she didn't want to call for someone to change it quite yet.

How had she not seen it coming? Dìomhair had been from Spring. The hostility of his entire Court should have been a huge red flag. She shouldn't have trusted him simply because he'd flashed her a smile and said he didn't think the same way others did about mages. He'd only been a corpse flower, lovely to look at but bringing the stink of death along with it.

Penny sighed and almost turned to move onto her side, but any movement of her torso hurt worse than the ache in her back.

A rustling came from her left, she turned and found a pair of dark, brown eyes staring back at her from atop her bedside table. Penny gasped and then bit back a groan. Flinching hurt worse than getting kicked by a horse.

"No need to be frightened, my lady," said the brownie. "I have only come to check in on you."

Penny watched the creature. Its wide ears hung down, the tips meeting the loose fabric hung over its shoulders. From the more feminine angles of her face and the skirt just reaching large round toes, Penny guessed it was a girl. It was the same brownie that had given her the Summer King's note in Crann Mòr not so many weeks ago.

"I'm only surprised. We've met before have we not?"

The brownie grinned, showing her large, flat teeth. "Yes, my lady."

"I didn't catch your name."

"Fee, my lady."

"Hello, Fee. I'm Penny."

The brownie sat on the edge of the table and swung her wide feet through the air. "I heard the humans calling you that. I thought your name was Penelope."

"It is. Penny is a nickname. Penelope is such a mouthful, and my mother always used it when she was angry with me."

Fee giggled, a childlike noise. "My *màthair* did the same. 'Feasgar, you better be washing those baseboards, young lady.'" She mimicked what was likely supposed to be her mother's bossy tone. "But I think Penelope is a pretty name."

"I like the name Feasgar as well."

Fee bowed her head in thanks. She looked to Penny's abdomen. "I'm sorry we weren't there when you were attacked. We could have helped you."

"What do you mean?"

Fee jumped off the table and sat on the bed next to Penny's arm. The brownie girl's tight curls sprang up all around her head. "We do not like to go outside often. The snow is cold on our feet, and we do not like to wear shoes. A few of us had known Dìomhair was plotting against you, but we are not supposed to share secrets unless asked for them by the High King or the Court rulers. It keeps us safe. But a few of us knew and had been keeping an eye on him. He had gone outside and with you inside, none of us thought anything of it. But then you went out and no one knew where either of you were. Prince Bruadair had already found you by the time we did."

Penny shook her head in amazement. "I didn't realize you were all watching out for me. I thought the fae weren't supposed to like mages."

Fee placed her little hands on her hips. "We brownies do not care what the rest of the Courts say. We only care that those with the

Goddess's blessing are taken care of, as She asked us to do before She departed."

Penny tried to sit up, but the wound in her abdomen didn't allow it. She took a few shallow breaths until the pain eased. "You're very noble."

Fee nodded as if it was an already proven fact. "We do the Goddess's will, though some of the other fae have forgotten what She charged us with. But we cannot judge them too harshly. We can only encourage them back into Her good graces and protect those the Goddess has chosen."

"What does that mean, exactly? Those the Goddess has chosen?"

"Oh, like High King Aedon and you."

"Like me?"

"Of course! Have you not felt the bond? Have you not seen how She has changed your magic? She has chosen you for a glorious purpose, though we cannot guess as to what yet."

"Wait, hold on. You're saying the Goddess has chosen me for something?"

"Absolutely. Why do you think She told you to eat the *toradh na beatha*?"

"No one told me to eat it."

Fee settled next to Penny's shoulder and grabbed her face between her four fingered hands. "Of course She did. All the brown-iekin in the Tree felt it. Did you not feel a nudge? Perhaps something caught your eye, or an idea sprang into your mind that you would have never considered before? I have heard you tell Our Sovereign that you know it was not a mistake."

Penny thought back to the revel. She had felt something, hadn't she? There had been a pull toward the fruit. And Fee was right, she had told Aiden it hadn't been a mistake. It still felt like she was supposed to be here, like she had a future here, though she didn't know how. Was it truly the Goddess giving her direction? Telling her this was where she was supposed to be?

"You see?" Fee said. "You were meant to eat the fruit, no matter that everyone believes you made an error. You were meant for something greater than all the other Tuatha can comprehend, and we brownies pray that, in time, they will grow to see it too."

Penny felt wet tracks trail down the sides of her face. "Thank you,

Fee." And she didn't care if the little brownie took the words and used them against her.

Fee gave her a little smile. "You are welcome, Penelope." She hopped off Penny's bed and onto the floor. Her big eyes and the top of her curls were the only part of her Penny could see at the angle. "Now get some rest. You need all healed up if you want to be ready to fight for your place here."

With those words of encouragement, Fee disappeared.

Finally, a dark blissful sleep claimed Penny's senses, and a dream took over her consciousness.

Penny only knew she was asleep because the colors around her blurred. It looked like the winter solstice ball she'd attended with Aiden at his birthday, but the floor was that of the Great Hall in the Winter Palace and the walls were made almost entirely of wood.

She danced in her dream, her gold gown flashing under her and a pair of amber eyes making her melt. She allowed herself to swim in their depths as she was led out of the ballroom. She followed Aiden through the crunching snow, but instead of Olympia's palace walls surrounding them, it was those of the Winter Palace. The sky turned dark; the stars angry instead of joyful. A cold wind rushed through the garden, making Penny shiver. Blood began to seep from the skirt of her golden dress.

Aiden let go of her hand. She watched as his face turned angry. "The only time I haven't left of my own free will was when I was brought here, but apparently that's a strike against me as well. I refuse to be bullied and beaten into staying silent on things I don't agree with. I've had enough of that to last a lifetime."

He morphed before her eyes until it was Dìomhair leaning over her.

"Thank you for making this easy for me," he whispered in her ear.

She closed her eyes, preparing for the blow, but nothing came.

She peeked and found Dìomhair frozen in place, the vague outline of a knife glinting in his hand.

"How are you feeling, Penelope?"

She spun and found Dair standing in the snow behind her. In her dream.

"Dair?" This hadn't been how the night had played out.

"I came to check on you a moment ago but found out you were finally asleep. I did not want to risk waking you, so I thought meeting you here would be better for your body."

"Wait, are you saying this is real?" She looked about, but the vague outlines and blurred images told her it was still a dream. The blood-soaked dress she'd been wearing was gone, replaced by the simple work dress she'd worn in the orchards back in Eleusion.

"We are still in your dream, Penelope, but our conversation is very real. It is my *tiodhlacan an spioraid*, my gift. I can walk in other's dreams."

"I've never heard of such a thing," Penny said.

"Apparently our family has a history with interesting gifts, but we are not here to talk about me. I just saw what happened." He glared over at the fading form of Dìomhair. "Did Aedon actually say that to you?"

Penny shrugged. "More or less." There was definitely more, but she wasn't going to admit it. "I deserved it."

Dair shook his head, lavender hair swinging. "Deserved or not, my *athair* would have boxed our ears if he ever heard us talking like that to a lady, mage or no."

"Your father sounds like a good man—I mean *fae*."

Dair's face fell. "He really was. The best." He looked up at her. "I think he would have absolutely adored you. We told Aedon you had to go back to Olympia, that a relationship between the two of you would have never worked, but after seeing you and Aedon together, I think *Athair* would have been the first to say you made my cousin a better fae."

Penny shuffled her feet in the dreamed-up snow. "I don't know what to say."

"What I am trying to say is that I think we were wrong. I think we allowed prejudice to blind us to Aedon's feelings for you. He has been miserable and the only time I see him brighten is when you are in a room, or he gets a report on you from a brownie that you are in good health. We thought he could forget you, that we would be able to send you home and that Aedon would move on. But now? I think it would break him to let you go. You should have seen his face when he found out you were hurt again. Nearly took out the guard captain's study, the shadows were so thick."

"He knows? How?"

"I went to Crann Mòr to get him. He is facing a pack of feral Spring fae as we speak."

The dream went dark at the edges.

"Wait, do not wake up quite yet. I do not know if he is in a good state of mind just now. Give him time to gather information." He played with a wisp of color from her fading dream. "They were able to capture Durant."

Penny gasped. "Are you serious? They got her?"

Dair smiled. "Yes. The old windbag is behind bars in Crann Mòr. We just have to work to keep her there and get ahead of the rebels."

"Let's hope we have enough time. Adira Durant isn't one to allow a little thing such as capture to thwart her plans." *I certainly hadn't.* It was only a matter of time before Adira made her escape if they didn't figure out how to keep her in the dungeon. Perhaps the Andàn had some insight. They had been threatening to have tea with Penny for a week. Perhaps she needed to take them up on their offer.

"We are doing our best to come up with a plan," said Dair, "but we do not quite know how it will all play out. All we can do at this point is pray to the Goddess."

"I know we can beat her. We just need to work together." She began pacing in the snow. "Do we have any word from Olympia yet?"

Dair shook his head. "We know not to expect anything for at least another few days. Farrah should return by then with news."

"Great Goddess, I hope you're right." The capture felt like a win, but knowing Adira Durant, it could easily turn against them.

14
STRIDE

King Falaichte threw his hands in the air. "Something must be done. Immediately!"

Aiden bared his teeth in what he hoped was his most lethal smile. "And what would you like me to do, my lord?"

"The mage needs to face retribution!" called one of the Spring courtiers.

Aiden held up a hand, silencing them. Skies, the lot of them had been harping since he burst through the portal. He hadn't even made it out of the Great Hall yet. "We are in the process of an investigation. I will let you know our findings when I'm ready to deliver them."

"And when will that be?"

Aiden allowed his shadows to ripple over the floor toward them and his voice to magically carry across through the room. "When I very well please." He strode toward them. "I am your High King. I do not answer to you or your Court. I answer to the Goddess and the Goddess alone. Remember that next time you wish to throw accusations my direction."

The courtiers huddled down, the air thick with magic. The corners of Aiden's vision went blurry with the sheer force of it.

A vision of black and silver came up beside him. "Can I help, My Sovereign?"

Aiden didn't turn to look at her, but he could hear the obvious question in Shirina's voice: *do you need backup in this fight?*

Aiden reined in his magic, the Land settling to the back of his mind. "No," he said, his voice back at a normal volume. He finally turned to her. "I'm going to see Thaen. Will you see to this mess in the Hall?"

Shirina nodded, but he saw her obvious anger.

So, Thaen had been right. Penelope had been winning over the rest of the family.

Aiden paced in the sitting room outside of Penelope's door. The shadows along the wall told him of the coming night. He couldn't go in there. Not after he'd been the one who had sent her running out into the garden where she'd been stabbed.

Great Goddess, she'd been stabbed. When he'd found Thaen and seen the blood on Penny's dress, he had nearly lost every semblance of control and buried the entire Spring Court beneath the mountain.

Having Annalysa in the palace had been nothing short of a blessing from the Goddess herself. The blade had only nicked Penelope's liver, giving the healer plenty of time to heal the wound before Penelope bled out. The fae who had stabbed her obviously hadn't been a trained killer. If he had been, Penelope would be dead.

He raked a hand through his hair. His lungs ceased to work at the very thought and shadows pooled around his feet. He'd nearly lost her today. Penelope, the love of his life, could have truly died.

And everything in him would have died with her.

How could he have been such a cursed blackguard? She had been right here, with him in this crazy kingdom of magic and wonder that he was now king over, and all he'd done is push her straight into the arms of an assassin.

Why is it so easy for you to push me aside when all I've ever wanted was the future I dreamed up with you?

Penelope's words echoed in his ears. Why had he ignored the fact that she'd come for him? He should have been shouting for joy that she was here, with him, not trying to push her away and ruin whatever chance he had of winning her over. Ruining the little time they could have left.

His steps paused right outside her door. He set a hand on the handle. He should march in there and show her how much he truly loved her. He should tell her he was sorry and—

"Aedon?"

Dair's voice whispered across the hall. Aiden gritted his teeth and turned away from the door. "Yes?"

Dair came up beside him. "She is asleep."

Aiden nodded, still unwilling to let go of the handle. The brownies had reported to him that was the case. The need to speak with her still burned through him.

"Come, cousin. There will be plenty of time for apologies tomorrow after we have all had a moment to breathe. You and I need to talk."

Aiden nodded and followed Dair away from the door. He'd go back tomorrow, after he went over in his mind what he was truly going to say to her.

Dair led him through the halls to the study he'd taken over. Shirina had claimed it was an extra, Fiadh's having been closer to their rooms on the level above. Shirina still had not moved their things into the royal apartments. Aiden imagined it was hard to leave the place she'd made with her husband in their other rooms.

Aiden shut the study door behind him. He rubbed a hand over the back of his neck as he slumped into the chair behind the desk.

"I learned of the conversation you and Penelope had before she found Dìomhair on the grounds."

Aiden felt his ears heat. "Oh? What did you hear?"

"It is not so much what I heard, but how Penelope must have interpreted it. Did you ever stop to wonder how she would feel if you cut her to the quick and then left her behind as you so blatantly mentioned you had in the past?"

Aiden's stomach sank. "I wasn't thinking—"

"No," Dair cut in, "you were not. I watched her subconscious process that information, Aedon. What I saw was not something you should be proud of."

"I'm not," Aiden said, subdued. What did Penelope think of him? What had Dair seen in her dream?

"She needs to feel safe here. She needs to feel like she has a safe place to go to and allies she can trust."

"I know, Dair. I know." While he was glad to see the shift in his family, he still couldn't figure out how to get the rest of the kingdom to do the same. Not before something truly terrible happened.

"What are we going to do, cousin?" Dair twisted a thick silver ring around his thumb.

Aiden blew out a breath. "I have no idea."

"We may have to hide her somewhere," Dair suggested. "There is a lodge at the base of the mountain we use during the late summer months. Perhaps she could go there."

"If we do end up sending her somewhere, she'd need to be guarded, and we don't have anyone we can trust to do it." Not to mention the fact that sending her away didn't sit right with him. "One of us would have to go, but we need every available person working on beating the rebels."

A knock on the door preceded Thaen's arrival. "I have completed my investigation."

Dair gave him a look that said their conversation about Penelope wasn't over yet. "And?" Aiden prodded.

"It certainly looks like self-defense. With the way the tracks in the snow lay and where the blood was, you can tell he attacked her and suffered the consequences."

Praise the Goddess Penelope knew how to use a blade. "So, she won't be faced with any repercussions for it."

Thaen hesitated.

"Maybe not any that would be legal," Dair supplied. "You can definitely bet on the Spring Court retaliating for the loss of their citizen—especially such a high standing one."

Aiden frowned. "They attempted to kill her, outside of their home and jurisdiction, and we should expect her to face them?"

Thaen nodded gravely. "If you think this is the last we hear of it, you would be mistaken."

Aiden folded his hands over his eyes. Wind and snow, would they ever catch a break? Guilt churned in his gut, acidic and heavy since leaving her alone after they'd fought. All her concerns made sense now that he thought about them outside the heat of the moment, but he didn't know if she'd forgive him, not after leaving her alone to face a murderer. And now she would face more enemies for protecting herself.

A small clearing of a throat came from under his desk. He ducked down and found a large pair of brown eyes peeking out from the shadows. A small mustache covered the brownie's upper lip. Aiden recognized him as one of the ones who had taken to reporting on Penelope.

"Yes?" Aiden asked.

"Lady Penelope has been asleep for the last half hour," said the brownie. "No one has ventured into her rooms, My Sovereign."

These reports had come three times before, arriving every half hour. Even the bwbachod were worried for her. "I'm pleased with the report, then."

"Also, the Andàn have arrived, My Sovereign. They are heading to the family sitting room. They have requested you come alone."

"I will attend them," Aiden replied. The *alone* part sounded rather ominous, but his misgivings were pushed aside with the hope that they'd found something. "Anything else?"

The brownie flashed him a small smile and touched his four fingered hand to his face. "It will be all right, My Sovereign. You will get it figured out." With the soft words, the brownie disappeared.

Aiden lifted his head, finding his cousins watching him curiously.

"What?" Aiden asked.

"I have never seen the brownies take to someone as they do to you, cousin," Dair said. "Or to Penelope. It is odd, to say the least."

Thaen nodded.

"Well, the Aunties have just arrived." Aiden would have to let the brownie mystery lie for now. "Hopefully they've come with the solution to all of this."

The three of them left the study, Thaen and Dair drifting off in the opposite direction as Aiden went to greet the Andàn in the family sitting room.

When he arrived at the door, he found the Aunties seated next to one another. Aiden stepped inside and joined their large circle of chairs. The number of family councils had facilitated more chairs added to the room, considering they also sometimes involved the cousins, Penelope, Sgiath's family, the Aunties, the Eiles up until they'd left, and everyone else who was poking their nose into Aiden's business. He sank into the wingback leather chair closest to the fire. "Please say you learned something."

"You will not like our answer, Little One," Auntie Niomi said, sitting on a sofa across from him. "We know it will be what you most wish not to hear."

That was it then. Penelope would be trapped here for the rest of her life, threatened by a people he had responsibility over and forced to live in hiding. "What have you found?"

"Nothing," Auntie Taddie said. "We have communed in the temple for three weeks, and we have even more questions than we went in with."

Aiden didn't know whether to be overjoyed or completely frustrated. "Why more questions, Aunties?"

"We were able to commune with Our Mother," said Auntie Niomi, "but what She said did not make much sense."

"Not that she likes to make much sense often," Auntie Taddie mumbled.

"What did she say?"

Auntie Taddie stood from her chair and shuffled over to a table where her overly large carpet bag sat. She rummaged through it, pulling out a slip of paper and squinting at it. "To save Penelope, you must keep the promises you made in the place of unkept promises."

Aiden blinked. "What does that even mean?"

Auntie Niomi patted his hand. "In time, we will understand Her ways, but for now we must have faith that She does everything for a reason and remember that no one can stand in the way of Her purposes. We must seek within ourselves what the Goddess desires of us and do our best to follow Her plan."

"Regarding Penelope's bond," Auntie Taddie continued, "that which was Hers has become Hers once again, and She will bring in new life with the power She has regained. The bond of magic has been sealed, and no one but the Goddess Herself can separate them."

"So that's it?" Aiden shot out of his seat. "Penelope is subjected to this bond no matter what?"

Auntie Taddie nodded. "Afraid so, Little One. Our Mother has accepted the bond and was very clear She will not relinquish it."

"What do I do?" he pleaded.

"What can any of us do?" Auntie Niomi said, her blue nest of hair wobbling atop her head. "We must do our best and be valiant."

"That," said Auntie Taddie, "and eat plenty of cake."

15
SCARS AND APOLOGIES

ANNALYSA SET A HAND ON PENNY'S STOMACH. "CAN YOU TAKE IN A DEEP breath with your abdomen?"

Penny did as requested, only feeling the slightest pull where her skin had scarred together. After four days under Annalysa's care and there was only the slightest pucker of flesh left of the gaping stab wound she'd sustained by Dìomhair's hand.

"Excellent." Annalysa pulled her hand away. "It seems you have made a full recovery with both your arm and your abdomen."

"You really are a miracle worker," Penny said, wincing as she sat up on the sofa in her sitting room.

Annalysa waved off her words, though the tips of her ears peeking through her long, white hair turned pink. "I am simply doing as Danu would have me do."

"And we are indebted to you for it."

Penny turned around and found Aiden standing in the doorway. A piece of his dark hair fell into his eyes. Penny's fingers twitched with the desire to push it out of his face. What he offered Annalysa was no small thing. Being indebted to the fae was not a situation anyone in their right mind would wish to be in.

"I appreciate such a boon, My Sovereign," said Annalysa with a bow, "but I am truly happy to use my gift in such a way."

"Not many would agree with what you have done," he said in a low voice. "I would be remiss if I did not show proper thanks for it."

Annalysa scoffed. "They also would not agree with having a sliver of decency in their bones. Goddess forbid, it might give them an itch."

Aiden smiled and Penny felt her own lips mimic the movement. She'd never seen him smile in Olympia as much as he did here. Even with the stress, this place suited him.

His eyes met hers and she tried to keep his gaze, but concern and hurt still swirled in their amber depths. They hadn't spoken since their fight three days ago. She pushed down the lump growing in the back of her throat. Was he still upset with her? Would he be open to talking about what happened? She looked away.

"The scar should fade to white within the week and the tightness will ease as you continue to exercise," Annalysa asked as she hoisted her bag on her shoulder. "Is there anything else we should be concerned with, Penelope?"

Penny shook her head. "I feel right as rain."

Annalysa gave her a funny look. "Right as rain?" she muttered as she lugged her heavy bag toward the door. She stopped next to Aiden. "Call for me if there are any more problems." She took another step forward but paused. "Though, if I come back and find that once again Penelope has been put in a position like this, I will start to question her safety within this palace."

Penny gaped, but Aiden met the healer's eyes and gave her a firm nod.

Annalysa returned the gesture and stepped out into the hall.

Aiden closed the door behind him. "For such a terrifying mage, you're doing quite a good job at making friends here."

Penny blinked at him. "What do you mean?"

"Shirina, Dair, Farrah, and now Annalysa. I think even Thaen is warming up to you."

Penny gave an unladylike snort. "Not likely. He's as cold as this mountain."

Aiden's lips tipped up. "All right, he's tepid at best, but I have had nothing less than a dozen comments like Annalysa's within the last week. Everyone here is concerned for you. The brownies have given me a report on your welfare every half hour since your injury, even though I didn't ask for it."

The brownies? The little folk had come into her room several times this morning, leaving flowers or bits of honeycomb on a plate on her bedside table. A few had smiled at her, and one had even winked. Every time, she'd found herself mystified after the encounter. "I still don't see what any of that has to do with making friends."

Aiden came and sat beside her on the sofa. "The folk here see how amazing you are. Skies, they flock to you like pixies to a sugar bowl."

Pixies like sugar? Penny would need to start keeping a list.

"The point is," Aiden continued, "they've all helped me see the error of my ways."

"What does that mean?"

Aiden leaned back and let out a long sigh. "It means I have been making a mull of all of this, and it's high time I rectified it." He reached out and took one of Penny's hands. A shock rippled through her, as it always did when he touched her. Why did it always do that?

He cleared his throat awkwardly. "I need to apologize. Again."

Penny met his eyes. "So do I. I'm sorry about throwing all those accusations in your face. It was completely undeserved."

"I don't know if it was *completely* undeserved," Aiden said. "I shouldn't have treated you the way I have been. By the Goddess, Penelope, I should have seen how hard everything is for you here. I should have realized what Angelica's leaving meant for you and how much I'd been neglecting you."

"It's not like I've been seeking you out either." She pulled her hair over her shoulder and tightened her hold on his hand. "I didn't want to be a burden on top of everything else."

"I've told you before, I will never think of you as a burden." His head fell against the back of the sofa. "If I'm being honest, I think I was trying to protect myself."

Penny rubbed her thumb over the knuckles of his fingers. "From what?"

He opened his mouth a few times as if trying to find the right words. "The Andàn came with their answer."

Penny's stomach flipped. "What did they say?"

"A lot of things, but the gist of what I got is that they have no idea what the pomegranate seeds have done. They don't know if you are safe going back to Olympia."

So, I can't go back. Penny closed her eyes, waiting for that reality to sink in. She waited for the gut wrench, but it never came. Instead, peace settled over her, warm and pleasant like the first rays of sunlight after a thunderstorm. This was what she had been asking for.

An answer.

And she found that she'd already come to that conclusion on her own. She'd never wanted to leave Aiden. Sweet Gaia, just sitting next to him was as healing as Annalysa's magic. She needed him and she knew he needed her.

She opened her eyes and looked at her and Aiden's joined hands. "Does this change anything for you?"

Aiden rubbed a hand over the back of his neck. "I think I was waiting to find out that you were going to be able to return to Olympia. I wanted you to—for your own happiness mostly and partially for the ease of the Courts. I knew it was the best option for everyone... except me."

Penny felt her mouth turn down. Before she could speak, Aiden continued.

"The selfish part of me wants you to stay, really wants you to be here alongside me. But since I found out I would never be truly able to return to Olympia, I knew you would have to go back without me. I knew it wasn't safe for you here—perhaps not *how* unsafe, but I'll be apologizing for that misstep for the rest of my life. I knew that you would have to return to Olympia, so I latched onto it so hard I tried to push you away when you were near. I didn't want my heart to break all over again."

Penny scooted closer to him. "What gave you the impression that I would consider leaving?"

Aiden shrugged, a bit self-consciously if Penny interpreted it right. "Why wouldn't you? Your entire life is back in Olympia. Your friends. Your work. Eleusion is still under rebel influence, and I know you wanted to work to take it back. You have so much potential there, while here you'll be persecuted for what you are and not for the kind, loving person I know you to be."

Her eyes prickled. "You're right. I do have a life back in Olympia." She pulled his hand into her lap and began lightly stroking his fingers. That sense of peace swelled in her. "But I want to stay here. I want to be by your side. I'm willing to work with you to get through all the hard stuff. I always have been."

"I know and I'm sorry I didn't believe you. I'm sorry that I trusted what I thought you truly wanted more than what you said you did."

"Thank you," Penny said.

"And I'm so sorry about what happened with the Spring Court—in both instances. I trusted that you would be safe simply because I said you weren't to be harmed, but I should have realized that hate and prejudice would supersede anything I said. I haven't gained the respect or trust of my kingdom yet, and I should have remembered that Winter isn't like the other courts. I should have protected you."

"It doesn't matter now," Penny said. "We'll just know better going forward." She tapped the small blade on her wrist that the Lòchran had returned to her. "I guess I'll have to keep an iron blade on me and start up a more rigorous training regimen."

"Nothing too intense until you're feeling better," Aiden said.

"Aiden, I'm fine. You heard what Annalysa said. I *should* be exercising."

"I'm not just talking about your body, Penelope, but your heart as well. It's taken a brutal beating—especially from me. I don't know how I'll ever make any of this up to you."

The words eased something in her, and she wove her fingers through his. "I think, perhaps, we should make the decision, right here, to leave it behind us."

His fingers tightened around hers. "Just like that?"

"Yes. Just like that. We've both made so many mistakes when it came to our being together." Tears gathered and she tried to blink them away. "I know I tend to rush without thinking things through."

"And I seem to overthink everything when it comes to you." He brought their hands to his chest. "Penelope, I'm going to be better. I swear to you, I won't leave you again. If you still want me—*us*—after everything I've done, I promise not to let anyone else hurt you."

"Aiden." She pulled their hands over to her heart. "I'm not some damsel that needs saving all the time."

Aiden quirked a brow in answer, looking down at her abdomen.

Penny shoved him over on the sofa. It must have surprised him, because if he'd been expecting it, he wouldn't have fallen over. A small giggle burst from her chest. "See? I'm strong enough to push you over. I don't need you to protect me, I only need you to trust me. I need you to be my partner again."

A breath, so small no one else would have even noticed, slipped between his lips. "How do you keep finding it in yourself to forgive me?"

"Well, it comes easy since you're High King of a magical land I've always wanted to explore." She laughed. "All you have to do is promise I'll get to see a unicorn and you've won every argument we ever have."

He gave her a halfhearted glare and stood up. "I've changed my mind. Grab your sword and come with me."

Penny's laughter died off, but her smile remained. "Where are we going?"

"You're right about needing the exercise."

Penny followed Aiden into the sand. His gaze lifted to the domed ceiling above them, and she took a deep breath of the metal and sweat smell soaked into the wooden benches.

"This is a much nicer sparring ring than Olympia's," Penny remarked.

Aiden looked around and shrugged. "A sparring room is a sparring room."

Penny glided toward the wall of weapons, almost as if they were magnetic. She ran a finger over the flat sides of a few blades and looked over the tips of a handful of arrows. "They have some talented craftsmen." She drew her sword from her waist. "Though nowhere as good as Heff."

Aiden flashed her a smile. "I agree. I'm still lamenting the loss of my own sword. Evan's probably stolen it by now. He's always been jealous of it."

Penny had the urge to laugh but held it back. "I'm sure Rissa found it first and made a shrine. She's sentimental enough to have done something like that."

Aiden took up his own sword and swung it in a circle. "How long did you wait?"

"For what?"

"How long did you wait to come after me?" He sliced the sword through the air lazily. "I know it was soon after I disappeared."

Penny pursed her lips. "How about we play a game?"

Aiden's right brow curved up. "You won't answer my question?"

"I never said I wouldn't. I just propose we turn it into a game. We spar and the winner of the round gets to ask a question which the loser has to answer honestly."

Aiden still looked slightly confused. "Penelope, you've never won a round against me. It's hardly fair."

Penny batted his sword with hers. "Then it should be easy for you."

Aiden chuckled, then moved. In one moment, he stood a few steps in front of her. In the next, Penny's sword went flying out of her hands and Aiden's sword stood level with her heart—which took up an irregular beat.

Aiden grinned. "I win."

Penny's gaze flicked back and forth from him to the sword. "How did you—"

"Now, now. Winner gets to ask questions." He retrieved her sword from the ground and handed it to her. "How long did you wait?"

Penny spread her feet. "I didn't wait. I left the temple moments after you disappeared. Lady Alvis took me to the portal before sundown that day."

"You really—"

Penny smacked the sword hanging loosely from Aiden's hands. It slipped from his fingers and fell to the ground. She grinned. "My turn. Where did you learn that move with the sword?"

"That was a dirty trick." Aiden took up his blade once again. "Thaen's been training me pretty much since I arrived."

"Oh great," Penny muttered and went at him again. He didn't lose his sword a single round, but Penny did.

It took him a whole three seconds and a smack on the back of her hand with the flat of his blade to get her to drop it again.

"How long were you in Durant's camp?" he asked.

Penny rolled her eyes and picked up her sword from between her feet. "Three weeks."

She held up the sword.

This time, she was able to keep it in her hand for probably ten seconds before he came under her guard and used his elbow to pop her arm up. She kept hold of the blade for a second, but he grabbed her wrist and twisted her around, making her loosen her grip. The sword smacked into the sand.

"Why did you bring Spot with you to Faerie?"

"Because I knew he could help me find you." She picked up the sword and met his eyes. "And I knew you'd miss him."

A soft smile twitched at his lips, but his amber eyes grew playful as he brought his sword to the ready.

Penny only lasted two seconds before her sword flew across the sparring ring. By the Goddess, she knew he'd always held back when they'd sparred in the past, but this was embarrassing.

"Stop holding your blade so tight. Don't you remember I taught you to hold it looser?"

"Yes, and that counts as a question." She smirked, grabbing her sword and holding it properly in her hand.

The loosened grip did help. She defended herself well, keeping him at bay until he was able to get behind her. He grabbed her waist with one hand and held his sword at her neck. It wasn't anywhere close to her skin, but between the blade and his proximity, she shivered.

He leaned in, his lips nearly brushing her ear. "When I told you I've been in love with you since I saw you during the debut ball, did you actually mean it when you said you'd loved me for a long time too?"

Penny paused at this one. "Yes, though I don't think it turned into love until later. I was fascinated by you, after our encounter in the garden. But I don't think I truly fell in love with you until I knew you. Learning under you as Lou and being close to you in Olympia cemented it for me, but it's been a slow progression of love instead of an instant manifestation of it. Though our first meeting was certainly unforgettable."

Aiden dropped his sword from her neck and spun her around. "I think I know what my next question is going to be."

Penny looked up at him, but his eyes were focused on her lips.

She bit her bottom lip and shoved him back. "You haven't won this round yet."

Aiden's gaze burned through her. "But I plan to presently." He gave her a wild grin and charged toward her.

Instead of raising her sword, Penny turned and ran across the sand. "You're going to have to catch me first."

Aiden laughed, that deep laugh he only saved for when he was truly surprised or pleased by something. It made Penny smile.

Her smile fell away when she heard him finally give chase.

The sound was the scariest part. Aiden rarely made a sound when he moved, but this time he made sounds on purpose.

Penny looked behind her and saw him closing in. She squealed and put on a burst of speed. He could obviously catch her anytime he liked, but he was drawing it out, making her heart race.

She spun around to face him, sword drawn, but continued walking away.

His grin was almost feral. "Why are you running, Penelope?"

A giggle burst out of her. "Why are you chasing me?"

He lazily knocked his sword against hers. "I want my question."

She dodged his sword. "Are you sure? What if I say 'no?'"

"You don't even know what the question is."

She pointed the tip of her sword at him. "You want a kiss."

The moment the word came out of her mouth, her cheeks began burning. They'd kissed before. Multiple times. But this felt different. They were different people now. There was the enormous gap between them called "Faerie." While they may have fixed things between them, she could admit she was frightened. Not of *him* exactly, but what being with him would mean.

Aiden crept closer still, the gold of his eyes blazing. "Yes, you're right. I do want a kiss." He zipped toward her and grabbed her hand around the red leather grip of her sword. "But that wasn't what I was going to ask for."

The doors to the sparring ring opened and a group of fae walked in.

And not just any group.

"It has a sword!" one of the Spring females cried.

Two of the males drew their own swords as Penny repositioned to hold hers between herself and the newcomers.

Aiden moved to stand between them. "Yes, we're sparring."

"You think it is safe to give that thing a weapon?" one of them sneered. "After it *murdered* our poor Dìomhair?"

Penny's throat clogged and she had the faintest urge to vomit. She sheathed her sword, not willing to become a pawn in their game. She would be innocent in this. Aiden would handle it.

And if not, she had an entire wall of weapons next to her.

"She did not murder *anyone*," Aiden objected. "Dìomhair stabbed her, and she protected herself."

King Falaichte's consort scoffed. "It can lie, of course it said anything it needed to stay out of trouble. But we saw it! The thing used iron against our Dìomhair!"

"*I can lie,*" Aiden seethed. "And I would expect anyone in this kingdom to attack when provoked. I do not condemn a single one of you for protecting yourselves."

"But the mage killed our friend!"

Shadows wrapped around his arms. "And your friend tried to kill *my future wife!*"

16

STAKE

Wind and snow, had he really just said that out loud?

Why?

Why had he said that?

Everything had changed since his arrival in Faerie.

Yes, he still wanted to marry her, but what he wanted didn't matter in the grand scheme of things. He could never actually hold Penelope to the promises they'd made under the tree in Olympia. She might have changed her mind. He couldn't just assume she would still want him.

Something within him stirred, and the shadows winding around his arms smoothed out.

To save Penelope, you must keep the promises you made in the place of unkept promises.

The Land's quiet voice echoed what the Andàn had told him. By the Goddess, was this what it meant? Would she truly be all right as the *consort* of a kingdom where her subjects would hate her and ridicule her?

Something in him didn't feel right about that.

The entire arena stood stock still, including Penelope. Her face had lost all color.

"Your what?" King Falaichte demanded. "I do not believe I heard you right."

Aiden narrowed his eyes. To the Mist with the lot of them. "No, you heard exactly right. That is my future wife."

A few of the fae gasped.

The king took another step forward. "Do you mean to tell me you will desecrate our kingdom by taking that *thing* as a consort? Blend your already tainted blood with hers?"

There was that word again, and it still rang wrong within him.

Consort.

Why did that feel so wrong? Having her be his wife was everything he'd ever wanted, but his consort? The very idea sent his heart aching and his stomach twisting into knots.

"Aiden?" Penelope whispered from behind him.

He turned to look at her.

Her eyes were wide with questions, her mouth set in a firm line and her brows low. She looked ready to battle, whether against these fae or perhaps even whatever answer he would give. Just then, she didn't look like a consort.

The magic of the Land rose up in him again, making every nerve in his body tingle almost unpleasantly. The whisper of intent in that magic nearly had him gasping.

Aiden drew on every piece of command and severity he could muster.

"No, she will not be my consort." The magic inside of him almost purred with pleasure.

The fae before him visibly relaxed.

He went to his knees before her, placed a fist over his heart and bowed his head. "She will be High Queen."

Shirina whirled on Aiden after Thaen shut the door behind their group. "Why the blowing, biting, *blasted* blizzards would you say and do that in front of the entire Spring Court?"

The Spring Court had nearly trampled one another trying to get to the highest power they could to tell them what Aiden had done. Shirina had called the entire family, including the Aunties, for a family council after being harangued by the Spring Court.

"Did you think you could get away with such an insult?" she asked. "You just put a giant target on Penelope's back! They will be coming for her as soon as they can now. You cannot lie and say you are going to make her High Queen."

"I didn't."

Shirina frowned. "You did not think you could get away with it or you did not say you are going to make her High Queen?"

"I didn't lie." Aiden found a spot on the sofa next to Penelope. "I meant what I said with every fiber of my being."

Shirina paused in her pacing. "You mean you are actually going to try to make her High Queen? It cannot be done!"

"Why not?" Dair asked.

"You blasted know why not!" Shirina nearly screeched. "We cannot just decide who the High Rulers are. It is not our decision! The Goddess is the one who decides."

"What if She has decided?"

Thaen looked at him sharply. "What is that supposed to mean?"

"It means that I can prove Penelope has already been chosen to become High Queen."

"You can do what?" Penny squeaked.

He turned to her beside him and took her hand. "Do you trust me?"

She bobbed her head almost automatically, though there was still a wariness in her eyes, one he swore to himself he was going to work every day to diminish until he had her full trust.

"Aunties," he said, turning toward the Andàn, "will you please tell everyone else what the Goddess told you in regard to saving Penelope."

Auntie Taddie frowned. "She said you must keep your promise."

"I must keep my promise made in the place of unkept promises." He turned back to Penelope. "Do you know what Olympia's palace used to be before the Faerie Wars?"

Penelope shook her head.

"It was a temple," Shirina answered. "It was built when I was a child. Every Season had one. There's another further into Olympia, though I could not tell you what has become of it now."

Penelope gasped. "It's Iatrus Castle, isn't it?"

Aiden nodded. "I had forgotten until recently. The Olympian

royal family had the one in Olympia renovated, but originally it was a temple. The ceiling in the ballroom still has the original artwork of the heavens painted by the fae before they left it."

"But what does that have to do with promises?" Thaen asked.

"What else do we do in the Goddess's temples except make promises? We promise to cherish our spouses and do the Goddess's will. It has been a long time since any of that has happened in that temple."

"Hence 'unkept promises,'" Penelope said.

"Precisely."

"But what promises were made there?" Dair asked.

Aiden smiled and met Penelope's eyes once again. "That's where I asked Penelope to marry me. I promised to love her always and make her my wife under the oak tree in the palace gardens."

"But even that prophecy could be interpreted in many ways," said Thaen. "Is that all the proof you have?"

"Not at all." Aiden sidled up to Penelope, her expression vacillating between hope and terror. "Aunties, what did the rest of the Goddess's words say?"

Auntie Taddie had pulled out the note she'd made when the Andàn had been communing with the Goddess. Aiden kept his eyes on Penelope as she read. "That which was Hers has become Hers once again, and She will bring in new life with the power She has regained. The bond of magic has been sealed, and no one but the Goddess Herself can separate them."

Penelope's face grew paler, but he saw the understanding dawn in her eyes.

"Penelope, what has happened to your magic?"

Her throat bobbed. "I can't use it anymore."

"Why?"

"Because when I try it's so overwhelming it hurts. There's too much and I can't do anything unless—" She paused.

"Unless?" Aiden straightened. She hadn't told him of anything else happening.

She ducked her head. "Unless I don't reach for it. I've had a few moments where it's worked without my actually trying. It's mostly when I think about it happening or sometimes it's random."

Aiden's eyes pulled wide. "Like the white daffodils."

Penny looked up. "How did you know?"

"I saw your hands glow. I thought I'd imagined it, but white daffodils don't grow anywhere close to here."

"Actually," Shirina said, "we do not have any that grow within Faerie's boundaries anymore. Not since the Farraige Gaineamh was created."

Hadn't he seen the flowers in Faerie before though? Aiden's mind reeled. "But I have seen them here. There was an oasis in the dunes."

Penelope ducked her head timidly. "I may have had something to do with that as well. I accidentally summoned up quite a few oases during my first few days out of the Mist. I couldn't get my magic under control."

Auntie Niomi cackled. "It is the same magic, and it has returned to the Goddess's power. She has been working with you for Her own purposes."

"You mean *She* was the one who created the daffodils in the vase and hit Dair upside the head?"

Dair sat up from his lounge on the floor. "The Goddess did what now?"

"I agree that the Goddess has had a hand in this," Shirina admitted, "but I still do not see how this qualifies her to be queen."

Aiden took both of Penelope's hands in his. "The night of the revel, you arrived at the party dressed in branches and what appeared to be blue pomegranate blossoms. Where did you get them?"

Penelope licked her lips and glanced around the room. "I found the room, with the faerie glass throne. The branches above the room drooped down and gave them to me."

Shirina actually gasped. "The Great Tree *gave* them to you?"

"Of course." Aiden smiled at Penelope. "We matched. Like true partners."

Shirina took up the seat closest to them, leaning forward to look them both in the eye. "I need you both to listen very closely. Marriage in Faerie is not the same as Olympia's. Mortals are married in Olympia for this life and this life only. Without the magic, there is only the bonds they make on this earth. In Faerie and in the Isles of Aigean, a marriage, a *seulachadh anama* is forever—unless the Goddess Herself does not choose to accept it or breaks the bond as She sees fit. Once done, it will not be undone. It will link you together, not just as husband and wife, but your very souls will be linked."

"How did you prepare for it?" Aiden asked.

Shirina visibly deflated and silver limned her dark eyes. The fingers of her right hand fiddled with the pinky of her left. "Fiadh courted me for five years before we decided. With him being so much younger than me, I never wanted to take him seriously, but he always knew we would be married. He said it was destiny, and he was right. We were *taghadh*."

"What is that?" Penelope asked.

Auntie Niomi stepped up beside Shirina's chair. "It is a pair of two beings that Danu put on a collision course since their creation. Two mates that find one another in this made world and choose whether to accept the pairing the Goddess believes to be the best."

"Like soulmates?" Aiden asked. Even that sounded like a myth.

"Not so much that you are soul-bound as it is that you are always meant to meet," Dair answered, rolling his eyes. "But it does not happen for everyone. Like, could you even imagine someone choosing to shackle themself to my brother?"

He laughed, drawing chuckles from the rest of the room, but it was quickly cut off by Thaen tackling him to the floor and then proceeding to smother him with a pillow.

Shirina shook her head, but Dair's plot had done the trick. Only a history of tears remained on her face as she turned back to them. "Danu has given Her children the freedom to choose their own paths, but She knows us better than we know ourselves, and puts those in our lives that will help us grow and progress. She allows us to collide with those that would ultimately make us happy in this life and the one to come, but we are the ones who must listen to Her council and decide whether or not to except such a thing. The bond that is created is a sacred thing, and if you are lucky enough to find your *taghadh*, there are many responsibilities that come with it."

"What does that mean?" Penelope asked.

Shirina held up her hand, showing a light gray mark around her pinky that Aiden had never noticed before. "If such a thing were to occur for the two of you, his magic will be your magic and your magic will be his. You will be linked in a way nobody else could ever be—more than even Fiadh was to Morana. It also connects you to the Goddess, making the connection with the magic of the Land that much stronger. It is a magic in and of itself and if you are not prepared for that kind of commitment, you need to decide right now."

"And you married because you found out you were... this... *taghadh*?" Penelope asked.

"No. We did not even know until we were standing across from one another with our hands tied in marriage. You discover your chosen mate after you have already made the decision to choose one another."

"But what if you aren't fated?" Penelope fiddled with the fabric of her purple skirt. "What if you're just two people who get along with one another?"

"Then those that choose to be are still happy. Not everyone has the opportunity to find their perfect match, but everyone can still find complete joy in the Goddess's plan for them. It is She that brings joy, not us who go and find it."

"But I'm a mage," Penelope said. "Can mages even be a chosen mate for a Fae?"

Aiden pulled her toward him. "Why does it matter?"

"Because"—twin tears fell down her cheeks—"if there's a fae here that is supposed to be your spouse, who would be even more perfect for you and your kingdom than me, why would I risk getting in the way of that?"

He took her face in his hands and wiped the trail of tears with his thumbs. "I chose you, Penelope Barclay. No matter what Danu may have put into action, I chose you and I'll continue to choose you for as long as we both live and then far longer after that. I'll come out of our wedding happier than I will be going into it because I will have married the girl that makes me a better man and cares so much about what is right that I won't even think about some other, mythological being out there that may or may not exist. I have you, Penelope. And I'm not ever planning on letting you go."

More tears ran down her face, and he pressed a small kiss to her nose. "Now, I am still entitled to ask you a question."

"What?" Penelope asked, confused.

"I was about to ask you a question when we were so rudely interrupted in the sparring ring. I would like to ask it now."

She lowered her voice as pink stained her cheeks. "I'm not going to let you kiss me in front of everyone."

"Tempting as that may be, that was never the question I intended."

"Then what were you going to ask me?"

Aiden slid from the sofa and knelt on the ground by her feet. He took one of her hands in his and brought it to his heart. "Will you still marry me, Penelope?"

17
WEDDINGS AND QUEENS

"Are you being completely serious right now?" Penny asked, voice shaking slightly. *Dumb voice.* She cleared her throat. "You still want to marry me? You don't even want to think over what Shirina said?"

"Penelope, there is no thinking about it. I've been thinking about it since before I asked you in Olympia. I want to do it. I want to marry you. Right now."

"*Right now?*"

He smiled at her. "Yes. Right now."

"We can't get married right now!"

"Give me one good reason why we should not get married right this second."

Penny spluttered, her mind whirring with every good reason why not. "Because! What about your people? What about my mother? What about—"

"Penelope." Aiden silenced her words. "Do you love me?"

"Well of course I love you, you dolt, but I don't see how that has anything—"

Aiden's lips silenced hers, capturing them so completely she forgot how to speak.

Or think.

Or even breathe.

His hands moved from her cheeks to her shoulders, leaving a trail of sparks wherever he touched her. He deepened the kiss, and she fell into the fathomless expanse of it. Great Gaia, how could she have forgotten what this felt like? Like sun and life and happiness and love. With the simple press of his lips against hers, the world was right, and everything was as it should be.

"Ahem," a voice called.

Aiden broke the kiss much too early. Penny's eyes remained closed. Their breaths mingled in the space between them. His forehead settled against hers, her nose less than an inch from his.

"Please marry me, Penelope."

"All right."

He leaned back. "That's it? Just 'all right?'"

She grabbed the lapels of his jacket. "Yes, I'll marry you. I'll risk the magic, the danger, all of it. I'll be your wife in this life and the life to come. Now take my acceptance and kiss me again." Honestly, right then, she'd do anything to make him press his lips to hers again.

And he did.

And it was as glorious a kiss as the last one. Warmth and serenity sank into every fiber of her being. She didn't even hear the conversation buzzing around them until she actually remembered there was an entire audience still in attendance.

"Ugh," said Auntie Taddie, "young love."

"Makes you want to just sing, does it not?" Auntie Niomi trilled.

The Lòchran grunted. "Or vomit."

Penny pulled away this time, hurrying to duck her head to hide the very hot and likely extremely red cheeks she was sporting. By the Goddess, if she'd done that back in Olympia, they definitely would have had to get married now. What had gotten into her?

She looked up to meet Aiden's warm, honey gaze. "Are you sure about this?"

Aiden retook her hand in his and pressed his lips to her fingers. "I've never been so sure about anything in my entire life."

"For the love of all the snow on these peaks, will you please stop kissing her?" Dair groaned.

Aiden smirked at his cousin, finally breaking eye contact. "You can leave if you don't want to watch."

Penny smacked Aiden on the chest. "Enough. We obviously have some things to do." She turned to the rest of the room. "I know this wasn't what you wanted for Aiden. I know you all love him and wanted his rule as High King to be simpler rather than harder. I'm grateful he has such a loving family. I can't promise that I'll be a perfect wife—in fact, I can promise that I *won't* be—but I do promise to do my best by him and to always work to deserve his love. I want us to be partners. I'm willing to sacrifice myself for that."

"I know you will, my girl," Shirina said. "I only wish it were easy for you both. I wish Fiadh were here to see it." Shirina stood, tears pooling at the edges of her lashes again. "He would have been jumping for joy that our Little Shadow has found a match that can keep up with him."

Penny stood as well and wrapped her arms around the female. "I'm sorry for what part I played in his death."

Shirina pulled back. "You have nothing of the sort to apologize for. My husband died at the hands of Adira Durant and no one else."

Penny wiped a stray tear from her own cheek and gave a short nod.

Shirina turned back to the room, one arm around Penny. "We must make this quick. We will need to perform the ceremony tonight. If anyone finds out what we are up to, Penelope will be even more of a target."

"Tonight?" Penny squeaked.

Aiden laughed. "Did you think I was joking when I said 'right now?'"

"I thought you were being romantic!"

Dair lifted himself from his spot on the floor. "No, Aiden is right. Best we do it now before the Spring Court can get up in arms about it and either kill you or have you killed. Once you're High Queen, they won't be able to touch you."

High Queen. By the Goddess, they were actually doing this. In Olympia, there had never been the chance of her becoming queen. It would have been as simple as them getting married and Aiden remaining as spymaster while she continued to run the duchy, depending on what happened with Mother. Even when she hoped— no, *wished* they might still figure out a way to be together, she only imagined the possibility of being his consort. But High Queen?

She swallowed. "I don't even know what to do. Are there customs I have to follow or preparations that need to be made? What about ceremonial clothing or words to recite?"

Aiden stood, but Shirina turned Penny to face her. "Little Sapling, all you have to do is say 'yes.'"

Penny brushed her hands over the skirt of her gown. The pale lavender nearly matched the color of Dair's hair. Dair pinned her hair up into an elaborate braid thing.

"How did you learn to do hair?"

He quirked an eyebrow and pointed to his own head. "Learning how to braid is basically the first thing any fae learns. That, and how to lie without lying." He took a step back and looked over the simple net of braids holding her hair back. He plucked a few crocuses from the vase on the table next to him.

If only we had more white daffodils.

Green flashed out of the corner of her eye. From the mirror, Penny watched one of the vases behind her fill with white. Daffodils sprang up between the other blooms so quickly the vase wobbled before toppling over onto the table.

Dair jumped back before the water from the vase could splash onto his boots. "Did you just do that?"

"I—I think so?" Penny replied. "I don't know. I can't consciously do it."

Dair plucked the blooms from the ground. "Would you rather have these instead?"

Penny pinched her lips together but nodded. She had wished for them after all. She wasn't going to just leave them to sit scattered all over the table and floor. Aiden would definitely appreciate them.

Dair set the crocuses down and began weaving the white blooms into her hair. "Why white daffodils? Are they special?"

Penny couldn't help but smile. "They're the reason I'm here."

Dair paused. "I thought you were here because you ate the fruit."

"Aiden and I met because I was fixing white daffodils that had been trampled. He was chasing a rebel through the palace courtyard. I followed him and trapped them both. I thought he was attacking a servant, but realized he was actually pursuing a trespasser."

It had been such a small moment, such a coincidence that had changed her entire life. Yes, perhaps she still would have met him the night he saved her from being kidnapped in Eleusia or if he had come to Barclay Manor to work undercover, but without that first night in the garden under that oak tree, would any of it have mattered?

Without that rebel, the two of them would likely have never been set on this course.

He tucked in the last flower and pulled Penny to her feet. "How are the two of you going to manage after all of this rebel business is over? It seems to be the thing keeping you together."

Penny laughed, long and clear. She couldn't hold it back. There was so much bubbling up inside of her that that laugh seemed the only way to get any of it out. "I have no clue."

Dair joined her in her laughter.

A knock on the door quieted them and Shirina swept through. "Is everything in here all right?"

Penny wiped tears from her eyes and straightened. "Actually, yes." For the first time in a long time, and even though it hadn't come from the best circumstances, everything in that moment was just right.

Shirina tilted her head but shrugged. "Well, it is time to go."

"Where are we going?" Penny asked.

"To Crann Mòr."

Penny fidgeted outside the throne room. The large tree spanning the massive doors loomed over her. Her stomach twisted this way and that. She shouldn't have been so nervous. This is what she wanted. But her instincts were screaming at her to run.

Am I really about to do this? Become High Queen of Faerie? Rule over a people who would despise her for the rest of her short, mortal existence? Marry Aiden?

The last part was a definite *yes.*

So why was she so afraid?

The door opened and The Lòchran slid out of the throne room where everyone else waited. His eyes scanned the room but stopped once he reached her. "Aiden should be here any moment. He said he forgot something back in Eagallach that he needed."

Penny twisted her fingers. "And I thought he was the one that wanted this done as quickly as possible."

The Lòchran grunted. Penny guessed in agreement, but she hadn't yet gotten a good grasp of him yet. He was very brusque in his use of words. He did not mince them, but he also didn't give large heaps of them like his twin. It made it difficult to figure out how to talk to him.

She took a step in his direction. "Lòch—Thaen, I want to apologize. I don't feel like I treated you very well for the first several weeks I was here."

Thaen gave her a flat look. "Do you really want to have this conversation right now? Because I do not."

Penny nodded quickly. "Right. Me neither. You're still a blockhead."

Thaen gave her a small smile, which she returned. Perhaps the start of some kind of truce between them.

She'd take it.

"I'm here. Sorry it took me..." Aiden's words trailed off as he came around the corner.

Penny watched him approach, his wide eyes and gaping mouth likely reflected on her own face. He'd put on a jacket, trimmed in silver and embroidered with leaves and flowers. A handsome cravat encircled his throat, and his hair was combed back in a way that would be easily mussed by his fingers if he put them through it. Sweet Gaia, she wanted to run her fingers through it.

"Stop gawking, you two," Thaen said. "Everyone is waiting for you inside." He went back into the throne room, leaving Penny and Aiden alone in the hall.

Aiden closed the remaining distance between them. "You look radiant."

Penny felt her cheeks grow warm. "It was all Dair. He really knows his way around a vanity."

Aiden shook his head. "It's not the hair, or even the dress. You're always radiant, I just think I'm taking note of it at this moment because I'm about to be gifted you as my wife. I can't express how that makes me feel in more words than just telling you how lovely you are and how much I'm looking forward to this."

Penny felt the grin pull at her cheeks. "I always forget how poetic you are until you blurt out stuff like that."

He took her hand, threading his fingers between hers. "Am I poetic?"

"You can be, when you want to."

Aiden shook his head and reached into the pocket of his jacket. "I have something for you." He pulled out a small leather pouch.

"It better be a snack. I was too nervous to eat before we got here, and now, I'm regretting it."

That pulled a laugh from him. "Sorry, my love. I promise to remedy that as soon as I can though." He cupped his hand under hers and upended the contents of the small bag into her palm.

A single ring fell into her hand.

Eight perfectly round, amber stones winked at her from around the dainty band. Five smaller diamonds were pressed into the gold on each side of the stones. The artistry alone would have made the ring unique, but the jewelry wasn't what made her hands shake.

"The fae don't exchange rings at their weddings," said Aiden, "but I thought we could add a little Olympian tradition to ours. We gave up so much of what we planned already."

She looked up at Aiden then back down at the ring. "How did you even have time to do this?" she whispered.

Aiden stuck the bag back in his pocket and plucked the ring from her palm. "I've been carrying this around since your birthday. After I found out you were in Faerie, I asked Shirina to have it made for me. I needed you to have something from me that would remind you of how I felt. I wanted it to be a birthday present, but that night, I realized I couldn't give it to you."

Her voice softened. "Why not?"

He turned her hand over and slid the ring over the finger next to her pinky. The band fit perfectly.

"That night, I started to believe that you couldn't be mine. I saw the world for what others knew it to be, and I trusted what they said over my own heart. If I'd given you this ring that night, I would have given us both hope I didn't fully believe in. I couldn't do that to you. I couldn't subject you to the torture I felt every time I looked at this ring and thought about you. If you were going to have to leave, I wanted you to be able to forget me too."

She blinked back tears. This beautiful, kindhearted man cared so deeply, so fully sometimes it was hard for Penny to wrap her head around. Mother had always instilled a wariness of men in her, but Aiden disproved every single one of Mother's fears. He was kind. He was generous. He thought about others in a way not even most people did. Loyalty had engrained itself so deeply in him that he'd become the embodiment of it. There was no way on this earth or even in the worlds beyond that Penny wouldn't have fallen in love with him.

"Aiden, I would have never, ever, forgotten you."

Their conversation stopped there as the holy man—the *èildear* as Shirina said he was called—slipped out into the hallway.

"Are you two ready?"

Aiden nodded, but Penny had too many questions, no matter that they needed to hurry. "What exactly do I need to do?"

The èildear smiled. "All you have to do is follow my directions. I promise, it will not be confusing or put you under too much pressure. Just focus on what you are feeling rather than what I am saying. Those are the things you will carry with you for the rest of your life."

"All right. I think I can handle that."

The èildear looked to Aiden. "Are you ready, My Sovereign?"

Aiden looked to her. "Are you ready?"

Penny pulled her shoulders back, thumb running over the amber stones now circling her finger. "Yes."

"Then let us begin." The èildear opened the door and gestured for them to precede him.

18

SAFE

Aiden felt Penelope's hand shake. He clasped her fingers in his and gave a reassuring squeeze—though who he was reassuring, he couldn't actually say. He probably needed as much comfort as she did.

After all, they'd told each other they'd take it slow.

Their wedding could wait until the right moment.

It would be grand, and all of their friends and family would be there.

It would be right.

They never said it would be this.

Penelope might have said she was ready—stars, he had been ready since the moment he realized what the Goddess had intended for them—but it didn't mean it would be easy.

Shirina, Dair, Thaen, and the Aunties sat in the front row closest to them in the circle, all fitting on a single set of chairs. An emptiness muffled the room, the only sound being Penelope's sure steps across the carpeted floor. Everyone else moved silently, barely breathing. The tension in the room was almost palpable. It felt like a funeral more than a wedding. The family had come around to Penelope, but if anyone caught wind of this, it would all go awry.

Penelope pulled up beside Aiden at the base of the dais to the throne. Her wide eyes took in everything around them, but he could still feel that tremor in her hand. He pulled her hand to spin her toward him and he leaned down to look in her eyes.

"I know this wasn't how we wanted it to be, but I promise there's nowhere else I'd rather be than right here, in this moment."

Those bright green eyes softened. "I know how you feel."

Aiden wanted to kiss her right there and then, erase every bit of doubt drawing the line between her brows, but the èildear cleared his throat.

"For a pair of High Rulers," the èildear began, "the *seulachadh anama* should probably be grander and the public would be made known of it. But at the moment, I am finding the intimacy of this occasion to be much more poignant than it would be if this were a grandiose wedding. This is a time for family. For love. This is a time when two of the Goddess's children come before Her and ask for a bond that will last longer than a lifetime."

Aiden glanced back at his family gathered as witnesses. While they watched intently, he could still see the love and approval shining in each of their eyes. Auntie Niomi dabbed at her cheeks.

The èildear drew a thin, red ribbon from his pocket, tying it around Penelope's hand first. Something in Aiden's stomach quivered at the sight. He couldn't exactly say why, but he knew without a doubt that this scrap of cloth was important.

"Penelope Barclay. Daughter of Olympia. Child of Mages. Maiden of Spring and Nature Partaker of the Fruit." He tied a knot around her pinky. "The decision to marry is not one to take lightly. In Faerie, once your life is sealed with your other half under the *seulachadh anama* there is no going back. Only by Danu's will can the bond be undone. This is a sacred promise, a trust you will share with your spouse, even after you reach the Goddess's waiting arms. It will be your responsibility to care for your other half. To comfort him, find joy with him, mourn with him, celebrate with him, and continuously be a support to him. Do you promise to do all of these things in this life and in the life to come? For eternity and far beyond it?"

Penelope didn't hesitate. "Yes."

Even standing beside her, knowing this was what they had planned, the word sent something akin to elation coursing through him. In fact, not even all of the emotion was his. The Land hummed with pleasure. She'd said yes. By the Goddess, she'd said yes. There hadn't been any doubt in his mind that she loved him, but *this* went far beyond just love, and he couldn't help but want to kiss her right there and then.

The èildear turned to him, distracting him from his awe.

"High King Aiden. Son of Faerie. Born of Olympia. Lord of the Dead." The èildear took the ribbon attached to Penelope's hand and secured it around Aiden's pinky. He repeated the words he'd only just said to Penelope. "It will be your responsibility to care for your other half. To comfort her, find joy with her, mourn with her, celebrate with her, and continuously be a support to her. Do you promise to do all of these things in this life and in the life to come? For eternity and far beyond it?"

He met Penelope's eyes. He saw the hope and the fear swirling in them. They'd already been through so much—together and apart. And he never wanted to be apart again.

"Yes."

The ribbon around their hands began to glow. The binding brightened until Aiden had to squint to look at it. A tingling began around his pinky, and he heard Penelope gasp.

Then, his soul opened up to hers.

In that moment, he felt her.

Joy.

Hope.

Sorrow.

He felt the life beating like a drum inside her and it felt like taking a breath for the very first time. Energy and growth and magic filled every part of him. How did all of this fit in her petite body? Her green, life-giving gift wove itself in his dark, death filled magic. How would the two of them fit? How could her gift even get close to Aiden's? They were the complete opposite, antitheses to one another.

But somehow, it did. The magic of the Land wove through the connection, easing Aiden's overwhelming emotions and settling them between the two bodies. How was he going to hold all of it?

"By the Goddess," Penelope whispered.

Aiden opened his eyes and found hers looking down at their hands.

Where the red ribbon had once been, now only a thin line of color encircled their pinkies. Penny's was encircled with amber, and Aiden's was lined a shade of emerald so bright it seemed to glow.

"This is also a time," said the èildear, "in which we sometimes discover a missing piece of ourselves. Every so often, the couples beseeching Our Mother find that they, in fact, were a pair made in Her kingdom. Two people whose fates were meant to intertwine if they so choose. A *taghadh*."

Penelope was his *taghadh*.

Of course she was. And he was hers. The green settled under his skin as if it was always meant to have been there. It felt so right he couldn't even imagine his life before he'd had it.

And then there was the green glow seeping into his skin.

The green spread up to his forearm, melding with the black veins so prominent against his alabaster skin. And the black of his magic bled from his fingers into Penelope's hand.

Black veins sprouted along her skin, stark against the green glow of her magic.

Aiden yanked his hand back, trying to pull his magic back from Penny. He wouldn't taint her magic with his, not with the price it came with. Not with the darkness that followed it.

But his efforts did little good.

She raised her hand up to eye level, her green eyes wide as she took in the magic still webbing across her skin. There wasn't fear or pain on her face.

Only wonder.

"Wind and snow," he heard Shirina gasp from her chair.

"Well, this is certainly interesting," the èildear said, his grin pulling wide as his eyes trailed the magic being exchanged back and forth. "Since Tuatha Dé Dannan do not have tells, we do not share them, but the *taghadh* do often find their magic irrevocably linked when they perform their *seulachadh anama*. What this means for the two of you, I do not know. There could be repercussions we are not yet aware of."

Aiden watched as the black settled against Penny's skin. He felt her magic nestle in next to his, a spark of life in his shadows of death. It didn't hurt. In fact, it felt almost like he finally had a missing piece restored to him. Like his magic was finally balanced. Light and dark. Life and death.

Slowly, gently, he grabbed Penelope's hand and pulled her close until he rested his forehead against hers. "And we will face whatever repercussions. Together."

Penelope squeezed his hand, their magic still pulsing between them. "Together."

By the Goddess, would he ever deserve her?

He brushed his nose against hers. His *wife*. The desire to kiss her crashed into him. She must have felt it too because her eyes fluttered closed.

"Excellent," the èildear cut in. "Then we can get on with the coronation."

Penelope straightened, her eyes flying open. "Wait, the *what*?"

19

CORONATIONS AND
INTERRUPTIONS

"You didn't think we were only getting married today, did you?" Aiden asked.

That was *precisely* what Penny had thought. "Doesn't there have to be, I don't know, councilors and nobility and witnesses to the oaths and stuff?"

Aiden shook his head, a bemused smile on his lips as he pulled her up the three steps. "Not at all. Once the Land decides, it's simply a matter of anointing you—which isn't even totally necessary because, well, you've already been chosen. It's mostly for spiritual significance I think and to be able to show off the wooden crown that tells people you've been chosen. But we won't really need to do that. Honestly, the crown will probably just go straight into the vault."

Sweet Gaia. "So, what exactly do I have to do?"

The èildear came to Aiden's side. "It is as easy as what you just did. All you have to do is say 'yes' and I will do the rest."

Penny took a deep breath and let it out slowly. "All right. I can do that."

"I know you can," Aiden said. "I did it and I swear you can do anything I can and do it even better." He let go of her hand and the green and black of their combined magic faded while the amber circle around her finger did not.

Penny gave him a little shove. "Now you're just flattering me."

"We all know it is so he can avoid upsetting you before you have the chance to be alone tonight," called Dair from his seat. A thump and a muffled curse came from his direction before the warmth in Penny's cheeks turned into an inferno.

"This is a sacred space, Bruadair," Shirina chided.

The èildear took her hand and led her to the throne. "Aiden," he said over his shoulder, "since you are High King, you may stand with her during the anointing, indicating that you are equals in the Goddess's eyes."

Aiden skipped up the steps as the èildear helped Penny onto the faerie glass throne. It wasn't cold like she expected it to be, but warm and comfortable. Her hands settled over the arms of the throne, the light shining all around them reflecting off of the magical glass and scattering in fractals all over her.

"Now, Penelope, this will be slightly different than Aiden's anointing. We do not have to put you on display as we usually do for the Courts and so I will be able to recite only the most important parts of our anointing. Does that sound acceptable to you?"

"I'll do whatever you deem necessary."

"Then let us begin. Do you Penelope, accept the title of High Queen over all of Faerie and Her habitants until the Goddess, Danu, prepares the way for another, whether from your own seed or that of Her many children?"

Was she really doing this? She looked up at Aiden. She didn't have to become High Queen. Settling for consort would have been more than enough for her. Becoming Aiden's true partner came with so many risks. What would the fae think? It was obvious they still had a few reservations about Aiden having mage blood. They would riot when they found out she had sat on this very throne. And even if the fae didn't care, was she really a good choice for a High Queen? Not even Mother had given her much in the way of authority back in Eleusion. Why would Aiden trust her with an entire kingdom? To allow her this much of his power? His influence? Was he really prepared to face the consequences of this?

He looked her straight in the eye, and as if reading every thought that sprang into being in her mind, he gave her a firm nod.

That nudge she had grown so accustomed to on this side of the Mist reared up.

Without any more thought Penny opened her mouth.

"Yes," she said.

The magic under her feet sang.

Light suffused the throne, casting beams of color onto the walls and into the branches above their heads. The leaves above them shook, almost as if dancing.

The Land sang along.

She saw the fae. Ellyllon and Bwbachod all together. The cities under the ground and the cities above it. The rebels hidden in their glamours and the Aigeans stepping up onto dry sand. The refugees in both Winter and Autumn. She saw the place the Andàn called home. The harpies' nests in the mountains. The goblin dens in the forests. She saw it all and, for the first time since arriving in Faerie, she truly understood why Aiden could never leave. This was life, not the small, insignificance of humanity, but the everlasting magic of the Goddess's grace and love. This was what life was truly meant to become and to Penny it was like waking up.

A voice, a kind warm tone, cut through the chaos.

"Blessed Penelope, I have watched you since your creation. You have done wonders with My gift and performed miracles no other on this earth could. I have witnessed your steady strength in the face of trial and perse-cution. Because of your unyielding spirit, I give you a new gift. You shall never fear pain from My children. When you call upon the magic of this Land, it will attend you."

The magical well within Penny changed. When she'd eaten the Faerie fruit, it had felt like something had been ripped apart inside of her, as if her magic had broken open and was spilling around inside her body. Now, it felt like that well had never existed. Now she had an ocean of magic, a sea of life and light and death and darkness all woven together to create this new instinct inside of her.

"You no longer need ask me to perform that which you desire. Now go, save My children not only from this threat, but also from themselves."

Penny opened her eyes and tears blurred her vision. She turned and found Aiden beside her, his amber eyes filled with the same love, joy, humility Penny felt.

"Stars above," the èildear said. His face was turned up toward the branches, where hundreds of blue pomegranate blossoms opened up into the room.

"Is that normal?" Penny asked in a whisper.

Aiden laughed, a deep joyous ring from his chest. "Not at all, but when do you ever do anything normal?"

Penny tried not to look too chagrined, but Aiden kissed her on the cheek which deepened her blush. Her arms flickered green, the glow reaching up past her shoulders. Black veins protruded from the amber circle around her finger and spread over her hand and up her wrist. That would take some getting used to.

"Hopefully we can postpone any more fun surprises until after the anointing," the èildear said. The lights dimmed but did not fully dissipate as the èildear reached into the bag at his waist. "I anoint you with this oil, taken from Crann Mòr Herself. There are many things we receive from the Great Tree and each of them has special significance. This oil is representative of the essence of the Tree, symbolizing the connection our ruler has with the Land and Her people, just as the *toradh na beatha* connects us individually—as you well know." He chuckled and sprinkled droplets of liquid on her head.

"Now, this is the best part." He corked the bottle of oil. "By the authority passed to me and gifted by our Great Mother, I bless you with an unbreakable will and a compassionate heart. You have not come to rule during a time of peace, but a time of struggle from both within and without your kingdom. You will have to fight every day for that which is right even though many will say you are wrong. But know this, you are a daughter of Danu, a queen, and a bringer of life. Always remember the promises you have made here, and you will never find yourself without hope."

The èildear stepped back and reached his arm toward the branches above them. One of the still quivering boughs descended and placed a ring of leafy branches in his outstretched palm. "We do not have a crown of gold or jewels in our kingdom as they do on Olympia. Only the leafy crown that represents the connection our ruler has to the magic of this land and the blessing of our Goddess."

He turned to place the ring of branches and leaves on Penny's head. His hands held the dainty circlet of greenery up.

And then he stiffened.

With a single gasp, he fell to the side and tumbled down the steps onto the carpet. A single bolt sticking out from between his shoulders. Blood seeped into the bright yellow fabric of his tunic.

Aiden snatched Penny up from the throne and shielded her behind him.

"What? I didn't get an invitation? And here I thought this was the reason you let me stay."

Penny peeked around Aiden's arm.

Adira.

She stepped fully into the throne room. Her clothing was streaked with blood, her silver hair wild and untamed. A large sword hung from one hand and a dagger was firmly gripped in the other. Both blades were nowhere as sharp as her smile.

"My, my. Our little Penny has certainly come up in the world. Hasn't she, Aiden?"

"Don't you *dare* speak her name," Aiden growled.

"Oh, dear. And here I was just coming to congratulate you on your nuptials. Once the guards alerted me that you were here, I had to come say hello." She looked down at the blood staining her tunic. "Unfortunately, the small company of guards won't be able to join us."

Penny put her hand on Aiden's back. His muscles coiled under her palm, ready to spring across the entire room should Adira make another move.

Adira sighed. "But don't fret, Aiden. Her name is of little use to me. In fact, I've come bearing a much more important one."

Penny felt Aiden go completely still under her hand. "No," he breathed.

"Yes," Adira bit out. "Come here..." Her mouth moved, but the sound disappeared, like she formed the words with her mouth silently. Penny could feel the magic in the air ripple toward them.

Pain tore through Penny and she nearly fell to her knees. Something inside of her ripped at her magic, at the freshly tied bond she had with Aiden. What was happening? What did Adira say? Penny blinked at Aiden, who had been standing beside her.

He'd taken two steps from the faerie glass throne.

And two steps was all she would give him.

Penny called on her gift, and it answered immediately. The branches above their heads came crashing down around them and the carpet tore into pieces as the flooring sprang up under Penny's command. Four walls made up of the tree encased him. Penny held tight as his magic pounded against the cage, splintering the wood only to be replaced by another piece.

Rough hands grabbed her from behind.

She grabbed the dagger hidden in the pocket of her skirt and swung around, landing a nasty blow to Dair's face.

"Blizzards, Penelope," he cursed, holding his nose. "You have to let him out. She used his true name. He will kill himself trying to get to her because that was her command. He must fulfill it."

Penny turned back to the cage she'd erected. She could hear Aiden's bellows of pain and anger through the crunch of the breaking wood. Even worse, she could feel it. Every blow he made had her hands shaking. She could feel his pain, though his mind seemed not to register it. That was focused on one thing and one thing only.

"It'll kill him if we allow him to go to her," Penny answered, jaw tight with the strain of her gift and the effects of the true name tearing through her. With another surge of magic, she tightened the box so it limited his movement. "Let him go, Adira!" she shouted. "I won't let him out and you know it."

"How long do you think he'll last in there?" Adira asked. "I hear the command of a true name is something to be feared, a bodily compulsion to only follow orders, complete and utter lack of self will except within his own mind. He'll attempt every manner of escape until his arms are bloody stumps and that self-healing heart of his ceases to beat."

Penny's stomach twisted as Aiden screamed, but whether if it was in anger at Adira's words or his futility in getting to her, she didn't know. But what else was she supposed to do? She closed her eyes, sinking back into the newly forged connections within her. The bond between her and Aiden remained, but it grew thin, strained as if it were fading under the weight of Adira's command.

His name. Adira was using his true name against him.

Penny opened her eyes. Dair stood next to her, shadows circling his hands and curving over his shoulders. Shirina stood close to Penny's haphazard cage, using her own magic to fortify the edges. The Andàn stood sentinel over the èildear's body, watching the proceedings with wary eyes.

But where was Thaen?

Adira's voice cut through her thoughts. "You know you can't just keep him in a box indefinitely, Penny. Soon you'll have to let him out, and when you do, he'll be coming with me."

Penny turned to Dair. "Will killing her stop this?"

Dair shook his head. "The command lasts even after death. If she dies, he will still follow."

Penny's eyes stung and she turned back to face Adira.

A flash of black and purple stopped behind her and Thaen's blade stilled at her throat.

"Listen well, Cartographer," his voice rumbled. "You will release My Sovereign from his bond, or I will release your head from your neck."

Three men burst from the hallway, swords pointed at Thaen's back, but he didn't release her.

The rebels had made it into the Tree. Of course they had come for their master. Had Adira planned this? Had she made sure to be here when Aiden returned to the capital? Penny's stomach churned and she took deep breaths through her nose.

"Ah, Lòchran," Adira said, "I knew I should've kept a better eye on you."

"Release him!" Thaen snapped.

Penny gasped as Aiden took out a huge chunk of the wall. Something inside of her writhed in pain as the wall reformed. She couldn't separate her feelings from Aiden's or the Land's. Perhaps there was no difference at that moment, all three experiencing raw panic and pain.

"See, I don't think I want to," said Adira. "If I release him, what's stopping you from slitting my throat?"

"Absolutely nothing," Thaen bit out.

"And therein lies the problem. I release him, you kill me. I don't release him, you kill the both of us. In all honesty, the second scenario sounds much more appealing. I'd much rather go out with a bang than all on my lonesome."

Thaen gritted his teeth. "An exchange then."

Adira's eyes sparkled. "Ah, now there's an interesting proposition."

"No one will be going with you, Adira," Penny said. Aiden would be heartbroken if anyone in this room was to go to the rebels. Who knew what the cursed woman would do to them? It would be a death sentence. They needed to keep Adira in the dungeon, but that door was closing with every crack of Aiden's magic against Penny's.

"And that's where you're wrong, Penny. I had planned to take Aiden with me to escape my imminent demise and then chain him up somewhere in my camp until this whole thing blew over and I could get to all of the fun bits I had prepared for him. However, I hadn't anticipated him actually making you High Queen. The little ring ceremony in the hall nearly drew me to tears! I thought I taught him better than to share power. And now you'll keep him from me until he dies, and your assassin friend ends my life.

"But the Lòchran has already played that story out in his head and realizes that isn't an option, not if he wants his king to make it out of this alive. And so, he makes a proposition that would spark my interest." She chuckled. "And believe me, my interest is certainly piqued. Now we get to see which one of you is going to be the martyr in our little tale. Will it be the misunderstood guardian? The unprepared queen? The self-deprecating younger son—"

Shirina stepped forward. "It will be me."

Adira turned her eyes to Shirina, appraising. "Ah, the broken-hearted widow."

Tears ran in tracks down Penny's face, but she held the cage around Aiden firm. Aiden's ceaseless pounding on the walls grew weaker, but he continued to rage.

Dair took a step toward his mother.

"Stay where you are, Bruadair," she ordered, her tone brokering no argument. She met Adira's eyes. "You will release Aiden from your command, make no move to harm my family, and I will go with you. Willingly."

Adira nodded. "I would also like to add to the list of stipulations that you will assist me in returning to my camp and stay with me until one of us is dead."

Penny sucked in a breath. Before she could run over such implications, Aiden's hand burst through the cage, black veins swelling with the power he was exerting.

Shirina stepped forward and thrust her hand out for Adira to take. "Do we have a bargain?"

Adira smiled, a predatory thing. "I always knew I liked you, Councilor." She struck like a viper, her hand encircling Shirina's before either of them could pull away.

With Shirina's hand still in hers, Adira turned back to the rest of the room and met Penny's eyes. Her mouth moved again. "... you are released from my command."

The pounding of flesh on wood ceased. Penny sagged to the floor, her limbs trembling. She dropped the walls and found Aiden crumpled on the ground, his fingers bruised and bleeding as he swayed on his knees. His chest rose and fell in heaving gasps, sweat pouring down the sides of his face. She crawled to where he knelt and wrapped her arms around his middle to hold him up.

"Drop your weapon, Bàsthaen," Shirina said.

Thaen dropped his sword with a yell and said something quietly to Shirina, but she only kissed his cheek and pulled away. She looked between her sons. "Take care of each other. I love you."

"*Màthair!*" Dair protested.

Shirina raised her hand to silence him. "I willingly give my life for my king. Do not allow my sacrifice to be wasted."

"Yes, yes," Adira drawled. "We'll be going now." She grabbed Shirina's arm and led her to the door.

"You won't get away with this, Durant," Aiden said. He pulled himself up, his limbs trembling. The flesh of his hands hadn't healed in the slightest which told Penny his magic was still recovering. Even the Land was still slightly shaken if Penny could translate the swirl of emotions inside her correctly.

Aiden got to his feet, blood dripping onto the floor. "I am going to stop you."

Adira smiled back at him. "I'm looking forward to watching you try. Don't attempt to follow. I will kill her if I see a single shadow out of place, am I clear?" She pulled up short. "Oh, one more thing."

Again, her lips moved and that pain tore through Penny's middle

"... the next time you see either of your brothers, kill them." She yanked the door shut.

Aiden fell to his knees beside Penny, and Thaen let out a thunderous roar.

20

STOLEN

Annalysa removed the careful wrappings from Aiden's fingers. He winced as his wounds met open air. The mutilated flesh looked far better than what he vaguely remembered. His mind had been so foggy after Durant had used his true name.

Skies, he almost couldn't believe it happened. Durant had used his name only twice in his memory. Having her use it so blatantly felt almost blasphemous. To the fair folk, it was blasphemous, but he hadn't been raised in the ways of Faerie. He'd been raised in the ways of Adira Durant, and she was turning out to be more of a heretic than he'd ever thought she could be.

The Council was calling it a massacre. Durant and her men had killed fifty of the guards in the Tree before they disappeared. Aiden had sent Thaen after them, but the rebels had used magic to barricade the doors out of the top level of the tree. The Tree had given him a route to go after them, but by the time he'd caught their trail, they'd made it out into the city and disappeared.

Guilt sat heavy in Aiden's gut. If he hadn't been compromised, if he'd gone after her, they wouldn't have escaped.

He was useless.

And Shirina was gone.

"Both your body and your magic have been worn to the bone," Annalysa said. "While the magic of the Land will help speed along the healing process, I will have to reset a few of these fingers and your recovery will take longer."

Aiden nodded, his jaw tight as he prepared for what came next.

"Wait, wait, wait," Penelope cut in from her seat beside him. "You're actually going to break his fingers? Again?" Her eyes were ringed in dark circles and her face drawn. She'd looked like this since he'd woken to find her sleeping in a chair next to his bed that morning.

He only remembered bits and pieces of getting back to the Winter Palace, but he remembered seeing her face again and again.

"Yes, My Sovereign," Annalysa replied to Penelope. "It is the only way to get them to heal properly."

Aiden turned to Penelope. "Perhaps you should step out..."

"I'm not going to leave, you muttonhead." Penelope scooted closer to him on the sofa, wrapping her arms around his torso tightly. "I've seen far worse than broken bones."

"Muttonhead?" Aiden huffed a fragment of a laugh. "That's a new one."

"I picked it up from Farrah while we were together."

Annalysa smiled. "That child always has some new epithet in her arsenal." She lightly grabbed Aiden's hands. The sensation ached on his raw skin, but she must have been working a bit of her magic because that soon eased. The pressure of her fingers tightened, and a resounding *crack* echoed in the room.

Aiden sucked in a breath as the bones in his fingers realigned.

Penelope gave out a pained gasp.

"Are you all right?" he asked.

Tears pooled in her eyes and a green glow flickered in her hands. "This whole *taghadh* thing really stinks."

Aiden frowned. "Why would you say that?" He stretched out his fingers, feeling the bones knitting back together under Annalysa's gift. The swelling had gone down immensely, so he was able to bend them a bit, though they were stiff.

Penelope sniffed, her breathing growing ragged. "Because, instead of actually being happy and married and having fun, instead we have broken bones and kidnappings, and I'm just so blasted tired of fighting everything, and I just want to crawl into a hole somewhere."

Aiden watched as vines grew out from under their seat. "Are you all right, love? It was just a couple of broken bones." Penelope usually had good control of her gifts. She was one of the most emotionally strong women he knew.

The green of her hands flared. "No, I'm not blasted all right! You literally broke your cursed hand trying to beat down a magic wall, and now your bones had to reset, and it *hurt* you, and I know it hurt you and yet you just go on acting like it's nothing but it's not nothing, and we can't even have one blessed day where something isn't going out of control."

The vines carpeted the room now. Annalysa stood and crossed over to Penelope.

"My Sovereign, is there any way you can calm your breathing?"

"I am calm!" Penelope snapped, but her breathing only grew more ragged.

Aiden grabbed her hands. "Penelope?"

She started shaking her head, tears running down her face. "It's too much. It's all too much."

"What is too much?" Annalysa asked. "You were married only yesterday. I know it can be a lot to take in."

"It's *all* too much. I can feel everything. I can feel him, I can feel you, I can feel all the little brownie feet pitter-pattering all over the palace, and I just can't breathe."

Aiden watched her as she ran a hand down her face, one now marked with an amber ring and black veins. Understanding dawned and he cupped her face in his hands and drew her face close to his. "Let it go, Penelope. You need to stay inside of your own body."

Annalysa took one of Penelope's wrists, connecting her magic to Penelope's body. "By the leaves in the trees, what is happening?"

"Penelope," Aiden said, "just stay right here with me. Can you do that? Breathe with me."

She shook her head, eyes wide and tears pooling in his palms still cupped at her cheeks, but she watched his chest as her breathing slowed to match his.

Aiden kept his breathing going but continued on, "All right, listen to me, Penelope. I need you to find five things you can see. Can you do that?"

She kept her breathing with his as her eyes flicked around the room. "Uh, vines. Flowers. There's a clock on the mantle. The door. Your eyes."

"That's great," Aiden said. He moved his hands to her shoulders. "What four things can you touch? What do you feel on your skin?"

Penelope blinked back her tears. "So, your hands are warm on my shoulders. I can feel the silk of my chemise on my back and the lace of the skirt on my ankles. Four? Uh, I can feel the warmth of the stones warming my feet."

Her coloring was already turning normal, and her eyes were less frantic. "Perfect, love. What about hearing? Can you give me three things you can hear?"

Penelope stared down at his chest, but her eyes were unfocused, obviously straining for any sounds. "I can hear the clock ticking over there. And, um, your breathing. Oh! Spot just barked outside."

Aiden moved his hands down her arms and grabbed her hands. The green had faded into the warm bronze of her skin color. His pale fingers looked so stark against her beautiful fingers. "Fantastic. Can you smell two different things from where you're sitting?"

"The plants," she answered quickly, "and leather. You always smell like leather."

Aiden smiled. "Do I? I guess that makes sense." He put an arm around her and settled back into the cushions of the couch. "What is one thing you can taste?"

She thought about it for a moment. "Nothing besides my own spit."

Aiden chuckled, but he let out a breath of relief as she settled against him. He looked over to Annalysa, whose brows were raised.

"Care to explain?" she asked.

He shook his head. Explaining how he had learned to center himself under Durant's tutelage would do nothing for Penelope's emotional state. He had learned the technique for high stake missions and for keeping his mind straight under the influence of drugs or torture. It was not something he needed to share with anyone at that moment. All that mattered was that it had helped Penelope.

He turned to her. "Do you feel more centered?"

She scrubbed at her cheeks. "Yes. I'm sorry for losing myself like that. It's this blasted bond, the *taghadh* or what have you. I can feel everything you do, and the bond with the Tree isn't helping either."

Aiden ran his fingers lightly over the side of her arm, doing his best to give her something to focus on while she spoke. "Why?"

"Since we married, the two bonds have been wrought with emotions. My gift allows me to connect so naturally with plants. I've never had to do it with things going through dynamic emotions all the time. It's been... hard."

"So, when I reset the bones," Annalysa said, "you felt something, even though I numbed him?"

"I felt his hurt. Not so much the pain, but the hurt he felt. His heart."

"I'm sorry, love," Aiden said. "If I'd known..."

Penelope shrugged. "I didn't quite know what would happen either, but now we understand it a little better."

Annalysa stood. "You said you feel this with the plants as well?"

Penelope nodded again.

"Perhaps, My Sovereigns, it has to do with how the two of you connect to your emotions." She picked up her bag of supplies from where it was hidden under the leafy vines. "Please let me know if there is anything else you need."

"You are too good to us," Penelope said, sending the healer a warm smile.

As Annalysa left the room, Aiden continued to stroke Penelope's arm, and she settled her head on his shoulder. Within moments, she was breathing softly, exhaustion taking her. He leaned back, settling his cheek on the top of her head. His mind turned over with what Annalysa had shared. He reached for the bond he now shared with Penelope. He could feel the quiet hum of peace that now settled along their connection, but he'd had no idea how much she had been struggling. If this new bond was tied to their emotions, why could he only feel a drop of insight versus Penelope's bucket full?

Aiden stood at the table in the war room, his fingers finally having healed a few days ago. Apparently, shattered finger bones took longer to heal than a stab wound. Something about the tiny pieces having to be carefully positioned. The large map of Faerie took up every square inch of the tabletop along with the scattered pieces representing the separate forces. His eyes stared at the empty spot at the table between Sgiath and Deireadh and kept meeting Dair's hollow gaze.

Was Shirina even still alive?

Thaen walked in uncharacteristically late.

"Cousin," Aiden greeted.

Thaen nodded but said nothing as he took up post against the wall. He'd been quiet in the two weeks since Shirina's capture, spending most of his time running soldiers through drills at the training grounds. Dair seemed to be hiding out as well. Aiden didn't know how to help either of them, especially because the events of that night had all been his fault.

Aiden had decided not to tell the High Council about Penelope's new status as High Queen. The other Court members had been in an uproar over Shirina's capture, and he didn't think it wise to stir them up any more than that for the moment—especially with their new additions.

Three new members had joined their war council after Aiden had reached out to the Courts for their best strategic minds. Chieftess Sgrios, a dwarf leader from the city under Crann Mòr who would take up training the fae that came to the encampment at the base of Eagallach; Stallion Mealladh, leader of the largest centaur herd in Faerie who now led the scouts all over the kingdom; Commander Fàil, the alpha werewolf, would lead the trainees in both Winter and Autumn.

"Sona is too close to the border to be deemed as *safe*," Rìgh said.

"While I agree," said Chieftess Sgrios, the dwarven leader, "we have not had much cause to think they are moving out. We are now in the middle of the summer months, quickly approaching autumn. It would make sense for them to either strike soon or hunker down until winter passes and the snows begin to melt. Laying siege to the mountain will get them nowhere if they cannot accomplish it in time."

"They likely will attack before the frost," Commander Fàil said. He pointed at several groups of gold pieces on the map collected in Spring with a claw tipped finger. "If these groups come up around the capital and regroup at the Teine, they would cut us off from one another—excepting the two folk we have that can portal."

"It also does not bode well that both refugee camps are closer to the capital than either of the Court seats are," said Thaen. "They would be attacked first."

"Perhaps we really should bring the camps into the cities," Aiden said.

"That would bring about an entirely different kind of blood bath," Mealladh whinnied.

"But honestly, which would they truly prefer?" asked Dair. "Being enslaved and drained of all of their magic, or having to live down the street from folk they may or may not get along with?"

The room remained silent, but the lack of voices was answer enough.

"This is absolutely ridiculous," Aiden said. "You've all lived together in this place for centuries!"

"Yes, and we have kept very specific boundaries for the last several off them," Fàil quipped.

"How is it possible the humans fell under your command and only broke away from you two hundred years ago?"

"Cursed mages," Rìgh hissed.

"Listen here, Councilor," Thaen said, "I am getting rather tired of your slandering."

"Do not preach to me from your pedestal, assassin."

Thaen glared at him from across the table. "I will do as I please, especially when you are the one cursing My Sovereigns."

Aiden bit his lips together. The family had decided not to include the Council in on his marriage to Penelope and the true reason they had gone to Crann Mòr. With Durant's escape and the new members finally coming in from the other courts, it didn't seem like the best time. They needed a plan, but now, any kind of preparation they could have made went up in smoke.

The slip was so unlike Thaen. Shirina's capture had rattled them to the core. Aiden watched his cousin as realization flashed over his face, just a slight raise of his eyebrows. Thaen glanced around the room, watching for any of the other councilor's reactions.

Chieftess Sgrios looked up at him sharply. "Did you just say 'Sovereigns?'"

Thaen's eyes widened and he looked in Aiden's general direction. Aiden tilted his head to the side and gave a surreptitious shrug. The proverbial cat was out of the bag now.

"Was that in error, Prince Thaen?" Commander Fàil asked.

Thaen opened his mouth, but he could not lie. "No."

Every eye in the room turned to Aiden. He quirked a brow at them.

"Who is he referring to, My Sovereign?" Deireadh asked.

Aiden met every eye. "My wife."

By the Goddess, it still felt like a dream calling her that.

Even the crickets were silent. All five males turned their heads, a motley crew of confused faces. The chieftess watched him with intensity.

"There was a wedding?" Stallion Mealladh asked. "We were not aware you took a consort."

"I didn't take a consort."

"Oh, that's a relief," Rìgh said. "I do not know that the Courts could handle such a thing—"

"I took a High Queen."

Deireadh's staff slipped from his hands and clanged against the floor.

"You did *what*?" Rìgh bellowed.

Sgiath began chuckling until the small noise turned into a roaring laugh. "Please," he said between wheezes. "Please tell me it is who I think it is."

Aiden squared his shoulders. "The Goddess has made Penelope Barclay High Queen of Faerie."

Sgiath's guffaws rang over the room as Rìgh raged.

"How *dare*—You cannot possibly—This is unprecedented. *A mage!* As *High Queen*?"

Dair took Rìgh's arm. "Best sit down before you injure something."

Rìgh jerked his arm away from Dair. "This is unacceptable! The Day Court will never bow to a mage queen. It is an affront to all Tuatha Dé Dannan, and I demand the usurper's head at once!"

Thaen materialized in front of the Summer Councilor. "Are you telling me my Goddess made a mistake?"

Rìgh jumped back in fright. "No! No, not at all. I would never—"

"I think am just beginning to see a very faint mark right... here." Thaen pressed a single forefinger onto the Councilor's head and pushed him back into his chair. He set both of his hands on the arms until he was looming over the quivering male. "If you seek to harm my queen, in any manner, I will be the last face you ever see. Danu has chosen Her queen, and those who disregard her edict will find themselves marked for death with my sword in their stomachs soon to follow. Do we understand one another?"

Rìgh may have nodded, but Aiden couldn't tell with how badly he was shaking.

Deireadh came up beside Aiden. "Have you really married a mage, My Sovereign? And she was made High Queen?"

Aiden nodded. "If you would like witnesses that you can make certain will not lie to you, both my cousins were in attendance as well as the Andàn. An èildear performed both ceremonies and Shirina was also present, but with the èildear's murder and Shirina's capture, you will have to rely on those present."

Sgiath's laugh tapered off. "I am guessing you did not actually go to Crann Mòr to interrogate The Cartographer before her escape, as you claimed."

Aiden shook his head, his chagrin definitely peeking out through the confident mask he tried to maintain. He didn't regret what he'd done, only that it had ended in such a horrible way. Penelope had deserved better than what she'd gotten.

The door burst open and a tall, bedraggled fae practically fell into the room. A short crop of black hair brushed against her jaw, the shortest Aiden had ever seen on a fae besides himself. A gash was rapidly healing along her cheek and her brown eyes flashed with a mixture of fear and excitement.

She held up a large envelope. "I have come with news from Olympia."

Sgiath gaped. "Farrah? Great gourds, what did you do to your hair?"

Farrah ran her long fingers through the short strands. "Had to go undercover. Though, I'm enjoying the length. Makes it much easier to glamour away."

Aiden's thoughts exactly. *Finally, someone in this kingdom understands me.*

Sgiath wrapped his arms tightly around his daughter. "Your *màthair* is going to strangle you."

Farrah pulled away and delivered the package into Aiden's hands. "This passed from Angelica Eile's hands directly into mine. She said it explains everything that's been happening."

"What about my brothers?" Aiden said. "The others in the capital?"

She pushed the packet toward him. "Just read it."

Aiden tore open the package and out slipped three envelopes along with a map. Angelica's familiar handwriting stood out on each envelope, all of them addressed to Penelope with one titled 'Read first.'"

"I don't understand. Why did you only bring things from Angelica?"

"It was too risky to transport anything else."

Aiden felt his brows pull together as he tore open the first of the letters. The others gathered around him.

Dearest Penny,

Y riho qhtv nix rsalyes ons rsudmodoyih ondo ndm...

"It's ciphered," Aiden said, trying to decipher the words written in Angelica's curvy handwriting. He passed it to Sgiath to try to decipher it and turned to Farrah. "Did Angelica say what the key was?"

Farrah shook her head. Her father hummed and tucked the letter back into the envelope. "I suspect our new High Queen may have some insight, considering it was addressed to her."

Rìgh grumbled something under his breath but wisely kept it to himself.

Aiden tucked the papers back into the wrappings and turned to the Council. "We will break for the evening. Let's return after supper to discuss what action we can take."

The Council departed and Aiden swept toward the family wing.

"Where are we headed?" Farrah asked.

"I need to go speak with my wife."

Farrah practically skipped out in front of him, then turned and proceeded to do it backwards. "So you did end up marrying Penny!" He could only guess how she knew it was Penelope. The Council room was shielded from eavesdroppers. "How did it go? Everything you ever hoped it could be?"

Aiden frowned, but Thaen ended up being the one to answer.

"They discovered they were *taghadh*. Penelope was anointed High Queen, then the cursed Cartographer showed up and used Aiden's real name on him. Penelope had to restrain him, keeping him sealed in a wooden box that he beat until he bled while we exchanged his life for my mother's."

Farrah's skipping halted. "Oh, pumpkins."

"I do not think squash had anything to do with it," Dair said. He pushed ahead of the group toward the family wing.

"I am sorry," Farrah said.

Aiden blew out a breath but nodded in acknowledgement of her apology.

The War Room they left behind had no windows, so Aiden hadn't realized how late it was. The stars were out in full force, dancing across the black velvet curtain. His heart ached for Shirina. He did his best not to get caught up in the grief of her loss, but it still showed up at random times. Evenings were the worst. It was like the entire palace felt her loss once the sun fell below the horizon.

Aiden left everyone in the family wing and went to Penelope's door. As husband and wife, they could have moved into the same room, but with everything going on they hadn't done it yet. In truth, they hadn't had time to do *anything* together since they returned from the capital, something Aiden was beginning to chafe at.

He opened the outer door carefully, cautious of any traps she might have laid after the multiple assassination attempts. Sure enough, a faint glimmer caught his eye, and he saw the thin string near the bottom of the door. He closed his eyes, sending a bit of shadow out and using his connection with the Land to disassemble the trap. She'd had two crossbows and a bucket of silverware set to spring. If the crossbows didn't do the job, at least the silverware would alert her and anyone else close by. Aiden would likely hear such a clatter from his room next to hers.

After the trap was taken apart, he stepped quietly into the room.

Penelope lay in the middle of her canopied bed. A faint trickle of moonlight limned her covered feet. As he got closer, he could better make out her features. Her dark hair cascaded over her pillows. The blankets bunched around her shoulders and as he came close to the bed, she shifted and turned toward him. Skies, she was beautiful. Breaths came out between her full lips and her dark lashes brushed her cheeks. The desire to touch her, to be with her, slammed into him.

The murmur of voices in the sitting room just outside doused his thoughts. Penelope's brows scrunched and her eyes flicked back and forth under her eyelids. The noise was likely waking her.

Aiden sat on the edge of her bed. "Penelope, love."

Penelope stirred but didn't wake. He spoke louder but to no avail. Carefully, he reached out to touch her. The only time he'd ever really woken a woman from sleeping was one time Rissa fell asleep on a job, and he'd nearly lost an eye.

He prodded her shoulder. "Penelope."

She stilled, a frown deepening on her face.

"Penelope, can you hear me?"

She gasped awake, sitting straight up in bed. Aiden stood and held his hands out, not willing to touch her in case something was wrong. She blinked a few times and then looked up at him. "Aiden? What's going on?" She sat up and rubbed her eyes with the heels of her hands. "Great Gaia."

"Are you all right?" Aiden asked.

Penelope rubbed her palms down her face. "I think so, though I just had the most horrible dream..." She shook her head and looked to the slightly parted curtains. "It's dark out. Has something happened? Is everyone all right?"

He brushed away a curl sticking to her cheek. "We've gotten word from Olympia, but we can't decode it."

Penelope frowned. "Why not?"

"It was written by Angelica in a cipher we do not have the key word for."

A hint of a smile teased Penelope's lips. "Oh? The great Lord of the Underworld never figured out my cipher, huh?" She laughed. "Angelica will love that."

Aiden stood and grabbed her dressing gown from its place near her bed. He held it up as she slipped her arms inside of it. "Now I really must know what it is."

She turned to him and gave him her radiant smile. "Come now. It's not impossible to guess. Angelica writes it in every letter. *Dearest Penny.*"

21
LETTERS AND SEALS

Dearest Penny,

I don't know how to even describe the devastation that has occurred since your departure. Olympia is not the same as it was when you left.

Olympia's palace has been taken. The king and queen are now in hiding. Prince Evan has been trapped in the Isles of Aigean since the spring, the queen holding him hostage until King Dion agrees to surrender himself to the rebels. Tauros has been completely overrun and the vineyards destroyed. Delphine seems to be the only one holding its own, though likely only by the sheer power of Lord MacGregor. Diana is regularly seen with a hunting party along the coast, causing what havoc she can for the rebels and their allies.

Your mother is nowhere to be seen.

No one has heard from the duchess in weeks. She arrived at my parents' estate several weeks ago but disappeared. I cannot tell you where allegiances lie. Father believes she's been looking for you, but since the MacGregors and Lady Alvis were the only ones who knew of your location, we cannot devise where she went to find you. Now that everyone is aware of your situation, we'll do our best to find her. I'm sorry I don't have better news.

The other two letters I've included in this parcel are actually addressed to High King Aiden, but Father suggested we write them to you to mask their intended addressee. Included are a map of Olympia and the reported rebel encampments as well as a letter from King Dion, and a formal declaration of war against both the Aigeans and the rebels as demanded by the tri-kingdom treaty. Great Goddess, I never imagined something like this could ever happen.

I fervently pray these reports make it safely to your hands. You are constantly in my thoughts and prayers.

Your Fearful Friend,
Angelica

"BY THE GODDESS," PENNY WHISPERED. FIRST HER TERRIBLE DREAM AND now this. Her emotions were a tumult inside of her and she had difficulty separating dream from reality. Tears fell from her chin onto the paper, and she quickly set the letter onto the table next to her before any more damage could occur.

Mother was missing. How had no one seen her? Where could she have gone? It was possible she'd gone to Paulo, and he'd explained everything that had happened the morning of Dion and Shaunie's coronation. But where would she have gone after that? Mother was friends with the Hermens, though Penny didn't know if Lord Hermen would have divulged the location of the portal. It wouldn't have worked anyway since the Mist had been closed off. Would she have gone to the rebels? It seemed like someone would have seen her with them if that were the case, but what other option was there?

"Is it so bad?"

Penny looked up and met Aiden's eye. His mouth turned down in a frown, though if it was because he was worried about the letter or if it was still targeted at Thaen after he slipped into the room when she'd sat down at her writing desk, she couldn't tell. She grabbed the other two envelopes, one with a plain seal and another with the Olympian royal crest. She opened the unmarked one and decoded the message within it. Her attention was focused more on the decoding than what was actually said, but what she did manage to catch didn't improve her outlook any more than Angelica's letter had.

It also didn't keep her mind occupied enough to distract from her terrible dream. The night was still out in full splendor, but thankfully it would make way for dawn soon enough. Her dream had been cast under the stars, the fires glowing and the men shouting. It had been worse than the rallies she'd seen in Olympia. Those had been raucous and vile, but what she'd seen tonight?

A shudder ran through her, and the quill slipped a bit on the page.

Praise the Goddess it had only been a dream.

She finished and held out both the transcription and the unopened envelope to Aiden. "These are for you."

He gingerly took them and broke the royal seal first.

Thaen stood just behind him.

Penny turned back to the letter addressed to her. First the intense dreams, now this? She pulled her robe tighter around her torso. Sleep would certainly elude her for the rest of the evening.

"What is it?" Thaen asked. Penny noticed his attention on the page in Aiden's hand, obviously not able to read the parchment over Aiden's shoulder.

"It's a declaration of war against The Cartographer and her allies, signed by my brother." He slipped it back in the envelope. "I will need the Council to also agree to it. This document would begin the break of the alliance between the three kingdoms. We will need to make sure it all goes according to the dictates of the treaty."

He pulled out the other letter. Penny's fresh handwriting stood

stark on the page, but she knew the words were from one king to
another.

22
SIBLINGS

Denny,

I would first like to congratulate you on your acquisition of a kingdom. Not even I could have seen that coming. I think Ev may have gotten jealous. Both his older and younger brothers having their own kingdom? Sounds a bit unfair, don't you think? Though, of course he and the ambassadors had to go and get themselves captured. Blasted idiot.

The palace was infiltrated. We lasted as long as we could, but during the skirmish we lost some very valuable treasure, and it had a bearing on our success. We did our best, but decided it was best to leave our newly coronated life behind. You know I'm a simple man. Shaunie, as always, remains strong in the face of adversity, even when our good friend with the golden touch tells her she needs to relax after the loss of our treasure. She is a tough queen, and these rebels don't know who they're messing with.

Being locked out of the palace has many downsides, but many excellent ones. I've discovered your armory and can't help but admire your collection of weapons. Some have been quite a struggle to learn to work with, but you know I've never backed down from a challenge. I look forward to playing with all of them in my spare time.

There has also been the issue of your Nell as well. That has been quite a pain in the neck, if I do say so myself. The tree seems to not fall too far from the apple, and this particular tree has been barking quite a bit in my ear, though it's quieted down in recent weeks which worries me. We cannot reap that which is not planted you know.

All in all, I would say we're faring well. I have enough wine to drink, but not nearly enough shiny objects to look at. Perhaps I could borrow some of yours sometime? Might help me get through this absolute boredom.

Shaunie has asked that we take a visit sometime to your new home. We had planned on taking a twelve-week vacation, but Lord Hermen simply wouldn't allow it. Said with such a riot after our wedding, we'd only get one shot to make it right.

Best of luck to you, little brother. May the Goddess bless you.

King Dion of Olympia

"ABSOLUTELY NONE OF THAT MADE SENSE," THAEN SAID, FOREHEAD scrunched as Aiden finished reading the letter aloud. "I figured King Dion a bit of a lout, but with that drivel, I am surprised they allow him to be king."

Penelope stood, wiping the remnants of tears from her face. "King Dion may be a scoundrel, but he's certainly not a complete idiot." She turned to Aiden. "It was some kind of code."

Aiden smiled and lifted the letter up once again. "Dion and Shaunie are safe and have found reprieve with the Hermens and my previous operatives. My brother Evan has gone to take Aigean for himself. He was captured on purpose and is attempting to take them from the inside, though Dion doesn't agree with it." He cleared his throat. "Shaunie lost the baby prematurely. Somehow, the rebels had a hand in it, but it doesn't say exactly how. Doctor Ashton seems to have been able to help her though." Knowing the miracle-working doctor was still with Dion eased a bit of the panic in Aiden's mind.

Penelope gasped. "They both must be heartbroken."

Aiden nodded, not yet ready to think about what the consequences of such a thing would be like for Dion and his new wife. "He goes on to say that he's taken over the Underworld network and has been using them to fight against the rebels. And then he references Penelope, saying Lady Barclay has been causing problems."

"Angelica said my mother has been missing."

"It seems that's the case, though Dion has heard word from her, and she's been causing him grief which probably means either our suspicions we had about her were correct, and she'd fighting with the rebels, or she's figured out where you are and is trying to make Dion fetch you. But that's all conjecture at this point. I think he mostly mentioned it for your benefit." Aiden continued to the next piece. "With the capital taken, they are down men and ask for aid."

"We have no fae to give," Thaen said.

"I know that, but he doesn't. I didn't give Farrah leave to explain our situation more than the fact that we're also under attack and wish to open up communication."

Thaen nodded, and Aiden finished the rest of the letter, his hand shaking. "He then says he's made plans to go to the Hermen residence so that he and Shaunie can come here in twelve weeks—though I can't guess at why it'll take so long. And they only have the one shot to pull it off."

Penelope stood. "But he can't! Not after what Adira did to you."

"I know." Durant likely knew Dion would try to come to Faerie which was why she commanded Aiden to kill him on sight. The woman had no soul, he was learning.

"How do we tell him no?"

Aiden shook his head. "The Hermen lands are closer to Eleusion than they are to Olympia. He's likely already set to travel, especially since they'll have to leave false trails. Besides, we could really use this."

"You would risk your brother?" Thaen asked.

"We'll figure it out. Perhaps he can go to Crann Mòr."

"Not with Adira so close," Penelope said. "She would do everything she could to get to him there and she already knows the Tree. He needs to come here, but he can't if you're here."

"The problem," Dair said, speaking for the first time since they had gathered, "is not that he cannot be here, but that you cannot *see* him."

"So, I should just lock myself in my room the entire time he's here?" That sounded... miserable, but he would do it for Dion. He'd already rid Olympia of one king, and that had been for the kingdom's benefit. Killing his brother was not an option.

"Nothing so drastic." Dair untied the rather lacy, black cravat from around his neck. "You would just need a blindfold."

Penelope snatched the fabric from Dair's hand. "Of course!" she said, a laugh in her voice. She came forward and wrapped the fabric around Aiden's eyes. The soft fabric brushed his cheeks and completely blacked out everything in the room. "As long as you didn't *see* him, it wouldn't be a problem."

He took the silky fabric from Penelope's fingers. "I suppose I could use my magic to see around me."

Dair pursed his lips. "I do not think that would go well either. You would still technically be seeing him and could trigger the command."

"You're right," Aiden said. "It's a risk simply letting him in the palace."

Penelope gestured to the missive in his hand. "Are you ready for your brother to see the kind of king you've become?"

Aiden's gut jumped about like a couple of goblins were bouncing around inside of it. "Not one bit."

She set a hand on his arm. "There's nothing to be afraid of. You're a wonderful king."

Aiden barked a laugh. "In the almost six months I've been king, I've had rebels kidnapping folk, two of our cities overtaken by the enemy, and the one shield we had from Olympia obliterated by the death of one of the Court's kings. I would not call that *wonderful*."

Penny set a soft hand on his cheek, and he looked down into her deep, green eyes. "None of what has happened is your fault. Yes, you've been dealt a tough hand and perhaps you aren't the perfect king, but you are *trying* and that says more about you than anything else. You're a *good* king and you are trying to do good things. As long as you are continually seeking Gaia—I mean *Danu's* will, you can't fail."

Aiden pulled her hand from his face and set a kiss on her knuckles. "When did you become such a devout follower of Danu?"

"Since I became a High Queen and learned that she practically owns my magic. Best to learn as much as I can about Her so I can better understand what's happening to me."

Aiden squeezed her hand. "Penelope, I am sorry—"

"Hush," she said. "I don't want to hear any more unnecessary apologies." Her lips pressed a warm and entirely too brief kiss on his cheek. He would need to remedy that soon. "We'd best get going. We have a king to prepare for."

Aiden took her arm before she could walk too far out of reach. "Penelope, there is one other major thing I should discuss with you."

"What's that?"

Aiden kissed her on the cheek and whispered, "Thaen let it slip that you're the High Queen in our meeting."

Penny whirled on Thaen. "You did what?"

Thaen held up his hands. "It just came out."

"So, the entire war council knows?" She set a hand to her chest. "What did they say?"

"Oh, mostly that you will likely bring ruin upon our kingdom," supplied Dair, "and that it was a rather idiotic idea."

"Thank you, Dair," Aiden said. He glanced up at the clock on the mantle. They had already spent a good hour of their break from the war council talking about other matters. He was tired of being king at the moment.

"Thaen, Dair, Farrah, I'd like a little bit of time with my wife before supper."

Thaen frowned at him. Dair smirked. Farrah's eyes flicked from Penelope to him and back to Penelope.

Thaen held up the missives they'd received. "We should discuss—"

"You know what?" Farrah interrupted. "I just remembered I left, uh, something in my pack. A very dangerous Olympian thingy that needs disposing of. Can't have the brownies discovering it and blowing up the palace."

Thaen's head whipped in her direction. "You brought explosives into the palace?"

"Yes, uh huh. Explosives." She grabbed Thaen's and Dair's arms and led them toward the door. "Both of you will have to take care of it. Awful business. Great gourds, Nonnie always said I was a bit of a nut."

Her voice faded as they disappeared down the hallway. Aiden immediately locked the door behind them. His stomach flipped as he turned around and found Penelope, alone in the room with him.

"What was that about?" she asked. She picked up the parcel from Dion. "Don't you want to take all of this to the war council?"

Aiden strode to her and took the package from her hand and promptly set it on the side table. "No, I don't want to take it to the war council. In fact, I don't even want to *look* at the war council until after supper."

Penelope looked at the window. "It's well past supper."

"We lost track of time." Aiden took a step closer, wrapping a finger around one the loose curls laying over her shoulder. "But I think food will have to wait."

She turned back to him, one dark eyebrow curved in curiosity. "Oh? Was there something else you needed to do?"

Skies, yes. There were a million things he should have been doing, but there was only one thing he needed. "I need to kiss you," he said softly.

Her green eyes widened. "What? Now? You don't want to talk about Dion or the Council knowing my title or anything?"

"To the Mist with every one of them," Aiden said, taking her hand and tugging her closer. She didn't resist, which told him perhaps she didn't really want to talk about any of those things either.

"*Aiden*," she chided him.

He settled his forehead against hers, those deep, emerald eyes capturing his. "Stars, I love when you say my name."

Her eyes crinkled with a smile. "Aiden," she said, but not with chastisement. It sounded more like a sigh or a wish.

"Penelope," he said back, pushing every want and wonder and desire into his voice. They'd been married for days, and this was the first time they'd actually been alone with one another. The first time there wasn't an entire kingdom vying for their attentions.

Her eyelids closed, her chin titled up. He could feel her warm breath on his neck, then his mouth. Then, her lips lightly brushed his. A whisper of a kiss.

"Penelope," he breathed, heart beginning to ache with want, "I need you to tell me if you don't—"

Her lips silenced him, word and thought completely evaporating in the euphoria the kiss elicited. By all the stars in the sky, kissing her made the world around him stop, made the constant buzz in his head completely disappear. It was like waking up or coming back to life every single time.

Their lips never parted for more than a breath. Her arms came up around him and he slid his hands up her back and into her soft curls. The kisses grew deeper, fuller. He didn't know if she was pulling him closer or if he was pulling her closer until they were completely flush against one another.

Her fingers were at his neck, his hair.

His hands trailed the back of her bodice, stopping at the swell of her hips before moving back up.

Skies, she was perfect.

She nipped at his bottom lip, driving him to near insanity.

He stepped forward, pushing her back until her knees met the edge of the divan. His lips followed hers as he picked her up and laid her on the cushions. He moved over her, holding himself up with one arm while the other continued to explore every delicious curve. She was a goddess and he her most devoted worshiper.

His mouth roamed from her full lips to her jaw.

Her ear.

Her neck.

A soft moan escaped her, and he nearly lost all semblance of control.

His mouth returned to hers, his tongue parting her lips. Skies, she tasted like moonlight and the sweetest fruit he'd ever partaken of.

Her back arched, and he splayed his hand against her small of her back, holding her to him as his kisses moved to the soft skin of her jaw. He pulled away slightly to shed his jacket, the heat between them building to an inferno. The cravat went next until all that was left was the white linen shirt he wore underneath.

Penelope's gaze trailed over him, her lashes low and her green eyes heated. She bit her bottom lip between her teeth and reached out a hand. He shuddered as her fingers softly ran along the open collar of his shirt, her warm skin against his sending goosebumps all over his body.

He closed his eyes, returning his lips to the skin of her neck. Her shoulder.

Her trailing fingers stopped at the top button of his shirt, just under his clavicle. "We could..."

Aiden opened his eyes and found hers.

There was a question there. A wish. An invitation.

Her cheeks flushed and she turned her head to the side.

He followed her gaze to her bedroom door, heart pounding at the idea of what she was offering. His eyes returned to hers, desire and awe burning through every particle of him.

Penelope pushed him up and set her feet on the floor. She grabbed his hand and pulled him up with her to their feet.

Slowly, she led him toward the door.

Aiden called for the council to gather the next morning in the war room. He hadn't returned to the war room after supper. In fact, neither Penelope nor he had even gone down to supper the night before. Aiden had expected to hear the sky was falling and Durant's army was at their door when he arrived at the war room, but the council was not discussing either when he walked in.

"My Sovereign, we come with grievous news," Rìgh said.

Aiden's stomach sank. "What's wrong?"

Rìgh's face fell and Deireadh stepped forward. "King Comhachag has returned to Danu's arms."

"He's dead?" Blizzards, Aiden didn't like the fae, but he had enough of a leadership problem as it was. Having another Court without a ruler was worrisome. "How did it happen?"

Rìgh glared over Aiden's shoulder.

Aiden turned and looked at Thaen, whose face had turned grave. "Thaen?"

He stepped away from the wall. "Danu called for Comhachag's death. I delivered justice on Her behalf." He looked at Aiden. "If you'd like to know, his death was requested in the form of hemlock seed."

The others in the room all gasped, but Aiden didn't think they fully understood what Thaen was saying. It took much more than a handful of hemlock seeds to kill a fae. It was certainly a punishment. The Goddess didn't request King Comhachag's death simply because it was his time. She requested it to protect Penelope.

"Why would the Goddess do such a thing?" Stallion Mealladh cried. His forelegs danced under him in agitation. "King Comhachag was a good fae. He took care of his people. Why would she ask for such a horrendous death?"

Thaen slowly crept around the table, the sword at his back shimmering. "I do not question the Goddess's will, and I suggest you do not either."

Aiden knocked his knuckles on the table and turned to Rìgh. "We will be sure to have his funeral arrangements made by this evening so everything can be done by the end of the week. I am sure the Summer folk would like to be present at the Tree for his burial. Please send my condolences to his consort." While there was a small sliver of relief that he wouldn't have to worry about the Summer King coming after Penelope again, his heart still ached at the thought of another fae gone. They would have to have another funeral, another goodbye.

Rìgh nodded, his face still a mask of distress.

"Now," Aiden said, trying to keep his emotions under control, "I've received word from Olympia and there's much that needs preparing for." He went over what Dion had shared and brought out the war proposal as well. All the council members went back and forth about how they would accommodate the Olympian royalty as well as how to keep their visit a secret.

"Farrah will have to retrieve King Dion from Olympia," Sgiath said. "I have not been to that part of the kingdom in over a century. Much has changed."

"And where should we place them?" asked Chieftess Sgrios.

"Do we have an appropriate space for a visiting king in the family wing?" Aiden asked his cousins. "I would like to at least allow them comfort while they're here and keep them close."

Thaen shook his head. "I do not think that wise. We do not wish for you to cross paths with them without a blindfold."

"What is this?" Rìgh asked. "A blindfold?"

Aiden rubbed his eyes with his thumb and forefinger. "After my curse by The Cartographer, we have decided that the best course of action to take while my brother is here is to have me wear a blindfold for the entirety of his stay."

"But how will you get around?" Sgiath asked.

"Is that dignified?" Rìgh sputtered.

Deireadh pursed his lips. "Are you sure that is your best course of action?"

"I assure you, it won't be so cumbersome. Actually, it'll likely help King Dion feel more at ease, especially because of who I have asked to accompany me to all of our meetings."

"You cannot mean the mage queen," Rìgh scoffed.

"I very well mean my wife, Councilor." Aiden was quickly growing tired of Rìgh's snide tone. "Penelope is acquainted with both my brother and his wife. It'll do them all good to have more familiar faces than only fair folk."

"I have to agree with My Sovereign," Deireadh said. "We do not wish our distinguished guests any discomfort."

"I suggest we include Penelope and the palace housekeeper in anymore plans regarding my brother's visit." Aiden stood. "Besides, it's high time you all got to know one another."

"I would very much like to formally meet our new queen," Sgiath said jovially. "While I am somewhat wary of the prospect of having a human on our throne, I delight in the chaos that will surely ensue."

"Is mayhem all you think about?" Rìgh snapped, finally getting up from his chair.

Sgiath gave an exasperated sigh. "My lord, a life of mayhem is much better than a life of obscurity. You should try it sometime. You may just find you like it."

23
COUNCILORS AND FIRES

PENNY FIDGETED IN HER CHAIR ACROSS FROM AUNTIE TORI—AT LEAST, THAT was what Aiden and his cousins referred to her as, and Penny hadn't been given any other name to call her by. She glanced down at the cards in her hand. Two queens, but no crowns. Auntie Tori had somehow snatched one of them up already and the other sat three cards down in the deck. Auntie Tori grinned as she lifted another card from the draw pile and laid it in front of her. A king, blast it all. If Penny hadn't been so distracted, she would have won this round three turns ago.

"Cursed husband," she muttered under her breath. Now that the funeral had been finished for the Summer King, he'd called for her to meet him and the rest of the council in the family sitting room after supper, but she hadn't been able to eat more than a sip of her soup. Now, she was off her game against Auntie Tori who happened to be an unabashed cheat at Cruin.

Did Penny have to meet the High Council now? Right before Dion and Shaunie arrived and everything turned on its head again? She gazed at her lackluster cards as she twirled the amber ring around her finger—the finger next to the one with the bright amber line all the way around it. Her just being there was enough of a shock to delicate fae sensibilities. Why couldn't she just be a silent, in-the-background queen that no one had to know about?

She snorted aloud. *Like I could even keep quiet for more than five minutes.*

"What is so funny?"

Auntie Niomi stopped whatever knitting project she was working on. Penny couldn't tell if it was a hat or a very large stocking.

Penny set her cards face down on the table in front of her. "Nothing of consequence." She wasn't going to win with that hand anyway. Not unless Auntie Tori didn't see her sneak a crown out of the deck.

Auntie Taddie wiggled in one of the large leather chairs, searching through her pile of skirts. "No need to lie, My Sovereign. We see everything after all."

"I assure you, it was not so important."

"Yes, but now you are High Queen," Auntie Niomi hummed, the blue bird's nest atop her head swaying in time with the clack of her needles. "Every thought in that brain of yours will be important from here on out. Best remember that, dearie."

Auntie Tori tapped her hand of cards on the table impatiently.

Penny ignored it. "My thoughts are not generally ones sought after. I've done my fair share of allowing others to think for me."

"Bitter, are we?" Auntie Taddie cackled. "I like a girl with a bit of bite, and I imagine you have quite a set of teeth behind that charming smile, High Queen Penelope."

"I'm not bitter, per se. Just... amenable to change." There were so many things that Penny could do if others allowed her to. She struggled at Barclay Manor with the constraints of Mother's rules. The fae continued to pose a problem, believing she needed to go when the Goddess Herself told her to stay. Even Adira wanted her to be a slave, using her Goddess-given gifts at the will of another.

Why couldn't everyone simply be happy to be themselves without pushing her around too?

"Well, that is good," Auntie Niomi said, "because you are about to see a whole lot of change in the coming months."

Penny straightened. "What do you mean?"

"Simply that there is much you have yet to face," Auntie Taddie said. "War is not an easy thing, especially not for a new ruler."

"But let us not get too far into such dire subjects." Auntie Niomi slipped a hand in the pocket of her vest and came out with a small, leaf wrapped package. "For you and Aiden, dear. A wedding gift. We were asked to deliver it."

"I was looking for that," Auntie Taddie grumbled.

"And I knew you would lose it in that pile of rags you are so keen on wearing, so I took it for safe keeping."

Penny gingerly took the small parcel between two fingers. She studied it, recognizing the bluish leaves making up the wrapping and running her fingers over the coarse twine made up of what looked like gray hair and long strips of grass tying it together. "It's not poison, is it?"

Auntie Niomi pouted, but Auntie Taddie gave her a smirk. "Do you think we would go through all this work just to kill you?" She chuckled. "If Danu wanted you dead, you would have found your end at someone else's hands. We are far too old to be playing such games."

"And how do you know it's not poison?"

"It is definitely not poison," said the blue-haired fae. "In fact, it may just be the cure."

"What do you mean 'the cure?'" Penny turned the package over in her hand. What could such a small gift remedy? Curiosity tugged at her willpower. It wouldn't do to open it without Aiden. It was a wedding gift for the both of them. She would save it for when she and Aiden could carve away some time alone.

Their conversation was halted by the sounds of voices coming down the hall. All three of the Aunties' heads turned toward the door, and Penny's hand moved to the pile of cards on the table. How was it that every time Penny asked those with oracular powers what they meant, she was always interrupted? It had happened more than once with Paulo back in Olympia and she was fairly certain all of them did it on purpose.

Auntie Niomi gave her a toothy smile, showing off her pointy teeth.

Penny slipped the parcel and her extra queen into her dress pocket. Praise the Goddess Aiden had family. As an only child with only Mother and no close relations, Penny grew up without the camaraderie she witnessed between extended family members. The Hermens and the MacGregors were the closest thing she had to it, and she knew Aiden had had nothing close to that growing up. It was wonderful to see his family eagerly bring him into their fold, even after everything that had happened between the mages and the fae.

The voices drew closer, and Aiden sauntered through the doorway. His eyes grew slightly wider as he took in the Andàn, who all gave him each their own kind of small greeting. The cheeky ladies knew he'd be surprised apparently.

Aiden held a hand out to Penny. "Penelope, love, would you join me?"

Penny laid her cards out for Auntie Tori to see. A queen, a king, and a crown stared up from the table. "Full throne. I win." She grabbed the small pile of coin in the middle of the table and dropped it into the small purse at her waist.

Auntie Tori frowned at the cards, but Penny took Aiden's hand and stood, not entirely certain what she should do with herself. Aiden placed her fingers in the crook of his elbow as if he were escorting her to a fancy party and not the gallows.

She straightened her spine as the High Council swept into the doorway in all their finery. Even so late in the evening and after the many hours of meetings they'd been involved in, they all looked immaculate. All three filed into the room, followed closely by the twins. The Councilors huddled in a group close to the door while Dair sank into a chair and Thaen closed the door.

The Councilors stared at her, all three a mix of trepidation and curiosity.

And none of them spoke.

After a few painstaking seconds, Penny cleared her throat. "Good evening."

"Is it?" the Summer High Councilor asked. "We have had some of the most outrageous news, as I am sure you can guess."

Penny took a deep breath. "And what has you so outraged, Councilor? The rebellion? The infighting between the Courts?" She gestured to the large glass windows framing the snowy peaks of Eagallach. "Or are you simply finding the weather not to your liking?"

Aiden pulled her a little closer to him, a hint of a smile at the corner of his mouth.

The Summer Councilor huffed. "You know exactly to what I am referring, since you so blatantly—"

"Rìgh," Aiden snapped. "You will speak to my wife with respect, are we clear?"

The Councilor bowed, but Penny could see the fire still burning in his eyes. It would take more than just a title to convince him of her right to be there.

The Spring High Councilor took a step forward. He bowed in the show of deference Penny had seen others give Aiden, though she didn't know if he'd intended it for her or just her husband. "How did all of this come about? You claim the Goddess had a hand in it, but we were completely oblivious to any plans for not only your marriage, but your coronation as well."

A snort came from behind Penny, and she saw Auntie Taddie roll her eyes. "If you all did not have those wretched staffs stuffed so far up your—"

"Alltadair," Auntie Niomi balked, "that is no way to speak in polite company."

"Go titter in someone else's ear, Snìomhadair. If these preening pansies had simply watched our young queen before her anointing, they would have seen the way the Goddess had chosen her—not to mention that she and Aiden are *taghadh*."

"They are *what*?" Rìgh gasped.

Sgiath leisurely strode toward Penny and held out his palm. "May I?"

She offered him her empty hand, the one with the very vibrant amber ring around her smallest finger. A wide smile bloomed across his face, and he held out her hand for the other Councilors to see. "They have chosen their mates, and the Goddess has blessed their union from the start."

"*Sands*," muttered Rìgh. "What is the Goddess thinking putting *two* mages on the faerie glass throne?"

"While we do encourage questioning of the Goddess's will, I cannot say I am liking your tone, Councilor," Auntie Taddie said. "Penelope is a smart girl, wise too. The Goddess has chosen her as a vessel not only for Her throne, but for Her power as well."

Rìgh opened his mouth, but the green-clad Councilor silenced him with a look. The Spring Councilor frowned. "Our concern is what the folk will say. There are many who frown upon High Queen Penelope just being here. They will not take kindly to finding she has stolen the heart of Our Sovereign, especially those who had hoped to possibly win it for themselves. It will be even more of a shock since we have not had a pair of High Rulers in several generations."

"Pish posh," Auntie Niomi said. "Those drama queens you call potential suitors would have wilted like daisies in the heat wave these two will face in the coming months."

"Then how do we convince them?" the Councilor asked. "If the Goddess has chosen her as High Queen, how do we prove it?"

"A trial by the Courts?" Rìgh suggested.

"A battle to the death?" Sgiath popped in.

"How about combat training?"

Everyone turned to where Thaen stood by the door. He shrugged. "We have more recruits coming in every day. Nothing inspires loyalty like watching those with power have to roll around in the mud with the lowest of their subjects. We can have High Queen Penelope join in with the rest of the new recruits." He met Aiden's eyes over Penny's head. "If she inspired even an ounce of loyalty out of any of them, we would at least have a few names to sift through to assign for her personal guard."

Penny turned to Aiden. "It's a good idea."

He frowned, eyes still locked with his cousin. "But not one I'm very fond of."

Penny grabbed Aiden's face and tilted it until he was looking at her. "It would give me a chance to win over some of our folk. I won't tell them I'm their queen, not yet, but I could at least show that I'm willing to work with them."

"What if something happens?" He lowered his voice. "What if someone tries to kill you again?"

"Did you forget one of the main reasons you married her?" Dair asked. Everyone turned to face him. "As High Queen, the Tuatha Dé Dannan cannot lay a single hand on her with intent to harm. They may go in with a mind to hurt her, but it will go very much awry for them."

"We do not yet know how the magic works for our new queen," Sgiath said.

"You are right," Auntie Niomi said. "It could be even more potent and the whole jig will be up the first day."

"But we won't know until we try," Aiden said. He let out a long sigh. "All right, my love. This is your decision."

Penelope gave him her most confident smile. "I can do this."

Rìgh folded his arms over his heavy stomach. "You lot better not come to me crying when all of this goes awry."

"Trust me, Rìgh," Sgiath chirped, "no one will ever go crying to you about anything."

Auntie Taddie stood shakily from her chair and settled a wrinkled hand on Penny's shoulder. "Our Mother will do much with this child of mages, just you wait and see."

Darkness filled Penny, whole and complete. It was peaceful, restful.

She was half aware that she was somewhere and coming out into another somewhere. She could hear noises, but they were far off.

Her body floated, trying to push herself in the direction of the sounds half-heartedly. She didn't want to leave the calm, tranquil nowhere. It was quiet in the dark. Restful.

Light began to give shape around her, stars speckling the sky and warmth underneath her feet. Warmth that quickly turned hot.

Hotter.

Burning.

Flames licked at Penny's skin, rising from her feet firmly planted in the ground.

She couldn't move.

She couldn't escape.

She couldn't even scream.

The tiny men dancing below her threw charm after charm and each one hit their mark. More flame exploded over her until even her limbs were aflame.

So much fire.

So much pain.

So much fear.

She pulled into herself, into the two connections tied to her, laying close to one another.

She felt Her screams, Her anguish.

She felt him wake up and followed after.

Penny woke, the scream still caught in her throat. She kicked at the constraints around her feet, her arms. Her limbs were immobilized, just as they were in the dream. Sweat soaked her back. Flashes of fire sparked across her vision. Smoke still clogged her throat.

"Let go, Penelope!"

She froze when she finally realized where she was.

Aiden sat over her, his hands at her wrists and his eyes wide with fear. The same horror she felt sat heavy in his eyes. "You saw it, didn't you? You saw the fire?"

Penny could say nothing as a sob broke through. He let go of her wrists and pulled her into his arms. Penny settled her cheek against his chest, listening to his heartbeat as it settled in time with hers. Her mind didn't register the door to their bedroom opening until Thaen appeared at the end of their bed, wrapped in shadow, sword sparking at his back.

"What has happened? What is wrong? What—"

"The rebels," Aiden said, cutting off any more inquiries. Penny realized how raw his voice sounded. His grip on her tightened. "We've been watching the border from Spring to Winter, but we weren't watching the capital. They sent a team and lit the Tree on fire."

Thaen turned to a corner of the room. "You there."

A brownie stepped out from the shadows. "Yes, Your Highness?"

"Send for the Council. This is an emergency."

The brownie disappeared.

"We will need to send someone to get a grasp of the situation." Thaen's face fell. "There are sure to be casualties. Praise the Goddess you both decided to stay in Eagallach or there would be much more."

"If we had stayed in Crann Mòr," Aiden said, "perhaps we would've been able to stop this from happening."

Thaen narrowed his eyes. "Or you would both be dead."

The possibilities tightened Penny's ribs around her lungs. The Goddess only knew what kind of terror Adira would have managed if Aiden had still been in residence. Not only would there have been more fae, but she could have easily taken control of Aiden through his true name. Penny's heart swelled while her ribs stayed tight. While she was beyond grateful Aiden hadn't been there, she still couldn't move past the horror of her dream.

Aiden opened his mouth, but Penny set a hand on his chest. "How did I see it?" she whispered.

Aiden looked down and readjusted his hold on her. "I was going to ask you about that. How long have you been able to connect with the Land in your dreams?"

Penny shook her head. "I haven't—at least, this was the first time I noticed." She squealed as he got to his feet, wrapping her arms tightly around his neck. "What on Gaia's green earth are you doing?"

"This conversation—and our present company—should be taken out of our bedroom. I'm sure the Councilors are already up and headed toward the war room."

Aiden strode down the hall, Thaen on their heels. Penny told him over and over that she could walk and that attending a meeting in their night clothes wasn't appropriate, but he must have felt her tremors, because he didn't put her down. If she was being honest with herself, she didn't know if she *could* walk, and she really didn't want him to put her down anyway.

Thaen opened the nondescript door ahead of them. Penny hadn't been allowed in the war room until tonight, and she likely couldn't have guessed where it was based on the door and the very empty hall around them. Aiden strode in and headed toward the fireplace but quickly changed direction and set Penny down on a sofa pushed against the wall. He walked over to the fireplace and stacked the wood before igniting it.

"She will not get warmed by that fire all the way over there," Thaen said.

Aiden crossed back to where Penny sat, a thick blanket from who knew where in hand. "It should warm up the room quick enough. Besides, Penelope doesn't like fireplaces, and I'm feeling rather standoffish about the flames myself tonight."

"How does one not like fireplaces?" Thaen asked.

Penny burrowed into the blanket, not wanting to admit to the reason. He'd probably call her a coward for it. Something sparked in her chest. *Thaen's the coward.* She was surrounded by them. Well, except for Aiden of course.

"Penelope has had a rough history with them. I found her in one when her house was burning down around her. I imagine that particular instance left a mark, since she hadn't had any discomfort before then."

"But we don't need to tell everyone about it." Penny narrowed her eyes at Aiden, but the small flashes of anger sparking in her chest mellowed. He'd noticed her discomfort, understood it, and had never judged her for it. She lifted the edge of her blanket, allowing him to slip in next to her.

The shuffle of feet preceded the entrance of the three High Councilors, the war leaders, and Dair who yawned as if he'd awoken right outside the door. A pang hit Penny in the chest as they hurried into their seats. Would Shirina ever return to her rightful place beside these other fae?

Blasted Adira. When Penny got her hands on the cursed woman, she was going to strangle the very spirit from her body.

Penny shook herself. The anger bubbled hot in her chest, but it didn't fit quite right with the other emotions she was feeling.

"How did they slip past our defenses?" Sgiath asked, starting the conversation right off. "We have been monitoring their movement, even when they used glamour. The watch set around the capital should have seen them coming."

"It wasn't a large force," Aiden said. "Perhaps two dozen men."

"There were thirty-two," Penny added. "Thirty-two blasted blackguards circled beneath me, laughing and jeering and..." She trailed off when she met Dair's questioning amber eyes.

She felt a frown pull on her lips. What was going on with her?

Sgiath straightened in his chair. "You saw them? How?"

"The connection to the Land extends to her as well," Aiden answered offhandedly. He had his eyes closed, and she guessed he was reconnecting with the Land to check the damage at Crann Mòr. His brows drew together, and Penny watched his breathing grow ragged. She reached out to touch him, but he shook his head, obviously in some sort of pain. With a frown, she clenched her hands in her lap instead.

"*Sands,*" Rìgh cursed. How many times a day did he say that? By the Goddess, he was such a whiner. Since Penny had met the fae a week ago, she'd heard nothing from him but complaints.

"How did they do it with such a small force?" Deireadh asked.

Aiden opened his eyes and took a few deep breaths. "I can't say exactly. The connection I have is being muddled by the devastation. The Land is angry. It's almost difficult to keep myself more subjective."

The Land is angry. The inferno in her chest simmered a bit. It was the Land's anger, not entirely hers. She sank back into the cushions and closed her eyes. Her magic reached out into the connection she shared with Aiden and the Land. She saw Aiden's side trying to sooth, relax the Land. Did he even know he was doing it? Penny dug deeper and saw the deep gash and felt the Land mourn over the loss of Her heart.

She also saw the root of her fury.

A blaze settled within the core of the tree, angry and hot. The absolute fury boiling just under the surface was enough to make anyone mad, but Penny better understood why she'd been acting so out of sorts. The connection between her and the Land grew stronger every day. Penny would need to start being more aware of her connections to both Aiden and the Land.

Penny pulled back, better able to separate her feelings from the Land's now that she realized what was happening. This was a heinous act on Adira's part. There would be much the rebel leader had to answer for.

Penny opened her eyes and met with the silent stares of the rest of the room.

"What?"

"Do you not think it a wise choice?" Thaen asked.

Her brows furrowed. "What choice?"

Aiden scooted closer to her. "I asked you if you think it would be a good idea to send a team out to evaluate the damage. I suggested Thaen, Sgiath, myself and a handful of trustworthy guards here in Eagallach."

"Oh." She hadn't even heard what they'd said. How long had she been connected with the Land? "All right. Yes, that's probably smart." She bit her lip. "Can I go?"

Aiden opened his mouth, but Dair was the one to answer. "Actually, I have a few things I would like to work on with you. Here."

Penny met his eyes once again. The desire to fight him on it swelled up with in her, but when she opened her mouth to argue, she felt a nudge not to. She pursed her lips. That nudge had happened more than once, and it was always in her best interest to listen.

"All right."

Aiden looked at her, perplexed, but she shook her head. They could discuss it when he got back. This was his chance to do something about Adira. He didn't need her and her riotous emotions getting in the way of the very gruesome work he was about to take part in.

He nodded. "Well then, there's much to pack." He looked at Sgiath and Thaen. "We leave before dawn."

24
SMOKE

AIDEN CLOSED HIS EYES AS THE WIND WHIPPED AT THE WALLS OF THE TENT surrounding him. It had taken a little over an hour to collect supplies for the short journey to the frozen edge of Lake Truaighe. He'd pitched his tent and crawled into it, reaching for his connection to the Land.

That searing anger blew through him, and he gritted his teeth as he pushed his consciousness through the connection.

"Let me see," Aiden said, like a doctor to an injured child.

The capital opened up under him.

Aiden hovered where Crann Mòr had once reached into the sky.

It was gone.

Long lines of black ash stretched over the city. Flames still sprang up, casting shadows against the black of soot and ash coating the city. He could hear the voices of those that had called the capital home, crying out in distress.

What had once been a city full of color was now a ruin of gray.

He looked down and allowed himself to draw closer to the stump left of the Great Tree. The scar over Her heart almost resembled the black marks stretching across the Faerie capital Aiden had seen from above. He felt his body somewhere behind him shudder.

His eyes opened and he sat up in the tent, shivering despite the warm furs strewn all over the floor. Thaen, Sgiath, and a handful of guards from the Winter Palace had set their tents in a circle just inside the trees bordering Lake Truaighe's edge. The crystalline water looked completely solid, and Thaen told him it had not once melted in Shirina's eight hundred years.

But it wasn't the cold seeping into his bones.

He got up and threw open the flap, finding Thaen standing sentinel just outside.

"And?" Thaen asked.

"It looks like a horde of dragons were released on the city. The top half of the Tree is completely gone. The rest of the city littered with ashen limbs and rubble." He shuddered. It was a good thing he hadn't allowed Penelope to accompany them. It was a nightmare— almost as terrible as witnessing the heinous act in progress. While she could handle tough situations, this was something he was grateful she didn't have to witness.

"But the people? Was it deserted? Have the rebels taken refuge there?"

Aiden shook his head, looking toward where the capital lay as the first colors of the day spread across the sky. He swallowed. "There are still fae in the city, still fires being put out. It looked like the attack was targeted at the Tree, but there's destruction everywhere." He rubbed a hand over his sore chest. The Land's sorrow still ached next to his own heart. "Why would someone do something like that?"

Thaen set a large hand on his shoulder. "If we understood, it would make us like them. Perhaps it is better to not know the *why*, but rather the *how*."

Yes, how did someone burn an entirely magical tree to the ground without magic of their own? "The amount of power that would have taken..."

"The number of souls that blackhearted villain must have reaped." Thaen shook his head. "It is absolutely abominable."

"What do you mean?"

"To get that much power? Aiden, she is not enslaving these fae. She is forcing them to drain the entire stores of their magic and kill themselves."

"How... how could she even do that?"

"There is only so much a being can take before they will do anything—*give* anything just to make it stop."

And if anyone knew about breaking points, it was Durant. She'd always been able to find them, even for the most stalwart of men.

Aiden paced back and forth in front of the tent. "We have to stop this. We can't keep losing. We need to figure out how to fight back, no matter that the numbers are against us."

"I wholeheartedly agree."

Aiden ran his fingers over the branch laying limp in the street. Whatever his fingers touched crumbled to ash, floating away on the breeze.

He thought he'd be prepared, having seen from above with his connection to the Land.

He'd been wrong.

Fae called out in the streets, searching for lost loved ones or seeking help.

Smoke still blackened the air, the embers in the split trunk of the Tree popping and shooting up like a volcano, landing in the already charred ring of the neighboring buildings.

Flying fae swooped through the smoke, hauling buckets of water or those with power to stop the fires. A werewolf helped load a cart pulled by a pùca, packed with the ash smattered faces of children, ellyllon and bwbachod alike. A group of ellyllon used their Court magic to pull away debris off the road so more traffic could go through. Beams of light and shadow worked together to create a path out of the massacre destroying their homes.

It was the first time Aiden had seen the Day and Night Courts working together. The first time he'd witnessed them stand shoulder to shoulder without any hint of disdain for the brother or sister standing next to them.

He only wished it hadn't come at such a cost.

Their group finally reached the base of the Tree. Sgiath had left after dropping their team off on the outskirts of the city. He planned to return with those that could organize a force to help the folk and get the fires under control.

Thaen went to his knees. "Even the Green Man himself will not be able to restore the Tree." He stood back up, a large chunk of charcoal in his hand. "If he even survived the attack."

Aiden walked closer to the trunk, boots crunching in the dead coals beneath his feet. Heat radiated from the Tree, but Aiden pushed through whatever discomfort he felt. The raw pain crackling through his limbs distracted from everything else.

He finally reached the roots and dug his hands through the ashes until he found an unblemished piece of wood. He grazed it with his hand and searing pain shot through him. He cried out and Thaen was on him in an instant. Aiden brushed him off and knelt again for the root, this time bracing for the pain.

It still punched him in the gut and dug its claws into his soul.

He muddled through the burning, the aching, and found the roots. Still whole. Still intact. The city beneath still hummed with life, though the hum was that of fear rather than joy. Aiden moved on and found the core of heat at the very center of the trunk. The Tree had tried to protect itself, had bottled up the magic and kept it at its core to keep it from harming anyone else. Aiden looked a bit closer.

The Tree had mimicked what Penelope had done to him. It had created a box to keep all of the raging inferno inside to protect itself and the folk under its branches.

But it wouldn't hold forever.

He pushed at the magic, but the Land shoved him away. "You have to let it out," he said.

A fierce denial followed his words. The magic beneath him writhed, pained and weak.

Aiden felt the cry build up in his chest. *By the Goddess, it hurts.* "You can't hold it. If you don't let it out properly, all of this work will be for nothing."

The Land turned frantic, holding tighter to the ball of magic and looking about for what to do.

"You don't have to send it out. Send it up. There's nothing else for it to catch on. You can send it into the sky."

The ground underneath Aiden shuddered, and he felt the magic begin to move. "Wait! I didn't mean right this second!"

The Land panicked, but the foreign magic was already on its way toward the sky.

Aiden shouted at the fae swooping above them, using his magic to cast his voice out as far as it would go. He grabbed Thaen's arm and tugged him away, but before they could make it to where the wall of trees had once stood, a roaring inferno of light magic shot into the sky. Aiden went flying onto the cobblestoned street, Thaen crashing next to him.

The white-hot magic soared into the sky in a cloud of searing heat and the clouds above the Tree hissed as they evaporated into nothing. The column of light expanded until it fully dissipated into the sky above them.

Aiden pushed himself onto his knees. His chest ached with the sorrow the Land felt, at the magic torn from those of the Day Court used against the Tree. The folk around him all knelt as well, sobs and prayers abounding. Aiden's own lips formed into prayers, sending his up with the rest of them and hoping the Goddess would receive them. He closed his eyes and bowed his head. The voices around him quieted, fading out until only one could be heard.

If these desecrations continue, it will not only be the humans who pay. All magic will be lost.

Aiden opened his eyes and turned to Thaen, whose own eyes were wide.

He'd heard it too.

Thaen growled. "It is time to figure out how to end this rebellion once and for all."

Aiden looked up at the sky, ash raining down in large flakes. "Call for the Hunt. We need everyone on this no matter where their loyalties lie."

25
COUSINS AND KINGS

Penny sat on the edge of her bed and rolled the leaf-wrapped package the Andàn had given her in her hand.

It may be the cure.

The parcel had been sitting on her desk, though she thought she'd left it in the pocket of the dress she'd worn when she'd met the Council. Before the Tree. The brownies must have found it and placed it in plain sight. She hadn't had the chance to open it, but she didn't want to without Aiden. It was a wedding gift for the both of them.

The curiosity only slightly distracted her from the worry over Aiden. Their team hadn't returned for supper, sending a note with Sgiath saying they would return sometime the next morning. Penny hadn't been able to eat more than a few bites of food, praying constantly that everything would be all right.

That nagging heartache still sat heavy in her chest. She couldn't imagine seeing the devastation—

A knock sounded on her door.

Penny pulled her dressing gown snug around her and went to answer.

Dair leaned against the doorframe on the other side. "Are you ready to work?"

Penny blinked at him. "What?"

He slid past her into the room, gesturing for her to follow him.

"Come now, we have no time to waste. Best get you to sleep so we can get some real progress before Aiden comes back and takes up all your time."

Penny's brows pulled together, and she shut the door behind her. "Is this why you asked me to stay behind?"

Dair nodded and plopped himself onto the bed. Her bed.

She stopped in her tracks. "I'm not sharing a bed with you."

Dair rolled his eyes and rolled off the side. He sprang up quick as a dandelion and planted himself on the chaise against the wall near the wardrobe. "Fine. I will doze here while you hog the bed." When she didn't move, he clapped his hands. "Move it, queenie! We have lots to do and not enough time to do it."

Penny moved warily toward the bed. She tucked her legs into the blankets but remained sitting upright. "What are we going to do?"

"We are going to sleep."

He snapped his fingers.

Penny opened her eyes and found herself above Eagallach. Her arms wheeled, and she screamed as her body swayed.

"Relax," a voice said from beside her. "You are not going to fall."

Penny whirled and found Dair hovering only a few feet away from her. "What—How—You—"

"Yes, all right, do not get your shadows all twisted up in knots. We are accessing your connection to the Land in your sleep."

"You knocked me out!" Penny swung a fist at him, but the blow passed right through him.

He smirked. "We are incorporeal beings, Penelope. You cannot hit me."

"How did you knock me out?" she demanded.

He waved a hand around them. "I have power over dreams, remember? Did you not think I could have power over sleep also?"

Penny glared at him, though the connection made sense.

"Come on. We have lots of things to do."

She set her hands on her hips. "What are we doing here, Dair?"

"*You* are going to use that connection with the Land and the one with your husband and find him. I hoped with Aiden out of Winter, we could have a crash course on how to navigate your connection to the Land. Aiden had weeks to work on this, but you do not have the luxury of time."

Penny took a deep breath. "All right."

Dair quirked a brow. "All right? That is it? You are simply ready to go?"

Penny glared. "What would you have had me do instead?"

"Do you even know where to start?"

Penny closed her eyes, reaching for that connection instinctively. The magic of the Land and her magic were so similar, it was easy to access it. She attempted to use the bond with the Land to go to Crann Mòr.

Instead, she ended up cartwheeling over Spring.

She screamed as she headed straight through the tops of the trees, though none of them actually touched her.

Dair caught her by the foot right above the ground. "Honestly, My Sovereign. This is most unseemly."

She kicked at him. "I thought you said we were incorporeal."

"Focus, Penelope. You are connected to both the Land and Aiden. We do not have time for you to dally about Faerie. We need to see what is going on."

Right. She had ties to both. Instinctively, she tugged on the connection she had to Aiden until she found herself standing next to a fire. Aiden and the rest of their team circled the blaze as the warmth melted a ring of snow powdering the ground.

"Well, that went better than I expected."

Penny turned an annoyed frown on Dair. "Don't underestimate your queen." She crept closer to Aiden and watched as the wind tousled his dark hair. Streaks of ash brushed across his cheeks. They'd gone to the tree then. He spoke with Thaen, who sat beside him.

"Are you certain we can get the refugees to the base of Eagallach before winter?" His eyes flicked over the landscape in front of them.

Thaen nodded. "With the summer heat melting the passes, we should only have to wait a few more weeks until they are clear. We will have a few more after that to get them all through." He rubbed a hand down his face. "It will be quite a strain on the Winter Court though, especially without..."

Without his parents, Penny filled in. She reached out to touch his shoulder, but Dair smacked her hand away. "He is too in tune with the Goddess's magic. We do not want to give him any way to know we are here."

Penny tucked her hand against her chest. "You could have just said that." She tried to kick at him, but her foot went through his leg again. "Why can you touch me, but I can't touch you?"

"Magic dream powers. Now shush!"

"About that," Aiden said, bringing her focus back to the conversation. "I've been trying to commune with the Goddess about what to do. With regards to the High Councilor position, I only know that Shirina is still alive and that there's more yet to happen before her position is to be questioned."

A well of relief and gratitude surged up in Penny. Not only would losing Shirina hurt Aiden and the twins, but Penny as well. While their relationship had started off rough, the Councilor had proven herself to be a wonderful member of Aiden's family. Penny would be crushed if anything happened to her. But she remembered what happened to fair folk in Adira's camp, and it might be better to wish Shirina did meet an early end.

"But with Fiadh's death so raw," Aiden continued, "I didn't want to even think about calling a new Winter King until everything was more settled. However, with guidance from the Land, I think it imperative we discuss it, and now feels like a good time for some reason."

Thaen blew out a deep breath. "I do not want it."

Aiden nodded. "I know you don't. And I think the Goddess has more plans for you than having to rule over a Court."

"So that leaves Dair."

Penny heard Dair's sharp intake of breath, though no one else was aware they were there. Except perhaps Aiden, who kept looking about as if watching for someone.

Sgiath stood from his seat on the other side of the fire and drew close to them. "We have discussed it amongst the High Council, but we are not sure which of you would be better suited. We think Dair would be a fine leader, but Thaen, your magic is far stronger."

Thaen shook his head. "Dair is far better than I for such a role. He knows the workings of the Courts inside and out. He has been my *màthair's* right hand for several years. As for his power, he has far more talent than anyone gives him credit for. I think we have yet to see him at his full potential, and when the Courts finally do, they will be astonished."

Dair glided closer to where his brother sat, tears in his eyes.

Sgiath nodded sagely. "You are likely right. We have yet to see much of Dair's gifts, but I think that is more from their nature rather than potency. The High Council will discuss it further, though it seems the best course of action."

Aiden nodded and they all stood, dusting bits of snow and ash from their clothes and trudging toward their beds.

Dair's eyes finally met Penny's over the fire. "I think we should go now. We have much more to work on before the night is over." He lifted his fingers and snapped once again.

Penny stared out toward the city nestled on the peaks. The seat closest to the tall window in the family sitting room had quickly become her favorite place to sit. It gave her a full view of the room as well as the frozen garden outside and allowed her a slice of invisibility. Folk sometimes forgot she was there if she didn't move.

An unwanted queen. Invisible and easily forgotten.

Her fingers met the frosted glass separating her from the kingdom she was now High Queen over. Would the fae ever accept her? She'd read some of their sacred texts, learned about the creation of magekind and the abominable treatment of the Goddess and Her gifts. There wasn't much about the mages themselves, but there was enough about how the fair folk regarded them. Would these immortal beings change the way they'd lived for centuries and bow down to a queen they abhorred?

Not likely.

The sound of multiple footsteps pulled Penny away from her musings and the sight out the window. She stood just as the door opened and Aiden strode into the room. Even after only a few days apart, her heart jumped at the sight of him. Flakes of snow melted in his dark hair, the enchantment on the palace and the warmth of the fire doing their work to warm the thick stone walls. She'd read about that in the library too. His gaze immediately found her, and the amber glittered with a sort of relief as he crossed the room to her.

There were dark circles under his eyes, but he didn't look ill. Merely tired. The expression on his face attested to the weariness as well.

"How did it go?" she asked when he was only a step or two away.

Instead of answering, he wrapped his arms around her and pressed his face into the crook between her neck and shoulder. His arms enveloped her smaller frame, and her toes barely brushed the ground as he straightened a bit. She felt his heart beat in time with hers as he clung to her. Even with only being apart for a couple of days, she still felt a piece of her move back into place with him holding her.

She embraced him without further provocation. "Was it that bad?"

His fingers trembled were they pressed into her back, and he only nestled his face further into the side of her neck.

She ran her fingers through his soft hair. The sides of his hair were shorter, but the top was long enough for her fingers to comb through it. The thick strands slipped between her fingers as smooth as silk. His hold on her relaxed a fraction, and a soft sigh slipped between his lips. She stilled for a moment but quickly returned to her ministrations. She would offer whatever comfort he would allow her to give while she held him.

But her mind could only allow a moment.

"Tell me," she whispered.

His hold on her tightened before he set her back down and met her gaze once again. That weariness still tugged at the corners of his eyes and the center of his brow.

His voice came out in a hoarse whisper. "The Tree is nothing but a blackened stump. It was agonizing just being next to it."

Penny could easily imagine. Even now, the deep ache in her chest throbbed as constantly as it had since Aiden had left.

"What about the city?"

He blew out a deep breath and found a spot on a brown leather sofa, pulling her down beside him. "It was in shambles," he said, his voice growing in tempo but that hoarseness still clinging to it. "The branches had come down from above and crushed buildings and cut off streets. We were able to get a team there to help get the rest of the citizens out, but the casualties..." He shut his eyes and squeezed her hand almost painfully. "Stars, it was *devastating*."

Penny moved closer to him, grabbing a handkerchief from her

pocket and wiping the small smears of ash he still had in his ears. It was a testament to his exhaustion that he wasn't in the bath that instant.

"The folk are so afraid," he whispered, eyes wide as he stared down at the ground, "and I don't even know the first thing about how to help them." He ran a hand through his hair, his eyes turning glassy. "I don't know how to help them."

Penny set the handkerchief down and wrapped her arms around him. She couldn't speak as sobs tore through him. She set her cheek against his hair as he broke apart in her arms.

I don't know how to help them either.

26

SPIRITS

REPORTS HAD BEEN COMING IN ALL MORNING ABOUT THE EVACUEES OF CRANN Mòr arriving in Winter. Aiden had sequestered himself in the study, his thoughts a blur and his mind needing to do something. Anything. He'd taken up the task of going through the missives from their contacts around the kingdom.

He'd also invited Penelope to come with him.

Since his return from Crann Mòr six weeks ago, he couldn't seem to stay away from her. He asked her to come along with him everywhere he went, even the war councils. And she'd stayed with him without complaint. If he read the bond right, she needed him as much as he needed her.

At the moment, she was curled up in one of the chairs they'd moved into the study so she could sit on the same side of the desk as he did. If Spot could have fit through the door, the three of them could have pretended it was just like when Penelope had joined the Underworld in Olympia. A small pile of missives was tucked into the nest her skirts created in her lap. She had insisted on helping him rather than sitting around doing nothing. He had been too grateful to say no.

A brownie popped up on the arm of Penelope's chair, making Aiden jump slightly. The brownie grinned under her mop of long brown hair and held up a folded piece of paper. Penelope didn't even look up as she held out her hand.

"Thank you, Fee," Penelope said.

The brownie tucked the new missive into Penelope's hand and disappeared.

"Fee?" Aiden asked.

Penelope looked up as she broke the seal on the missive. "The brownie's name? Fee has been a great friend these last couple of weeks."

Aiden's mind reeled. Penelope had obviously made an impression on the brownies since her arrival, but now she was claiming friendship with them? He didn't even think he knew a single one of their names, let alone was on friendly terms with any of them. Sweet Gaia, he rarely saw them, let alone had regular conversations with them like she did. His reeling mind stopped. Skies, Penelope was stealing moves right out of his strategy book. She'd befriended the servants before he even had the chance to.

She handed Aiden the new letter. "This is the newest report on the Crann Mòr evacuation."

Aiden took it from her. Apparently, he'd need to shape up his game if he was going to keep up with his wife.

Most of the Tuatha had made it out of the city, though the casualties had been many. It had been nothing like Flùranach. There was no reason to it except to incite terror and desecrate something the fae held sacred—not that he'd put that past Durant. But the folk were nothing if not resilient. More letters about the Tree's removal and possible clean-up of the city came in as well. Of course, he wouldn't be able to instigate any of the suggestions until after they found a way to stop Durant, but it was good to see the folk looking to the future.

A knock on the door lifted Aiden's attention from the note in front of him. Thaen's head popped into the room, his eyes instantly zeroing in on where Penelope sat behind the desk.

"May I come in?"

"Of course." Aiden quickly finished reading the note as Thaen made his way across the room. The status of the evacuation was what he expected, but he was still grateful for the updates he received every few hours.

Penelope straightened in her chair and stacked her papers neatly on the corner of the desk.

Thaen settled in the chair across from them. His eyes flicked back and forth between them before stopping on Aiden. "I have a favor to ask of you."

A favor? From Thaen? Aiden's interest instantly piqued. "What can I do for you, cousin?"

Thaen looked down at the top of the desk, his already blind eyes growing more vacant. "I..." He blew out a breath. "I would like—well, Dair *and* I would like if we could have the chance to speak to our *athair*."

Aiden straightened. "Of course." He'd been wanting to offer for weeks, but with everything going on and with Shirina gone, no time had felt appropriate. It had found a place in the back of his mind, but he was relieved Thaen wished to speak with Fiadh now.

Thaen nodded. "I grieve that my *màthair* cannot be here to participate, but I believe we need his advice. With everything that has been going on, I do not know how we will handle all of this without a piece of his guidance. Dair has been begging me to ask you since our return."

After the fire, Aiden could use some wise words himself. "I will warn you, I have never done this particular summoning for a full blooded fae. I can't guarantee that it'll work." While he'd met fae through his connection with those that had killed them, the magic of the Tuatha Dé Dannan was so different than that of humankind. The world beyond theirs was a complete mystery, even with Aiden's direct ties to it.

"I am grateful for whatever effort you give, cousin." Thaen rubbed a hand down his face. "Wind and snow, I do not know if I am at all ready for this."

"I don't think there's really any way to prepare for this." He turned to Penelope, but she was already standing.

"I think this is something that needs to be just family," she said.

He grabbed her hand. "You are family, my love."

She leaned down and pressed her lips to Aiden's. His blood lit in his body, and all he wanted to do was pull her closer. He reached around her to do just that, but she pulled away.

"I know, Aiden, but this is something the three of you need to do alone." She set a comforting hand on Thaen's shoulder before walking out of the study.

Thaen took a deep breath and let it out slowly. "She is kind to let us do it alone. I do not think I could do this with an audience."

Aiden stood and came around the desk. "It will be all right. Perhaps your father will give us some much-needed answers."

"I hope you are right."

They decided to gather in the family sitting room. Aiden had found out Penelope liked to spend time in the conservatory on the east side of the palace and had decided to take tea with Farrah in there that afternoon. The guard at the door had been ordered to not allow anyone but Penelope through the door, but Aiden suspected not even she would interrupt. They would not be disturbed.

Aiden turned to Dair beside him. "Did you get what I asked for?"

Dair's leg shook, making the sofa he sat on beside Aiden vibrate as he pulled a small miniature from his jacket pocket. The long face of an equine stared back at him, a scraggly mane puffed up around the gray, crooked horn between its ears.

"What is that?" Aiden asked.

"Meet *Athair's* first love, Plàigh the Unicorn."

Aiden shook his head. "That thing does not at all look like what we saw on the beach in our travels." The unicorns he'd seen on Summer's coast had been magnificent beasts, teeming with power and majesty. This creature looked like someone had stuck a knotted root onto a donkey's face.

Dair chuckled. "*Màthair* has told him since he showed her that picture that he had obviously been duped. We think it was some sort of crossbreed, though we have never been able to figure out where it had been purchased from. Plàigh had been a gift for one of his birthdays, but he could never remember who had given it."

Aiden plucked the small picture from Dair's hand. "And this picture meant something to him?"

"He had it on his night table since before we were born," said Thaen from his seat in the leather armchair next to them.

Aiden nodded and cradled the old parchment in his hands. "This should work then. Place your hands on my arms." He closed his eyes and tugged on the deep well of magic inside of him. His gift came roaring to life, black snaking through his veins until they were dark as tar around his fingers.

A flicker of black appeared in front of him. He pushed a little further, his heart twinging for the first time in months as all of the shapes cleared, and the spirit appeared in front of them.

Fiadh smiled, his lips pulling wide as he looked between them. "Hello, my little shadows."

Dair gasped and Thaen's hold on Aiden's arm tightened to the point of pain.

"Blizzards, I am so happy you called for me." Fiadh blinked as if to banish tears. "I know we cannot be together long; the tether is that much thinner for fae than it is for humans and Aedon's magic will not last as long as I would like, but I am glad for this time all the same."

"*Athair...*" Dair's voice broke on the word, and he had to take a deep breath. "There is so much that has happened. So much we have to tell you, to ask you."

"I know. I know there has been so much trouble for you boys. We are not hidden away on the other side. We are aware of you."

Thaen's hand shook against Aiden's arm and the strong male's head dipped down.

"Thaen, my son," Fiadh said. "You are carrying heavy burdens. I know the capture of your *màthair* troubles your heart. I know the bond you have struck between you and your cousin is a heavy burden but know that you are doing the right thing by staying at his side. Know that we are proud of you for the work you are doing. The Goddess is proud to have you as Her hands."

A slip of a noise—a sob, a cry—snuck out between Thaen's lips, and he shut his eyes tightly against the struggle Aiden hadn't even realized he had been dealing with. Aiden wanted to wrap his arms around his cousin, but he didn't want to risk losing the connection to Fiadh.

Fiadh turned his amber eyes on Dair. "Dair, my boy. You have carried such heartache in your heart, such pain in your soul. Let it go. You are so much stronger than you realize. I know it. I know you are a great leader, and I know you will do so many wonderful things with the gifts you have been given. Do not doubt yourself, son. You are so much more."

Dair was not as discrete as Thaen was with his emotions. Tears trailed down Dair's face, his shoulders shaking with emotion.

"And Aedon."

Aiden straightened as Fiadh's attention turned to him.

Fiadh gave a long sigh. "You have faced so much change, so much trouble, and it is not even close to being over. There is so much the Goddess has yet to do with you, so much you have yet to face with Her at your side. I am sorry, Little Shadow, but it is only going to get harder before it is over."

Aiden closed his eyes, letting his head fall back as if in supplication to the Goddess Herself to relieve him of this burden.

"But do not lose hope. You have so many around you who will help you. I am so glad you were able to take Penelope as your wife."

Aiden's head shot back up.

Fiadh chuckled at the shock probably playing on Aiden's face. "I am. While I know I attempted to turn you from this path, now that I know the things I do, I know it was the right choice. Even without the two of you being *taghadh*, I know she is meant to be at your side for reasons even I cannot comprehend. She is a true gift from the Goddess to this world. Protect her. Listen to her. Cherish her. Trust me, you will find yourself to be a much happier man if you council with your wife for everything. I was lucky enough to have such a gift of my own."

Dair's sobs grew. "Why? Why did all of this have to happen? Why did Danu do all of this?"

Fiadh's gave his son an empathetic smile. "Innocent people die because guilty people make bad choices or simply because they were not meant for the long life attainable in this mortal plane. We cannot always see the Danu's wisdom, but there is always a *reason*. Just as I was always meant to be here, to help you now as I could not if I were alive. We can try to guess what the Goddess's reasons may be, but it is not our job to do so. Our job is to remember Her and follow the path She has paved for us."

Dair huffed. "You sound like Thaen."

Fiadh leaned forward, his elbows resting on his knees. "Our Mother has many plans for all of you, but I am not privy to them. All I know is I was meant to come here to offer comfort and wisdom. That is all She told me."

Thaen leaned forward. "You have seen the Goddess? What is she like?"

Tears gathered above Fiadh's lashes. "Oh, My Shadows, you would not believe me even if I was allowed to tell you. There are things, sacred things, I am not allowed to divulge, but just know that She loves all three of you and wants your happiness in this life and the next, as She does with all Her children."

Warmth spread through Aiden's chest. The love that Fiadh spoke of bloomed along the connection Aiden shared with the Land, and he realized this kingdom really was an integral part of the Goddess's plan. That his connection to this magical place was another connection to the Goddess. A tear trailed down the side of his face, and he had to use the shoulder of his tunic to wipe it away.

Fiadh shook his head. "But enough of that. I have also come with a warning from Our Mother. The loss of Crann Mòr was a blow. The magic of the Land relied on the connection that came through the Tree. There are laws that must be fulfilled in order for the Goddess's power to remain. There must be a source. When She left, She created the Tree to allow an open connection to Her children, one they can use to continue to grow and become like Her until they finally returned to Her presence in Her home. Without the Tree and the fruit continually feeding the fae and then the magic being fed back into the Land, magic itself will fade as it does in Olympia."

"Skies," Aiden said under his breath.

"What are we to do?" Dair asked. "We cannot regrow the Tree, not without help. And the rebels will simply burn it down again."

Fiadh lifted his chin. "You must win against The Cartographer and rid the kingdom of all rebels. You must free the enslaved fae and the kingdom must work to restore the balance."

"How?" Aiden asked, leaning forward. "How do we defeat her?"

Fiadh shook his head. "I am sorry. I do not know. All I was meant to say was that the Tree must be restored."

"How is that helpful?" Dair bit out.

Fiadh sent a chastising look his way. "Do not question the wisdom of Our Mother. I know we cannot guess why She does things the way She does, but trust that She knows what is best. In time, you will all understand, but that knowledge is not needed now. For now, we must have faith that we are on the right path, even if it leads to our own destruction."

"Does Danu desire our destruction?" Thaen whispered.

Fiadh shook his head. "Of course not, but what is the loss of a mortal flesh in the grand scheme of eternity? Even if you do not win this battle, know that Danu is waiting for you with open arms to return to Her home."

"That does require a lot of faith," Aiden said. He grimaced as his heart twinged again, the magic beginning to drain him.

Fiadh gave him a knowing smile. "Keep going. Fight this fight. Become the fae I know you all to be. Even if I do not know the Goddess's plan, I know that if you all work together, you will come out victorious. You three are brothers, even if Aiden is only your cousin." He looked both of his boys in the eyes. "You will bring your *màthair* home. As your *athair*, I have no doubts about it. You will help your cousin. Help his wife." He narrowed his eyes at Thaen. "You especially. I know it is difficult to see beyond the prejudices of the past but know that the Goddess is using our High Queen for purposes which none of us can even comprehend. There is much work to be done, and Danu's work cannot be halted, only accepted."

Aiden's heart beat somewhat sluggishly, but he held on to the magic with an iron fist. "I don't want you to go."

Fiadh's eyes glimmered and his form began to fade as Aiden's hands shook with the strain. "And I do not wish to leave you, but our time is up. I love all of you. Even if you cannot see me, I am always with you. I will be in the shadows at your back and the kiss of frost on your cheeks. Always, my sons. Always."

27
SPARRING AND PREJUDICE

Penny lifted the padded cloth and held it up against her waist. When the leather pant legs fell well past her feet and onto the floor, she looked over at where Fee sat at the edge of her bed and gave the brownie an unimpressed look.

"Don't they have anything smaller?" she asked, rolling up the pair of thick, black leggings.

Fee shook her head. "Unless you are as wide as a trow or short as a gnome, these were the best fit in the palace. The Lòchran told us you needed sturdy clothing for your training, and these were the best we could come up with on such short notice. Of course, we brownies will have an entire dresser full of training clothes fit for a queen by tomorrow, but for today..." She gestured toward the mismatched pile on the bed next to her.

Penny sighed and gathered the rest of the clothing to take to her dressing room. With a few discreet folds and a wide belt, she emerged in what she would call a passable training outfit. The shirt was a bit baggy and nearly fell to her knees, but the material was sturdy and would likely be able to handle the tousles Penny was positive she'd find herself in today.

She grabbed a leather vest already hanging in her closet and slipped on her new pair of boots. The palace staff had been hard at work creating her wardrobe for the past couple of months. She'd had a handful of dresses before her anointing, but Dair had made it his personal mission to make sure she was properly attired afterward. To say nothing of his manners, he certainly had a way with style that even Mother would have appreciated.

Penny stepped out of the dressing room and Fee burst out in applause.

"You look ready for battle, My Sovereign."

And Penny felt anything but. Between the ill-fitting clothing and the anxious beat of her heart, her self-confidence plummeted. Penny nodded her thanks to Fee anyway and grabbed the sword leaning against her bedpost. No use hiding out in her room for Thaen to come drag her away.

"Let's pray the only battle I see today is with this outfit."

"Welcome to the arena, Penelope," Thaen said.

Penny followed Thaen through the large gates of the stone fortress. The walls towered above her, probably thirty feet tall and at least ten feet thick, not to mention teeming with magic. Within, a large hall stood in the center, surrounded by other stone structures. Hundreds of fae dashed to and fro between the few large buildings or in training exercises. Thaen led her toward a crowd gathered near one of the many buildings.

"I hadn't expected it to be so grand," Penny said.

"It is one of the last great fortresses from before the Faerie Wars," Thaen said, leading her through the crowd of trainees. At the center, a pair of soldiers sparred with one another, Day and Night Court magic flashing between them. The male with the light under his skin blocked the shadowy spears thrown by the female opposite him with a wall of solid rock. He then pushed his hands outward, and the ground beneath his opponent's feet buckled. The female cast a sheet of ice over the hole and charged across the muddy ground.

"Is it wise to pit the Courts against each other like that?" Penny asked, keeping her voice low as to not draw attention to herself. Her fingers fiddled with the edge of the gloves hiding her *taghadh* mark. She'd had enough glares cast her way walking through the command center on the other side of the camp. None of the folk watching the fight had noticed the mage in their midst.

Not yet at least.

"Sometimes, it's the only way to keep the peace," Thaen replied. "The tension between the Courts is nearly palpable and allowing them to blow off steam like this can be helpful."

"But why not get them to work together instead of against one another?" she asked. The separation between the Courts had been apparent even in the camp. "Don't we want them to see each other as allies instead of competition?"

"How do you propose we do such a thing when the two Courts have been at war with one another since the Goddess ascended?"

Penny pursed her lips. She wouldn't admit she didn't have any ideas at present, but that didn't mean there wasn't a solution. The Tuatha were of the same lineage and had more in common than not. There was sure to be common ground somewhere, it was just a matter of someone finding it and helping them see each other in a new light.

The bout in the ring ended, the female coming out victor much to the disappointment of the male's comrades.

"Come on, then," Thaen said. "It is your turn."

Penny's head whipped to the side so fast it cracked a few joints. "What did you just say?"

He nudged her toward the center of the crowd, the faces closest to them beginning to turn in their direction. "I signed you up for the next round."

Penny's eyes pulled wide, and she shoved the heels of her boots into the ground, though it did nothing to stop Thaen's shoving. She gave up on that tactic and twisted out of his grasp. He reached for her again, but she dodged him. "I am *not* going in there."

"Oh, yes you are." Thaen squinted in her direction and grabbed for her again, this time catching the sleeve of her shirt. "It is time to prove your mettle."

Penny wriggled, but Thaen's grip on her didn't lessen in the slightest until they were in the center of the ring. Penny jerked her arm free and gave her most menacing glare.

"If you are attempting to communicate something with your expression, I cannot see," he said with a smirk.

The whispers around them turned into hisses.

"Filthy mage."

"What is it doing here?"

"Who let the thing out of its cage?"

"I bet it has fleas."

Heat rose into Penny's cheeks, and she took a step back in Thaen's direction. "I don't think this is a good idea."

Thaen shrugged. "Then you had best adapt to the concept quickly." He turned and strode toward the rest of the onlookers.

Penny followed. "Aren't we going to spar?"

Thaen looked back. "Us? No." He pointed behind her. "She is the one you are up against."

Penny whirled and found a female striding into the circle. Hair the color of liquid gold was pulled back from her face in a thick braid and her magenta eyes flashed with anger. Penny's stomach sank to her toes.

Fearg. The Huntress.

It may have been four months since Penny had seen the fae, the disgust radiating off her hadn't diminished in the least.

Penny grabbed Thaen's arm before he could reach the ring of onlookers. "Please don't make me fight her," she pleaded. "She's one of your greatest warriors. I can't imagine how this will help anything."

Thaen leaned down. "Do you think you cannot win?"

Penny glanced back at the prowling Huntress and then returned Thaen's questioning look with an annoyed one before realizing once again that he couldn't see it. "That's not the point."

"Is it not?" He lowered his voice so only she could barely hear. "I thought the point of me dragging you out here was to show all of these folk that our High Queen would not back down from a challenge." He slipped from her grasp and disappeared into the crowd as if he'd never been there.

Penny growled. *Blasted Lòchran.* She spun to face the Huntress as she reached the center of the ring. This would not end well; she was sure of it.

Fearg pointed one slender finger in Penny's direction. "I may not be able to destroy you in front of all of these folk, but I am going to show you what a true magic wielder looks like."

Well, this should be fun. Penny held back an eye roll. She took her place before Fearg and drew her sword.

Fearg did the same, her form natural and apprehensive. They had fought in the forests of Spring only a few months ago. While Penny had been practicing with Aiden at the palace for the last couple of weeks and wasn't sickly from being prisoner in a rebel camp, she still didn't know if she could beat the mighty Huntress.

Penny heard the ring of a gong somewhere to her left, and Fearg charged. Her sword swung high, and Penny ducked past her. With a lithe grace only accomplished by the fae, Fearg swung around, barely skidding in the mud with her forward momentum. Penny's sword came up to block a blow, and she felt the strength of her opponent through the vibrating metal.

Sweet Gaia, why did the fair folk have to be so much stronger?

Penny pushed Fearg back, giving herself more space to take up another defense. Something tingled her senses, and Penny watched as Fearg thrust her hand toward her. A wave of magic crackled in the air between them.

The crowd roared in approval, happy to see their comrade getting a leg up on Penny.

Penny felt the wave, practically smelled the acrid scent of it as it washed over her. A warm fury bloomed in her chest. This *fae* believed she was better than Penny. Thought Penny was beneath her. The sword in Penny's hand felt light, felt hungry. Penny would show all of these cursed fae what a real magic wielder looked like. They wanted her to feel small? They had another thing coming.

The cursed nudge grabbed hold of her.

She looked over the crowd and found Thaen again. He had a stupid smirk on his face that made Penny's blood boil. Who was he to look at her that way?

Another nudge.

Penny gritted her teeth and reached inside for the insufferable bond that constantly tried to tell her what to do. The moment she touched it, the blazing heat in her chest dissipated. She gasped and looked over at the Huntress, still holding out her hand, brows furrowed.

Fearg was doing this. She could manipulate emotion. And not just any emotion. She could make folk angry.

As long as Penny held on to the bonds within her, the anger disappeared. Besides a slight tingle between her ribs, there was nothing left. She looked down, expecting to see something wrong with her, but the anger was completely gone.

Fearg growled, bringing Penny's attention back to the fight.

Fearg rushed to the table of weapons and ripped a shield from the pile.

Penny looked about and found Thaen staring at her from the crowd, and she threw him her most put out expression even if he couldn't see it. Had he pitted Penny against the Huntress because he knew she couldn't use whatever magic she'd been gifted? Did he honestly think that would be wise considering how Penny's connection to the Land had changed her magic and that all of the fair folk despised her for the very gift she'd been given? If she beat this Tuatha with magic after she wasn't able to use hers, it would be absolutely humiliating for her.

He tilted his lips up with mirth and she wanted to scream.

Fearg swung her blade once again, tucking herself behind the thick shield she'd grabbed. Penny batted the swing away and tucked into the female's side, knocking the shield arm away and dislodging the barrier from her arm.

The female screeched in anger as she defended against Penny's attack with only her sword. "How dare you come in here and pretend to be one of us!"

Fearg kicked out, but Penny avoided the blow. The fae nearly slipped in the mud but caught herself and swung her sword in Penny's direction. The female had strength and speed on her side. It was only Penny's constant training for the last couple of weeks that remotely evened the fight.

Penny avoided the slice toward her arm, but it grazed her leg when she turned.

Why on Gaia's green earth did Thaen think it a good idea to allow them to fight with actual blades?

She righted herself just as Fearg came around and thrust her sword in Penny's direction again. In a stroke of anger, she overextended her swing. Penny jerked her elbow up and disarmed the fae. The sword went flying and landed with a *thunk* in the mud at the feet of the audience.

Fearg roared. Penny allowed her sword to drop to her side.

"Well, that was—"

A fist connected with her cheek.

The crowd around them thundered their approval as Penny felt her head whip to the side. Her sword was up a moment later, but

Fearg had already grabbed a spear from the weapons pile and the point pierced the side of Penny's shirt.

Penny grabbed the shaft of the weapon and pulled it from the fae's hands. A gaping tear exposed her undershirt at her ribs. "This is borrowed!" She stabbed the tip of the spear into the mud and raised her sword.

But the female faltered. Her mouth opened wide, and she fell to her knees with her hands around her throat. The spear fell from her hands, and she took ragged breaths.

Penny watched with horror as the girl struggled to breath. In a moment of sanity, she rushed to her side, holding her up.

"Breathe. Come on, breathe."

The female looked at her with wide eyes, her skin draining of color as her breath was stolen from her lungs. The rush of Fearg's magic happened again and Penny immediately shoved it aside.

Penny prodded her chest, looking for anything that could have stopped her breathing, but there was nothing there.

"Someone help!" Penny called. "She can't breathe!"

Someone grabbed her from behind and pulled her away from Fearg.

"What did you do?" the blue-skinned fae holding her asked.

"I didn't—" Her voice cut off as someone else grabbed for her.

"It is using its cursed magic to kill her!" another voice yelled.

"Stop it!"

"Restrain it!"

Penny kicked out, panic taking over as fae clamored for her blood. She fought her way free from her captor, but another one took their place. She looked everywhere for that cursed purple blade Thaen always carried around, but it was nowhere to be seen. Someone shoved her and she fell to her hands on the ground.

As she fell, she saw other bodies fall, each with the same gasping as Fearg in the middle of the sparring ring.

By the Goddess, what was happening to them?

Then she saw the absolute fury in all their eyes.

Fearg was enhancing their hatred.

Penny glanced around, looking for the Huntress, but the folk kept coming at her.

Her arms sparked and green and black flared up her skin through the thin fabric of her shirt. She gritted her teeth for the pain that accompanied her gift, but no pain came. Instead, the ground rumbled beneath her hands.

In a wave, plants sprang from the ground and shoved the rest of the crowd away from where she knelt. Fae went flying, even the ones that couldn't breathe.

The wave stopped against a wall of black and purple.

Thaen's sword cut through the plants in front of him, revealing where he crouched beside Fearg. Her head was bowed, and she had a hand over her heart. Her shoulders rose and fell with deep breaths, and she looked at Penny in shock. The magic she had been sending out ebbed.

The other fae around them were rallying, their emotions still fueled by their anger. But the bodies kept falling, all of them gasping.

Penny got to her feet and ran to Thaen. "How do we stop this? We can't have all these folk dropping dead!"

Thaen quirked a brow and turned to the thickening crowd. The commotion had drawn more of a crowd, the fae having fetched their friends to help. The entire fortress was probably standing around the arena.

"Cease your hateful thoughts!" Thaen roared. "See what your sister has realized that you are too blind to see."

Penny looked down at Fearg in front of her with everyone else. Fearg's eyes were still wide on her. She hadn't stood from her pose, fist still set against her heart.

"My Sovereign," Fearg whispered.

Penny felt that nudge again and she pushed her magic into the muddy ground under her boots. Flowers bloomed from where she stood, out across the sparring ring. White daffodils rose their heads, all pointed toward Penny in supplication.

"Behold," said Thaen, "High Queen Penelope of Faerie."

The crowd around them stilled. Penny heard a thump and spun. A fae had been trying to come up behind her, but had fallen, breaths stolen just like the others. Dozens of fae were on their knees. Penny crossed her arms over her middle. If they didn't stop, if they didn't just give up trying to come after her, they would die.

"Kneel, you morons!" Fearg hollered. "This is the queen Danu has chosen for us, and if you do not get that through your thick skulls you are going to die right here in the dirt before you even see battle."

Penny glanced around and pulled off her gloves. The amber ring around her pinky glowed with the green and black winding up her arms.

Then, like a wave, the rest of the fae fell to their knees.

Those gasping were helped to their knees, and they beat their fists against their chests. Soon, the sound of gasping transformed to the sound of whispers and prayers.

"My Sovereign," Fearg said again, "if I had known…"

"Stop," Penny said. "It doesn't matter." She turned to the rest of the fae. "Get up, all of you. It wasn't my intention to be a distraction. I came to spar, to meet all of you. I didn't want any of this. Please, go back to your training. I'll leave."

She turned to walk away, but Fearg grabbed her pant leg.

"No, you should stay." She finally stood. "No one else here has skill like yours and I need the training." She spread her arms out. "We all do."

Murmurs broke out, and Penny could see the wariness in the other trainees' eyes.

She looked down at Fearg. "I don't think the others quite agree."

Fearg stood. "If I want you to stay, they will learn to follow suit. A few might need convincing, but you leave that to me, My Sovereign." She gave another bow.

Thaen stepped to Penny's side. "I pray everyone here learned a lesson. We should not forget it is the Goddess who rules over us, not our own opinions."

Fearg gave another bow. "I do not believe I shall ever forget again." She smiled and walked away.

Penny turned to Thaen. "This was not the plan."

He smirked. "This has always been the Goddess's plan. You were the only one that was unaware."

28

SIEGE

THE BLACK SWATH OF DARKNESS FELL OVER AIDEN'S EYES. THE SILK WAS SOFT against the sides of his face, but the all-encompassing blindness wasn't nearly as welcome.

Dion and Shaunie had arrived only half an hour ago.

Penelope had thought it best that Aiden give them a moment to refresh themselves after the journey. He wouldn't begrudge the time he could take to mentally prepare to meet them.

Aiden reached his hand out and found Penelope's arm easily. She'd been the one to tie the blindfold around his head and even without their new connection he would have been able to tell where she was.

"How is that?" Penelope asked. The sound of her voice soothed him. Penelope didn't have a high voice, not like Shaunie or some of the other young ladies he'd overheard tittering in Olympia. It also wasn't husky and smooth like Rissa's. It was steady, commanding, but there was always the hint of joy, like a laugh was just waiting at the back of her throat. It wasn't derisive, more like she wanted to laugh with pure elation at the wonder of the world around them.

He pulled her closer until he felt the warmth radiating from her. "I don't particularly like that I can't look at my wife."

She poked him in the ribs with her free hand. "It's not as if you haven't seen me all day."

He grabbed the offending finger and kissed the back of her hand. "Yet it feels that way."

Penelope's skirt brushed against the front of his trousers and her lips met his. Almost unconsciously, he reached up to cradle her face between his palms. He deepened the kiss without second thought. As she pressed into him, he could feel her heartbeat against his chest, the same wild rhythm beating under his own ribcage.

He pulled back just a fraction of an inch. "You know, I think Dion can wait just a bit longer."

Penelope laughed but took his hand and pulled him forward. "Please. We're likely to be late enough as it is. Are you ready?"

"To see my ridiculous brother with a cravat wrapped around my face?" Aiden shook his head mirthlessly. "You know he's going to laugh about the entire situation."

"Yes," Penelope agreed, "but we also know he'll take the threat seriously."

Aiden pressed a quick kiss to the side of her head. "You're right, of course. But still..."

Penelope chuckled, a warm, beautiful sound that he was truly able to appreciate without being distracted by the smile he knew came with it. "You'll simply have to bear it."

Aiden allowed Penelope to pull him into the hallway and toward the more formal sitting room.

He heard doors open and close, some within the hallway they walked in and others farther away. One never realized how much a certain sense could affect the world around them until it was gone. When he'd been a boy, Durant had often put him in situations where one of his senses would be nulled—sight, touch, hearing. All of them. She'd used magical suppression as well just to make it more difficult. Looking back, it made sense why she had done it. Her plans to become The Cartographer had likely gone back as far as that.

The voices of the High Councilors met his ears before they joined them outside the family wing on their way to the east side of the palace. The group was to present a united front to the King of Olympia. Dion couldn't know that anything was amiss.

Not until Aiden could be absolutely sure what was going on back in Olympia.

The High Councilors had made the point not to divulge anything until Dion gave his full account—especially not about why Penelope couldn't return to Olympia or about what happened at their wedding. For the most part, they weren't sharing anything at all. They didn't want anything "bandied about," as Rìgh put it, and Aiden had to agree. Dion was Aiden's brother, but he was also a shrewd ruler over a kingdom with many more citizens than Faerie, including Penelope's missing mother. Dion's priority would be to his people, not to any familial connection to Aiden. Penelope hadn't agreed with the Councilors, saying Dion was not so unfeeling, but Aiden could see their point. If he had been the one in Dion's shoes, he didn't know how he'd react to finding out one of his most valuable mages was now Faerie's High Queen and that Aiden had captured Durant only for her to escape.

Penelope pulled to a stop. He heard the rap of her knuckles on the door in front of them and felt the change of air flow as the door opened. The rustle of fabrics and the faint sound of multiple heartbeats told him there where people in the room before him. He felt Thaen's presence near the door, the aura of predator always giving him away even without Aiden's magical senses. He smelled Dair's unique mixture of scents, the mint of his soap and the beeswax of his hair products. It mingled with Penelope's cinnamon and citrus and earth. The latter had grown even stronger since their wedding.

Penelope stopped a few steps into the room and lowered slightly. Aiden realized what she was doing and pulled her back up before she could perform the elaborate curtsy. He would not have his High Queen bow, even if Dion and Shaunie were not aware of her new title yet. The very thought rankled him.

"Hello, Dion," Aiden greeted. "I hope your trip was not too eventful and you made it here mostly intact."

He heard the deep rumble of Dion's voice before the words formed. "Everything went fine, Denny. Your extraction team did a remarkable job. It didn't even tickle."

Aiden's lips twitched. Dion had never gone through a portal, he knew. Remembering his first time going through one back in Eleusion, he highly doubted Dion wasn't at least slightly affected.

"We brought a gift," Dion said. The syllables slurred slightly, though probably not enough for anyone who didn't know him to notice. He'd likely found something to drink while they'd been waiting.

There was movement and the temptation to remove the blindfold emerged for the first time. He felt Penelope reach her arms out and gasp.

Aiden leaned down to her ear. "What is it?"

"It's a helmet," Penelope answered.

"Heff insisted I bring it to you," Dion answered a little too cheerfully. "I'd tell you to try it on, but the blindfold may inhibit such a thing. I'm sorry you felt I was so much more kingly than you that you had to shield your very eyes from me as to not grow jealous. It's unfortunate that I don't think that very regal helmet will help any either."

"What does the helmet do?" Penelope asked.

"It's just a helmet," Dion answered.

Aiden rolled his covered eyes and turned to where he guessed his sister-in-law stood. "Hello, Shaunie. How are you?" Aiden hadn't told anyone besides his family members about the pregnancy and he didn't want to put her on the spot now, but he couldn't help asking.

"As well as can be expected I think," she said. "The effects of whatever poison was used have fully worn off, praise the Goddess. Doctor Ashton had his hands full for a while." Without being able to see her, Aiden could better hear the weariness, the sorrow in her voice. A weight deepened in his chest.

"I'm happy you're here," he said.

"As am I," she answered.

"And Nell," Dion drawled, "what a surprise to find you here." It was very obvious from his tone that he was not at all surprised.

"Hello, Your Majesties." Penelope wobbled, catching herself before she curtsied.

"Dion," Aiden cut in, "allow me to introduce you to the rest of our party." Dion had already met Sgiath and Thaen as they had helped Farrah get Dion to the palace. So, Aiden made the rest of the introductions, beginning with the Councilors Dion hadn't met and then ending with Dair. He then invited everyone to sit, knowing Penelope had led him to one of the large meeting rooms on the east side of the palace.

"We are happy to find ourselves in such good company," Dion said civilly from across the table. "However, I wish it were under better circumstances."

"As do I," Aiden said. "Tell us what's happened since your coronation, Dion."

Dion began his tale. There had been riots in Olympia's streets, and they'd begun a strict curfew in the first few weeks, but the city guard as well as the small army they had gathered outside of the city hadn't been enough to subdue the rebels. They had gone under siege just before the spring equinox and lost the palace within hours. The rebels had then begun to spread out from Eleusion, taking the lower part of the kingdom and moving toward the capital. Assassins from the continent had weaseled their way into the palace, poisoning trustworthy members of the guard and finding positions in high stations in the palace. Every waterway was now patrolled by the Aigean Trident. The forest around Discordia had been burned using fae magic. The vineyards of Tauros destroyed, and the land blighted. Iatrus Castle under siege for weeks.

"It's been absolute madness," Dion bit out. "The Underworld operatives have finally infiltrated a few key points in The Cartographer's chain of command, but their ranks are as tight as a drum. We haven't been able to break through any inner circles and are still weeding out moles within our own ranks. After Shaunie lost——" He cleared his throat. "After the rebels took that treasure, the hunt for traitors became even more thorough. It's been the Underworld that has found out most of them."

A small breath sounded from beside Dion. "Rissa has quite taken to the task," Shaunie said in a quiet voice.

"I'm sure she did." He tried not to allow any pity to creep into the smile he attempted to send her way. Shaunie wouldn't welcome it. But the knowledge that Rissa was taking care of Olympia and was working on taking down this poisoner eased his mind. Rissa—and even Heff—had a deep fondness for children. Aiden knew they would be merciless in their hunt for the one who had hurt Dion's family.

"And I can't forget about the pain in the neck Duchess Dominique has been." Dion let out an audible huff. "Forgive me for saying so, Nell, but your mother has gone absolutely mad."

Penelope tensed at Aiden's side. "What's happened? Did you figure out how she's connected to the rebels?"

"What?" Dion asked. "Oh, I forgot that she was a suspect. Well, I don't think we need to worry so much about that right now. She's been gallivanting all over the kingdom trying to find *you*. At first, she believed you'd been abducted by the rebels after the hubbub of the coronation, which is one of the reasons I began to question her involvement with them. She came to me every day for two weeks before the castle was taken, pestering me to search high and low."

"And we can assure you," Shaunie added, "we were completely prepared to send a search party out until Lord MacGregor told us what actually happened."

"Yes, yes. We didn't want you getting into Durant's hands, but we were sworn to secrecy and had to prioritize the palace over a pointless search. That's when the duchess went off by herself."

"What do you mean?" Penelope asked, alarm sharpening her words.

"She instigated her own search," Dion answered. He then lowered his voice, but in his state, it wasn't nearly as quiet as he probably meant for it to be. Aiden would have to talk to the brownies about hiding the drink during Dion's stay. "That's when I realized she couldn't be part of the rebellion. I can't tell you how many times she was caught sneaking into someone's home or attempting to break into the dungeons to interrogate a prisoner. Her antics grew until I told her she wouldn't be allowed to interfere with the work the Underworld was getting into. Then, she left."

"Where did she go?" Penelope asked, her voice urgent and her emotions plucking the string of their connection. If Lady Barclay wasn't involved in the rebellion, it would change so much for her.

Aiden heard the quick rustle of fabric across from him. *A shrug maybe?* The blindfold grew more tedious, and he had to smother the desire to rip it off.

"We don't know," said Dion. "She left the capital right before the riots began and we had to lock down the city. Last I heard, she'd gone into Delphine, but that was before summer solstice. We've been trying to find her. We need her help, and I was somewhat hoping you would know where she is."

"I haven't a clue," Penelope said. "Why do you need her help?"

Shaunie took over before Dion could answer. "We need food. The rebels haven't taken the valley on the other side of Olympia's mountains. If we can have Lady Barclay work her magic on those fields, we can keep people fed. We have plenty of grain stored in warehouses manned by Lord Hermen's limited number of men, but with winter coming sooner rather than later, we don't have the means to grow anything before the frosts. The weather mages have made all the plans they can to hold back the cold, but they can only fight it for so long."

Aiden tilted his head. "I thought we'd talked about how the Barclay magic wasn't a good option." Lady Barclay had gone to great lengths to dissuade Dion from growing magically enhanced food. When was that? It felt like years since he'd been in Olympia.

"No food will kill people faster than magically enhanced food," Dion said.

"She hasn't offered her help at all?" Penelope asked. It didn't make sense. If she truly wasn't part of the rebellion, she should have jumped at the opportunity to feed people. It was her life's work.

"No," Shaunie answered. "We don't even know if she's heard. She could be searching the continent across the sea for you, and we would have no idea. Once Angelica told us you were here, we came to ask for your help."

"I'll do anything I can," Penelope said.

Aiden could feel Penelope's worry bubble in his own gut. First, the palace was taken, now Lady Barclay was missing. How had everything gone so awry? Durant was a mastermind to be certain, but how had she managed all of this in little under a year? The pieces of Aiden's fortitude crumbled slightly. How much more would they lose before all of this was over?

"And even if we do find her, we aren't going to last forever," Dion added. "We need aid, Denny. With the palace taken, we cannot gather men. The only noble house besides the Hermen's still in control of their militia are the MacGregors, and while he may have beat back the rebels for now, I believe even Paulo is holding on by a thread. The rebels are likely lying in wait until they receive reinforcements."

"So, what are you asking us for, Dion?" Aiden asked. "Besides helping locate Lady Barclay."

Dion blew out a breath. "We need men—well, *fae*. After reviewing reports and gathering more intel, I believe if we can take support back with us then, perhaps, we can use the divided forces to push the rebels—"

"We can't," Aiden interrupted.

Dion paused. "You can't get on board with the idea, or you can't help?"

Aiden leaned forward, hoping to portray his discontent with the situation even through the blindfold. "We can't help."

The room was silent. The air began to crackle, attesting to Dion's mounting frustration. The hairs on Aiden's arms stood up.

"What Aiden is trying to say, Your Majesty," Penelope cut in, "is that we wish we could help—we *want* to help, but the situation in Faerie is much more precarious than anyone has led you to believe."

The Councilors seated in the room had been completely silent until Penelope spoke. Their clothing rustled as they moved to protest Penelope's explanation.

Aiden took hold of the conversation before they could get a word in. "Penelope is correct. Dion, we don't even have an army to protect our own kingdom, let alone give aid to yours."

The electricity in the room disappeared.

"How bad is it?" Shaunie asked.

Aiden swallowed. "We no longer have any Tuatha Dé Dannan within the boundaries of the Day Court. We have refugee camps scattered throughout the Night Court. The Aigeans have blocked our entire eastern coast, and we are waiting for them to move in on the western side before the first frost. Just last week, our capital was ransacked, and our sacred Tree burned to the ground. There was no way we could have stopped it. We're in the process of training fighters, and while the folk are quick learners, our seasoned warriors are spread thin."

"How is this possible?" Dion demanded. "How was Durant able to do this?"

Aiden bowed his head. "I don't know."

"Are we to surrender?" Shaunie said in a shaky voice Aiden had never heard from her in all the years he'd known her.

"No." To Aiden's surprise it was Penelope's voice that brokered no argument. "Adira has not offered us a surrender. She has only given us a death sentence. If we give up, we will be doing more than handing over our crowns, but the lives of our citizens."

Dion sighed. "While I agree with the sentiment, Nell, I don't see a clear way out of this."

Aiden's sigh came out an exact echo of his brother's. "Neither do I."

29

PRESENTS AND SURPRISES

Penny flopped back onto the coverlet on top of the bed. The door to their bedchamber snicked shut and Aiden lifted the blindfold over his head.

"That did not go at all as I'd hoped," he said.

Penny closed her eyes. She couldn't even muster up the words of agreement. Dinner had been quite the somber affair. After their meeting, it seemed not even Shaunie and Dion had any hope for their kingdom. And while they put on a good face, Penny knew the two of them were crumbling to pieces inside. She saw it in the way Shaunie stayed quiet as Dion drowned himself in wine.

Penny rubbed her eyes with the heels of her hands. All she wanted to do was fall into the swift oblivion of sleep, but that wasn't going to happen. Not with all the stress eating away at her heart.

Mother was nowhere to be seen. Where had she gone? If she wasn't working with the rebels, what was she doing? Had she come into Faerie after the Mist went down? Faced the rebels themselves? The questions and scenarios swirled in Penny's mind like bees buzzing from one blossom to the next. They wouldn't stay still, and the swarm of them grew louder and louder. A sob bubbled up in Penny's chest and she pushed it down, as far down as it would go. She'd settle for somewhere between her knees and her toes if she could manage it, but it stopped around her stomach for the moment.

"Penelope?" Penny opened her eyes and found Aiden holding up the small, leaf-wrapped package that had been sitting on the desk. "What's this?"

She pulled herself into a sitting position on the edge of the bed, grateful for the small distraction. "The Aunties gave it to me weeks ago. They told me they were tasked with delivering it."

Aiden turned the package this way and that, much like Penny had when she'd looked at it in her alone time. "Who sent it then?"

Penny shrugged. "They didn't say. Only that it was a wedding gift. I didn't want to open it without you." Between the fire, dealing with the High Council, and Dion's visit, everything had been so busy she had nearly forgotten about it.

Aiden met her eye. "Do you want to open it now?" His mouth curved up into a smile, like a child on their birthday.

"I suppose," Penny said slowly. His eagerness didn't match the frantic buzzing in her head, but she had no good reason to deny the request.

He gave her a look of chagrin. "Sorry, I don't often receive presents. Well, I *didn't*. Faerie has changed that somewhat."

Every bee zipping about in Penny's skull quieted. "Of course we should open it." She patted the thick blankets beside her. "Bring it over."

Aiden crossed the room in two strides and sat beside her, his leg bouncing as he held up the tiny package.

"You go ahead," Penny said, a smile pulling at the corners of her lips. "Open it."

Aiden tugged at the knot at the top. The entire thing came apart in his palm, revealing the gift within.

A ragged strip of blue, satin ribbon.

Penny cried out, the sound bursting from her chest as she cradled Aiden's hands with her own. Her sight blurred and the sob she'd managed to push down to her stomach raced back up and broke out.

"Is this what I think it is?" Aiden asked, surprise clear in his widened, amber eyes.

Penny reverently trailed a single finger over the frayed edge. Tears burst from between her lashes. "It's"—her chest shuddered— "it's Sissy's lucky ribbon."

"I thought you lost it."

Penny nodded, the thoughts in her mind incoherent even to her. Aiden gently settled the ribbon in her hands, and she wanted to press the cool fabric to her heart, but worried about damaging the tattered strip further. The lucky ribbon had seen some hard times under Penny's care.

"There's a note," Aiden said, holding up a slip of ragged parchment Penny hadn't noticed within the package. Aiden began reading the note aloud.

> **MY SOVEREIGNS,**
> **I HOPE THIS GIFT FINDS BOTH OF YOU WHEN YOU NEED IT MOST.**
> **AM FEAR LIATH MOR**

Aiden set the parchment on the bedside table and turned back to look at the gift cradled in Penny's palms. "Do you want to see her?"

Penny's head shot up. "What?"

"Do you want to speak with Sissy?"

Penny looked back down at the ribbon and then up at Aiden. Of course. Why hadn't she thought of it? Aiden's gift was over the souls of the deceased. He could communicate with the dead. He could help her talk to Sissy—to apologize for her part in the maid's death.

Aiden fidgeted in the silence. "Though, with everything going on, I can understand if you don't—"

"I want to," Penny blurted out. "I want to speak with her."

Aiden's concerned expression remained, but he nodded. "All right. Where do you want to do it?"

Penny stood. "Let's go to the sitting room." While she had no idea what things dead people saw on a daily basis, having her young maid in the bedroom she'd been sharing with her husband the last few weeks would be... awkward.

Aiden sat beside her on the settee in the small sitting area separating their two rooms. They still hadn't moved their things from the separate rooms since their marriage, but there hadn't been time or care over the fact. There were more important things to do than worry over how big the room was where they slept.

"What do you want me to do?" Penny asked. Excitement and trepidation battled for the forefront of her feelings, but she tried to remain calm.

"I'll just hold your hand with the ribbon between our palms," he said, offering his palm.

Penny took a deep breath. How would this go? What would she say? A thousand questions burned at the tip of Penny's tongue, but she hesitated.

"What if it doesn't work? Or what if she blames me for her death?"

Aiden set both of his hands on each of her shoulders. "And what if you were given that ribbon as a way to assuage your fears and unfounded regrets? My gift can offer both peace and restitution. If it does become too much, you can simply let go."

Penny nodded quickly, probably more times than she should have. Aiden offered his hand once again and this time she didn't hesitate. Her palm met his, the blue satin ribbon pressed between their skin.

Magic tugged at Penny's core, and Aiden's veins glowed green and black down his arm toward where her fingers entwined with his. Penny felt the magic react to the tether, and she gasped as the vision of the golden-haired girl blinked into existence.

A wide smile broke across Sissy's face. "Hello, Lady Penny."

Penny heard herself cry out again, though she hadn't wanted to. Tears raced down her cheeks, and she nearly folded over completely, but Aiden wrapped his free arm around her middle to catch her.

"Please don't cry," Sissy pleaded. "There's a prickling where my eyes should be, and I don't know how spirits are supposed to cry when they aren't made up of anything other than the Goddess's power."

Penny covered her mouth, trying to contain the sobs. Sissy stood right in front of her. Penny didn't know what she'd expected, but Sissy was just as she'd always been, except for the wispy edges of her spirit. Penny took a few gulping breaths, trying to calm herself, but it wasn't working as well as she would've liked.

"I'm very pleased to officially meet you, Sissy," Aiden said, taking some of the attention from Penny, praise the Goddess. "I've heard much about you."

"Hello." Her lips turned down into a thoughtful pout. "I'm sorry, but I don't know whether to call you Lou, Aiden, or Your Majesty. I don't quite know how the whole hierarchy system works, what with me being dead and never having met you in person like this. I mean, I met you when you were staying at my parents' house, if you even remember that five second introduction. Until I died, I'd only known you as Lou, but now..." She shrugged.

He smiled. "Aiden is fine. Besides, I consider anyone who saves my wife a friend."

Sissy turned back to Penny and winked. "I knew you'd find your own path. Papa always said you were meant for something fantastic."

Penny swiped at her eyes with her free hand. "By the Goddess, I can't believe you're actually here." The tears had slowed, but they simply wouldn't stop. Even her hands had begun to glow with her loss of control.

"Oh, Lady Penny, you've no need to cry!" Sissy reached out but stopped. "I suppose I won't actually be able to wipe any of those tears away."

Penny shook her head. "I'm so sorry, Sissy."

Sissy tilted her head. "What do you have to apologize for?"

"You died!" Penny swiped her silk sleeve over her face, which didn't much help. Aiden handed her a handkerchief with his free hand, and she wiped her nose. "You died because of my choices. Because I got caught up in adventure and what I believed was justice for my duchy. If I'd paid more attention, used my brain, those rebels would never have had the chance to get into the house. I would've hidden myself better, thought through things more—"

"Even if you had actually done something wrong, you would've been forgiven long ago."

"What about your life? Your parents?" Even thinking about Aaron and Ada sent a sharp pain through her ribs. Their faces had still held that deep grief when she'd seen them last. "You had your whole life ahead of you. You had so much left to do."

"But what about all of this?"

Penny met Sissy's eyes. "All of what?"

"You and Aiden. Your exodus to the capital. Learning who The Cartographer really is. Coming to Faerie." She gave Penny a seeking look. "You do realize none of those things would have happened if that fire hadn't started and I hadn't pushed you out of the way. The Goddess does things for a reason, even if they may seem horrible. Her work will always push forward, in spite of the machinations of Her children."

"But you were innocent. How could the Goddess allow such a thing? There was no reason for you to die."

"Penelope..." Aiden began, likely noting her direction toward blasphemy, but Penny's attention remained on Sissy, who only shrugged.

"If I had to die so all of this could happen, it was worth it."

Penny bit her lips together and shook her head. Why was it that the dead had to be so... *reasonable* about their deaths?

"I don't think I could measure your death in such a way." Penny pressed the heel of her hand to her aching chest. "You were one of my closest friends, Sissy."

Sissy scooted a little closer. "You were one of my closest friends as well, Lady Penny."

Penny wanted to chastise her further, tell her to stop calling her 'lady,' but the words wouldn't come out. Sweet Gaia, she was a blubbering mess. She wiped her eyes again, the full green and black of her gift swirling up her arms. A few small blooms of alyssum popped into existence around her feet. She couldn't control the magic any more than she could control her tears.

Sissy's face drew close to Penny's. "I'm only sorry I couldn't be there to help you more."

Penny reached out, her fingers going to brush Sissy's face. The green glow met Sissy's cheek and Penny's fingers met skin.

Penny startled, her spine bumping against the settee and releasing Aiden's hand, making Sissy disappear before her, though where she'd just touched her cheek took longer.

"What?" Aiden asked. "What just happened?" His eyes remained on where Sissy had been, still able to see her with his gift while Penny couldn't unless she were touching him.

Penny returned to her place beside him and took his hand. Sissy's form returned.

"—and then I could feel her fingers on my cheek!" Sissy finished. Her eyes turned to Penny, fingers prodding at her cheek. "How did you do that?"

Penny opened her mouth, but without a proper explanation, no words emerged.

Aiden shifted, looking at their joined hands between them. His amber eyes danced with curiosity. "Let's do it again."

"What?" Penny and Sissy both blurted.

Aiden pulled Penny up to stand next to Sissy. "Touch her again. Let's see what happens."

Penny lifted a shaky hand toward Sissy once again. Sissy's wide, brown eyes met Penny's as she leaned forward, and Penny placed the tips of her fingers against her cheek once again. The green glow washed over Sissy's face as it lost its vaporous quality and continued to solidify all the way to where her bare feet met the stone floor.

A puff of air slipped from between Penny's lips, stirring the curls around Sissy's face.

The tears Sissy had been holding back finally slipped from her eyes.

30
STUDIOUS

"By the Goddess," Aiden whispered.

But Penelope's reverence flew out the window. She cried out in a ragged, relieved shout and wrapped Sissy in a hug with her free arm. Aiden, not having thought to take his hand from hers before being tugged toward the crying girls, gently extracted his fingers from Penelope's, allowing her to fully wrap her arms around the maid and taking the ribbon as to not damage it further.

The moment he did, Sissy lost her solidity.

Both girls cried out, passing through one another and stumbling forward. Aiden caught Penelope around the waist before she could fall to the floor.

"What—what happened?" she gasped out, head whipping around to look for Sissy who had likely disappeared from her sight again.

Sissy straightened and whirled in their direction. "Can we do it again?"

Aiden led Penelope back to the settee and returned his hand to hers. He felt her tension loosen as she saw Sissy once again.

"I don't understand," Penelope said. "How was she here?"

"I'm not sure yet." Aiden chewed on the inside of his cheek. "Let's do it again. This time, however, I'm going to let go and watch what happens."

They repeated the encounter, though Penelope only touched

Sissy's shoulder, and both were seated. When Aiden let go, Sissy faded back into her spirit form.

"What if I keep the ribbon?" Penelope asked next.

Dozens of different trials followed after that. Penelope would keep her magic connection open even after Sissy was whole. Aiden would be the one to touch Sissy. Sissy would hold both their hands as she became whole.

All of them failed to keep her there.

After the thirtieth, Penelope fell back into the cushions, defeated. "I don't understand why the Goddess would torture us in this way. Why allow her to become whole at all if she would have to be attached to us the entire time to keep it?"

All three of them kept their hands connected, both girls unwilling to lose the connection and Aiden not willing to watch his wife cry any more than she already had.

"There must be something we're missing," Aiden mused. He thought about their gifts, combined and divided. His magic hadn't changed since becoming High King, but Penelope's had. Even the Aunties had said—

The Aunties.

Aiden pulled the two of them to their feet. "Let's go ask for some advice."

"From whom?" Penelope asked.

Aiden led the two of them toward the door. "We have three of the most knowledgeable fae on this planet. If anyone knows anything about the Goddess's will and the way Her magic works, it's them."

"Wait!" Penelope pulled him back toward the desk. "You need your blindfold in case we run into Dion."

"Right." With one hand, Aiden maneuvered the black silk onto his eyes. "You'll have to take the lead, Penelope."

Penelope pulled them forward and he opened the door. Aiden walked straight through and ran into a wall of leather and steel.

"Cousin?" Aiden asked.

"Aiden," Thaen said, confirming Aiden's guess. "I felt a... Who is that?"

Aiden's brows rose, shifting the blindfold on his face slightly. "You can see her?"

"Her? Who? Skies, she... I don't quite understand what I am

looking at." He spluttered for a few moments, which was very uncharacteristic for him. "What the blizzards is going on here?"

"Thaen," Penelope said, "meet Sissy, my maid. Although, I suppose she hasn't been my maid for quite some time."

"What does that even mean?" Thaen asked.

Aiden pulled their group into the hall, still not relinquishing Penelope's hand. "We'll explain on the way."

After divulging all the information to Thaen, they found the aunties in the library. He removed his blindfold and spotted the Aunties pouring over old scrolls Aiden couldn't even decipher. All three sets of eyes widened as Aiden recounted their story.

"My, my," Auntie Niomi said. "This is an interesting development." She lifted Sissy's hair. "Tell me, child, has your hair always had this hint of green?"

Sissy used her free hand to pull a section of her blond hair into view. "Actually, no. But now that you mention it, there is some green, isn't there?"

"Your skin too," Auntie Taddie said. "I imagine it might even darken with some sun."

"What does that mean?" Penelope asked, her hold on Aiden's hand tightening.

"I have a suspicion," Auntie Taddie said. "Bàsthaen, what do you see?"

Thaen stepped forward and squinted in Sissy's direction. "A number of things. Her magic looks like a mixture of the Goddess's magic mingling with Aiden's. Though that could be because Penelope's magic looks like the Goddess's. I can see her form, decidedly human, but it is not so much what I see as what I feel."

"And what is that?" Auntie Niomi asked.

"Before I went to investigate what Aiden and Penelope were up to, I felt this odd tugging on my soul, then the magic in the palace began acting strangely and when I found them, I knew the Goddess had done something no one had ever seen before."

"So, this is part of the Goddess's plan," Penelope said matter-of-factly. "But how do we make it permanent?"

The room remained silent. Aiden could feel everyone's contemplation as they thought it over.

A low murmur sounded from the table where the Aunties had been studying. "Binding."

Aiden turned with the rest of the group to where Auntie Tori sat in her chair, watching the group with trepidation.

"Of course!" Auntie Niomi exclaimed. "She is not actually bound to anything."

"What do you mean?" Aiden asked, not willing to broach the topic of Auntie Tori actually speaking.

Auntie Taddie sagged back into her chair. "When she was mortal, she was bound to her body the way every child born of a mother is. The Goddess created a system where a soul could be bound to flesh until that flesh withered away or no longer could hold the spirit. Since our young friend has already passed from this plane to the next, she must be rebound to something here in order to stay."

"And this new form won't work?" Sissy asked.

Auntie Niomi shook her head, the swirl of blue hair shaking as she did. "This form is still the form of your spirit and of magic. You need something here, created or born of this plane to bind your spirit to if you wish to remain."

"Like what?" Penelope asked.

"We cannot use something already inhabited by a spirit," Auntie Taddie warned.

"I can supply a body," Thaen said.

"Oh, gross!" Sissy said, her nose wrinkling in disgust. "I'm *not* going to inhabit someone else's corpse."

Thaen's face flushed slightly, and Aiden wouldn't have seen it if he hadn't been watching. Wind and snow, he didn't know Thaen *could* be embarrassed.

"I do not believe a corpse would be the right direction either," Auntie Taddie said. "But it needs to be something linked to the Goddess's magic as well."

"What about a tree?" Thaen asked. The Aunties grew quiet, and Thaen straightened from his embarrassment.

Aiden rubbed at his chest. With Penelope's magic linked to the growth of plants and the absence of a spirit within the plant, it might work.

"It is worth a try," Auntie Niomi said.

Aiden summoned one of the servants to fetch a sapling from the conservatory. They had a selection of trees for the palace staff to use for various things—most of which Aiden couldn't even guess at.

A werewolf returned with a potted tree and set it down in the middle of the library.

"How do we do this?" Penelope asked.

"Feel it out," Auntie Niomi suggested.

Penelope closed her eyes, and Aiden could feel her gift reaching toward the plant. He felt the tugs on his own connection as she pushed the magic this way and that, but his connection to Sissy didn't change.

After several minutes, Penelope frowned. "I can't seem to link the two, the magic of the tree being somewhat different than mine and therefore Sissy's."

A thought breezed across the front of Aiden's mind. "What if you grow the tree yourself?"

They called for another pot, this time only filled with dirt and a seed instead of an already growing sapling. Penelope easily brought the tree to life and a trio of oak leaves burst from the soil.

"What about now?" Aiden asked.

Penelope's concentration seemed to double as she pushed the connections further. Aiden felt the tug on his magic.

"It's working, but I can't get it to stay together. It's keeps coming apart like it doesn't quite fit right."

"What else do we know about the Goddess's magic?" Aiden asked. "Perhaps there's something we're missing."

"Names," Sissy mumbled. All eyes turned to her, and she blushed, though the color was a bit greener than normal for a human. "Before I met with you, I was told not to forget my name."

Penelope gasped. "Like the fae." She turned to Aiden. "Names are part of your magic. They bind you to those who use them."

"How do we use a name?" Thaen asked.

"The same as anyone uses a fae name." Penelope turned to Sissy. "Sissy, bind your spirit to this tree." Penelope closed her eyes, but nothing happened.

"Why didn't that work?" Aiden asked.

All three of the aunties turned to Sissy, a knowing glimmer in their eyes.

Sissy gave Penelope a guilty look. "Actually, Sissy isn't my real name."

"What?" Penelope gaped. "But even your parents called you Sissy."

Sissy blushed again. "Because they did it at my insistence. My name is awful, so I attached to the nickname Papa always used."

"What is your actual name?" Aiden asked.

Sissy grimaced. "Brighid."

"*Brighid* is not an awful name," Penelope said, pulling both Aiden and Sissy closer to put her hands on her hips.

"It is when no one can say it correctly because the more popular pronunciation is 'Bridgette.'" Sissy—or rather, *Brighid*—rolled her eyes. "Papa always made a point to correct people, since it's an old Sireadh name, so I simply stopped going by it."

"Let us try it again, then," Auntie Taddie encouraged, obviously as eager to figure this out as Aiden himself was.

Penelope closed her eyes, connecting with the tree once again. "Brighid, bind your spirit to this tree."

Aiden felt a tug in his chest and a flash of green blinded him as the magic took hold. When the light faded, he blinked back spots until he could see Sissy standing beside the tree. On her own.

Penelope squealed and let go of Aiden's hand to rush into her friend's embrace once more. Tears streamed down both of their faces. Sissy caught one on her finger and looked at it with awe. More followed.

"Well," Thaen said, coming up next to him, "this could certainly change things."

Aiden pulled his gaze away from the crying girls. "What do you mean?"

Thaen pointed at Sissy. "If we can bring others back the same way we did this girl, we may have a chance of doing this for more souls and gather an army big enough to fight this war."

Aiden grabbed Thaen's arm. "Your father."

Thaen's eyes went wide.

Aiden whirled on Penelope. "Love, we could bring everyone back."

The possibilities were endless. They could revive Fiadh. They could make their family whole again. And not just the family Aiden had met. Stars above, he could bring back his mother if he found something to link to her.

A faint throb of fear spiked within him, but the possibilities shoved it down. Death had no power over them, so long as they had the ties to bring them back.

Penelope's eyes spilled over with more tears. "Fee?"

A brownie appeared at Penelope's skirts. "Yes, My Sovereign?"

"Will you fetch what we need to summon King Fiadh's spirit?"

Fee disappeared for only a few minutes before returning at Aiden's side with the small portrait of the mutant unicorn. "Here you are, My Sovereign."

Aiden held onto the painting and pushed his magic out from him. Like before, it took more effort to summon Fiadh's spirit. His heart already ached slightly after their experiments with Sissy, but if he could bring Fiadh back, it would be worth every bit of discomfort.

Thaen held Aiden's wrist as Fiadh finally appeared.

A sad smile sat on his face.

Aiden's shoulders sagged, his small flame of hope extinguished before it could even light his soul. "I can't do it for you, can I?"

Fiadh shook his head. "I am sorry, Little Shadow, but there are limits to this new power you have been given."

Thaen dragged in a ragged breath.

Fiadh turned to him. "I am sorry, son. I know it is not what you wish to hear."

Aiden wrapped a tight arm around Thaen's shoulders, doing his best to keep the connection to him so he could see his father. "So, what limits has the Goddess made?"

Fiadh clasped his hands loosely in front of him, and his head tilted to the side as if he were listening to something. "The biggest is that you cannot bring full-blooded fae back to this plane of existence. We were created from the Goddess's womb and our bodies cannot be recreated. Humans, however, are born of the earth and the earth can be used to give them life once again. In addition to fae, you cannot bring back those that have died a natural death. No matter how young they were, if the Goddess called them home, it was for Her purposes alone. While She has Her hand in all things, She does allow those taken by another's will to return to this plane if they wish."

Aiden nodded. "Then, Sissy agreed to this from the beginning."

"She did," Fiadh said. "You have figured out most of the rest. The binding must happen, and you must have the tree magically grown. Penelope is an integral part to this. Both of your gifts combined are the only way to perform this feat."

"So, if we are to bring more humans back, it will take both of us."

Aiden rubbed a hand down his face. The possibility of bringing an entire army back to life was dwindling.

"Do not forget about the tether either," Thaen said, nodding down to Aiden's hand still holding the miniature portrait.

Aiden hung his head. Faerie didn't have access to many humans nor things that could be used to connect them to the Aiden's magic. To create the army they would need, he would have to collect thousands of items, and Faerie simply didn't have that many humans. Even if he could go to Olympia, it would be nearly impossible to collect such things.

It was hopeless.

"Do not give up hope so easily, Aiden," Fiadh said as if reading his mind. "There is a way to do it, and I will not leave until we have uncovered it together."

Penelope approached them. "Well?"

Aiden stuck out his elbow and she connected to him. Her eyes went wide as she took in Fiadh's form. "By the Goddess, you two could be twins."

"I will take that as a compliment," Fiadh said. "We were just trying to figure out how to use your new connection with my young cousin to win this war."

"And what have we come up with?"

Aiden—with Fiadh's input—brought her back up to speed. Saying it all aloud again made the hopelessness more real. Durant still had the support of thousands on her side. It would take thousands of trees, thousands of items, in order to bring all of those souls back to this plane. There was no logical way they could put possibly pull this off.

"So, what kind of tether would we need?" Penelope asked. "Any kind of loyalty to something would do?"

Fiadh shrugged. "Possibly."

She turned back to Aiden. "What about Olympia herself?"

Aiden tilted his head. "What do you mean?"

"Wouldn't the very ground hold some kind of link to her people? I know with plants the earth works with them which is why I can sense things under the ground as well as what the plants can see. There's some connection there. Wouldn't the loyalty to a kingdom also connect someone to it? What if Olympia herself were the tether?"

Thaen cocked a brow. "It would weed out any unscrupulous individuals. Only those loyal to Olympia would return."

Aiden turned back to Fiadh, only to see him slowly fading.

"I told you I would stay until we uncovered it. Well done."

"Wait!" Aiden said, hope finally regaining its strength within him. "I have more questions."

Fiadh shook his head. "The time for questions is over. Be well, my sons. The battle is only just beginning, and your army awaits your orders."

31
REUNIONS AND BETS

Penny sagged back into the chair of the family sitting room, a sliver of peace easing the aching of her heart that had plagued her for so many months. Aiden rested just down the hall, his spirits sunken, but hope growing within him. She prayed he got some rest before the stresses of tomorrow arrived. If they really could raise an army, it would change everything.

Sissy sat in the chair across from her, an equally pleased smile on her face. "So, you thwarted all of Her Grace's plans and ended up marrying a king of a different kingdom and got yourself trapped here in the process?" Sissy chuckled. "If you would have told me when I was working in Barclay Manor that this was in your future, I'd have said you were insane."

Penny laced her fingers in her lap. "I would have called myself insane, yet here I am."

Sissy leaned forward and placed a hand on Penny's knee. "And I'm so glad. I know this path has been wrought with strife, but I can see how much you've grown since I last saw you. Then, you were a girl trapped under her mother's misguided protectiveness. Now, you're High Queen and you are changing the world."

"When did my *younger* maid become such a beacon of wisdom?" Penny asked a little sarcastically. She fidgeted with the end of her braid. "It feels more like those changes are leading us to ruin."

"Nonsense," Sissy said. "There are so many people who dream of things like this and you're living it."

"Then why does it all feel like such a nightmare?"

The corners of Sissy's mouth pulled down. "I don't know why some people can't see the Goddess's path. I don't understand how they can think they're doing the right thing when people are being persecuted. But it's also not my job to understand them. It's my job to stand up for what I know is right and hope they can one day understand why."

Penny shook her head. "You talk about my miraculous change, but you've failed to acknowledge yours. The Sissy I knew wasn't so wise about the ways of the world, though perhaps I only took it for granted before now." It may have been less than a year, but Sissy still didn't look a day over sixteen.

Sissy sank back into her chair. "I learned a lot on the other side, Penny. There are so many things I wish I could share with you, that I wish you could know for yourself. Even if I could explain what life is like in Danu's realm, I don't think you'd believe me."

"You can't try?" Penny asked.

She sighed. "When I was told I would get to talk to you again, I made a promise not to reveal certain things. A sort of geas if you will. What I can say is this life, while so important to what the Goddess has made for us, is nothing compared to what waits for us beyond."

A sinking feeling pulled at Penny's gut. "Do you miss it? Was I selfish to keep you here, with me?"

"Absolutely not," Sissy said certainly. "I know now that this is what I was meant to do, why you were given back my ribbon and why your magic works the way it does with High King Aiden. While I'm no longer fully human, my work on this planet is not finished quite yet."

"Why do you think the Goddess has done such a thing?"

Sissy brows drew together in contemplation. "While I cannot begin to guess at the full reasons of the Goddess and Her plans, I know that my return is part of the answer to winning this fight and restoring balance to the magic of this land. I think your very striking assassin was onto something when he mentioned creating more of my... kind."

Penny's mind caught on that last sentence. "Striking? You think Thaen—The *Lòchran*—is *striking*? What kind of striking?"

A hint of green deepened at her cheeks and she opened her mouth, but a knock cut her off.

"Curses," Penny muttered as she got up to see who was at the door. Sissy blew out a relieved breath, but Penny was not going to let her off the hook that easy. She thought Thaen was *striking*? The only striking Penny associated with that brute was with swords or fists.

Penny opened the door and found Shaunie standing on the other side, her eyes determined, and her lips pressed tightly together. They'd seen one another earlier at supper, but after everything that happened with Sissy, there hadn't been much time to speak besides at the meeting with the Council earlier. It had all been so official, but Shaunie's expression said this was to be somewhat off the books.

"Is Denny here?" she asked, glancing over Penny's shoulder.

"He's asleep in the other room," Penny answered, "but I can go wake him if it's something important."

"No," Shaunie said quickly. "I just need to speak with you."

Penny moved to the side and allowed Shaunie to pass by. Sissy stood and gave a deep curtsy and a welcoming "Your Majesty." Penny introduced the two of them as simply as she could, then pulled another chair close to where she and Sissy had been talking. Shaunie fell into it as if the world were pressing her down into it.

"What's going on, Shaunie?" Penny said.

Shaunie pressed her fingers into her forehead, hiding part of her face from Penny's view. "I didn't want to come here tonight, Penny, but I had to." She pulled her hand away, revealing her growing tears. "We leave to return to Olympia tomorrow night, and we need your help."

Penny took one of Shaunie's hands in hers. "What can I do?"

Shaunie took a deep breath, regaining some of her stalwartness. "We need you to come back to Olympia."

A breath caught in Penny's throat, making her choke. "What?"

"I know you've found happiness here with Denny, but we need you to help us. With Lady Barclay off only the Goddess knows where, your magic may be the only thing that saves us. We need the food you can provide, the strength of your magic."

Penny shook her head. "You know we can't grow food like that." Too much magical influence on the crops could cause more problems than less. Her magic could help for a short-duration crop, but anything with a growth cycle of more than a few months would lose too much nutrition to be a viable source of food. Mother had been quite vocal about that particular aspect of their gifts. There was no rushing nature without consequences.

"Then come back to help us figure something out. The king's council has fallen into disarray since your disappearance, and I know it's partially because of Her Grace's departure. Even Dee has been less sure of himself. He hasn't been able to do anything, and I fear he's going to lose the will to try anymore. We need people who can lead. We need you and your mother, if we can find her. Without you, we can't get our kingdom back."

"I—I can't," Penny said. "I can't leave Faerie."

"I know you just reunited with Denny—"

"No, you don't understand." Penny's hands flickered green and black with emotion. "I physically can't leave. If I leave the kingdom, I could die."

Shaunie's face paled. "What?"

Penny let out a breath. They hadn't revealed this particular news to Shaunie and Dion because they hadn't thought it relevant at the meeting. They'd apparently been wrong.

"I ate the Faerie Fruit. My life, my magic, is tied to these lands."

"But the fae can leave and they have magic. We know the humans can't leave because of the lack of magic, but why can't mages?"

"The Andàn told Aiden I had to stay here, that I am supposed to be here. Being High Queen might change all of that too. Aiden can't leave for more than a few days, or he would die." Penny snapped her mouth shut when she saw Shaunie's expression.

"The two of you married?" she asked, shocked.

"That didn't come out the way Aiden wanted it to." Penny swallowed. "We were supposed to tell you and Dion together tomorrow at breakfast. We wanted to give the news in a more private setting."

Shaunie wiped her face with a handkerchief she pulled from her sleeve. "That must be a lot, considering the whole mage thing."

Sissy huffed a laugh from where she listened in. "You could say that."

"Are you certain?" Shaunie asked, desperation tinging her words. "Are you absolutely positive you can't leave? If we found your mother, if you could help us get food to the people, it could be what wins us this war. We need you, Penny."

Penny opened her mouth to deny her again, but something stopped her. She *wasn't* certain. She couldn't be. She reached out and set a hand on Shaunie's knee. "I'm not going to tell you that I can, but I'll see what I can do."

Shaunie threw her arms around Penny. Shock zipped through Penny, making her limbs hesitate before returning the woman's embrace.

"I know it's a lot to ask but thank you."

Penny tightened her hold on the other queen as her heart raced and her mind spun. What could she do? The risk even just an attempt to cross the border could be too high to ask of Aiden, of Faerie. If she was simply Penny Barclay, heiress to the duchy of Eleusion, it would be a simple decision. She would do anything she could to help her people, but now? Now, she had an entire kingdom under her protection, a magic land that needed her, chose her to be its guardian. Leaving could upend everything.

But not going could ruin all their plans. Faerie needed the border open in order to get aid from Olympia. If what they discussed with Fiadh was correct, they would need access to Olympian soil, which was now heavily guarded by the rebels.

She pulled away from Shaunie, holding her by the shoulders. "You should get some rest. I'm sure Dion is wondering where you've run off to."

Shaunie looked at the door, face crestfallen. "Perhaps." She pulled away before Penny could ask why she seemed so sad. The door closed behind her with an almost inaudible click.

"So, what are you going to do?" Sissy asked.

Penny stared at the door, an idea forming in her mind. A wild, yet necessary idea.

"I'm going to talk to a *striking* assassin."

If anyone could convince Aiden to let her go to the border, walk across to her possible doom, and leave to save everyone on that side while everyone on this side dealt with Adira, it was Thaen.

"Absolutely not," Thaen grumbled.

"Come on," Penny said, jogging to match the fae's longer stride as they made their way to the training grounds. Shaunie's words had echoed in her head for the week since she and Dion had returned to Olympia, but this was the first time she'd been able to get Thaen alone. "Don't you think there's even a small possibility I'm not as tied to this Land as Aiden is? If I'm made up of the Goddess's magic, I should be able to carry it with me rather than have the source cut off."

"And what if we test your theory and you die, leaving my cousin ragged and broken?"

Penny's steps faltered. "Aiden is stronger than that."

Thaen raised a brow but kept marching forward.

"You and I could test it out."

"Have you told Aiden about your theories?"

Penny bit her lip. No, she hadn't, and Thaen obviously knew as much. If she had discussed it with Aiden, they wouldn't have been having this conversation now.

He harrumphed. "Your silence is answer enough. I will not go behind his back and risk your life to test a theory. Why are you pushing this? Are you so determined to meet your end so quickly?"

Was she? Penny couldn't exactly name what was driving this line of thought, but since Shaunie and Dion had left the night before, she hadn't been able to stop thinking about it. She hadn't figured out how to broach the subject with Aiden, but it was an avenue that needed to be discussed. It had haunted her dreams as she'd slept as well, but more than that, it felt... possible.

They made it to the training grounds, a few of the younger recruits nodding in Thaen's direction. He was a source of hope for them, but only a few of them even acknowledged Penny's presence. How could she change that? Now that they knew she was their queen, they were certainly less vocal about their disdain, only glaring at her from afar. However, it still wasn't what she hoped for. She was their High Queen. She would be, Goddess willing, for the rest of her life. Would she really live the rest of her life only being barely tolerated by the fae? It just didn't feel right. But she supposed it was better than fighting off assassins left and right. She had bigger worries to deal with anyway. She needed to help win this war.

"What would I have to do to convince you?" she asked as Thaen led her in the direction of the sparring ring. Penny tried to make eye contact with those she walked by. Most of them turned away, but she kept her head high and a genteel smile on her face.

Thaen hummed, dramatically deliberating her question before stopping outside one of the tents. "Nothing. You cannot convince me to go against Aiden's wishes or desires."

Penny grasped for straws. "What if I do all of my exercises without complaining?"

Thaen gave her a flat look and entered the tent, letting the flap fall closed between them.

She followed behind anyway. "Or what if I spar and beat every one of my opponents?"

"Not so difficult seeing as how you are more trained than most of them." Thaen began taking stock of the piles of weaponry.

That was true and she'd stopped sparring because of it. It wasn't polite to keep winning over fae who were already perturbed with her presence in the ring. And there was the whole thing about them not being able to harm her which made most of them wary to raise a blade against her.

"What if I beat *you*?"

Thaen huffed a laugh. "As if."

"What's that supposed to mean?" Penny set her hands at her hips. "Are you scared?"

Thaen turned back to her. "No, I am not afraid. You cannot beat me in the sparring ring."

"So why won't you agree?"

"Because I am not willing to see you injured and incur the wrath of my cousin." He summoned a weapon out of thin air, an abacus with rows of tiny, black beads to keep count as he went.

Penny almost asked how he did that but didn't want to get off track. "I could just stick my hand over the border. We'll bring Farrah with us in case she needs to whisk me back to her mother for quick healing."

He jotted something down in his magic notebook and then sent it back out of existence. "Or we could just not go at all."

Penny grabbed Thaen's arm before he could walk away. "Please, Thaen. If I have even the slightest chance of knowing my mother's all right, I need to take it."

It was easy to see the heartbreak in his face. She knew it had been a bit of a low blow, but it was true. The worry gnawed on her insides. She could see that same worry about his mother swirling in the back of his eyes.

Thaen rubbed a hand along the back of his neck. A family trait, Penny was learning. "All right."

She clasped her hands together. "You'll agree? You'll go with me?"

"Yes." A flicker of a smile tugged at the corners of his lips, halting Penny's near celebration. "If you beat me in a sparring match."

He walked out of the tent, leaving Penny to follow.

"Curses," she muttered. Yes, she'd been the one to suggest it, but actually beating him was likely impossible.

Thaen strode to the arena. Penny had to jog to keep up with him. A group stopped as they passed.

"Where are you off to so quick?" a member of the group asked.

Thaen didn't look up, but he answered, "We have some business in the sparring ring."

The group all turned to one another before promptly following behind, excited whispers branching out and spreading the news of the Lòchran's bout like water down furrows in a field, reaching every ear until the entire fortress trailed behind them.

Thaen reached the sparring ring first, sending the partners teamed up for practice out and taking his place at the far end. The crowd gathered around the perimeter, ready to watch the mage get taken down a notch. If anything, this fight might help her gain some empathy from her fellow trainees.

"Mage scum," someone hissed behind her.

Or not.

"Are you sure you want to do this?" Thaen asked.

Penny straightened, holding her head high even as imminent defeat stared back at her through Thaen's pale eyes. "Yes."

A savage grin stretched across Thaen's face. "Then draw your weapon."

Penny undid the belt at her waist, setting her sword and scabbard on one of the tables holding other weapons. Going against Thaen with a sword would have been an obvious mistake. The sword at his back looked more like a scythe, ready to reap souls like wheat offering up no resistance. Thaen chuckled and placed the glowing blade on the table beside hers. Next went the daggers and even the gloves Penny always wore when she sparred to make the fae around her more comfortable.

"Unless you have a hammer hidden somewhere up your sleeve, I do not know how you are going to fight me."

"Magic only," Penny said in her most steady voice. "You and I will only fight with magic."

Thaen stepped closer to her as murmurs circulated in the crowd around them. "Are you certain about this? It could cause more problems."

Penny looked about, catching the narrowed eyes of a few of the onlookers. "I'm tired of trying to play by their rules. I'm going to make my own."

Thaen pulled away, but not before Penny saw the glimmer of respect flash in his eyes. Oh, he was definitely starting to like her. She just knew it.

Penny had to stop herself from skipping to her side of the ring.

Commander Fàil stepped forward, his eyes—one blue and one brown—scanning the arena.

"Everyone knows the rules," he drawled, seemingly bored. "One weapon, first to yield. If your magic makes it out of the ring, you are disqualified." He gave Penny a look which obviously meant that last bit was for her. "On my mark, you may begin. Ready? Mark!"

Thaen rushed forward as soon as the fae jumped out into the protective shield.

Penny squealed and jumped back as he thrust a sword of shadow in her direction. "Hey! He said only one weapon!"

Thaen smirked. "When the weapon is magic, you can do whatever you want so long as it is created with magic." The sword morphed into a spear which he jabbed in her direction for longer reach.

"Curses," Penny spat as she summoned a shield of plants to block the blow. If Thaen hadn't hardened the shadow, it would have reached her through the physical shield for certain. She hurried back, out of range of whatever Thaen's next weapon would be.

A bolt of shadow shot past her face.

"Blizzards," Thaen bit out and drew another arrow.

"How are you doing that so *fast*?"

"It is my gift," Thaen said, as if that were an actual answer. He summoned a whip next and aimed for Penny's ankles. The end wrapped around her ankle, and Thaen yanked it hard enough to send her to her rump. She summoned a small dagger of wood and slashed the cord before he could drag her to him. Then, she was up and running. It was a game of cat and mouse, though Penny was finding she did not at all enjoy being the mouse.

She splayed her hands, her magic charging into the ground beneath their feet. Vines shot up from the ground, no seeds or water necessary. Penny stumbled a bit, still taken aback at how little encouragement the plants needed from her with her enhanced magic.

Thaen leapt over the plants, his increased strength sending him a dozen feet in the air. Penny cursed under her breath and raced to the side as he landed only a foot or two from where she'd just been standing.

"Give up yet?" Thaen asked, not even winded.

"Absolutely not," Penny said, breathless. By the Goddess, they'd barely started, and she was already gasping for air.

Thaen charged her with another shadow sword. Penny summoned a wooden sword of her own along with a shield. Both materialized in her hands, and if she hadn't been facing off with Thaen, she would have stopped to admire how quickly her magic responded.

But the looming shadow of Thaen's blade didn't allow for such thoughts.

Penny gritted her teeth and lifted her shield to defend against his strike. The wooden shield shattered against her arms, cutting through the thick fabric of her jacket and shirt all the way to her skin. She hissed as the shield was torn from her arm. The broken shield shattered against the packed earth. If Thaen had been any more care-less, her limb would have followed behind it. She lifted her sword to take back some control of the fight, but it was no use. Within a half of a blink, her sword joined its broken companion on the floor.

When she finished the second half of her blink, Penny found herself on the ground, a black blade hovering between her eyes. She closed them and allowed her head to smack back on the ground behind her. "Yield," she groaned.

The crowd around them cheered for their obvious favorite.

Penny opened her eyes as the sword that had called the end of their game dissipated into the vapors it had been made of. Penny reached out a hand to trail her fingers through the curling magic.

Thaen stuck his hand out to her. "You did better than I expected. You lasted an entire five minutes."

Five minutes? It had felt like an hour. Her body would be loudly protesting it later. Penny groaned again and took Thaen's proffered hand. He hoisted her up onto her feet. Doing her best to paste on a smile, Penny faced the onlookers. Many grinned at Thaen, the hero who had taken down the horrible mage queen. Penny would be somewhat jealous, except for the fact that there weren't any glares cast at her. If anything, only a mild sense of disregard in her direction. An improvement to be sure. She moved to follow Thaen out.

"Ho there, mage!"

Both Penny and Thaen stopped in their tracks and turned slowly to the speaker. The rest of the crowd hushed as well.

A centaur stepped into the ring. Penny recognized her as the Huntress, Dìoghaltas. She stopped a few paces away and bowed her head. "It is no small thing to face an opponent such as our illustrious Lòchran. I commend your courage and fortitude, My Sovereign."

Penny felt herself gaping and snapped her mouth shut. "Uh, thank you."

Dìoghaltas gave a short bow. "May Danu bless you with many glorious battles in your future."

Penny searched for words. She settled on "For you as well." It seemed to be the right answer, as the Huntress gave her an excited whinny and trotted back to the circle where a few other centaurs waited for her.

After looking around to make sure everyone had seen that and it wasn't just her wild imagination, she turned back to Thaen. "Maybe being pummeled into the mud by you wasn't such a bad thing after all."

Thaen led her back out of the ring, allowing the next pair of combatants to make use of it. She looked over her injuries, noting a few large scrapes down her arms that would need tended too, but nothing pressing.

The biggest injury was to her plans.

"So, you really won't allow me to go?" she asked.

Thaen continued walking, his face giving her no indication to his thoughts—as usual. "No. I will not give my consent to take you behind Aiden's back."

Penny's shoulders sagged.

"But"—he stopped and turned back to her—"I will back you up if you take the issue up with him yourself."

32
STUCK

"Are you out of your *blasted* mind?" Aiden stood at the head of the table of the war room, glaring daggers at Rìgh across from him. They'd been in there for hours that morning, trying to figure out how to get refugees moved into a more defensible location as well as the reports of rebel movement going back across the border.

"I only mean to say that now that the border is open, we should discuss a possible arrangement with King Dion," he huffed. "They were our lands once, before we had to remove ourselves behind the Fuath. With him indebted to us for aid, I am sure we could come to an arrangement for the kingdom to gain more land."

"You mean for the Day Court to gain more land," Sgiath barked back.

Rìgh shrugged, but Aiden cut him off before any more stupidity could fall out of the male's mouth. "We will not be discussing any sort of annexing on any kingdom's part. The Day Court should be more concerned with having *any* land by the end of this war, not trying to take that which hasn't been theirs for centuries."

Honestly, was it too much to ask that they get through this cursed war without having to cause any more problems?

A knock sounded on the door.

Perhaps it was too much to ask.

Thaen's head popped in, his recent return from the training

grounds made obvious by the mud on his boots and the armor he wore.

"Pardon me, but might I have a word with My Sovereign?"

Wind and snow. Thaen never called him *My Sovereign* unless he was waiting to deliver something Aiden wasn't going to like.

Aiden turned back to the High Councilors. "We can return after supper. I have duties I need to attend to, and I think it would be good to come back into this discussion with fresh eyes."

The Councilors filed out of the room, their voices low and quick as they bickered back and forth. The discord between them had grown in the last several weeks. It seemed no one was immune to Shirina's absence.

Aiden took a deep breath. "You needed something, Thaen?"

"Actually, it is your wife requesting your presence. I am simply the messenger."

Aiden tilted his head. "I'm surprised Dair didn't take the opportunity to play the page boy."

Thaen's expression stiffened, a thick mask falling into place. "Dair has not been acting much like himself lately."

Aiden had noticed it as well. Since Shirina's capture, Dair had withdrawn into himself, no longer flaunting about the palace or making fun at his family's expense. The twins were rarely together now. Even Aiden's family was falling to shambles.

By the Goddess, if only Durant would leave his family be.

Aiden followed Thaen to the family sitting room. It seemed an entire crowd sat scattered about the room. Auntie Niomi took pieces of bright-pink fiber from Sissy's hand and added it to a long line of twisted yarn wrapped around a whorl that spun on the floor between her feet. Auntie Tori quietly snored from her place on one of the large armchairs by the fireplace. Auntie Taddie muttered near one of the desks, fiddling with her carpet bag and pulling out item after item, all of which should not be physically able to fit inside. A hat stand, a mirror, a potted plant, and a lamp all came up and out. Aiden could create objects with his shadow, somewhat like using clay, but a sack that could carry actual things would be nice. Perhaps he could ask the Aunties if they had any spares.

His eyes found Penelope on the far side of the room, once again seated in the spot by the window she'd claimed as her own. Her green eyes watched him, the shine of adoration he'd grown accustomed to swirling with a shadow of trepidation.

"Aunties," Thaen called and then gave a quieter, "and Lady Brighid, would you allow us a moment of privacy?"

Auntie Tori's snores cut off abruptly.

Sissy wrinkled her nose. "Please don't call me that."

She stood to leave, but Auntie Taddie tsked and pulled her back into the seat. "Why would we do that when we know why you have gathered here? This conversation is important, and we do not wish to miss it."

"And Dair should be here any second," Auntie Niomi added.

Aiden quirked a brow. "I didn't realize a simple conversation with my queen warranted so much attention."

Auntie Niomi snorted. "If you think anything about this will be simple, you are much mistaken."

The beating of Aiden's heart took up a gallop. He drew up next to Penelope. "What's going on?"

Penelope rubbed her palms against the bodice of her dress. The vibrant purple of the fabric brought out the green of her eyes and the hints of red in her hair. His fingers twitched to run a hand through the long waves trailing down her back. They hadn't had nearly enough time together in the last few days. In fact, he couldn't remember the last time either of them had made it to bed without the other one already having fallen asleep.

"Aiden?" Penelope's eyes watched him.

"Yes, my love?"

"I have an idea, a theory about something that I'd like to test."

"What do you want to test?"

Dair's shuffling gait came through the doorway before she could answer. "My presence was requested?"

Aiden waved a hand, not taking his eyes of Penelope's expression. It was tight. Nervous. "Yes, yes. Close the door and find a seat."

The audible click of the door cued Penelope's continuation. She bit her bottom lip; a motion Aiden could not help but stare at as she stood from her seat. By the Goddess, he loved her. If no one else were in the room with them, he'd take her face in his hands and kiss her soundly right there.

A moment later, the glint of steel entered her eyes, and she straightened her spine. Aiden's wandering thoughts seemed to disappear. Her duchess—no, *queen*—persona slid into place.

Which meant nothing good for him.

"Aiden, Shaunie approached me the night before they left. She asked for my help with... with Olympia. I need to find my mother."

Aiden pulled her to one of the sofas. The rest of the family soon followed, encircling them in the other chairs. Skies, it was like being in a drama with a raptured audience.

"How is that supposed to help Olympia?" Aiden asked, ignoring everyone else. "No one even knows where she is, and even if she wanted to be found, it's very obvious she didn't want to aid them."

She wrapped one of his hands in both of hers. "If anyone can find her and change her mind, it's me. You know I can get her to help. They need me, Aiden, and I need to know she's all right. I need to know if she was ever part of the rebellion."

"But you can't. You can't cross the border." Aiden's chest tightened. Was she seriously considering this? It was impossible.

"We do not actually know if that is true," Dair supplied, slouched in a chair across from them. "We only assume that is the case."

"And I don't want to risk something happening on a theory," Aiden retorted. "We don't know if you can, but that means we also don't know if you *can't*. The bond you have with the Land is strong, possibly even more entwined than mine, and I can't leave for more than a couple of hours without growing ill if the accounts of the past rulers are to be believed. Even if you don't immediately..." He couldn't say the words. "Even if you could walk across the border, we don't know how long it would last."

"Aiden, I have to try. If not for Olympia or my mother, for Faerie. We have to access Olympia to bring more souls back. I can't do that from across the border. We both have to be touching it. Together."

He stood and Penelope's hands fell away from his as he began to pace the few feet open in front of the sofa. His gaze darted around the room until it landed on Thaen. "And what do you think about all of this?"

"I think you married a wise woman, and she wouldn't have brought this to you unless she had to. In fact, she attempted to talk me into taking her without your knowledge because she knew you would react like this."

Aiden whirled back toward Penelope. "You tried to talk him into taking you?" His chest began to ache. "So what? You were just going to portal into the heart of Olympia and pray you came back with your spirit still attached to your body?" His voice felt loud, it probably was, but he could barely hear it over the pounding of his heart. A shadow skittered at his ankles and swirled at the lace-trimmed edge of Penelope's dress.

"Of course not." He could see the temper snapping in her eyes, but only quiet words slipped between her lips. "I understand you're scared."

"Oh, I'm absolutely terrified." He stopped in front of her and knelt at her feet. "Do you know what it would do to me if you... if you didn't come back? Penelope, now that you're here, now that I've finally been able to hold every dream I've ever wanted in my hands, I don't know if I can let them go. I don't think I'm strong enough."

Penelope's soft fingers trailed across his jaw until her hands cupped his face. Her touch was the only thing holding him together. He felt he would just crumble to pieces with the rest of his kingdom.

"Listen," Penelope said, capturing his eyes with her emerald ones. "High King Aiden of Faerie, Lord of the Dead and Son of the Winter Queen, you are stronger than a broken heart. We live on a mortal plane, a place where death dogs our footsteps and hardship sniffs at our door, looking for fresh blood. This will not be the hardest thing you'll have to face. As rulers, thousands of lives depend on us every day, and we're going to make mistakes. There's always going to be the chance that we might not make it. If the Goddess wished it, I could drop dead right here, and there's nothing any of us could do about it."

Aiden's hands curled in her skirts as he set his forehead against her knees. "Don't say that."

Penelope ran her fingers through his hair. "But it's true. We can't know what the future holds for us. We can't claim to know what Danu has in store for us. We can only do our best, and right now, I know that our best is helping our family. Dion and Shaunie need my help. My mother needs my help. I can't leave them to suffer when I know I can fix it. I love them—your rascal of a brother included—too much to watch them face destruction when I could've stopped it."

Aiden clutched the thick skirts of Penelope's dress as if they were the only thing keeping him anchored to that moment. "Both of my brothers can face eternal torment if that means I know you're safe."

Penelope placed her fingers under his chin and lifted his eyes to meet hers. "You and I both know that's not true. Your brothers mean the world to you." She took a deep breath, tears gathering at the corners of her eyes. "Please, Aiden. Please let me try to save them."

Aiden closed his eyes. "Call for Farrah. I want whoever is taking us to be able to run."

The portal spit Aiden and Penelope out onto the cold, moonlit sand of the Farraige Gaineamh and they found Farrah at the base of the dune. Dair, Thaen, and Sissy—who had insisted she be brought along when she'd heard them planning the night before—slipped out behind a moment later. Farrah dissolved the portal and the five of them crouched low as they scaled the sand on quiet feet.

Farrah had gone ahead to check for a save place and to measure the dunes before summoning a portal for all of them. With the way the dunes shifted, they could have ended up in the middle of a mound of sand or thirty feet above one.

She'd also scouted out the rebel encampments.

Thaen snuck over the top of the dune ahead of them. The clatter of soldiers caused Aiden's gut to quiver.

They were too close.

Aiden held onto the glamour he cast over the group and found his connection with the Land. His mind's eye flew above them, seeing their group from behind before turning to where Thaen crouched at the top of the dune. Aiden pushed himself forward until he stood beside Thaen.

A battalion of rebels marched over the sand.

The rebels had taken up sections of the border on the Olympian side. To the west of them, Spring's border swarmed with rebels. The patrols had been thick when Aiden had used his magic to search for any openings along the gray line where the Fuath had once stood.

Which left the border along Summer in the east. The dunes covering the Farraige Gaineamh prevented easy access to water, and the heat could be scorching this far into the summer months. It would roast a man in his armor to go across during the day.

But night would work for Penelope just as well as it would work for the rebels. They'd been monitoring the rotations on this side of the border, far enough from the coast where the Aigeans patrolled and the heavy rebel presence in Spring. The rebels had been sending battalions through Olympia during the heat of the day to watch the border, then sending them across as soon as the sand cooled enough not to burn their feet. Which meant she would only have this short chance to cross the border between the time the newest soldiers moved on and when the next group would arrive sometime within the next few hours.

It was now or never.

Aiden didn't speak as he held Penelope's hand in an iron grip and crept up the dune. The soft sands blew past their faces, the heat swirling and the dying sun creating mirages over the crests of the dunes around them. Could all of this be a mirage? Would Aiden get to the border only to realize none of this was real and the fear escalating with every step, every heartbeat, was all for nothing?

But the image in front of him was very real.

An entire army moved northwest over the sand, headed in the direction of Spring. Horses hauled supplies over the sand, wagons and sleds rendered useless over the dunes. Iron chains rattled and more than one fae slave staggered through the sand behind the horses.

Aiden's fists clenched and he felt his blood boil. Before he could do anything, Penelope pulled him back.

"Look," she said.

Aiden tugged the glamour he had around their party tighter then followed Penelope's gaze. The hills of Olympia's border stretched out before them. The sands ended with that gray line of gravel before giving way to lush trees and colorful blooms. Aiden had only seen it through his connection with the Land, but looking at it now sent a small hint of longing through him.

He looked over at Penelope, who had that same longing written all over her face.

Thaen stopped ahead, signaling for their party to join him at the base of one of the dunes. Penelope pulled Aiden toward the line of gray at Thaen's feet. The sand bled a few inches into the gray gravel. On the other side, tufts of yellow grass stuck out between the pebbles as well.

"Is this it then?" Farrah said, wiping a bead of perspiration from her brow.

"This is where the Fuath began." Thaen pointed forward. "It covered about a hundred feet of ground from here to there."

"It's so short," Penelope said.

"It's odd to believe such a powerful thing could be so small," Sissy added.

Thaen glanced back at the girl before clearing his throat. "Farrah, please get into position."

They'd formulated a plan before they'd left Eagallach. Farrah would stand on the Olympian side of the border, ready to whisk Penelope back to Annalysa if anything went wrong. Thaen would walk across with Penelope, claiming he was the best fae for the job. With his ability to see, it made sense for him to cross over with her in case there were any traps lying in wait that he could see in the sand. He also didn't want both his king and queen in a compromising position. When Aiden had tried to veto that particular part of the plan, Penelope had stopped him.

"We know you're safe to cross," she'd said, "and I trust that everything will go completely fine, but are you willing to risk our entire kingdom in the event that it doesn't?"

Dair and Sissy would stay behind with Aiden, Dair with the task of tackling him if he tried to go across and Sissy with the job of moral support. Aiden suspected she had wanted to see a piece of home, even if she couldn't cross over. With her very direct connection to the Land's magic, they decided she couldn't risk such a thing. Penelope had been very worried about it. A stark contrast to the concern over her own safety.

Aiden looked down at the marvelous woman walking beside him. What else could he have asked for? He'd always known Penelope cared about others. Deeply. It was part of who she was, part of what made her such an amazing woman. She cried over broken flowers. She raged at the unfairness of Aiden's upbringing. She laughed at Dair's jokes and put up with Thaen's mood swings. She walked into the training grounds every day, surrounded by folk who despised her, and worked to prove that she was there for them.

She was a queen. His queen. And right now, she needed him to trust her.

Farrah stopped about two dozen feet from them and turned around.

Penelope squeezed his hand and slid her fingers from his.

"Wait," Aiden said. He retook her hand and pulled her to his chest. He planted a firm kiss on her lips.

She shoved him away, dislodging the scarf that had been covering her hair. "Take that ba—"

"I'm not saying goodbye, love." He pulled the cloth back up to cover her head. "Only good luck."

Her eyes widened in understanding, and she pulled him into a tight hug. "Thank you."

Before he could utter the refusals clawing up his throat, she released him and took her place at Thaen's side.

"I do not know if I can even watch," Dair whispered.

Sissy swatted at him, a break from the usual decorum she showed around the rest of them. "Are you trying to make everything worse?"

Dair snapped back something, but Aiden had already tuned them out.

Penelope had reached the edge.

Aiden held his breath, his gaze glued to her boots as they stopped inches from the gray stones.

He could feel her trepidation through their connection. It should have relieved him that she was somewhat frightened of the insane task she was about to perform, but it didn't. If anything, it made him want to rush up there and hold her.

Thaen leaned over and whispered in her ear, but Aiden was too far to hear what he said.

Penelope took a visible breath and lifted her boot.

Within that single breath she left the kingdom.

Aiden's heart stopped as she turned around and flashed him her most glorious smile.

She took a few more steps, each one faster than the last until she was sprinting over the gravel. When she reached Olympia's side, she laughed, the joyous sound ringing through the air. She splayed her hands and white daffodils popped up around her feet. She ran back in his direction, a trail of flowers growing in her wake.

He opened his arms for her, and she leaped into his embrace. He spun her around in a circle and crushed his face into her hair. If he held her tight enough, maybe she wouldn't leave. Maybe, they could stay together.

But as he held her with everything he had, he knew it would never be a possibility. Penelope was a queen in every aspect of the word. She would do whatever it took to help her people—both on this side and that side of the border.

They stopped spinning, and Penelope pulled slightly away from him.

"Sissy, it's time to pack my things. I'm going to find my mother."

33
HOME AND FAMILY

Penny stood in the Great Hall, bouncing on her toes.

The pack on her back pulled at her shoulders, despite being lighter than the one she'd carried through Faerie those first few months. She didn't need half as many supplies this time.

Aiden paced in front of her, his High King mask firmly in place as they brainstormed places Mother could have disappeared to. "Have you thought about going to Lord MacGregor? With your family's connection, he might know where she is."

She had thought of it. Multiple times. Scenarios had been dancing about her head all through yesterday and this morning. "Yes. Paulo may also have seen something as well. He will be my next stop after the Hermens'."

"Do you think she would've returned to Eleusion?"

Penny nodded. "Perhaps, though she'll be harder to find there if she did. I'm hoping she's kept in contact with *someone* throughout all of this, and it'll just be the simple matter of finding out who."

"And you know what to do if you begin to feel at all poorly?"

Penny wanted to tease him for worrying, but she didn't have the heart to right then. "Of course. I'll have Farrah bring me directly back." Aiden had been so concerned about her growing ill and not making it back to Faerie. Farrah would be accompanying her the entire journey, making travel through the kingdoms faster, but also ensuring her safety if anything went wrong. Farrah would portal her straight to Annalysa if anything bad happened.

But Penny wouldn't allow anything to happen. She was supposed to do this. She knew it and the Goddess had told her so. Standing on the other side of the border had felt like destiny. Even though she knew Faerie would forever be a part of her now, she knew returning to Olympia was just as important as eating that fruit.

The giant doors to the Great Hall opened, and Thaen walked in, face contorted in anger. Dair followed on his heels, a pack slung over his shoulder and a furious expression hard enough to rival his twin's.

"What's going on?" Aiden asked.

Thaen actually growled. "Tell Dair that he is *not* accompanying Penelope into Olympia."

"What?" Penny asked.

Dair rolled his eyes. "I am not a child, Thaen. I can make my own choices."

"Not if they are stupid ones." Thaen turned back to Aiden. "Tell him he cannot go."

Dair pushed forward, knocking into Thaen with his shoulder. "Aiden is *not* my *athair*, and neither are you. You cannot keep me here."

"I will lock you in the frosted dungeon—"

"Enough," said Aiden. He stepped toward Dair. "Why do you want to go with Penelope?"

Dair's lips thinned for a moment until he probably realized Aiden was asking him in earnest. "Someone ought to go with her. We cannot guess what Olympia looks like from the other side. While I think it good that Farrah will be with her, I believe you should have someone with more diplomatic ties as well as another fighter. I know Penelope knows how to handle a blade, but it would be better if she had another to watch her back."

"You can fight?" Penny asked.

Dair rolled his eyes. "You know I'm *twin* to the frosted Lòchran, right? Who else was he going to spar with?"

Penny's thoughts began to whirl. If Dair went with her, it would open up a few things she hadn't thought of. His gifts with dreams may be able to help locate Mother through others' subconscious. Having another fighter alongside her would also be a boon.

She looked up at Aiden with interest. How would such an idea play out in his mind?

Aiden's head tilted to the side as he studied his cousin. "Convince me to ignore Thaen's obvious attempt at mental compulsion targeted my direction."

Penny smiled when Thaen folded his arms over his chest and averted his eyes.

Dair kept Aiden's gaze, almost like he was trying his hand at his own mental compulsion. "I want to prove myself worthy, Aedon."

Thaen's head whipped in Dair's direction, but Aiden only quirked a brow. "What are you supposed to prove yourself worthy of?"

Dair blew out a breath. "I know of your intention to name me King of Winter."

Thaen took a step forward, but Aiden held up a hand to stop him. "And why does that affect what's happening now?"

Dair looked at the dark marble beneath their feet. "I am not a leader, Aiden. I am not like my brother, that can fight off any attacker. I am not like my father that had enough room in his heart to fit an entire kingdom. I am not like my mother that could stranglehold an entire council of folk with a simple word. I have only ever been the jester. I cannot possibly imagine how to win the respect of those I would be asked to look after. I do not know enough about myself to even try."

Aiden shook his head, but Penny could see how much Dair believed that of himself. How long had Dair been suffering with this absence of purpose? She knew he had been struggling since his mother was taken and even before that with his father's death. It wasn't good for anyone to be without hope, without a cause to take up and to fight for. Even with his support of Aiden and the kingdom, Penny could see his struggle, see how he felt so useless and alone when everyone around him was making decisions so much bigger than what he could do. She remembered the feeling, that cage of uselessness.

Penny stepped forward and set a hand on Aiden's arm. "I think he should come."

"You think what?" Thaen demanded.

But Penny kept her eyes on Aiden. On her husband.

His amber eyes looked back at her, somehow reading what Penny thought without a word passed between them. She saw him come to his decision before he likely realized he had. He turned back to Dair, a serious expression on his face.

"I don't know why you believe you need to prove anything to anyone. I would name you Winter's king simply because I believe you're the best suited for the job, even in your current state. No one else knows the people of this kingdom like you do." Aiden blew out a breath. "But I'm also not going to say no to sending Penelope out there with someone I trust."

"You cannot be serious," Thaen said.

But neither of them acknowledged him, much to Penny's relief. Instead, Dair wrapped his arms around Aiden. "Thank you, cousin. I promise not to let you down."

Aiden pulled back and met Dair's eyes, two mirrors looking at one another. "You have never once let me down. I only hope this will show you how much you're truly needed here."

Dair nodded and stepped back. Thaen pulled him aside, and Dair let him, the steel in his eyes sharpened with hope.

Aiden stepped forward and blocked Penelope's view of them. He stood so close he blocked the view of nearly everything. "Are you sure this is a good idea?"

A small smile tugged at her lips. "I think Dair and I will be just fine. Perhaps this will help him understand better."

"Understand what better?"

"Us. Humans. Mages. You're the only member of the royalty that's been on that side of the border since your mother. Perhaps Dair will gain some insight none of us can see simply because he's a fresh pair of eyes."

Aiden hummed, but she couldn't tell if it was in agreement or not. Then he settled his hand at her waist and pulled her forward enough that his forehead pressed against hers. "Are you really doing this? Are you really leaving me behind to go battle our enemies and save my brother's kingdom without me?"

Penny tried to seem lighthearted, even as something in her very heart sank at the idea. "You've had enough turns saving your brother. I figured I could have a chance."

Aiden closed his eyes. "If anything happens to you, I'll portal straight to wherever he is and kill him, Durant's command or not."

"Nothing's going to happen. Dair and I are taking a little stroll into Olympia, and we'll be back before you know it."

Several deep breaths filled the space between them.

"I love you," she whispered.

"As I love you," he whispered back. "Come back to me, all right? At least so I can make sure you're safe."

Penny pulled back and tapped the soft cloth of his shirt over where his heart beat. "You will know, just as I'll know that you're safe." She pulled close once again, wrapping her arms around him. "Please don't do anything foolish while I'm gone."

Now it was Aiden's turn to pull away. "Foolish? When have I ever done anything foolish?"

Penny arched a brow at him.

A whoosh of black sprouted against one of the walls, and Farrah stepped through. "Hello, friends. Are we ready to set off on a grand adventure that could mean the balance between good and evil, possibly ending in our horrible and gruesome deaths?"

Penny shot her a glare, but Farrah only smiled as she walked in their direction.

"That is not the kind of preparatory speech any of us wanted," Dair said, coming to join them.

"Ah, but was it the one you needed?" Farrah asked. "This is a serious endeavor, Prince Bruadair. If you truly wish to join us as I suspect by that rather large sack on your back, you need to be sure you understand what's at stake."

"I know what is at stake."

Farrah's expression turned grave. "Let's hope so."

With a flick of her wrist, Farrah summoned another portal along the wall.

Aiden's arm tightened around Penny's waist. "I know this is what you're meant to do, but would it be horrible of me to admit that I wish you didn't have to go?"

Penny turned to look up at him. His height and regal bearing always made him seem so sure of himself, but she could see the fear swirling in his gaze.

Penny grabbed at the lapels of his coat and pulled his face toward hers. Their lips met, the touch sending sparks down her spine and flaring where his hands came around her back. His touch was darkness and light, only enhanced by the bond they shared. Aiden moved one of his hands into her hair, deepening the kiss. She let him. Sweet Gaia, she couldn't do anything else as he drew her even closer until she could feel his heartbeat under her hand. She was going to miss him as much as he was showing her he would miss her. If she was a weaker person, she'd have taken his hand and fled back to their room, leaving the Goddess to save Olympia if She willed it. Penny would lock Aiden in there with her and forget the world outside those walls.

But Penny wasn't weak, and she couldn't forget.

She pulled away, her cheeks flushed and breathing heavy. It would take her a lifetime to get used to the intensity of his love.

He pressed his forehead against hers. "Come back to me."

She pressed her mouth against his one more time before finally pulling herself from his arms. "I will. I swear it."

34
DIVIDE AND CONQUER

PENNY'S FOOT LANDED ON SOFT CARPET AND HER LUNGS TOOK IN A BREATH. The feeling of the bond on her heart tugged at her, like a string stretched taut, waiting for her to come reeling back.

And she would.

After she found Mother.

Dair stepped through in the next moment, his silky hair slightly mussed from the intensity of the portal. He looked around the space, his amber eyes wide. "Where are we?"

Yellow furniture with gray accents sat scattered about the room. The standard of a winged helmet hung over the door. A sleeping fireplace lay opposite the tall windows, showing a sunlit garden on the ground floor below. Yellow roses lined the pathways outside. Penny recognized the sitting room Farrah had dropped them in. She'd played here many times as a child while Mother had been doing business in the study across the hall. As a teenager, she and Angelica would have tea right next to the window to watch her younger siblings play tricks on one another.

Farrah closed the portal with a wave of her hand. "Welcome to House Hermen, Prince Bruadair."

Penny looked up when she heard the pounding of feet from the floor above them. A female voice hollered something, and more feet went scrambling.

"Are we under attack?" Dair asked.

Farrah stepped over to the window and looked in the direction of the front part of the manor. "There's no army at the gates."

A scream cut through the air.

Penny and Dair both ran for the door, swords in hand.

Recalling her time spent in the house, Penny directed Dair and Farrah toward the stairs. Most of the commotion was happening on the stories above them. If Penny remembered right, the house had three floors above ground and a cellar below. There were three staircases if she counted the servants', and the one they crept up led down to the front door. If there was an invasion, the intruders likely would have come through the front due to the larger gate on the front of the property with easy access to the road, but they could have already swept through the first floor, as it seemed eerily empty.

Another shout rang through the air as Penny stepped to where she could see the next level. A pair of maids rushed across the hallway, carrying bloodied towels. Fear stood stark on their faces.

The voices farther down the hall grew clearer.

"Shaunie, you blasted witch!" Angelica screamed. "I'm going to *murder* you when this is over!"

Penny paused. It hadn't been so long ago that she'd come into a similar situation. She did the math in her head. It was a bit early, but not so much to be frightening. Shaking her head at her own foolishness, she sheathed her sword.

"What are you doing?" Dair hissed.

Penny smiled. "There's no threat here except Shaunie's aggressive delegating skills and Angelica's dramatic tendencies."

Dair gave her a questioning look and turned to Farrah for an explanation, but Penny saw that she had guessed what was happening as well. She held Dair back while Penny made her way up the remaining steps and followed Angelica's angry voice to where the rest of the women were gathered.

Shaunie stood at the end of the bed, arms working to wrap a bundle. "We won't have much time between them. Get ready to do this again." She passed the bundle to Lady Hermen, who tucked it to her chest and looked down in awe.

Angelica groaned, sweat beading at her forehead and soaking the tight curls framing her face. "By the Goddess, I'm going to die."

Devan wiped a cloth at her brow. "You're doing wonderfully, my dear."

"Don't 'my dear' me," she snapped at him. "This is all your fault!"

Penny took the final step into the room. "You know that's far from the truth. I believe you had just as much to do with this as he did."

Every head whipped in her direction.

"Great, now I'm hallucinating," Angelica said.

Devan shook his head, bewildered. "That's not your overactive imagination, love."

Penny smiled and came to stand at the side of the bed. She turned to Shaunie. "Do you need any help?"

Shaunie shook her head. "Not yet. We're just giving Angelica a break before we deliver the next one."

"Next one?" Penny asked.

Devan beamed. "We're having twins."

"Cursed husband," Angelica hissed between her teeth. Her face scrunched and Shaunie returned to her position at the edge of the bed.

"Here we go, people!"

Penny went to step out of the room.

"Don't you dare leave me here, Penelope Barclay!" Angelica snapped. She pointed to where her mother stood with the bundle in her arms. "That babe is your namesake, so don't even think about scampering off when I have to deliver her sibling."

Penny's heart flipped in her chest. "My namesake?"

Lady Hermen glided over to her. "Meet Penelope Sage Eile. They're planning on calling her by her middle name." Lady Hermen passed the baby into Penelope's arms.

The infant's eyes were closed, the child having snuggled down into the blankets to get some rest. Dark, fuzzy hair peeked out from the folds of the blanket. Her tiny fist tucked against her cheek. Penny brushed a flickering fingertip over the tiny fingers.

"She's beautiful," Penny whispered.

Lady Hermen nodded, smoothing the tiny strands of hair by the baby's ear.

Shaunie's voice continued to bark out commands and the maids around them bustled back and forth with new towels and dishes of warm water. Penny cringed as Angelica worked to deliver her second baby, but it wasn't too much longer until the wails of another infant cut through the room.

"Another girl," Shaunie said, placing the tiny infant in her mother's arms. She gestured for Penny to bring the other and soon both babies were nestled in Angelica's arms as Shaunie shed the outer layer of clothing she'd been wearing to attend to the births.

"Two healthy baby girls," Shaunie said wistfully. "The Goddess must be smiling down on you."

Penny came around the bed and wrapped an arm around Shaunie's shoulders. She didn't have words she could use to comfort the obviously broken pieces of the queen's heart. While Penny knew this work was so important to Shaunie, she couldn't imagine the tole it took on her.

Angelica looked up. "We've already picked the name for the second since we found out we were having two a few weeks ago. Would you like to hear it?"

Penny nodded.

Angelica looked over at Shaunie. "Her name is Regina Carnation Eile." A smile spread across her face. "Since being in Faerie, the whole flowers and nature thing really made an impact on our name choices. With the way our world is changing, we also knew these babes needed names that would be as strong as their spirits."

Devan smiled down at the little bundles. "And what two women are stronger than the very queens in this room?"

Penny felt tears track down her cheeks and looked over to see Shaunie with the same. Shaunie wrapped an arm around Penny and let the tears fall between them.

"When was the last time you saw my mother?"

Penny sat across from Lady Hermen in the sitting room where she, Dair, and Farrah had portalled in only an hour ago. Dair and Farrah sat next to her, the four of them circled around a small table holding tea and cakes. With Angelica and the babies resting, Penny had taken the chance to pull Lady Hermen aside and discuss why she was really there.

Lady Hermen sighed. "She came here after she left the capital.

She knew Stone had some kind of intelligence network, though she didn't fully understand what we were involved in." A twinkle sparked in Lady Hermen's eye, the first spy in the Hermen family to have been recruited by Aiden when he acted as Dion's spymaster. "When we received reports from Rissa, saying she didn't even know where you went, your mother disappeared. It seemed that no one knew where you'd gone, but Dominique had her own suspicions."

"What do you mean?"

"She thought Prince Aiden had taken you."

"What?" Penny asked. "Why on Gaia's green earth would she think such a thing?"

"She told me she'd seen him looking at you during King Dion and Queen Carnation's wedding ceremony. Said he'd been watching you in a way she didn't particularly like. She felt her fears had been confirmed when he stepped toward you before he was taken. The crowd had gone wild right at that moment, blocking her view of you, and when she'd been able to get up to the dais, you weren't among the other attendants."

"So, she suspected Aiden grabbed me before he disappeared?" Penny asked.

Lady Hermen nodded. "She came to me only a few weeks later, asking if Angelica had sent word of you in Faerie. She assumed you would reach out to Angelica as soon as you could. When I told her we hadn't had any news from Faerie in weeks, she grew frantic. She'd learned about the Mist locking up—reports had come into the capital, and she'd been harassing King Dion about getting her through the border before she came to me. I think she'd hoped we would have a direct line to Angelica."

"Did she say where she was going after that?"

"No. She disappeared the very next day without revealing her plans to me."

"What I do not understand," Dair said, "is that if she was in the capital, why would the Councilor that aided you not reveal your path through the portal?"

"That portal is a closely guarded secret," Lady Hermen answered. "I can't fathom what Lord MacGregor had to do in order to get Lady Alvis's help, but she's under strict orders not to reveal its location."

"She couldn't tell my mother what happened without revealing the information about the portal."

"So, who else would she have gone to?" Farrah asked.

Lady Hermen grabbed a sandwich from the tray in front of her. "If she wanted help from her friends, she likely went to Luciana."

Mater. She had been one of Mother's closest friends aside from Lady Hermen. It would make sense that she would go to the MacGregors. Not only for Mater's help, but also to speak with Paulo.

Penny turned to Farrah. "Have you ever been to Delphine?"

"No, but I helped a family move to one of the outlying towns. I could easily get us there, and we can portal hop to Lord MacGregor's estate."

Lady Hermen shook her head. "I wouldn't advise that. The rebels have been wreaking havoc on Lord MacGregor's lands. Practically every town outside of Delphine itself is crawling with them. Lord MacGregor's been able to hold them off with his men and the towns-folk, but if anyone caught you using magic, you'd likely be killed."

"What would you recommend?" Penny asked.

Lady Hermen thought for a moment. A smile stretched across her face. "We may be more or less done with the physical aspects of spy business, but Stone and I still have a few tricks up our sleeves."

35
LORDS AND LADIES

Dark gouges scored the earth on either side of the road. Centuries-old trees lay on their sides. Smoke trailed up into the sky, lazy and dark. The fields were bare of all life—animal or plant. The MacGregor family was known for their wide plains and hearty grazing lands. Their livestock were some of the most prized in the kingdom. The faint stench of charred meat tickled Penny's nose, a hint of what might have happened.

"I cannot believe you have subjected me to this torture, Penelope," Dair hissed from the back of the horse-drawn cart. He tugged at the rough spun shirt for the hundredth time, his face screwed up in disgust.

Lord and Lady Hermen were geniuses.

The couple had gotten in touch with a contact, a Sireadh friend, that still ran a profitable trading cart in the southern part of Olympia. With the war, the few Sireadh traveling tradesmen had found much business within the kingdom. People still needed supplies, wanted trinkets of good fortune, or wished to send word home to their families through whatever means they could. Sireadh were known for being trustworthy, and though the Hermen's friend wouldn't allow them to confiscate what he had from the rebel's side, he did allow them to borrow one of his carts. With a promise that they wouldn't besmirch his good name, he let the group pretend to be members of his company.

It also made it easier on the fae. Dair and Farrah only had to glamour their hair and ears to look more human instead of having to cover up their obviously fae clothing as well.

"It's not as if the fabric will kill you," Penny whispered back.

Dair scratched at his neck under his now brown hair, a pronounced pout on his lips. "No, but it may just chafe every piece of skin off until I am nothing but a pile of bones. And this heat is sweltering."

"Oh please," Farrah said from beside him. "This isn't even bad for an Olympian summer."

Dair shuddered.

"We'll be at Lord MacGregor's estate within the hour, Your Highness," said Lord Hermen from the front of the cart. "I'm sure the marquess will have something more to your taste."

Penny chuckled. "Paulo probably pays as much attention to his clothing as you do."

"Then he is likely the wisest man I will meet on this side of the border." His eyes flicked about, taking in the country as we rode.

As they drew closer to Iatrus Castle—the only other castle built in Olympia pre-Faerie Wars—the land around them grew darker, more scarred. Penny's stomach twisted. She checked the bond with Aiden again, but nothing seemed amiss. She missed him something fierce. Would this be what Faerie would look like before they rid themselves of the rebels?

"How did Paulo manage to hold them off from taking the castle?" Penny asked.

"While he may be a prankster," Lord Hermen said, "Lord MacGregor is one of the strongest lords in the kingdom in terms of military standing and mage gifts. It hasn't been easy for him, but he managed to hold them off before a good portion of them headed toward the capital."

"Is that why there isn't any sign of the rebels close to the castle?"

Lord Hermen shrugged. "They halted the siege about three weeks ago, though I don't expect them to stay away for long. While Iatrus Castle may have withstood the barrage and become more nuisance than it was worth, I think The Cartographer simply put taking the castle on the back burner. The host in Eleusion has been having some upheaval from what I've heard. I suspect, if The Cartographer takes the north, she's planning to come back with the larger host and use both forces to overwhelm Iatrus Castle."

Penny's heart sank. "Oh, Paulo."

"That is why we are here, Penelope," Dair said. "When we stop The Cartographer and end this war, your friends will be safe."

Right. She just needed to find Mother, explain what happened, take her to the border to bring their army back from the dead with Aiden, and help King Dion win back his kingdom. Then, they could fix everything in Faerie and wipe the rebels from existence.

Should be simple, right?

The land around them continued to get worse, until they reached the gates of Iatrus Castle. Penny had never seen them shut in all the time she'd been friends with the MacGregor twins. The walls around the castle boasted quite a few scorch marks and gouges, but they held strong. How many marks were left on the family after such destruction?

"Who goes there?" A single guard peered over the top of the wall, a crossbow steady in his hands.

"It's Lord Hermen, my good man. His lordship should be expecting us."

The guard nodded and pulled away. After a few seconds, the front gate began to swing open, only just enough for the cart to squeeze through before slamming shut behind them.

The wheels of the carriage clicked against the cobblestone drive, loud and irreverent in the quiet of the inner courtyard of the castle. The castle itself looked a little worse for wear. One of the three towers had been destroyed, its top half lying on the ground below it. A large chunk of the roof had fallen in what Penny remembered was the ballroom on the left side of the castle. Many of the windows were boarded up, the glass glittering in the dug-up gardens around the base.

Lord Hermen hummed as he took in the destruction. "It is somehow worse and better than I imagined it would be since Paulo had last sent word."

Tears gathered in Penny's eyes. How many of her friends had to suffer because of Adira's sick need for revenge? And revenge for what? A lost love who didn't even want her? She was a broken woman, and Penny couldn't even comprehend how broken she must be in order to perform such heinous acts.

"How do bronties cause such destruction?" Dair asked.

"They have abused the magic of others," Farrah answered. "If nothing else, humans are very good at exploiting the powers of others for their own gain. I often wonder if they learned such ways from the Tuatha Dé Dannan, or if we learned it from them and that's why everything went wrong so long ago."

The cart stopped at the bottom of the castle steps. Dair hopped over the side and Farrah followed as Lord Hermen helped Penny from the front seat. Penny still took in the destruction around them when her eyes caught on a glimmer at one of the windows above them. She looked up and could have sworn she saw someone in a silver mask, but she blinked, and they were gone.

When her feet hit the first stair, the large doors at the top opened. Two heads of flaming red hair barreled out the door.

"Penny!" the twins both shouted. Diana reached Penny first, scooping her up into a hug just before Paulo joined in on the crushing embrace.

"We've been so worried about you!" Diana said, finally setting Penny back on her feet.

A mix of relief and weariness pushed a laugh from Penny's chest. "About me? I've been going mad not knowing what's been going on with you. When Angelica sent word that you'd been under siege, I was heartbroken."

"It was nothing we couldn't handle," said Paulo.

"Obviously," Diana added.

Penny looked between the two of them. While they looked whole and hale, there was light missing from their eyes. Both of them had lost something of themselves in the months Penny had been gone.

"I'm so sorry," Penny said.

Paulo reared back. "What on Gaia's green earth do you have to apologize for?"

"I should have stayed. I should have been here to help you, to help everyone. Perhaps none of this would have happened if I'd stayed in Olympia."

Paulo set his hands on Penny's shoulders. "Listen to me very carefully, Penelope Barclay. I saw that future. I saw where you stayed behind and tried to help from this side of the Mist. Let me just say that I had that pack ready for you after the wedding and would have told whatever lies I needed to get you to go. That should give you answer enough, *Your Majesty*." Penny swallowed then nodded, not at all surprised that he knew about her new title. How Paulo could stand the fickleness of time and fate, she would never understand.

"Don't you think it ought to be 'Your *Mage*-esty?'" Diana snickered.

Penny rolled her eyes, but Paulo grinned. "I think 'Your Mage-esty' suits much better. Glad we got that sorted as there are introductions to be made"—he looked between the four new arrivals and grimaced—"and obviously some clothing to be burned."

Dair visibly relaxed. "Stars, yes."

Diana snorted as she pulled Penny after her brother and into the castle.

After a quick bath and a change of clothing, Penny felt much more herself. While Mater's light-pink gown hugged Penny's curves a bit too tight and did nothing for her complexion, she found she understood Dair's complaints a bit more. The fabric and cuts were nothing like the wonders she had in her wardrobe back in Eagallach, but she felt more herself in the proper clothing.

A servant fetched her to meet with the MacGregors and the rest of the group in the formal sitting room. The others had been treated just as well. Farrah had borrowed some of Diana's fine hunting clothes, and it seemed Dair had a grand time going through Paulo's things. Lord Hermen had obviously had clothing stashed here, the cut of his coat too perfect to be anything but his own.

There was only one other person Penny had hoped would be joining them.

Penny sat down in the chair next to the divan where Paulo lounged. "Where's Mater?"

"She'll be down in a moment," Paulo said, his eyes glued to the door. "She just went to fetch the last members of our group."

Penny felt her eyebrow raise. "Who else is here?"

The sound of arguing came down the hall and Paulo smiled.

Mater walked through the door, towing Donnie and a very pretty girl in behind her.

"Penny!" Donnie exclaimed, turning away from his heated discussion. He rushed to Penny and swept her up in a hug. "I'm so relieved to see you in good health."

"And I you, Donnie." She pulled away. "I heard about Tauros."

Donnie nodded. "This war has taken much from many of us, but I'm glad it's brought so many of us together." He pulled away and Penny got a full picture of the girl that had arrived with him.

She looked about Penny's age. Thick lashes brushed against her honey-colored cheeks. Eyes as dark as freshly tilled soil flicked around the room, narrowing when they landed on where Paulo sat.

Penny looked to Paulo, but his attention remained riveted to the young lady being dragged into the room. He stood a moment later, going to her.

"Laurel, you look lovely."

Laurel's chin jutted up in the most obstinate expression Penny had seen on a person's face. "Take your compliments and stuff them with the rest of your unmentionables, Paulo." Brown eyes flashed with anger as she stared up at him.

Penny could almost swear she'd seen the woman before, but she couldn't say where.

Diana laughed. "You tell him, Laurel."

A grin stretched along Penny's face. If she could guess by the sparkle in Paulo's eye, she would assume he certainly had his hands full, and he was as happy as a crow in a cornfield.

Paulo led Laurel the rest of the way into the room and sat her down on the divan beside him.

"Penny, this is Laurel Flumen." A glimmer of his magic sparked in his eye and his expression turned strained. He covered it up quickly, but having lived with the fae for the last several months, Penny had learned to catch a mask falling into place. A sliver of panic bled through.

Paulo cleared his throat. "Laurel is a friend Diana and I recently made in the capital. Laurel, this is High Queen Penelope of Faerie."

Laurel's dark brows shot straight up, her keen eyes flicking over Penny's features. "But you're not fae."

Dair laughed from his seat against the wall across the room. "No, she certainly is not."

Laurel studied Penny, obviously taking in that revelation. "How did a human become High Queen?"

"That's a little anticlimactic," said Paulo. "Penny, do tell her what's absolutely worse than being a human queen."

Penny rolled her eyes but played into Paulo's dramatics. She summoned her gift and the green glow of her tell lit up her arms, still as far reaching as it was in Faerie. The black veins stretched up her wrist all the way up to her elbow.

Laurel tilted her head, eyes wide. "You're a *mage*. How are you not dead in a Faerie ditch somewhere?"

Mater tsked, going to sit between Farrah and Donnie across the room, but Penny couldn't help but find it funny. She chuckled. "Luckily, I have some very good friends... and extremely sharp knives."

Laurel stood and made Paulo switch spots with her. "If you insist that I sit by you, then you'll let me sit by her so I can at least pretend you aren't in the room, *my lord*."

Paulo set his hands over his heart. "You wound me!"

Laurel ignored him.

Sweet Gaia, Penny really did like this girl. Paulo needed someone who would give him a run for his money. As a marquess with the ability to see into the future and a twin sister that could shoot a bee out of the air from a hundred paces, he needed someone who could at least give it back as well as Paulo could dish it out. Laurel seemed to be keeping up just fine.

Mater cleared her throat. "Do tell us what's happened since we last saw you, Penny. While Paulo does keep us informed of possible futures and we can collect bits and pieces of what's going on, we don't always have the full picture."

"Of course." Penny recalled every major instance since she left Diana standing outside the portal until they arrived back in Olympia only four days ago and the reason for their return. When she spoke of the capture of Shirina and the loss of the Great Tree, she had to hold back tears. Had all of it really happened in a few short months? Yet it felt as if eons lay between her and the burning of Barclay Manor, which had only been a year ago.

Lord Hermen sipped at the cup of tea that had arrived during Penny's retelling. "We've done a discreet search since Dominique disappeared, but even I haven't discovered where she is."

"Last Lady Hermen heard," Penny said, "she was headed this way."

Diana uncrossed her legs, her boots thumping against the floor. "That was months ago."

"That was the last anyone has seen of her," Penny said. "Did anything happen while she was here?"

Mater pursed her lips. "She had discovered our involvement in your journey to Faerie."

Penny winced. She could only imagine how livid Mother would have been.

"She was none too happy about it either," Paulo admitted, as if reading her mind. "She started throwing out speculation that Prince Aiden had come to Barclay Manor to woo you and steal you away from her as if he could curse you into betraying her."

Penny withheld an eye roll. "My mother always said love was a curse."

Dair and Lord Hermen snickered while Diana rolled her eyes. "Stupid boys and their stupid faces."

"She left once she realized we couldn't help her get to you," Paulo continued. "The Mist had locked up by that point and the rebels were preparing to come try to knock our walls down."

Penny nodded. "King Dion mentioned he hasn't seen her either."

Laurel straightened. "You've spoken with the king? Is he planning on taking back his palace? Did you see the queen?"

"Oh, absolutely," Penny said. "I don't know what their plans are for taking back the palace right now. I've come to find my mother and then see about how we can get the king and queen back on their thrones. It was Shaunie who actually asked me to come, and I couldn't say no. Not after what she's lost."

Paulo tried to cut in. "Yes, it's all very—"

Laurel raised a hand to silence him. "It doesn't seem like you're only talking about a palace. Who did she lose?"

The entire room seemed to freeze.

Penny's eyes flicked from one face to the next. Diana's face was somber. Mater's eyes were trained with worry on the back of Paulo's head and Paulo had his eyes closed like he'd just been kicked.

But Laurel's eyes left no room for deception. Penny could almost see the predator lurking behind her eyes.

A soft nudge had the words falling from Penny's lips.

"She lost a babe."

Laurel was on her feet, a dagger in her hand and Paulo's cravat in her fist.Penny shot to her feet, reaching for the dagger tucked into her skirt. "What are you doing?" she demanded.

Dair beat her to it. He angled a sword at Laurel's side. "I suggest you let him go."

Laurel didn't even seem to notice the sword. "Did you know?" she asked Paulo accusingly.

Paulo met the girl's eyes with somber resignation. "Yes, I knew."

Laurel's face drained of color. "She promised. She swore to me no innocents would get hurt." She shoved him back, still ignoring Dair's outstretched sword.

Dair met Penny's eyes across the room, an obvious question in them. She could only shake her head. She knew as little as he did.

Paulo reached for Laurel's hand. "Laurel—Don't!" Her frantic eyes darted about the room. "I need to go." She hiked her skirts up to her waist—flashing a pair of leather breaches and a long, needle-like dagger strapped to her calf—and fled the room.

"Laurel, wait!" Paulo got to his feet.

However, a masked person filled the doorway.

Penny shot to her feet, magic surging. She *had* seen someone in the window. Dair was at her side in a moment, shadows flicking around his hands.

"Penny, it's fine." Paulo held his hands out, coming between them and the masked person. "It's just Mare."

Penny peered around him, but they were gone.

Paulo strode to the door.

"Give her some time, Paulo," Mater said, but he had already disappeared. Mater sighed. "That's not going to go well."

Penny allowed her magic to dissipate. Apparently, Penny wasn't the only one who had changed in the few short months since her departure into Faerie. Even the countenances of the MacGregor's faces had changed, each carrying their own wounds, their own scars.

Penny sheathed her dagger and set her hands on her hips. "What in Gaia's green earth is going on here?"

Diana, who hadn't even moved from her chair, blew out a breath. "Where would you like us to start?"

Mater waved a hand at her. "We don't need to regale Penny with the events of the last few months. There will be plenty of time for that later, and we need to make a plan for finding Dominique."

Penny looked once more at the open doorway as she took her seat. Just what had she walked into?

Mater took Laurel's seat beside Penny. Worry furrowed her brow as well. "If Dominique isn't at the palace and none of us have had any contact with her, where would she have gone?"

Lord Hermen stood. "The capital is swarming with rebels. Barclay House would be unsafe."

But Mother would never have returned to Barclay House. There wasn't anyone left that could help her there. Penny straightened. Mother had already exhausted her resources with her friends, and the Mist had been locked up to prevent any rebels from crossing. With her plans to retrieve Penny thwarted, there had only been a few things Mother could accomplish on her to-do list.

"Lord Hermen." Penny turned to where he stopped near a window. "Didn't you say there's been something going on in Eleusion?"

36
STRATEGIZE

AIDEN STARED AT THE EMPTY BED. HE HADN'T REALIZED HOW... WELL, HOW *empty* everything would feel without Penelope there. He hadn't noticed it before she arrived in Faerie. The palace had seemed whole then. But then she'd filled the palace with her light and from the moment she'd stepped through the portal back to Olympia, it had felt like something had torn from his chest. It had taken every ounce of willpower he had not to leap through after her, curse the consequences.

Their connection remained strong. Faint traces of emotion filtered through. She wasn't asleep at the moment either, though the hour was late. A beat of excitement plucked at the string. What was she up to? Did she miss him as much as he missed her? He shook his head and walked away from the neatly made bed. There would be no sleep for him again tonight. Not without her.

His thoughts carried him back to the study. He lived in this room more than any other, something he wished he could change. Being cooped up made him antsy, but tonight he was already buzzing with nerves, and the workspace couldn't possibly make it any worse. He slumped into the chair behind the desk, rubbing at the back of his neck as he looked over the mounds of missives he'd been neglecting all week. They needed tending to, but he couldn't seem to pick one up.

Perhaps the study wasn't a good place to be either.

He stood back up from his chair as voices echoed down the hall, coming his direction quickly. In a few steps, he was at the door just as Thaen and the entire war council reached it, their faces all panicked.

"What's wrong?" he asked.

"The rebels, My Sovereign," said the dwarf chieftess. "They are amassing near the border of Autumn."

Aiden closed the door to the study and strode toward the war room, the rest following close behind. "When? Where?"

"The rebel host was seen crossing over the Dearmad only a few hours ago," Thaen supplied. "They will reach the barrow mounds in two days."

"How many?"

"About three thousand, if reports are correct."

Three thousand. That wasn't a substantial number of their troops, but it was obvious they believed they didn't need that many to attack helpless refugees. Blasted rebels. Aiden would have been offended, but the worry over those fae overshadowed everything else.

He pushed open the doors to the war room. "What about the Aigeans?"

"Based on what some of Spring's pixie scouts reported," Deireadh said, "they have stayed near the coast in Summer." He pointed to the tip of the Court, close to where the river let out into the bay separating Summer and Autumn. "There has been an increase in sightings here over the last couple of days, but there were no more than a handful of water folk each time."

The centaur stallion pushed forward, moving the pieces representing the two forces to where they would be in only a matter of days. "Should we prepare for a two-sided attack?"

"Like what they did in Flùranach?" Aiden asked.

The stallion nodded. "Precisely."

Aiden turned to Thaen. "How long would it take the Aigeans to come up the river?"

"A few hours? They move slower on land, but they could still be a large enough concern for the folk near Brònach. We need to move them."

Aiden frowned at the map. "I'm so tired of running away."

Thaen shook his head. "There is not much we can do to counter their attack in such a short time. They are using brute force against us—the only thing they have in their favor."

"But it seems to be working," Rìgh pointed out.

"What about the folk?" Sgiath asked. "If they are to hit the barrow mounds in two days, then the refugees outside of Brònach will be attacked first. They are practically defenseless."

"We need to buy them more time to escape," Aiden muttered. His eyes narrowed on the barrow mounds on the map. He'd only visited them once before, in the early trainings he'd had with Dair. "Where would you say the largest grouping of mounds is?"

Sgiath tapped a spot on the map. "Here, in the heart of them."

"And where are the rebels supposed to be coming from."

"Here." Sgiath pointed to where the forest wrapped on the northern side of the mounds, just south of the refugee camp Aiden had visited only a few months ago. "If they did converge with a group of the Aigeans, it would happen just before the encampment on the other side of these trees."

Aiden's mind whirled. The mounds went on for several miles, creating a natural border next to the refugee encampment. Brònach and the newest training grounds for the Tuatha in Autumn were on the other side, closer to the coast where they could provide a better defense against the Aigeans. Not that it helped them now. Durant would use the mounds as natural cover, and the entire force would slaughter the refugees before they could escape.

But the thought gave Aiden an idea.

He shuffled a few papers around on one of the other tables. He snatched up the latest report on their growing army. The number of trained Tuatha in the two camps was still lower than he'd like, but it was growing. He set the page down where everyone could see it. "It's time to fight back."

"With what?" Rìgh squawked.

"We've been training folk for months now. A fight is where we always knew we were headed. Why not let it be now?"

Rìgh scoffed. "But with a force that large against us, you cannot believe our motley group will be any hinderance to them."

Aiden narrowed his eyes at the Councilor before pointing down at the mounds. "But if we trust in what the Goddess has provided for us, we cannot lose."

The centaur stallion dragged a finger against the parchment. "So, we start here. If the scouts' reports are accurate, the rebels will be coming through the marshes on the west side and the Aigeans up the river."

Aiden stepped back slightly and closed his eyes. He allowed his connection to the Land to pull him to where the fight would take place. The mounds were dark lumps in the night but would provide sufficient cover and allow them to stretch their fighters out.

"Our warriors will be fresher," the dwarf chieftess said.

Aiden hummed his agreement, coming back to the room. "We'd also have the element of surprise."

"Not that either of those things will do us much good," Rìgh grumbled, "if we do not have the numbers to take advantage of such things."

Sgiath's lips curled up, but it was the chieftess that smacked Rìgh on the arm. "We do not need that kind of talk here, Councilor. All of us are in dire straits and need to work together and lift one another. If you ever want to see your Court again, I suggest you find a better attitude or learn to keep your mouth shut."

Rìgh opened his mouth to retort, but Aiden sent him a glare that had him snapping it closed so hard his teeth clacked.

Aiden kept eye contact. "Since you're so worried about there not being enough fighters, you won't object to accompanying us, will you?"

The sun sank below the trees, but the sky remained bright with the last rays before its slumber. Aiden's steps carried him around the mounds after Spot, who bounded ahead of him, tail wagging. The piles of earth rose above Aiden's head, covered in thick, cloying grass and blood-red poppies. It was a good thing poppies only had a mild aroma. The smell of sickly-sweet flowers would have dulled his senses.

Something white flashed in the growing shadows between the mounds and Spot ran after it. Aiden watched as more beings showed themselves. A pair of eyes blinked out of the shadows between the mounds. Skeletal fingers settled around the trunk of a tree.

Thaen grumbled. "Even the wights can feel the stirrings."

"The wights?" Aiden asked.

Thaen's brows rose. "Have you not heard of them yet? I suppose you would not, seeing as they only live within the mounds."

"What are they?"

Thaen shrugged. "Some guess they are spirits, cast from the Goddess's presence for any number of reasons. Others say they are beings predating the birth of the Tuatha. Some speculate they are the undead. But no one truly knows. Even to the fair folk, there are mysteries that have not yet been revealed."

"And here I thought the fae knew everything."

Aiden's name rang out and he turned to see Rìgh calling him back to where the other leaders had gathered.

Thaen chuckled. "There are certainly some who think they do."

Aiden wanted to roll his eyes as he called for Spot, and they walked back to join the group. Rìgh, Sgiath, and Commander Fàil all stood in the middle of the hubbub. Trolls, satyrs, were-creatures, dwarves, and centaurs flitted through the mounds, distributing supplies as ellyllon did their best to set magical traps throughout the mounds. They'd brought as much as they could through the portals from Winter to give their fighters more to work with and left enough to guard Eagallach in case of an attack, but he didn't know if it would be enough to keep Durant from attacking the camp that even now worked their way toward Winter.

After helping deliver fighters and supplies, Sgiath had joined the Hunt, who had agreed to take on the task of helping the refugees. While they'd been upset to be left out of the fight, Aiden had needed their neutrality with the Courts to help move the two groups of fae out of the city and into the mountains near the border to Winter. If nothing else, Fearg could use her dracon friend to put an end to any fighting much more effectively than Aiden could have.

"There has still been no sign of the Aigeans?" Thaen asked as they joined the group of leaders.

Sgiath shook his head. "No. A parliament of harpies have been watching the skies over the river. They will report if they see anything."

"We need to move faster," Commander Fàil growled, his heterochromic eyes of blue and brown flicking over the Tuatha around them. Spot sniffed at his head and the alpha werewolf barked out a warning. Two of Spot's three heads retreated, but the last only yipped playfully and licked the brindle-colored hair of the alpha. The werewolf growled but turned his attention back to the leaders. "This plan will not work if the enemy comes upon us in such a state."

Aiden nodded. They had to find cover.

And quickly.

He raced forward and helped a dwarf cover a hole of spikes they'd dug. Thaen followed behind, hollering for traps to be glamoured and the fae to get into places quicker. Spot dug holes alongside the earth gifted fae. Aiden used his shadows to camouflage traps and smother the freshly smithed gleam of their swords.

He was helping a group of soldiers use a glamour to screen a pocket in one of the mounds when Chieftess Sgrios called out for him.

"My Sovereign," the chieftess said, running up to their group, "the rebels have been spotted three miles out."

"Douse the lights!" Aiden hollered. The torches around him went out in a wave. Ellyllon and bwbachod skittered through the shadows, their voices hushed until the only sound around Aiden was the creak of their armor as they shifted and Spot's quiet pants from behind him.

At least, until the cacophony of humans hit his ears.

How had he forgotten how loud they were? The ragged pant of their breaths. The squelch of their boots. The jingle of their iron armor. Aiden still couldn't see any sign of them, but the sound—

"Here," Thaen whispered, thrusting something soft into Aiden's hands.

Two rounds of hard wax rolled around Aiden's palm. "What are these for?"

Thaen pointed to the side of his head.

Oh!

The two of them had discussed attempting something to keep Durant from using Aiden's true name against them, but Aiden hadn't had time to figure it out. It was only necessary if they met in battle, but he couldn't afford the risk. Thank Danu the magic of the names prevented her from sharing it with anyone else. He would have been dead a million times over if that had been the case.

He thrust the globs of wax in his ears. The sounds of the incoming army disappeared, but he shuddered. Having his ears clogged had always made him extremely uncomfortable, but being able to avoid Durant using his true name was worth the discomfort. Aiden's magic may not be able to harm her, but he could at least try to keep himself from becoming her mindless slave.

Lights glimmered through the trees.

Thaen pulled Aiden toward where they planned to stand against the army. There were three main bodies, all separated by the traps that had been laid. Aiden and Thaen led one, the body on the eastern side of the mounds and the ones with the least likelihood of being attacked, much to Aiden's dismay. Commander Fàil led the one on the west, him being more accustomed to the terrain and the best choice to instill fervor in the warriors of their homeland considering his pack made up a large number of them. The middle group was led by Rìgh and Chieftess Sgrios. Pixies flitted back and forth, delivering handwritten messages and allowing communication between the groups. A blue skinned one dropped an acorn in Aiden's hand, which he immediately cracked open and read the paper inside.

The first humans had breached the border of the mounds.

The air around them grew still, the entirety of their squadron holding their breath alongside the Land under their feet.

Aiden counted under his breath. First would come the arrows and enchanted projectiles that would take out the frontline of rebels.

Arrows flew over the mounds like a flock of starlings.

Then would come the flashes of light used to stun the rebels.

Sparks of Day Court magic flew into the air.

And the fae would charge.

The ground beneath Aiden's feet shook with the tremor of hundreds of fae.

The battle had officially begun.

Aiden closed his eyes and connected with the Land. The magic buzzed, trying to speak to him, but he couldn't hear what it was trying to say over the beat of his heart and the taut connection to his wife. The line he had to Penelope ached fiercely, but he ignored it as he searched out toward the first group. Iron plated humans covered the ground, bodies charred or in pieces. The fighting had pushed farther into the mounds as the group led by Sgiath and the alpha directed the rebels toward where Rìgh and the chieftess lay in wait.

The magic of the Land pulled him away, dragging him across Autumn—

A jostling next to him broke his concentration. Thaen bounced on his toes.

"Are you fidgeting?" Aiden hissed.

Thaen frowned at him, his mouth moving, but the wax in Aiden's ears kept the conversation one sided. Thaen's eyes glanced around anxiously, and his shoulders tightened with every second. Perhaps the desire for battle was getting to him.

Aiden looked back at the other warriors in their group. Instead of eagerness, he saw trepidation.

Shaking his head, Aiden closed his eyes once again, returning his attention to the magic of the Land that had tried so hard to get his attention before. There was an urgency he hadn't felt since Crann Mòr had been destroyed.

"I don't understand," he said.

Water.

37
SUCCUMB

AIDEN'S CONSCIOUSNESS PRACTICALLY JERKED HIM TOWARD THE RIVER WHERE he found Aigeans—selkies, merfolk and sea hags—leaping out of the water and into formation on land. They called on the water of the marshes around them, making it carry them faster toward the mounds than should be possible.

The entire parliament of harpies lay on the ground, their wings shredded.

"Blast," he cursed. He blinked away the image of the dead bird women, turning to Thaen. He unplugged one of his ears. "The Aigeans. They came by the river."

"Blizzards," Thaen hissed. "I thought we had folk watching for them."

"Dead," Aiden choked out. He'd never had a problem with death itself, just the reasons behind it. The Aigeans would pay for their merciless act.

"They're heading this way," Aiden whispered. With the rate of the Aigeans' travel, it would take them less than half an hour to reach the edge of the mounds.

"We cannot outrun them," Thaen said.

Aiden looked around at the five hundred fae huddled around them. Their group was manned with the least number of soldiers, the smallest group only meant to fight off the dregs if needed or get word back to Brònach and get the rest of the refugees out of Autumn. The force coming against them was at least twice that many.

Aiden ran a hand through his hair. He took stock of the traps laid around them, looked over the faces of the fae. They needed to come up with a plan.

And fast.

"We need to spread out," he said. "If we can take the Aigeans by surprise, it may be our best chance. We need to use the mounds around us as better cover, give some of these folk a chance to make it out of this alive. It'll make a successful retreat more likely if we're in smaller groups, but we need to hold them off for as long as we can."

Thaen nodded, grabbing an ellyllon with a gift over earth and stone. Thaen whispered into the male's ear and Aiden watched the color bleach out of the fae's red-hued face. The Tuatha scrambled back toward the other warriors, spreading word.

Aiden stuffed the wax back in his ear and called on the pixie on hand to deliver messages. The violet glowing fae floated down, an open acorn in her arms. Aiden quickly jotted down a note to Rìgh and popped it into the hollowed-out shell.

"Take this to Rìgh and Chieftess Sgrios."

The dwarf chieftess had informed Aiden of dwarf trading tunnels near Brònach that could get them to the mountains on the border of Winter in case of a retreat. But with the water folk coming on them quicker than he could have imagined, Aiden didn't know how they would reach the tunnels.

Aiden used the Land to once again watch for the Aigeans. He followed the wreckage of a flash flood further into Autumn until he found them.

"Thaen!" he yelled.

Thaen grabbed him, eyes wide.

Aiden pointed in the direction of the shrinking wall of water coming over the marshes, just visible over the tops of the trees about a mile away.

Thaen let go of Aiden and began hollering at their squad, though Aiden heard none of it. He grabbed the helmet Heff had sent him and shoved it on his head. He turned to begin barking more orders and getting their groups into formation, but a yellow pixie flew into his face, brandishing an acorn. Aiden plucked it from the pixie and popped it open.

Only one word stood out on the page like a scream in silence.

Run!

"Thaen!" Aiden tossed the note in his direction.

He read it quickly and looked up at the incoming storm of water folk. He crumpled the parchment, drew his flickering sword, and gestured at the soldiers behind them. A handful of them turned and ran, but the majority stayed and raised their shields.

Aiden reached up to take out the wax, not wanting to be hindered in the fight, but Thaen stopped him. He shook his head and pointed in the direction of the rebels.

They'd already reached Rìgh's company.

Blast it all! Aiden's team was supposed to help them if they went down. It was barely sunset. The refugees wouldn't have made it more than a few miles past Brònach.

The wave of water folk crashed into the ground, reaching the end of the water source that had allowed them to travel that far. Soggy branches and slick rocks rolled toward Aiden's feet, setting off enchantments and exposing the traps the soldiers had so carefully laid earlier.

Aiden drew his sword, teeth bared. The first Aigean came over the mound in front of them, helmet gleaming with water and waking moonlight. Spot leaped from the side of the mound and took him in one of his maws, disappearing on the other side like a monster of death.

Aiden tucked himself close to the side of the mound, wrapping himself further into the shadows created by the night. He pushed more of his magic over the small group of two hundred gathered around him. He kept his connection to the Land open just enough to watch the Aigeans creep forward around the base of the mounds.

Nine steps away.

Seven.

Three.

One.

Aiden lifted his sword and cut off the head of the first Aigean.

The fae behind him charged forward.

Aiden's sword became a blur of steel in front of him. He cut into Aigeans left and right, his shadows shielding him from the splashes of boiling water or the sharp ends of flying icicles as efficiently as it protected from tridents and clubs. A barrage of harpoons flew over one of the mounds, bouncing off Aiden's shadow. The unshielded were not so lucky. Sharp spikes dug into their flesh, and they opened their mouths in screams as they were dragged through the mud. Aiden slashed at the ropes, freeing some of his comrades, but too many disappeared over the hill and did not return to the battle.

Thaen remained near him. They fought back-to-back. Shoulder to shoulder. A maelstrom of blood and death. Spot's enormous form came and went in flashes of gray and black. He took a water folk in each of his mouths and bit through their armor as he trampled the other Aigeans under his paws. Aiden fought against a trio with clubs, their weapons dull, but the pure force of their hits were bone shattering. His shadow shield dented with their attacks as he retreated farther into the mounds.

A wall of muscle knocked him to the ground. Aiden called on his gift to shove the attacker off, but stopped when he saw Thaen's pale blue eyes and the hundreds of arrows flying over their heads as a horde of Aigeans came running into sight. The arrows flew true, turning the incoming attackers into pincushions. The water folk fell, but another wave of them crested over their fallen brethren.

Thaen dragged Aiden to his feet and pushed him behind the archers. The arms of the bowmen drew back once more, taking out another line of Aigeans.

Aiden lifted his helmet enough to take the wax out of his ears. The screams of dying fae pierced his skull.

"We can't hold them off," he gasped. "We need to break cover and try to get to the caves." He looked about them to find Spot but stilled.

Shadows crept over the mounds behind the fallen. Aiden's eyes pulled wide. He grabbed the shoulder of Thaen's armor and pointed at the oncoming nightmare.

Thaen blanched. "Afanc."

The creatures skittered down the hill on four legs, their reptilian torsos weaving through the destruction. Long snouts of razor-sharp teeth clamped around the legs of fae, bringing them down to the ground before ripping into them. Their wide, leathery tails slapped the ground, spraying up mud and debris into the fighter's faces. The vibrations of those slaps shook the earth under Aiden's feet.

"*Retreat!*" Aiden bellowed. He scrambled after Thaen as more of the fae chased behind them.

Thaen wove through the mounds in front of him, and Spot joined the sprinting throng ahead. Afanc growled behind them, their powerful jaws snapping as they galloped over the muddy ground. The Tuatha around Aiden kept looking back, watching what Aiden was sure was their comrades falling prey to the ferocious creatures. The screams kept being abruptly cut off by the sounds of breaking bones and tearing flesh. Not even fae healing could counteract such wounds.

The magic of the Land screamed inside of him, sending his shadows flickering all over the place. He barely maintained control over them.

So many dead.

So many he had a responsibility to protect.

Not even the coup he'd waged against Father had been this brutal.

This bloody.

This devastating.

Wind and snow, what have I done?

The Aigeans swept in from the side. Thaen brandished his sword while Spot charged through them, and the two of them cut the water folk down as fast as they came. Aiden's own sword flew, desperation and protectiveness for his kingdom almost overtaking his common sense. An afanc snapped at his leg, and Aiden's sword severed its scaled head from its furry body.

"*Move!*" Thaen thundered over the soldiers. Their speed picked up, the fury of their commander overtaking their confusion for another moment longer.

But what was a moment to the Tuatha Dé Dannan?

The Aigeans caught up to the rear of their group, slashing heels and trampling bodies. It was a slaughter as they surged forward through Aiden's ranks.

Thaen shouted from ahead, and Aiden turned in time to see an afanc bearing down on him. Aiden moved to dodge, but the beast reared up at the last second and crashed into him. They went down into the mud, the wicked teeth of the beast snapping in Aiden's face as he braced his arms against the furry chest to hold it off. Sharp talons dug into his thighs and his shoulders, and Aiden let out a roar. The stench of the creature's breath felt like a punch to Aiden's senses.

Aiden's shadows twitched about, frantic as Aiden tried to call on them. They pushed and pulled at the afanc, but the creature bore down on him more.

A streak of purple and black speared through the afanc's side, sending the thing sprawling into a group of Aigeans moving in. The group went down in a heap, but others took their place.

Thaen hoisted Aiden to his feet, and they took off running once more.

Blizzards, his body ached as it tried to heal. The deep gouges in his shoulders closed quickly enough, but the scores of torn flesh on his legs seeped blood as they ran.

"Afanc venom," Thaen said, pulling him forward and doing his best to gage Aiden's physical injuries while they ran. "Their back feet have poisoned barbs like a platypus."

Aiden couldn't ask what on Gaia's green earth a platypus even was, pushing through the pain as he continued to move his injured limbs.

Swerving around a mound, they came face to face with a group of rebels, racing in the direction of Brònach. The entire fae army was in shambles, their formations completely obliterated as the rebels and Aigeans came together. Fae raced ahead of them, some from the group Rìgh and Chieftess Sgrios had led.

Aiden jumped into the melee. His sword was slick in his hand, though from the blood or the mud, he couldn't tell.

The gleam of silver stood out in the waning light.

Aiden turned, his eyes meeting the steely green of Durant's only a few yards away from him. Her hand shot out and a throwing knife sank into the back of a dwarf running in the other direction. She grinned, not caring that the fae was obviously retreating, and took a step toward Aiden.

He jerked back, realizing the wax he'd pulled from his ears couldn't protect him. He searched his vest, his pockets, never taking his eyes off her. Where had he put them? Where were they?

Durant's mouth opened.

A force smashed Aiden in the back of the head, sending him straight into darkness.

38
RETURN AND REPORT

PENNY PULLED BACK AROUND THE CORNER AS THREE SENTRIES BRANDISHING torches came around the bend on the street. She tightened the scarf wrapped around her face and willed the clouds to move quicker over the moon.

Her beloved city of Eleusia was not at all how she remembered.

Fires burned into the sky, casting wicked shadows all over the city. The sounds of people and business she always associated with the cobbled streets was gone. The ring of weapons and the shouts of angry people had replaced the laughter and music. Eleusia had never been a perfect city, but where life and opportunity had once reigned, now only war and death prevailed.

Penny tugged at the end of her braid. The scenery wasn't helping the charge of nervous energy running through her. Her bond with Aiden had been swollen with emotions all day, and she couldn't shake the feeling that something was very wrong. She prayed it was only her imagination, the days of separation tugging at her.

"Where do you think she is?" Dair asked from behind her.

Penny refocused and peeked around the corner just as the three men scanning the street walked in front of a coral-pink shop. The windows were boarded up, but the building itself didn't look nearly as derelict as its neighbors. With all trade blocked into the city, the businesses had most likely shut down months ago.

The watchmen walked out of view. Penny tugged on Dair's sleeve and pulled him across the empty street with Farrah following closely behind. On silent steps, they made it to the front of the building. Penny nimbly lifted the large padlock dangling from a shiny new hasp on the outside of the door. Claudia had always taken great care of her shop.

Penny gestured for Dair to follow her around the back. The moon glared down on the rear of the building. Penny wanted to hiss in its direction, tell it to go so it wouldn't expose them, but when she saw the flutter of a curtain in the second-story window, she began singing the moon's praises.

I knew it.

Penny found the back door, this one with a matching padlock. The front door wasn't the way in, but the windows in the front were boarded up and the only windows on this side were on the second story.

Dair nudged Penny's shoulder and pointed up at the roof. Anyone else likely wouldn't have thought anything of it, but there was a potted ivy sitting on the corner of the roof, vines dangling over the gutter.

Penny smiled and pulled on her gift.

The ivy trailed down, the leaves multiplying as the plant lengthened. Penny wove the vines until a rope ladder hung down along the building, right over the window.

Penny pulled herself up to the second story, where she found the window open just a sliver. She silently wedged her fingers under the pane and slid it up far enough to allow her and her companions to slip through.

Layers of fabric covered the window, and Penny pushed them aside to find a brightly lit room. Candles were scattered about, as well as a handful of magelights. Penny quickly set the curtain back in its place once Farrah and Dair were through and picked up one of the small, mage-crafted lights.

But where was the person who had lit them?

Penny crept forward, cautious of creaking floorboards. She made it to the closed door on the other side of the room. Her fingers wound around the door handle, and she gingerly twisted it. As quietly as she could, she pushed open the door.

A thick blackberry vine shot straight at her face.

Without a conscious thought, Penny connected with the plant and stopped it a mere inch from her eye.

Dair's sword sliced the vine a good six inches at almost the same moment.

A gasp cut through the silent room.

"Penny?"

Penny looked away from the plant to find Mother standing in the corner of the room, the sage green glow of her magic vanishing in a heartbeat.

Mother took a step toward them. "Penny?" she asked again.

Tears gathered at the edges of Penny's eyes, and she threw herself in Mother's direction. The two of them collided, and Mother's arms wrapped entirely around Penny. They sank to the ground, Penny's body too full of emotion to hold her up properly.

"By the Goddess, I can't believe you're here," Mother whispered into her hair. "Penelope Lucille Barclay, you nearly drove me to an early grave."

"I'm so sorry," Penny sobbed, tightening her hold around Mother's strong frame. "I'm sorry I didn't tell you what was going on. I'm sorry I put you in danger."

"Hush now," Mother said. "You're here, right where you're supposed to be. We'll get through all of this. Together."

Something in Penny's chest eased. Yes, she'd been doing what she was meant to do all this time, but being here gave her a peace only found within Mother's embrace. It felt like everything would be easier because they were together, even though there were still things that separated them.

Penny pulled away slightly. "There's so much I have to tell you."

"I would guess so." Mother gave her an arched look. She stood up, finally looking over Penny's shoulder. "Hello, Farrah. I imagine you're the one who helped Penny get here." She met Dair's gaze. "Penny, are you going to introduce me to your friend?"

Penny winced. "Yes, um, Mother, may I introduce you to Dair."

Dair's human glamour remained in place even as Farrah fully dropped hers, his lavender hair glamoured brown and his features softened. He bowed, flashing Mother his most charming smile. "Hello, Your Grace. It is a pleasure to meet you."

Mother parried his smile with an arresting one of her own. "The pleasure may end up being mine. I'm always glad to meet my daughter's friends."

"I am honored to call her my friend, Your Grace."

Mother smirked. "Are you going to drop the glamour?"

Dair's smile turned mirthful as well, and he allowed the glamour to fade away.

"How did you know?" Penny asked.

"While I may have been foolish enough to not realize that my steward was fighting for traitors and my daughter was secretly trained as a spy for the Crown, I can spot a glamoured fae. Especially one that has not traveled much on this side of the Mist. They don't use contractions."

Penny's mouth fell open.

Dair's amber eyes twinkled. "I knew Penelope was quick, but now I see where she inherited it from."

Penny found her voice once again. "How did you know about me? I mean, the spy thing. How did you find out I was part of the Underworld?"

Mother straightened the vest she wore over a dark green dress. "At first, I thought the fae had taken you. I saw how Prince Aiden had watched you during the entire wedding. I saw him try to go to you before he was taken, but the crowd had turned to a frenzy, and I lost sight of the dais until after you'd both disappeared."

She continued to explain what had happened after. When she began making inquiries, the people she thought would know about Penny—Queen Carnation's other ladies-in-waiting, the palace staff, even Adam Cyrus—had no idea about why Aiden would have singled her out. According to Mother, most of them didn't even know Penny was in residence at the palace, thinking she was still staying in Barclay House.

Mother pursed her lips. "But I kept remembering how Prince Aiden looked at you at the wedding. For some reason, it wouldn't leave me alone. When I'd exhausted all of the resources I thought you'd be acquainted with, I really began digging around. I stayed in the rebel-infested capital for weeks, and it wasn't until I cornered Lady Delmar that I had any leads."

"How did you know she was involved?" Penny asked.

"Lady Delmar reported to the Council as the newest leader of the Underworld in Prince Aiden's stead." Mother's eyes turned serious.

"You had joined them, which meant you had been training under Prince Aiden. I recall a young farmhand coming on during planting season last year. One with very unique amber eyes, similar to our new fae friend here." Mother gestured at Dair, who beamed at the attention.

"You figured out I followed him," Penny said.

"Yes, but then I had to figure out how you did it and why. Stone told me he saw you outside the temple, when you took his horse. You'd gone towards the palace though, not the Mist. I figured you went to get supplies, but I couldn't return to the palace to look for any evidence and the nobles had scattered."

"Which is what took you to Paulo."

Mother nodded. "After speaking once more with Lady Delmar, I left the capital and went to Paulo. I had enough of the picture that even with that misleading way of his I was able to put together the rest with what scraps he and Luciana gave me."

Penny swallowed. "So now you know... everything? Paulo told you about Aiden and I."

"Well, I know where you went and what you were after. There are certainly things you'll have to tell me about your spymaster leader, I'm sure. But now that you're back, we can leave the whole business behind us. We'll fight the war on this side, help Faerie, and then everything will go back to normal. You can return home, and we should have plenty of time to get reestablished before planting season."

A low chuckle bounced around the room. Dair's laugh grew until both Penny and Mother stared at him. "You... She... Penelope, wind and snow, she does not know. The frosted oracle did not tell her."

Mother's brows furrowed. "What don't I know?"

"You really haven't spoken with anyone in the last several weeks?"

"What *happened*?" Mother snapped.

"I, uh..."

Mother's face turned thunderous. "Do not mumble, Penny. *What. Happened.*"

Penny ducked her head. "I married Aiden and became High Queen of Faerie."

"YOU DID *WHAT*?"

Farrah slapped a hand over Mother's mouth, and Penny swore she could see the urge to bite the female flash through Mother's eyes.

"We can get into all of it later," Penny hurried to say, "but we need to get you back to King Dion. They need your help."

Mother yanked Farrah's hand away from her face. "Oh, no. You don't just get to brush away information like that. How did that happen? Did he force you into it?"

"Of course not!"

Mother grabbed Penny's face between her hands. "If there's any compulsion happening, we can get it remedied. I know a few fae here in Olympia—"

Penny shook herself from Mother's grip. "There's no *compulsion*. I love him and because I love him, I married him."

"You don't even know him," Mother said, indignant. "And love isn't a motivation to get married."

"I've known him for over a year, Mother. And what better reason than love, *true* love, to get married?"

"You cannot know it's true love."

Penny pulled off her glove. "Actually, I can." She showed her the gold brand around her finger. "The Goddess chose us for one another, and we chose each other. It was always true love."

"Even if the Goddess herself came down and told you the two of you were meant to be together, how could you possibly become High Queen? The fae would never allow a mage to take the throne. It would be a death sentence."

"Since she did not need any divine visitation to tell her to marry Aiden," Dair said, "perhaps the Goddess came down to tell her to be queen instead."

Mother's eyes flared wide. "Is that what happened?"

Penny opened her mouth to answer, but Farrah took over the conversation. "Not in so many words, but your daughter has been chosen by Danu not only to be Aiden's chosen mate, but also to rule over Faerie as our High Queen. And great gourds, she has been doing a marvelous job if it, if I say so myself."

Mother stared at Farrah and Dair, her eyes narrowed as they met her steely gaze. She studied them for something, but Penny couldn't identify what.

"None of this really matters right now," Penny said, stepping between them.

Mother's glare turned on her. "You think this doesn't matter? That my daughter's future isn't the most important thing to me?"

Penny deflated. "I know it matters. I know you care, but this kingdom isn't going to have a future if we don't focus on more important things right this second."

A few seconds passed between them as Mother studied her. Penny could practically see the desire to keep on her motherly tirade and the responsibility she felt toward her duchy clash against one another.

Gently, Penny reached out to touch her hand. "We need to get out of the city and return you to the capital. King Dion needs your help, or the entire kingdom will be taken by the rebels."

Mother gave an insincere laugh. "I'm not going back to the capital. That would ruin all my plans." She stepped around them, grabbing a bundle of supplies from the floor, including a dark cloak and a scythe of all things. "If you're so concerned about this kingdom, come with me. I could use your help."

Penny followed her out of the room. "What plans?"

39
SURFACE

Colors and sounds blurred around Aiden's head. He tried to pull his hands up to his ears, but for some reason he couldn't find them. In fact, he couldn't find his head either. He was simply another color, another sound in this miasma circling around him.

Something in what should have been his chest tugged. If spirits could feel physical pain, he imagined he would have been in a tremendous amount of agony just then. He came together, piece by piece until he could feel the two strings holding him down and keeping him in place.

As his consciousness reformed, the scene around him did too. Clips of sound transformed into words. Colors and shapes began to line up and the myriad before him took form.

"—lucky this time, Cartographer." One of the water folk, a gray-skinned merrow, dripped water from its mane of seaweed green hair onto the carpet of the tent Aiden found himself standing in. "If we had not come to your aid, you would have been beaten before even setting foot in the barrow mounds."

Aiden felt his pulse jump. He was in the rebel camp. He was dreaming. *Praise Danu!* He wanted to laugh but worried even the smallest sound would somehow be noticed, though he knew he'd never been seen before. He couldn't squander this opportunity, not when they hadn't been able to infiltrate any of the camps again after he and Thaen had snuck into Flùranach.

Durant sat at a large table, three others occupying chairs to either side of her. She drummed her fingers on the tabletop, seeming bored, but Aiden knew she likely imagined each beat as a whip cracked against bare flesh or a club thumped against a skull.

"And we appreciate your foresight," Durant said with her most genteel smile, "but we won't be straying from the plans we've already set."

"And what plans are those exactly?" the merrow bit out. "We have agreed to be your allies in this fight, and yet you treat us as your dogs, siccing us on your enemies without any forewarning. Why, you do not even allow us in your camp without a legion of guards surrounding us. It is as if we are some kind of plaything to you."

Durant tsked. "How do you think my men would react if I allowed your folk to walk through my camp unsupervised? These soldiers have been training to view anything with magic as the enemy. While we have agreed to work with you because we will both benefit from an alliance, I wouldn't presume to say you would be safe to walk on these shores once our business is concluded."

The merrow took a step forward, but one of the guards brought up a blade to ward him off. The Aigean bared his needle like teeth at the guard but took a step back. "You think you can keep us from claiming Faerie for ourselves?"

Durant blinked innocently. "Why would I not? You're the ones who approached me with this alliance, not the other way around. While I'm grateful to your queen for agreeing to work with us, I can't say the rest of my men feel the same way I do about such an accord. Believe me, most of them hope I'll turn my sights to you after we take Faerie under our control."

Aiden studied the merrow's reaction carefully. He'd seen Durant blatantly flaunt her power to soldiers lower than this water folk. Merrows could be vicious when they wanted to. The creature wouldn't get out of the room alive if he attacked, but he'd take out more than a few of the guards.

But Durant was nothing if not calculating, and she never gave a threat she couldn't deliver on.

The muscles where the merrow's eyebrows would be pushed up on his forehead, but that was all the movement he made. "And will you?"

Durant pursed her lips, pretending to mull over the question.

"Not yet. For now, your queen is being agreeable, but if I continue to be badgered about the way I am leading my soldiers and battles I'm waging, perhaps I could change my mind. What's that old Aigean saying?" She tapped her lips theatrically. "'The sea is a fickle mistress?'" She laughed. "Perhaps I should have gone by 'The Sea' rather than 'The Cartographer.'"

Those at the table laughed with her, but the merrow only glowered. Aiden could see the cyclone of thoughts whirling through his mind, trying to decipher if Durant was lying or not. No fae would ever speak things like that aloud. The cursed woman did it to keep her allies on their toes, to keep them from getting on her bad side. One never knew which threats she would cash in.

But Aiden did.

She would cash in every single one.

Durant stood from her chair, lazily flicking her hand as she came up to the merrow. "There's no longer need to fret, my friend. The Isles and their queen will get their spoils of this war..." Like the strike of a viper, she whipped a knife from her sleeve and slashed the blade across his cheek. A clump of green hair fell from the strands by his face.

The merrow jumped back, but Durant's blade was at his throat before he could take another step. "You will get your spoils so long as I deem fit to give them to you. Do you understand?"

The merrow nodded and the blade disappeared from Durant's hand as if it had never even been there.

"Good," Durant chirped. "Now, get out."

The merrow scurried from the table, his hand finally reaching to cup his cheeks as blood dribbled off his jaw. Durant strode back to her seat. "Now, where were we before we were so rudely interrupted?"

One of her generals unrolled a map. "We were discussing the charge on Winter."

Aiden crept along the edges of the open tent, trying to keep to the shadows though he knew no one could see him.

"Ah, yes." Durant grabbed a large conch shell from the table and used it to hold down one side of the curling parchment. Aiden recognized the shell. They'd had one almost identical to it in Crann Mòr. A very unique enchantment only crafted by Aigeans and gifted only to Aigean allies as a direct line to the Aigean queen.

Now, Aiden realized Durant had gotten her hands on one of her own.

"We've taken three Courts in under a year," Durant continued. "Our timeline has moved so much quicker than we thought it would. The fae have been putting up less of a fight than I imagined, though I can't be upset about that."

One of the others, the one Aiden recognized as the man from the continent, leaned over the table toward the map. "Yet we do not have all the powers we've been promised."

Durant gritted her teeth, but to everyone else it probably looked like a smile. "But the catch isn't as gratifying without the hunt. We're in the last act, about to reach the culmination of everything we've been working toward. We have camps scattered throughout the entirety of Faerie and only have a few measly mountains to cross until we reach our ultimate prize."

"Yes," said one of the others, "but those mountains are the most perilous part of this endeavor."

"And the winter months will begin closing in," piped another.

Durant raised her hands, gaining their silence. "That's why I've been so adamant about moving our troops. With the sabotages in Eleusion and our unsuccessful attempts on Delphine, it's paramount we take over Faerie and rid ourselves of the High King so we can finish it all off."

"While we all agree," the foreign man said, "why have we not used our shiny new weapon to overtake them? We could have struck the Night Court seat as soon as she was in our grasp. You have done nothing but play tea party with her since she arrived."

Aiden stiffened. *Shirina.* Skies, she's still alive. He'd prayed— begged for her survival, but he hadn't imagined Durant would allow her to live this long.

"The Winter High Councilor is *my* toy, not yours, Teagan."

Aiden watched Teagan closely. While the man gazed serenely at Durant, Aiden could see the coldness of the expression, the rage flickering in his eyes. This man was dangerous, not only to Durant, but to Faerie and Olympia as well.

Aiden crept from the tent, the Autumn leaves around him swirling together and the edges of the shapes beginning to fade. He was too tired to be doing this. Dair had warned him enough times not to allow himself to get trapped in the dreams.

But there was one more thing he had to see.

He floated through the tents, feeling out the magic connecting the Goddess's creations to the earth. Every few paces, he saw one of his folk in chains, tied to posts or under the guidance of a whip. A child drew charms on the side of a tent from a bucket of blood, the skin of his wrists red and puffy where the iron touched his skin. A group of females scrubbed laundry in dirty buckets of water, their eyes empty as they moved in agonizing movements.

His blood boiled. Durant would subject the entirety of his kingdom to this all because of prejudice and hate. All because of him.

Aiden wanted to scream, but he felt the edges grow darker and pushed himself to find what he sought. He reached out his magic and prodded with the connection to the Land.

There.

With a thought, he whisked through the camp and entered a tent on the outskirts of the camp. Five armed men stood outside, each watchful as they guarded the prize inside.

Luckily for Aiden, he was a dream himself.

He walked through the tent wall and found her curled up in the corner, her breaths shallow as she slept through the daylight hours. Her form was thin under the scraps of the dress she had worn to the wedding. Her dark skin looked a sickly gray in the faded light of the tent.

Aiden crouched next to her and hung his head. "I'm so sorry, Shirina. I'm so sorry you're in this mess because of me. I promise to do my best to get you out of here. To return you to your family—to *our* family." He reached out a hand to touch her boney shoulder, but his fingers only met air where her shoulder should have been.

A groan pierced through Aiden's unconsciousness. Then, a pounding came from somewhere close by. His eyes were bleary as they opened, and he had to blink a few times to get a clear view. Beams of light punctured through the holes in the stone ceiling above him. Dust danced lazily in the beams, only stirring when disturbed by the faint breeze coming from the left of him. The crisp scent of fresh snow trailed along on that small gust of air.

He moved his head in the direction the breeze seemed to be coming from, only now realizing the pounding he'd heard was beating at the top of his skull. Wincing, he turned and found himself in a cot in the middle of a small cave turned medic tent.

Sounds came rushing in once more, and he heard the hushed whispers of the medics as well as the whimpers and groans of the other patients.

He saw Sgiath and Rìgh at the mouth of the cave, their heads dipped together in quiet conversation. Aiden was happy to see the Summer Councilor in good health, though he looked a little worse for wear. There had never been such a deep furrow to his brow.

Aiden pulled an arm up, ready to push himself from the bed, but a hand latched onto his wrist.

"Easy, cousin. Let us get you checked out before you start moving around."

Aiden turned to find Thaen sitting in a chair on the right side of his bed. He slowly returned his head to the wadded-up cloth beneath it. "Where are we?"

"The mountains bordering Autumn."

Aiden's chest tightened at Thaen's solemn tone. "What happened? Are the rest of our fighters rallying? Did we get the refugees out in time?"

Thaen sighed and rubbed a hand down his face. "It was a massacre, Aiden."

Aiden sucked in a gasp. "How many did we lose?"

Thaen looked around the room. "This is all we have left of our company. There are around five hundred fae scattered about in the caves, but many of them are injured."

Aiden sat straight up, completely ignoring the piercing pain in his thighs as he took in the room. "How did we get here? What about Fàil and Sgrios? Where are the rebels now?"

"I carried you here after we were discovered by Adira Durant in the mounds. I could not risk you coming under her thrall during the battle, so I knocked you out and ran. Commander Fàil did his best to hold off the rebels, but once they breached the edge of the mounds, it was a massacre. The refugees only made it to the mountain because Sgrios collapsed the tunnel outside of Brònach on top of herself and fifty rebels. There's another thousand of The Cartographer's forces circling the bottom of the mountain, looking for another way in."

"Wind and snow," Aiden breathed. He took another deep breath, his chest trying to cave in on itself with the sorrow pressing down on it. Those fae had followed him into battle. If he hadn't talked the rest of the Council into fighting, many of those warriors would still be alive. He closed his eyes. Regret and guilt churned like curdled cream in his gut, thick and heavy and rotten.

But he couldn't let the emotions drag him down. Not after the discoveries he'd gained from the Land. He had to share what he'd seen with Thaen, but adding to his cousin's heartache was something he didn't want to do.

"I saw your mother."

Thaen straightened. "When? Where?"

"Durant's camp, somewhere in Autumn. She's isolated in a tent, surrounded by guards. She's still alive, but she's…" He swallowed. "She's still alive."

"Curses," Thaen hissed. He pushed the heels of his hands into his eyes.

Aiden could almost taste his worry in the air around them. He grabbed Thaen's shoulder. "We're going to get her out, Thaen. We are going to save her."

Thaen shook his head. "Please do not make me promises you do not know if we can keep."

Aiden slumped back onto the bed, the throbbing in his legs nearly outweighing the pain in his heart. "What the blizzards did that afanc do to my legs?"

"Some kind of anti-healing venom from what the doctor said," a cheery voice said.

Aiden looked around Thaen and found Sissy standing behind him, her arms holding a stack of clean linens. "I, of course, have no medical expertise, so I can't tell you exactly what that will mean for you for later. All I know is, you're going to have to heal like a human from those wounds unless the doctors can get you the right kind of treatment. That orange-haired fellow over there said something about getting you to his wife, but that's all I know."

Aiden looked to Thaen to see if he could elaborate, but he sat frozen, hardly breathing.

Sissy came around the side of the bed and laid her stack by Aiden's feet. "How are you feeling, My Sovereign?"

Aiden opened his mouth, but the amount of things he felt clogged his throat. How was he feeling? Hurt? Worried? Lonely?

Sissy hummed and sat primly on the edge of his bed. "Papa used to say there's light at the end of the tunnel, that if you feel like that light is nowhere in sight, it means you haven't reached the end yet."

"Was it light when you passed through into Danu's realm, Lady Brighid?" Thaen asked quietly.

She gave him a serious look. "I died because a fiery building fell on top of me. Of course there was light."

Thaen's face reddened and he ducked his head. "I will just shut up now."

Sissy snorted. "I'm only teasing." Her lips pursed in thought. "I think there might have been a light. Dying is such a quick thing that you don't really pay attention in the moment. I can't speak of it too much, but it was a whirlwind to be certain."

Aiden looked around the room. "I hope it was a quick thing for our soldiers."

Thaen rubbed a hand over the ropes of hair on his head. "I wish I could say it was, but I know some suffered until the end. War is not a quick flick of a knife or the seizing of a heart. It is slow, agonizing."

Sissy blinked at him across the bed. "Well, aren't you just a little ray of sunshine?"

Thaen frowned. "I am not anything like sunshine."

"No kidding."

As the two of them went back and forth, movement at the mouth of the cave caught Aiden's attention. Sgiath and Rìgh shuffled toward them, their faces masks of sorrow and rage.

"My Sovereign." Sgiath bowed, Rìgh following right after. "We have word from Eagallach."

"What news?" Aiden sat back up in the bed, and Sissy pushed an extra pillow behind him for support.

Rìgh stepped forward. "The rebels have amassed at Crann Mòr, crafting barges from the Spring forests and moving supplies toward Lake Truaighe."

"How many trained fae do we have at Eagallach?" Aiden asked.

"Just under fifteen thousand, My Sovereign."

"And how many left in Autumn?"

"We counted four thousand able-bodied fae after the massacre,"

Sgiath reported. "If we move quickly, most of them could be to the base of Eagallach within the week."

"How long until the rebels can amass on Winter's borders?"

"With the speed at which they are moving their forces," Rìgh said, "I would say no more than six or seven weeks."

"Then we have time to prepare." Aiden swung his legs over the bed, wincing at the pain, but pushing it deep down. "Sgiath, summon a portal. It's time to get everyone back to the Winter Palace."

40
DUCK AND COVER

"I can't believe I actually let her talk me into this," Penny murmured to Farrah as they pulled up the wide stones making up the street under her feet. Mother had been having her do it all week but tonight would be the last. "Honestly, she thinks I'm the crazy one for running off to Faerie, but she's the one running around a rebel-infested city trying to torment them on her own. At least I had a team when I was doing it."

"You do have to admire your mother's tenacity though."

Penny gave her a halfhearted glare but pulled an envelope of seeds from her pack. The thin envelope held between three to five seeds of the nasty variant of poison ivy Mother had created. When activated, the vines would overtake anything and anyone within reach.

Mother's tenacity was likely to get people killed. She'd been planting these packets of seeds all over Eleusia for months, waiting to set the perfect trap. Except she was the only mage that had the power to activate the seeds and would have made herself a pretty target for the rebels. Penny couldn't help but think a bit of divine intervention had brought them together right when Mother was preparing to launch her attack.

Dair's form dropped down next to Penny, where she was tucking a packet between the cobblestones. His face was flushed with excitement and exertion.

"Your mother is very fun," he said, a smile stretching across his face. The first real one she'd seen in weeks.

"Great Goddess, not you too." She shook her head and uncorked the waterskin at her side, sprinkling enough water on the envelope to soak it through. "Only you would think rigging plant bombs all over the city and putting ourselves in the direct path of our enemies would be *fun*. You may have more in common with your twin than you think."

Dair gasped, a hand coming to his chest. "How dare you? Thaen is the epitome of uncouth. He would not find planting bombs fun because he would want to be the bomb himself."

Farrah chuckled and a smile twitched at Penny's lips as she stood. "Perhaps you're right."

Penny led them further through the city toward the docks. Mother had told them to meet her at the family warehouse near the water before sundown. Penny had shown it to Aiden—well Lou—when they'd worked to stop the rebels in the city, but it had been almost a year since she'd been in Eleusia, and the rebels had torn down more than one building while they'd inhabited the city.

Dair drew them up short and put a finger to his lips. His amber eyes darted around the small side street they stood on and gestured for her and Farrah to tuck into the doorway of one of the houses. The recessed door gave enough cover in the late light of day for Dair to hide the three of them. He finished the glamour when a pair of men carrying a body sauntered onto the street—a fae. Dair deepened the shadows around them as the two men dragged the deceased male out of view.

"Blackguards," Dair hissed. He took a step in their direction, his hands curled at his sides.

Penny pulled him out of the alcove and directed him toward the river. "There's nothing we can do about them right now. We need to find my mother."

Dair didn't argue, but she could feel the anger, the sorrow, coming off him in waves. Farrah's face was cast in fury as well.

She understood it. That was one of her folk, a member of her kingdom. The rage pushed her feet forward.

The stench of fish preceded the slap of the water against the planks of the docks. Penny turned, running parallel to the sound, in the direction of the warehouse. She could feel the packets of seeds under the ground as they ran, one every hundred yards or so. Mother had been busy in the weeks she'd been in the city.

They made it to the large warehouse before Mother. Penny pulled open one of the small side doors and the others snuck in behind her. The warehouse had already been raided, the grain that had been waiting to be shipped taken and the building gutted. The rebels had taken every piece of furniture, every item of value, leaving the floor littered with paper and scattered grain.

"Over here," Penny whispered. She led them to the stairs, heading up toward the second story where the manager's office had been. Mother hadn't told her what had happened to the small number of employees they'd had working there. Hopefully, they'd made it out of the city before it got too bad.

Penny opened the door to the manager's office, the large desk she remembered buckled in half toward the floor.

Fabric swished behind her, and Penny turned to find Mother in the doorway.

"Did you plant the rest of them?"

Dair grinned. "Every one."

"Good." Mother's smile matched Dair's. "Now, it's time to take my city back."

Penny squatted under the leaning roof of Farrah's shop. Farrah said she'd taken everything she'd needed from it after the fire at Barclay Manor, but Penny was grateful in that instant she had neglected to take the small pieces of glass hanging from the eaves. They sparkled in the moonlight, bringing a feeling of home to Penny's heart.

She reached for the bond she shared with Aiden. His heart had remained heavy since the night before. She'd learned to separate herself from the connection a bit so it didn't incapacitate her, but it was like a small cut on her hand that wouldn't stop bleeding. What had happened? She tried to send comfort to him through their connection, but she had no idea if it even worked that way. All she knew was that she could feel Aiden's pain while he likely felt her wariness.

When the moon hit its peak, Penny crept out from the shadows.

She pulled the gloves from her hands, allowing the green and black glow of her magic to light up the world around her. Farrah summoned her red tinged shadow and allowed it to crawl over the ground at her boots.

Then, they began strolling.

The sound of people hummed through the air, but Penny had no idea where any of them actually were. Mother said the rebels worked on the docks most nights, bringing in and sending out supplies for the rest of the army scattered around Olympia. There had been a crew of about five hundred rebels when she'd first arrived. A small number of Eleusia's citizens had begun gathering to work against the rebels and had supported Mother when she'd returned to fight. Her interference with the rebels' work had called about a thousand men back from fighting against Paulo in Delphine, and she'd said the rest had gone to Olympia to aid with taking the capital.

Which led them to tonight. Mother's scheme had been in the works for nearly six weeks, and tonight would be the culmination of all her planning.

The satchel at Penny's hip bounced as she skipped through the streets. The trill of a whistle preceded the shadow zipping over the path in front of her and Farrah. A flash of lavender streaked between two buildings above them. While Dair couldn't activate the traps Mother had set, his speed made him an excellent scout.

Penny grabbed Farrah's arm and followed after him, her magic already swirling through her, seeking the little pockets of seeds in the ground. Her magic found one, but Penny pulled it away before it could activate the seeds.

The rasp of voices called ahead.

Penny let go of Farrah's arm and made her footsteps echo in the street. She pushed up her long sleeves and allowed the magic to surge through her body. The green and black glow nearly blinded her.

A trio walked through the intersection ahead of her, a woman and a man laughing at something the other man with them said. All three carried blades at their waists and iron rings circled their fingers. None of them stopped or even glanced her way.

Penny grumbled and stomped after them, not even drawing the sword hanging at her side.

"Hey!"

All three heads swiveled in her direction.

Farrah waved. "Do you have a minute to talk about My Sovereigns, High King Aiden and High Queen Penelope of Faerie?"

All three pairs of eyes widened, and they scrambled for the weapons at their waists.

"That's more like it," Penny said, pulling Farrah along.

They ran back the way they'd come. The pound of boots on the packed earth followed behind. Praise the Goddess. Penny pulled Farrah into the alleyway, the sparks of her magic leading her back to the pack in the ground. Farrah crossed over it first and Penny gathered her magic as she passed by. She looked back to see the rebels cross over the uneven ground and she shot her magic at the ground under their feet.

Vines shot up from beneath them. Blackberry thorns and vines of Mother's special species of poison ivy stretched up the buildings on either side of them. While regular poison ivy took days to go into effect, Mother's crafted species worked much quicker.

A trio of cries went up and Penny used her magic to craft a cage around the rebels. When they attempted to tear it down, the sharp thorns tore at their clothing and the ivy left lines of red rash across their skin. Curses shot from their mouths like dragon flame, but Penny brushed it off.

"If you wouldn't mind waiting here for a bit," Farrah said, "I'm sure someone will be along to fetch you eventually." The kind citizens Mother had recruited would be along to gather the trapped rebels and lock them in the bailiff house at the center of town.

A whistle crooned from above, and Penny followed Dair's shadow to their next target.

Over and over, Dair led them from one group to another. The rebels seemed to be in rotations of two or three, patrolling the streets and working to ship out supplies.

When Penny and Farrah finished with their fifth group, Dair landed beside them.

"Your mother has requested your help."

They followed him at a jog as he led them toward the west side of town. Smoke rose into the air and the clang of hammers reminded Penny of Heff. They found a group of people huddled behind a chandler's shop, their hushed whispers silent in the ring of metal on metal. Penny approached them, Dair and Farrah shadowing her. One of the women broke apart from the group and greeted them.

"Hello, Lady Penny. I'm Mystique." She lowered in a short curtsy. "Her Grace told us to meet you here."

"Pleased to meet you, Mystique. What's the plan?"

Mystique shook her head. "I can't claim to know. Lady Barclay only asked that we gather here and wait for more instructions."

Penny rolled her eyes. Always like Mother to keep things to herself. At least it was somewhat obvious they were going for whoever was inside the building across the street. It was the only place with any activity in the immediate area.

Penny turned to Dair. "Want to check in with the group? Make sure we have proper supplies?"

Dair swept into the group, checking for injuries and taking stock of the weapons they had. Penny followed behind him, adding numbers in her head. There were twenty men and women here, another thirty waiting on the other side of the building they were scouting out.

A weapons smithy.

Fae and mages had been sequestered in there for months, crafting weapons for the war. Apparently, there were multiple operations throughout Olympia, but this one was the biggest, having the easy access to supplies straight off the river. It was likely the very first smithy the rebels had established in Olympia.

Penny could smell the iron.

"Is everyone ready?" Mother asked, seeming to appear out of nowhere.

"What exactly are we supposed to be ready for?" Penny asked.

Mother pushed forward through the group. "We're raiding the weapons in there and freeing the gifted slaves."

Chatter broke out through their tiny group.

"I mean obviously we're doing that," Penny said, "but what's the *plan*?"

Mother grinned. "I have two dozen plant caches in the ground around the building. You and I will activate each one starting on this side of the building and going around to the other. We'll leave one door on either side open. The men and women here are going to push the rebels out from this side and into the waiting swords on the other."

"That sounds simple, but what are we going to do about the people in there? Aren't you worried about the rebels taking hostages?"

"I've thought about it, but I think we can take care of it if the situation arises."

Penny grabbed Mother's arm. "You *think*? Mother, you can't just barge in there expecting everything to go smoothly. We need to make sure everyone has the best chance for survival if we go in there."

Mother yanked her arm away. "I've been watching these rebels for months, Penny. I know what I'm doing."

Penny stayed where she was, allowing the others to flow past her. When the last of them did, Dair stepped into her peripheral. "Do you think we need to worry?"

She raised a brow. "Don't you?"

He nodded. "I think I will take lead then."

Penny caught the sleeve of his jacket. "Don't go in first. That entire building is full of iron, and we have no idea what kind of protections they made to keep the fae trapped in there. You and Farrah stay at the back and wait for me to go with you, all right?"

His jaw clenched, chaffing at the prospect of allowing the humans to go first no doubt, but he gave a sharp nod.

They followed at the back of the crowd, waiting for the rest of the group to get in position. Penny's gaze found Mother's. She pointed to the east side of the building while going in the direction of the west. Magic swirled inside Penny as she connected with the packets set at even intervals along the building. When she made it to the halfway point, she unleashed the magic.

Long vines of kudzu, one of the fastest growing vines Penny knew of, covered the entire building in seconds. While the plant wasn't poisonous or barbed, it completely covered the entire building like a blanket, only letting slivers of light in or out. Shouts from inside were muffled by the thick plants and eventually went silent.

Penny pushed forward to the front of the building, ready to use the vines to take down any rebels that came through with the group waiting.

Swords at the ready, the Eleusion citizens watched the one exposed door on this side of the building.

After a few minutes without sign of any rebels, Penny's stomach began to sicken. Her magic stirred within her, the Land so far away plucking at the connection they shared.

"Something's not right," Penny said quietly. She turned to the closest man standing by the door. "Open it."

"But Her Grace said—"

Urgency slammed Penny in the stomach. Her sword was in her hand before she even thought of doing it. "Open it now!"

The man grabbed the door handle and threw it open.

The image that greeted them did not match the silence.

Penny stepped through the door, passing over the invisible barrier she'd only just realized existed, and the sound came rushing to her.

The folk and the mages inside screamed as they were slaughtered right in front of her.

"No!" Penny shouted. She sprang into action, her sword slicing into the back of a man that had a knife to a defenseless woman's throat. The man slumped to the ground, his knife leaving a shallow wound on the woman's neck. Iron-shackled hands went to the cut, but she'd live.

Two rebels dropped the wounded fae they were holding, turning their crude blades in her direction. The long knives in their hands featured twisted blades, three edges winding around each other. The fae they had stabbed fell to the ground; their hands pressed against the quickly bleeding wounds.

They weren't going to make it out of this building.

With a cry, Penny lunged toward them, Farrah close at her heels. While the rebels' knives could inflict devastating damage, they were terrible for hand-to-hand combat. She easily disarmed both rebels and cut into the leg of one, immobilizing him before moving onto the next threat. Humans were much easier to subdue than fae. The second man grabbed a hammer from one of the tables and swung at her head. A miniature portal appeared between his hand and her head. His arm sank into the black before the black disappeared, taking half of his arm with it. Blood sprayed and he fell back into a table of tools.

Before Penny could send Farrah a nod of thanks, another rebel took his comrade's place. He swung a broadsword at her head. She ducked and grabbed her dagger from her boot. As she came up, she sank her blade into his gut.

"Mage scum," the man spat. A glob of bloody saliva hit her in the cheek.

Penny bared her teeth. "You're mistaken. I'm the cursed Faerie Queen." She pulled her dagger from his abdomen and hit him over the head with it. His eyes rolled back in his head, and he fell.

The door on the other side of the building crashed open and Dair stormed in, shadows writhing around him. With a snap of his fingers, several of the black masses surged across the large workspace. Each one shot into the rebels' ears. In a single moment, the rebels that had been attacked by the slivers of shadow crumpled to the ground. The other rebels turned from their captives; their eyes trained on the growing number of Penny's group.

Penny pointed her sword at one of them. "Surrender your weapons."

One of the rebels grabbed a little boy by the hair and brought a jagged looking knife to his throat. "Or what?"

Green light flared from behind him, and a kudzu vine snaked from the ground and wrapped around his arms. The little boy went to his knees and crawled under a table as the man struggled in the encroaching greenery.

"Or we will truss you up like the pigs you are and prepare you for a spit," Mother snapped as she came into view, her face smeared in dirt and blood.

The man's curses grew more venomous, and Penny's patience snapped. With a snap of her fingers, she grew an apple tree beside her and plucked a fully ripe red delicious from the branches. When the man's mouth opened with a holler, Penny thrust the fruit between his teeth.

Mother turned back to the rest of the rebels scattered about the room, her large scythe propped up on her shoulder. "Anyone else want to be put on the menu?"

The remaining dozen rebels dropped their weapons.

"Wise choice."

Within minutes, the rebels were carted off toward the bailiff's jail, and the slaves were set free. Penny knelt by the little boy hiding under the table.

"Are you all right?"

The boy's amethyst eyes flicked around. "Are you really here to let us out?"

Penny sat fully on the ground. "Yes, of course. Do you want to come outside with me?"

The little boy licked his cracked lips nervously but nodded and scuttled out. Penny stood and walked beside him, following the rest of the group out the doors. His shoulders started shaking when he glimpsed a man—a *fae* crumpled on the ground near the door, a pool of blood beneath him. He had the same dark blue hair and honey-colored skin as the boy.

Penny pulled him closer and ushered him past, her eyes prickling with tears. How many families had to suffer before this battle was over? How many little boys would lose their fathers? Their mothers? Brothers and sisters?

Penny hurried the boy from the gruesome building. Hopefully someone would be able to help him.

Seemingly from nowhere, Dair came forward, crouching in front of the little boy.

"Hello, cousin."

The boy's eyes met Dair's, still filled with tears. "Are we cousins?"

"I think I know your parents, though it has been quite some time." Dair gave him a smile. "Your father's name is Càirdeas, am I right?"

The boy looked back at the building they'd just exited before turning back and nodding.

"Then you are a distant cousin of mine for certain. In fact, you are also a distant cousin of the High King, whose wife you just happen to be standing next to." Dair looked up at Penny. "Càirdeas used to live in Crann Mòr with his wife and two sons."

Penny crouched down to their level. "What's your name?"

"Strì, My Sovereign." He bent in a small bow.

"There's no need for that, Strì. We're family after all." She looked around at the crowd moving through the wide street they stood in. "Do you know where your mother is? Or your brother?"

Strì shook his head, tears falling onto his cheeks. "Only *athair*." Tiny sobs wracked his small frame, and Penny wrapped her arms around him.

"It's all right, Strì. I promise, you'll be all right."

Dawn shimmered over the river as the cheers of two hundred brontes, mages, and fae rang through the air. Dair and Strì stood next to Penny as a celebration of sorts began. Food and drink were passed around, and someone had even managed to track down a lute from somewhere. Farrah plucked at the strings from atop a barrel.

Penny tried to smile, but she felt dead on her feet. Even without Aiden's low mood slightly affecting her, she'd forgotten what it was like to use her magic without the constant connection to the Land around her. She hadn't been this tired since before she'd gone to Faerie.

Speaking of being tired...

"Dair, what was that thing you did with your shadows?"

"What thing?" he asked.

"I saw pieces of your shadows go in through the rebels' ears and then they fell. What did you do?"

"Oh!" Understanding dawned on his face. "I put them to sleep."

Penny recalled when he'd knocked her out to help her connect with the Land. "Have you always been able to do that?"

"Yes. I do not do it very often. Sleeping does not invite good conversation after all."

"How many can you put to sleep at one time?"

He shrugged. "I do not exactly know. Once, I put the entire Winter Palace to sleep at winter solstice, so I could see what gifts my parents had got for Thaen and I. *Athair* gave me a good thrashing for that one."

Penny could only imagine a young Dair rummaging through presents with a mischievous grin on his face. "I think you've been playing us all for fools."

He stood and dusted off his pants. "I would never." He gave her a wink then turned to Strì, who was falling asleep against the crate his small frame was propped up against. "Come, cousin. Let us get you some food and find you a bed."

Strì nodded and stood. Dair led him in the direction of one of the impromptu tables set up around the street.

Mother joined Penny a few minutes later. "Good work tonight, Penny."

Penny frowned. "A lot of good people lost their lives tonight. I wouldn't call that good work, Mother."

Mother's head drooped. "I didn't realize the rebels could be so...

ruthless. I wish I would have known or planned better. I don't know." She straightened and looked about. "But I think we still did *good*. These people will live to see the coming dawn, and that is more than many others still under the thumb of the rebels. I can't regret that."

Penny nodded, but it didn't mean the regret lessened. She could see the same sorrow in the slump of Mother's shoulders, though she hid it well. Penny guessed Mother would be thinking about this night for long after this war was over. They all would.

She wrapped an arm around Penny's shoulders, her eyes circled by weariness. "Let's let them celebrate, and we can find a place to rest. There will be quite the clean-up happening after the huge mess we just made." She led her from the revelry, Farrah trailing behind while Dair helped with the party. When they made it a fair distance from the crowd, Mother spoke again. "That little stunt with the apple tree was quite impressive."

Penny nearly snorted. "Caught that, did you?" She looked down at her hands, the bronze of her skin showing again instead of the green and black. "I didn't realize I could do it on this side of the border."

"You mean you don't need seed in Faerie?"

"Not at all. I can grow an entire forest with a thought." Penny chuckled. "Though, I haven't had much time to experiment. It all changed again after Aiden and I married."

Mother's green eyes narrowed. "We really are going to have to have a conversation about that soon."

"Do you want to do it before or after we save the rest of Olympia?"

41
RANK AND FILE

"That is what all the fuss is about?" Dair asked, staring up the hill at the white walls of Olympia's palace. "The turrets do not even touch the clouds."

"Not every king has a palace like the one in Eagallach," Penny said, rubbing her eyes. She apparently hadn't slept enough the night before, the price of her magic still making her tired even after the two weeks it had been since they'd taken Eleusia back.

Dair flicked his long braid off his shoulder. "Perhaps King Dion should consider it. This tiny thing does not inspire much majesty."

Farrah elbowed him in the ribs.

Mother glared back at them. "Will the three of you be quiet?"

Wincing, Penny caught up to her. "Was it like this when you were here last?"

"No. This is much worse."

The entire capital was empty, the streets deserted and alleys gaping maws. Windows covered in boards glowered at the street below. Some of the homes they walked past had been broken into, doors hanging from their hinges and broken furniture thrown out onto the street. Penny couldn't imagine what the palace looked like.

"How are we going to get past the barrier?" Farrah asked. "My portals can't cross shields like that."

Penny could see it too. A translucent dome glittered over the palace, only the highest turrets breaking through the top. It reminded her of the small shields Aiden and Thaen often used when they sparred. How much magic had to have been taken to make such a large one?

"I sent word ahead," Mother said.

"When?" Penny asked. "To whom?"

"Why to me, darling."

Penny spun, her heart thumping in her chest as a grin spreading over her face.

"Who is that?" Dair asked, stars in his eyes.

Penny's grinned, knowing exactly how he was feeling. "Hello, Rissa."

The siren stood, tucked in the doorway of a silent tavern. Her boots clicked over the cobblestones as she came out into the light. Her wine-red hair hung in two long braids on either shoulder, her sea-green eyes sparkling with delight.

"Hello, Penny."

Penny closed the remaining distance between them and wrapped her arms around Rissa. "I've missed you."

The siren pulled away slightly. "How's our Lord of the Underworld?"

"A 'lord' no longer, that's for certain." Penny looped her arm through Rissa's. "He's certainly taken to his new role as High King with dedication."

"And you to High Queen, eh?" Penny's face heated and Rissa laughed. "I can't tell you how long I laughed when Shaunie told us. Heff was downright thrilled."

Mother coughed from beside them. "Excuse me, but could we please move this charming reunion to somewhere a little less public? I'm not keen on getting shackled and dragged to the palace."

Rissa straightened, but the twinkle in her eye didn't abate one bit. "Of course, Your Grace. I was only waiting for the rest of the team to arrive."

"What team?" Dair asked.

"'What team?' he asks!" Jolly walked out onto the street, his signature grin already on display. "Din't think you'd get into the king without a escort, did ya?"

Adele and Harper stepped out from behind the giant of a man. Harper's blond curls had been cut close to his head and Adele's petite frame looked even tinier than Penny remembered, her dark hair framing her striking face. The trio looked so incomplete without their leader. An ache Penny had almost begun to live with sharpened slightly. She could see that same pain reflected in the eyes of the spies before her. Hart's death still took its toll.

"I didn't realize we required an entourage," Mother said, her brow quirked. "I assumed Penny and I would be enough backup."

Rissa shrugged. "We were already out on assignment when I got your note." She pulled a slip of paper from her pocket and waved it at them. "I figured we could catch two fish with one hook."

"You mean kill two birds with one stone," Harper said.

Dair looked at him in horror. "Why would you stone a bird?"

"Never mind that," Penny said, pulling him and Farrah forward. "Rissa, I'd like to introduce Farrah of Autumn, daughter to the High Councilor Sgiath and a previous resident of Eleusia as well as Prince Dair, Heir to the Winter Throne and Aiden's cousin."

"Oh-ho! A cousin you say?" Harper asked.

"Absolutely none of this matters right now," Mother answered hurriedly. "What *does* matter is how we're supposed to get to King Dion, break into the palace, and free the city from these cursed rebels."

Jolly swung an arm around her neck. "You just stick with us, Yer Grace. We'll get you in."

Mother unceremoniously shoved his arm off, her face burning with indignation.

Penny turned away before she could see the verbal lashing Jolly was on his way to receiving. "Where's Dion?" she asked Rissa.

Rissa spun on her heel, her long jacket swirling around her legs. "Come with me."

Dion lay sprawled on a divan in the dimly lit sitting room, a bottle at the tips of his fingers and a snore rattling the wooden floorboards. Penny didn't recognize the house, but she did notice the thick layer of dust and the all-encompassing emptiness of its walls. Her gaze darted about, waiting for something to jump out, but everything besides Dion was silent as a grave. Whoever it might have belonged to, it hadn't been used in a very long time.

Penny walked fully into the room, only a few steps behind Mother, whose shoulders were bunched up like a hissing cat. "You brought him here of all places?"

Rissa shrugged. "Figured this was the one place no one would think to look for him."

Dair turned to Penny. "Where are we?"

Penny shrugged, but Harper answered from the doorway. "Durant House."

With new eyes, Penny took in the room. It was rather empty, most of the pictures torn from the walls and the barest amount of furniture left to collect dust, but now that Penny knew, she saw Adira in the small details. The intricate rug on the floor, the very symmetrical pegs in the walls where pictures would have hung. The shadowy corners, nooks, and crannies best for secrets. Even bare, the house screamed Adira.

Mother found a pitcher on the only side table still left and lifted it up, swirling whatever contents were left inside. She glided over to the divan where Dion continued to snore and dumped the contents of the pitcher over his head.

Dion sat up, sputtering. Sparks zipped over the water, and Penny imagined his hair would be standing straight up if it wasn't soaked.

"*What the blasted*—" He stopped when his eyes caught on Mother's very disapproving glare. "Oh, hello Duchess Dominique." He glanced around at the rest of the room, grabbing his cane out of the cushions of the divan and ridding himself of the electricity. "My, what a party I seem to have forgotten I was hosting."

His perusal stopped when he got to Penny and his brows shot straight up. He got to his feet, swaying. "My favorite sister, Nell! This is a pleasant surprise!"

Mother shoved him back into his seat. "What on Gaia's green earth is going on here, Your Majesty? Why are you holed up in the Durant's old house, and where is your queen?"

Dion attempted to strike an elegant pose, but the drunken limbs combined with the soaked clothing made him more ridiculous. "Can't you tell? This is where the king has come to be exiled. Shaunie has apparently decided she doesn't wish to see me anymore. Rissa and Heff were kind enough to smuggle me back to this cesspit and allow me to watch my city burn around me." His gaze locked on Penny once again. "How's my brother, Your Majesty?"

Penny reached for the link she had to Aiden. His life beat strongly back at her, something like determination mingled with sadness, but he was alive. "He's well, Dion. I saw Shaunie at the Hermen's."

His violet eyes cleared a bit. "How was she?" In those few words, it was obvious he missed his wife. Penny could see the worry, the stress it was to be parted from her. She felt that same knot in herself. But she couldn't empathize with the shame that seemed to weigh down his shoulders.

"She's as well as can be expected," Penny answered. She came around the group and sat next to Dion, trying her best to avoid getting the skirts she'd borrowed from Mother wet. "Why are you here, Dion? Why aren't you with her?"

Dion sighed and raked his soggy mane from his face. "I"—he swallowed—"I messed up, Nell. I ruined everything."

Penny set a hand on his arm. "What happened?"

He met her gaze, the amethyst of his eyes dull. "I was the one who let the rebels take the palace."

He laid it all out for her, with the help of the Underworld. Assassins had infiltrated the palace, working alongside the palace staff for months. They became trusted individuals, especially as chaos broke out over the city. The first riot had burned down the city council building, cutting the people off from meeting with their representatives. The second had seen the city watchmen cut down and their towers turned to rubble. The third had seen the murder of a member of the nobility, and that had been the end of it for the noble houses. Dion had instigated a curfew which only stoked the flames of the people. The siege happened in hours, the palace completely overrun by rebels.

"The siege wasn't even the worst thing to happen that night," Dion said, his voice quiet. "It was also the day Shaunie lost our babe."

"How did it happen?" Mother asked softly.

"Poison," Jolly spat.

"She was laid up for days," Rissa said, "throwing up everything until she couldn't keep even a glass of water down. The midwife had gone missing, and a kitchen girl had gained the trust of the king, claiming she could help Shaunie. When Shaunie grew more ill, the girl told all the ladies-in-waiting to stay away for her safety. What we didn't know was the kitchen girl was an assassin herself."

Penny's stomach sank. "How did you figure it out?"

Dion blew out a breath. "Good old Polly and his magic sight saved her, though..." He wiped at his eyes. "I can't say that she didn't die along with the babe."

That explained why he was here, alone. Why there were bottles piled in every corner of the room and why he couldn't look any of them straight in the eye for more than a second. Penny could almost smell the guilt, raw and sour on the stale air of the lonely house.

Mother crossed her arms over her chest. "How did they end up getting the shield up around the palace?"

"They gained access to the Royal Sitting Room." Dion turned his face to the floor. "My cursed father had it installed years ago. I imagine Adira Durant shared it with her little cohort, having known about it from her time as spymaster."

The back of Penny's throat tightened. Everything always led back to Adira. When would it end? When would this suffering be enough?

"We don't need to go into all of the details," Rissa said. "We can only look forward to the future."

"How are you planning to take back the palace?" Dair asked.

Rissa grinned. "I've made some interesting new friends in my time outside the palace walls. With my two favorite Barclay women now present, and a very dashing fae prince along with a portal wielding Tuatha to add to our retinue, I think we may have just enough to send those rebels running." She turned back to Dion. "But you'll need to convince the queen."

Smuggling the king out of the city wasn't the difficult part. With the capital still full of people and the roads not monitored because of the fight in Faerie, they made it out of the city unscathed. Rissa and Heff had split off from them once they reached the crossroads leading to Eleusion and Delphine. They promised to meet them back at the capital when the time came, leaving them to speak with Stone on the plan.

No, the difficult part was getting Dion to face his wife.

He stood in the front lawn of the Hermen's manor, unmoving, his eyes on the front door. Thin flashes of light trailed over his fingers, zipping toward the cane he held in a death grip.

"She won't see me," he whispered. "It'll be better for you to just go in there, Penny, and tell her why we're here. I can stay outside with the horses."

Mother set her hands on her hips. "Honestly, Your Majesty. You'd think we were sending you to the blasted guillotine with a look like that."

"She won't see me," he said. "You know she won't."

Mother rolled her eyes and moved to stand in front of him. "Are you going to let your kingdom fall into ruin because you're too proud to ask for forgiveness?"

Dion's head snapped in her direction. "You think it's *pride* that keeps me from walking in there?" He shook his head. "Then you have no idea what it is to love someone."

Mother slapped him across the face.

Penny's mouth fell completely open, as did the rest of the group's. Hitting a monarch wasn't just disrespectful, but borderline treasonous. Dion could have Mother's head simply for standing too close.

Instead of retaliating, as he had every right as king to do, he hung his head. Not even a spark bouncing off him now.

Mother took a step closer, getting very much in his personal space and somehow looking down on him even though he was a good two heads taller than her. "You think love is the only thing that makes a marriage? Believe me, I thought it too, but we were both wrong. Love can't save you when you fall on hard times. Love can't save you when the other decides yours isn't enough. Love can't heal illness, shield against hunger, or deliver you from calamity. Love is a great tool, but it can also be a great weapon, even used against oneself. It can force you to do things you never wanted to but also give you the chance to become something greater than what you could on your own."

Dion's words came out as something smaller than a whisper. "But what if I can't fix it?"

"I know what a broken love looks like," Mother said, "and believe me, what you have is nowhere near broken. But fissures can grow and become rotten, savage things. Go to your wife. Make it right. If you don't, you may discover she has better things to fight for than your love."

Dion took a deep breath, nodded, and walked to the door.

Penny had to keep herself from moving as she pressed her ear to the polished door. Dion and Shaunie had taken up the sitting room, and while there hadn't been screaming or lightning raining down on anyone, Penny couldn't help but feel an urgency to hurry. Even her magic kept sparking, the green and black of her hands flickering in the afternoon light.

They needed Shaunie. They needed her strength along with the love of the people she had garnered over the last several years. While Dion might have been ruling over the masses, it was Shaunie who ruled over the palace. If they wanted a smooth takeover, Shaunie was the one to get it done quickly and efficiently. Besides, Penny needed Dion's help raising an army at the border. No king in their right mind would leave his just-reclaimed palace behind if he didn't have someone to care for it.

"I don't want to go back to the palace," Shaunie said. Her voice held all the gravitas of a queen delivering orders to her subjects. "I am tired of the lies and the deceit that seems to grow between those cursed walls."

"That's our home, Shaunie," Dion said, voice as timid as Penny had ever heard it.

"That's *your* home," she snapped. "That place has only ever been a prison for me. From the very moment my father signed our betrothal contract, I knew I would forever live in that gilded cage. But I believed being queen would make it all worth it. That my sacrifice would at least put me in a position to help others. How wrong I was."

"You weren't wrong," Dion said, barely audible through the door.

Shaunie scoffed. "Look at where we are, Dee. We can't help anyone. We had to go crawling to Denny to ask for help, which we can't even reciprocate. I can't help anyone."

"That's not true. I know you helped the Eiles with their babes. I know you've been helping Rissa keep tabs on what's going on."

Dion's voice grew bolder. "You are everything this kingdom needs—"

"We don't even have a kingdom anymore. It was taken right from your hands by a pretty face."

"Then we'll take it right back!" Dion pleaded. "We'll take it all back."

Silence stretched between them. Penny had to rub at her chest. The bond with Aiden seemed to tighten. If he was here, he would be able to help them. He would know what to say to these two people he loved so much to help them see how loved they were.

But he wasn't here.

"We can't take it all back," Shaunie said, her voice now quiet. "We are broken beyond repair, Dee. You saw to that."

The sound of Dion's boots clipped on the hardwood floor, matching the beating of Penny's heart. They should be able to get into the palace without Shaunie's help but having both the king and queen arrive at the palace, united even through their trials, would give the people hope. Hope that wouldn't thrive if Shaunie and Dion couldn't nurture it.

"I don't know what to do," Dion blurted. "I don't know what you need or how to fix all of this. I don't know how to turn back the clock and make different choices. I don't know how to do all of this without you."

"You've certainly never needed me before now. Sweet Gaia, I wasn't even enough for you when you had it all. Why would I be now?" The scuff of a chair moving preceded the angry clip of steps in Penny's direction. She pulled away, glancing around for a quick escape.

The steps stopped right on the other side, but the door didn't budge.

"Please, Shaunie," Dion said, far too close for comfort. "I've lost my home, my kingdom, my brothers. I don't want to lose you too."

"*I lost him!*" The last word broke as Shaunie sobbed. "I lost *our son*, Dion. I lost him because *you* couldn't keep yourself from chasing after other girls even after we were blasted married. After you had sworn you were done playing games, and I finally let you into my bed. I lost my baby and nearly died because of you! So don't you dare try to tell me that you've lost more than me. Don't you dare come back to this place, where I am safe, and try to tell me that I have to sacrifice more for a sorry excuse of a man who invited my son's murderer—*my murderer*—into our home because she lifted her skirt for you. You have no right. *No right* to tell me that you need me when all you've ever done is push me away. When I've given my soul to this kingdom only to have you throw it back in my face. I am *done* being your lapdog. I am done wasting my time hoping that you'll finally give it all up for me. I'm done being the villain in whatever twisted fairytale you've decided to live in."

The doorknob finally twisted, and Penny jumped back. She really should have left them to sort this out without an audience, but she couldn't help herself.

She took another step away, but something in her made her stop. Wait. Listen.

"What?" Shaunie said, the doorknob twisting back into place. "What other excuses are you trying to fling at me this time?"

Penny took another step closer.

"I am so sorry, Shaunie." Dion's voice cracked, devolving into quiet cries. Penny heard him fall, his knees hitting the floorboards with a crack. "You are the best thing that ever happened to me, and you've never been given the credit you deserve. When you told me you were with child, you can't even imagine how much joy and absolute terror the news brought me. I couldn't believe I had finally done something right by you, that I could finally give you something you wanted. But I was terrified I wouldn't be the man that you both deserved. That I wouldn't be able to protect either of you from what was happening. You and our child were all that mattered to me, but I allowed my fear to rule me. I broke my promise. I gave into the weaknesses I had sworn to you I wouldn't. I know this is all my fault and I am so, so sorry."

"You don't get to fix this with an apology," Shaunie hissed. "This isn't about you anymore. You always make it about *you* while everything I've ever done has been for everyone else. I'm done catering to you and every other cursed person that wants something from me. Hang your kingdom, hang your brothers, and hang everyone else for all I care! This is about what I've lost. What was taken from me before I even had the chance to finally hold that precious dream in my arms. I suffered through hours of pain after losing my dream, praying the Goddess would just take me and be done with it. This is about me having to live after that, having to wake up every morning and find the will not to just lie down and never get up again. 'Sorry' will never, *ever* be enough."

Shaunie's voice cracked, like a whip. Penny could swear Shaunie hit flesh as she heard Dion's slight whimper. Could swear each word hit their mark again and again.

A low sob cracked a piece of Penny's heart. Dion's soft cries filtered through the small crack under the door. The cries of a broken man.

The whisper of Shaunie's skirts against the door trailed down to the floor. "I can't trust you, Dee."

"You have every right not to," Dion said, a hiccup cutting through his cries. "I know there's no going back for us. Sweet Gaia, I've known for a long time that I ruined any future where you would trust me to be the king, the husband, the *man* you needed."

He hiccupped again. "I'm not going to make you go anywhere, Shaunie. If you want to stay here with the Hermens and be pranked by their litter of tiny tyrants, I won't make you. You have earned every right—ten times, a hundred times over—to choose your own future."

"But?" Shaunie asked, still right next to the door.

"But..." Penny could practically feel Dion praying. "But if you did decide you wanted to be queen, that it did put you in the best position to help people the way you want, I would do everything in my power to help you. If you wanted to rule on your own, I would disappear. Go find a hole somewhere to live out my days."

"Maybe Denny would let you sleep on one of his fancy, faerie couches," Shaunie said.

Dion barked a laugh still heavy with sorrow. "Or I could try my hand at being a sailor. I'm sure they'd appreciate someone who could keep the storms away."

"You'd turn everyone into pirates."

"I'd be a pirate king! And whenever I came into port in Olympia, I would bring you priceless treasures from around the world. I would fill your coffers so you could help your kingdom."

"Like I would allow pirates into my port."

"I would find a way to get those riches to you." Dion's voice turned serious. "I swear to you, I would do whatever it took to make sure you were happy. That you had whatever you needed to accomplish your goals."

Shaunie's voice was soft when she spoke next. "And what if I don't need a pirate king, but a true king who is willing to help me take back our palace?"

"Whatever you want, my love, I'll give you."

Mother had holed herself up with Lady Hermen somewhere. Dair had gone off to get into trouble as usual and Farrah had taken the opportunity to race to Faerie and update everyone there. Rissa and her crew had left the Hermen estate to fetch another member of their crew. And Penny had been left in the dining room to worry about all of it.

"With all of that pent-up energy, perhaps I should make *you* hold Regina," Angelica said. Regina's tiny fists were bunched up in her blanket, but she didn't make any noise as Angelica bounced her. Angelica stood beside the chair where Devan sat, Sage curled up in a bundle on his chest, snoozing quietly as he read over the reports scattered over the tabletop.

Penny stood and reached out for the babe. "I'd love nothing more."

Dair sauntered into the room a few minutes later, silky hair draped down his back and a fresh tunic falling to mid-thigh, looking like the prince he was. He came to stand by Penny and peeked at the sleeping baby in her arms.

"Hello, Little One," he said when Regina's dark eyes stared up at him. He reached a finger forward to graze the still-clenched fists of blanket. "I have never had much experience with bairns. Such tiny things."

As she bounced the tiny infant, Penny reached for her bond with Aiden. Having children during wartimes was not something either of them felt comfortable with and they were a bit young to jump into it, even if it was somewhat expected of them. Heirs were important to a reigning house. Desired. But for Penny, it had to be the right time. She wouldn't bring a child into a war. Not when Adira loomed over everything. Not when they would be in immediate danger.

"Anything from Farrah?" Penny asked. She had left only that morning and didn't expect to be back until that evening, but Penny couldn't help asking even as the sun had only reached its pinnacle in the sky.

"She's still gone," Dair replied.

Penny's magic flickered again, that urgency flaring up inside of her. Dair frowned down at her capped sleeve.

"Penelope, why has your tell lessened?"

Penny looked over at her arm and nearly gasped. When they'd arrived in Olympia, the green tell had remained the same as it had been after she'd been coronated. The green glow of her magic had reached above the curve of her shoulder, nearly to her neck. Now it reached just below the sleeve of her gown, just above her bicep.

"What do you think it means?" she asked.

Dair shook his head. "I cannot claim to know, but we need to watch it. Have there been any other odd symptoms?"

Penny almost responded with a no but stopped herself. "I've been a bit more tired than usual."

A sliver of alarm tugged at the corners of Dair's amber eyes. "We need to be more conscious about you using your magic. We do not know what changes may have occurred with your eating the fruit and being coronated."

Penny nodded, unease slithering about in her stomach. She'd tried to get the rest she knew she needed to refill her magic, but was being away from Faerie draining her like it would Aiden? What would happen if she ran out of time?

Mother walked in next, and Penny pushed her tell away. She'd done the same as Dair and had donned more suitable attire than she'd arrived in, likely something of Lady Hermen's due to the blue color of the skirts. Mother almost never swayed from their house green or beige. She walked over to where Angelica now sat, and the two of them spoke in hushed tones.

Penny tiptoed over to them.

"—taking Devan to assist," Mother was saying. "Your mother said he would be the best option of getting us to the warehouse in Olympia."

Angelica nodded. "Take him with you. Devan knows all the best ways around the city. It was part of his job."

The door to the sitting room swung open, and Shaunie stepped in, followed by Dion. Both had red-rimmed eyes and sorrowful spirits, but they also shared small smiles with the rest of the room, and

Dion's hand rested on the small of Shaunie's back. Penny let out a sigh of relief. If she was allowing him to touch her, they were probably going to be all right. The two of them glided over to where Penny stood. Shaunie's tender expression softened even further as she looked at the sleeping infant.

"The Goddess truly does create the most beautiful creatures," she said.

Dion's expression turned sad as he watched his wife, but Penny was almost overjoyed to see an inkling of hope there too as he stepped closer to her. The overwhelming despair Penny had witnessed from him was nearly gone, replaced by somberness and determination.

"How are you, Shaunie?" Penny asked.

Shaunie met her eyes. A familiar fire crackled within the icy blue of her gaze. "I'm ready to take my palace back."

Penny smiled and gently passed the bundle into Shaunie's arms. "Then let's go."

"When?" Dion asked, glancing about the room.

Mother folded her arms over her chest and lifted her chin. "We leave at first light."

42

ARMED AND READY

A High Queen, a royal couple, a faerie prince, and a domineering duchess, walk into a city infested with rebels...

To Penny, it sounded like the start of a terrible joke.

Lord and Lady Hermen had offered to send men to the warehouse with them, but after discussing it with everyone, Devan had told them to direct fighters toward the palace instead. They would need the distraction at the front gates if this plan was going to work. It would be much easier to get a smaller team into the palace anyway. The seven of them were going to cause enough of a ruckus taking down the shields and freeing the fae from within the palace. If all went as planned, the palace would be theirs.

Devan turned back to their group and pressed a finger to his lips. Their already-hushed breaths went still as they crept closer to the large Hermen warehouse. The thing was gigantic, sitting on the north side of the city and at the closest point to Lord Hermen's lands. The only reason it hadn't been infiltrated had been because of the intense wards placed on the building, even more secure than those of the palace or anything Lord Discordia had.

Once they reached the building, Dion hissed, "The devil has been holding out on me. We probably could have defended the palace if he'd shared this shield."

Devan looked back at him. "You can't blame him too harshly. It would be bad business to give Olympia the means to defend against the fair folk when it was intended to protect their own assets rather than an enemy's. Stone would have never risked such an affront to his suppliers."

Dion frowned. "But I don't know how no one knew."

"Aiden knew the whole time," Devan said.

"Of course Denny knew." He grinned back at Penny. "He's turned out to be as much of a devil as Stone."

Penny rolled her eyes.

Devan unlocked a small side door with his key and gestured for everyone to wait while he looked inside. He came back with an *all clear* and the rest of them filed through the door.

"Why did we have to come here when the Hermen's had weapons at the estate?" Dair asked.

"The first thing we need to focus on is how to dismantle that shield," Mother said.

"We came to this specific warehouse because of its proximity to Faerie," Devan said. "Most of the enchanted items we'll need will be here." He led them to another door, this one warded within every grain of the wood. "If all of you would step back, I just want to make sure I do this right without causing anyone else harm."

"Are you sure you know what you're doing?" Dair asked, glancing over the charm engraved on the door.

Farrah whistled. "That thing will obliterate us faster than Nonnie can carve up a squash for supper."

Penny watched, wide eyed, as Devan slowly began touching the charms. Penny had seen Nonnie cut up a squash with her giant cleaver. It was nothing to scoff at. One by one, the engravings he traced lit up a faint white color. When he'd traced seven of the runes, they all flashed solid green, and the door slid into the wall.

Devan let out a breath. "I've only ever opened it once, and Stone had been right there to watch in case I messed up."

Dair paled.

As the rest of the group followed him in, Penny stayed at the back of the group with Dair and Farrah. "What would have happened if he'd gotten it wrong?"

Farrah shook her head. "You don't want to know."

Following Dion and Shaunie, Penny tentatively stepped inside.

Rows and rows of enchanted items lined the walls of the windowless room. Jars of strange liquids glimmered next to stacks of old parchment tattooed with indecipherable words. Pouches of minerals and gems hung from small pegs above boxes of boots in different sizes and colors. Enchanted pieces of jewelry sat in velvet-lined boxes. A desk sat in the middle of the room, a large, leather-bound inventory book laying open atop it.

As Devan headed straight for the desk, Penny couldn't help but gape at the treasure trove of magic. "How has this place not been ransacked?" If she had been Adira, this would have been one of the first places she hit.

"The protections on this room are like nothing else in Olympia," Devan said proudly. "Stone has taken great pains to ensure the safety of our business."

Dion muttered under his breath but walked over to a section of enchanted keys.

"What do you think, Penelope?"

Penny turned as Dair showed off a chain-mail jerkin made of a dark metal she couldn't name.

"What does it do?" she asked.

Dair shrugged. "I have not the faintest clue, but I thought it would go good with those boots over there."

Penny refrained from rolling her eyes. Leave it to Dair to make a fashion statement with enchanted objects.

"Here we go," Devan said, tapping his finger on the open page of the book on the desk. "We need three of the enchanted keys on the hooks, a jar of anti-enchantment, and at least a dozen magic suppressant charms, as well as an entire sack of magelights." He walked to the cases of jewelry and picked up a leather cuff and a simple, sapphire necklace. "It also probably wouldn't hurt for Your Majesties to wear some glamours either."

"What about weapons?" Mother said, leaning over to glance at a spear that stuck out of a pot of water. The yew wood shaft almost glittered with carvings, though Penny couldn't identify what language it was.

"The enchantments are going to be our greatest weapons for this endeavor." He tapped the book once more and walked over to a set of drawers. Locating the one he was looking for, he opened it and pulled out a spool of golden thread. "If you were worried about swords, I believe Rissa has that covered."

Through the night, they traveled around the outskirts of the city until they found themselves on the beach below the palace. Above them towered a sheer cliff face pockmarked with small caves. Devan had named himself the official tools keeper and was in the process of braiding together the golden string he'd taken to prepare for their journey through the cave network above them. Dair had gone to act as lookout, and Farrah was enjoying her time on the moonlit beach. Without a fire to keep warm against the autumn breezes coming off the sea, Penny huddled together next to Shaunie while Dion and Mother went back and forth about the best way up the cliff.

"I thought Rissa said she had a plan," Shaunie whispered. "I don't know why the two of them are arguing over what to do."

Amusement curled at Penny's mouth. "Because they're only happy when they are the ones in charge. They've never seen eye to eye, you know."

Shaunie pulled the shawl she wore tighter around her shoulders. "He's ridiculous sometimes."

"So is she," Penny said, "but it seems like we love them anyway."

Shaunie's frustrated expression softened. "Why do we do that to ourselves?"

"Because we're the best people to love them, even though they drive us completely mad most of the time." Penny put an arm around Shaunie. "The Goddess doesn't make mistakes, and I think you and Dion were chosen for one another even if it seems like it was the Tyrant King and your father who decided your fate."

Shaunie gave a small smile. "Thank you, Penny. I'm glad you were able to be here for all of this."

A clatter of stones made Penny turn. Farrah dumped a few more rocks from the folds of her tunic next to a pile of seaweed. She had a good size sandcastle coming together.

"Couldn't you just portal us up?" Penny asked.

"I don't think it would be wise. With the way the wind will have worn down the rock, we won't know what's stable. I could portal us up onto one of the ledges only for it to crack and send us plummeting to our deaths. Best to do it the old fashion way."

Dair appeared next to Penny. "The rest of our party has arrived."

Penny turned to see Rissa coming down the beach, Heff's hand in hers, with members of the Underworld on their heels. As she counted, Penny realized the number was one more than she'd thought. A head of black hair bobbed up and down, weaving in and out of sight behind Heff. They came into view and Penny couldn't believe it when the new member of their band finally stepped forward.

"Laurel?" Penny asked, breaking away from the others.

Laurel bobbed in a short curtsy. "Hello, Your Majesty."

"You've met?" Rissa asked.

"High Queen Penelope came to Paulo's estate at the beginning of her endeavors in Olympia," Laurel answered.

"What are you doing here?" Penny asked. She stood on her tiptoes to look at the rest of the group. "Did Paulo come as well?"

Laurel shook her head. "This isn't his battle." Her attention swept past Penny as footsteps crunched in the sand. Her dark eyes widened, and she knelt in the sand.

Shaunie came up next to Penny, her eyes locked on the kneeling girl before her.

"Your Majesty," Laurel said, "I can't begin to say how sorry I am. If I'd known—"

"Enough," Shaunie said, her voice jagged but soft at the same time. "I know it wasn't you. Dion told me everything that happened that night. You're the reason we all made it out alive and you being here now only proves you're on our side."

Laurel looked up, her eyes lined with silver tears. "If I'd known what she was going to do, I could have stopped it. I could have convinced her to leave. It's because of my own selfish blindness that this happened, but I swear I'm here to fix it."

"What?" Penny asked.

Her confusion must have been very apparent, for Rissa stepped between them. "Penny, may I formally introduce Laurel Flumen, a Daughter of Stellatus Hall and one of the Continent's most skilled assassins."

Penny's eyes widened. "You're an assassin?" The connection came to her. Aiden had mentioned him. The man that was with Adira in her camp. The one from the continent.

Laurel's head bowed. "Not anymore."

"Laurel is actually the one who's going to get us up this cliff," Rissa said, walking in the direction of the rock. "She's the only one to ever find a way through it."

"What do you mean through it?" Farrah asked.

Laurel pointed up the cliff. "See those caves? The mountains are full of them. I found an entrance on this side of the palace's outer wall. I figured out how to get through and used it as a tunnel for communication with my order."

"If you worked for the rebels, wouldn't the tunnels be swarming with them now?" Mother asked. She turned to Rissa. "Are you sure we can trust her?"

"Out of the people on this beach, Laurel is one I'd put at the top of my trust list." Rissa swung an arm over Laurel's shoulders. "Well, right under Heff and Penny, of course."

Laurel glanced at Rissa out of the corner of her eye, but nothing on her face revealed if she was pleased or not. Penny studied her for a moment longer, finding the small handles of blades tucked in her vest. She barely even moved. How had Penny not noticed the way she held herself? She should have at least had an inkling of what she was. Penny had been around enough spies to spot them now. Had become jaded enough to be suspicious of anyone. This woman—she looked a bit older than Penny—was an obvious predator.

What kind of magic had Paulo worked on this girl for her to have switched sides so entirely?

Penny shook her head. *Only Paulo.* "We should get moving."

Laurel led the way, Rissa and Devan close on her heels. Six feet above them stood the opening of the maze. Harper grabbed a rope out of his satchel, but Penny waved him off, calling on her magic to create a ladder thick enough to hold up Heff.

When they all reached the mouth of the cave, Devan took the golden thread he'd been braiding and tied one end to the ladder. "This thread is enchanted to never run out. If you use it to leave a path, you can find your way back out in case anyone gets separated." He passed it to Adele. "I have to go help Stone at the gate. I'll see all of you on the other side." His head disappeared as he went back down the ladder.

Jolly passed out the magelights they'd gathered from the warehouse. When one was pressed into Penny's palm, she squeezed it, activating the magic within. Dair followed her lead, but he gripped it too hard, and the light blinded him. Penny laughed and showed him how to use it.

"We do not have anything like this in Faerie," he said once he got the hang of it. "Perhaps I should be taking notes."

Laurel led the group at the front and Adele followed behind, constantly tugging more string from the spool in her hand. They wove through the tunnels, the sounds of dripping water and skittering rodent feet bouncing along the smooth hewn rock. The rock changed the farther they went, shifting from the rough drilling of wind and time to the precision of crafted walls. Penny brushed her hands over the smooth stone beside her.

"These tunnels are dwarf-carved," Dair whispered.

"I suppose that makes sense," Penny said, "seeing as the palace above was once one of Danu's temples."

"That still does not sit quite right with me," Dair admitted.

And Penny couldn't help but agree. Now that she knew the Goddess as well as she did, the sacrilege of such a thing rankled her. Yes, there was a new temple in the city, but why had the first kings of Olympia decided that they were worthy to rule from Danu's house? It really did feel... indecent.

"Almost to the exit," Laurel said. "Keep heading that way." She tucked herself into a shallow alcove where a dust-covered bag had been tucked into a corner. Laurel ripped it open and pulled out a silver mask. She placed it on her face, using clever clips on her hood to hold it in place, and joined the group at the back, just behind Penny.

"What does the mask mean?" Penny asked her, doing her best to keep her voice low.

Laurel was silent for a few heartbeats before she said, "It means I'm taking my fate into my own hands."

The quiet hush of wind replaced the other sounds, and everyone turned off their magelights as the growing light of dawn crept through an opening in front of them. A sink hole had fallen into the tunnel, and a steep pile of rocks and soil reached up to the edge of the hole, creating a natural ramp.

Rissa stopped everyone before they could climb out. "The opening here is just inside the shield. Once we climb over the palace wall, we'll be splitting up into three teams." She grabbed Heff's hand, placing a light kiss on his wide-knuckled fingers then letting them go. "Dion, Shaunie, Laurel, and Heff will be going off to take care of the shield. Since Dion is the only one here who knows how to deactivate it, the rest of you have to do whatever you can to get him there.

"The next group consists of the Barclay women, Dair, Farrah, and Jolly. Somewhere in the palace, the rebels are holding fae prisoners. If we can get them released, the rebels won't be able to use them in the coming skirmish."

She pointed at Harper. "You, me, and Adele will go into the Underworld headquarters beneath the palace. I know Durant would have had the place ransacked, but Hart"—her voice choked for the smallest second—"he had caches of supplies—maps, palace schematics, and even some defense charms—hidden in there just in case Durant ever came back." She turned to Penny. "I know Aiden prayed she'd never return, but Hart feared that more than anything else and always made sure we wouldn't be defenseless against her."

Rissa took the golden string and tied it off on one of the long roots sticking out of the side of the tunnel before tucking the rest of the spool in her pocket. "No matter what, we cannot fail. If we do, Olympia fails with us."

Penny crept ahead of her group, Jolly taking up the rear. Getting into the palace hadn't been difficult. With Stone and Devan leading a charge at the front gates, the back of the palace, naturally defended by the sheer cliff and fortified by the shield, had been left unattended.

Getting *through* the palace was another feat of its own.

They'd searched the bottom floor thoroughly, checking every major room from the kitchens to the dungeons. In the dungeons, they'd only discovered members of the council and loyal palace guards. Dair had summoned a glamour for all of them to pass by unseen. It wouldn't have helped them to cause a ruckus since they couldn't let the prisoners out yet anyway. They needed to get the shield down and the fae free before then.

Penny held up hand, stopping their group at the intersection in front of her. She peeked around the corner and found two guards, stationed at either side of the door leading to the conservatory. She cursed and pulled back.

"I think we found them," she whispered.

Dair crept past her and glanced at the guards. With a flick of his wrist, he sent two slivers of shadow down the hall. The thump of falling bodies echoed back to them.

Mother's mouth slowly stretched into a mischievous grin. "I knew our task was supposed to be one of the easy ones, but I didn't think it was going to be this easy."

Jolly took lead and hoisted the two bodies over his wide shoulders. He came back around the corner with them, and Farrah opened a portal along the wall. Jolly pulled a bit of rope from his pack and trussed them up before throwing them through the portal, where they would end up in one of the cells in Iatrus Castle's tower that Paulo provided for them.

Penny returned to the front, Mother at her side, as she walked toward the conservatory doors. Penny reached for the door handle, but Dair stopped her looking over the doors. "We should make sure they are not enchanted," he said. When he didn't find hint of any fae magic, Penny pushed the door open a sliver.

Fae lay in rows along the ground, the clothes on their backs the only thing separating their bodies from the ground. Long chains of iron stretched between them, ending in large spikes staked into the ground. At each spike stood a guard, some of them quietly chatting with the guard on the next spike or simply just staring at random spots on the floor. With all of the fae asleep and immobilized, it looked like these guards had a simple job.

Penny turned back to their group and Dair took her place. "There are ten chains reaching from one end of the conservatory to the other, I imagine. On each end, a rebel guards the spike holding the chain in place and I suspect there is a guard for each side of the chain. From the looks of it, they have the fae cuffed about six feet apart."

"Which means they've probably got over two hundred fae trapped in that room," Mother surmised.

Jolly chuckled. "And you said this was gonna be easy."

Dair's amber eyes sparked with anger. "I can take care of the blackguards on this side since I can see them, but we will have to get closer to the other guards if we want to put them to sleep as well."

"The vegetation on the other side is thicker," Penny said. "I don't think you will be able to see them all at once."

"Leave those men to Penny and me," Mother said. "Once you take down these guards, you and Jolly set to freeing the fae. I imagine seeing one of their own here to rescue them will be a balm."

Dair nodded.

"Farrah," Penny said, "set up a portal and get as many out as fast as you can. I don't want to lose one more Tuatha."

"Yes, My Sovereign," Farrah said.

"Ready?" Penny asked, hands on the doorknobs. "Go."

Penny shoved open the doors and Dair sent ten darts of black and gold dashing into the ears of the guards. They fell to the ground without a sound, caught on pillows of shadow Dair flicked under them, and Jolly set to finding the keys to the chains. Three black portals appeared along the walls and Farrah positioned herself to hold them all steady.

Penny followed Mother through the rousing fae toward the other side of the conservatory. Penny's magic reached out to the plants around them, the reduced glow of her tell hidden beneath the jacket she wore. While Mother glided through the plants in skirts, Penny had opted for a pair of men's trousers and a jacket for this mission.

They crept along the stone wall on the west side of the conservatory, the others made of glass and the coming morning light beaming through. When they reached the other side, Mother stopped and tucked herself behind the large leaf of an elephant ear. Together, they peered through the wide leaves at the line of rebels standing watch and the man sitting at a makeshift desk behind them. A familiar head leaned down over the top of it.

"Rich," Mother hissed, the sound of his name a curse on her lips.

Penny stared at the traitor, her emotions a fickle beast inside her chest. Rich had been part of her life for over a decade, caring for their estate and a part of their team. Mother had trusted him implicitly, made him steward over everything and often left Penny in his and the other servants' care. That trust had been broken so thoroughly, so abruptly, when Penny had discovered his true loyalties.

And now, judging by the hard expression on Mother's face, he would pay for it.

"Do you see the wisteria?" Mother asked almost silently.

Penny found the creeping vines full of drooping purple blooms above the head of the guard closest to them. Penny nodded.

"I need you to grow it as large as you can," Mother said. "We will use it for cover and—"

The leaves around them parted and three burly men jumped through, tackling them to the ground. Penny let out a shout as one pressed her into the packed earth, pulling her arms behind her back hard enough to hurt.

She felt the cold bite of iron around her wrists. While the pure metal didn't harm her as it did the fae, the charms did. Her magic was put behind a wall, the charms on the cuffs separating her from it. Exhaustion leaked into her limbs, the price of her magic unpaid.

Mother cursed soundly as she tried to shake off her attackers, but they had the upper hand. Between the four of them, the rebels were able to drag them out of the bushes. Penny and Mother were on their knees in front of Rich's ramshackle desk before they even had a chance to run.

"Lady Barclay, Lady Penny—or should I say High Queen Penny?" Rich asked, his voice as congenial as it ever had been. "We did not expect your visit. I'm afraid I am not quite suited to hosting visitors at the moment."

"You're the uninvited visitors here," Mother said. "This isn't your home to offer pleasantries."

Rich bobbed his head solemnly. "You're right, of course. But this palace has its role to play, just like the rest of us."

"So that's what we were to you, Rich?" Penny asked. "A role?"

Rich's almost bald head wobbled back and forth. "Yes and no. In the beginning, it was my entire life. I didn't believe there was any greater place to be for myself. I had every kind of luxury a man of my station could dream of, but when I learned of The Cartographer and the vision she had for the world, I couldn't let it go."

Mother scoffed. "So instead of continuing your loyalty to us, you chased after a bunch of radicals."

"She approached *me*," Rich insisted, his voice growing a bit louder. "I didn't even have to seek her out. She found me, asked me to join her cause because she saw greatness in me that you never did."

"You were my blasted steward, Rich," Mother said. "I put all of my trust, my very life in your hands."

Rich sneered. "Please. You don't even trust your daughter that much. I worked every day to gain your favor, your trust, but nothing I ever did was enough. Not even burying my first master was enough. I never told anyone what we did that day, that you killed your husband and that I helped you get rid of his body. I did everything I could, but still, you didn't even look my way once."

Penny felt her eyebrows pull together and a frown pull on her mouth. Something was still off here. Yes, there were many disgruntled people with jobs they didn't like, but even Rich had admitted he'd had every luxury a man could dream of. And Mother had trusted him.

Penny looked up at the man, his eyes only on Mother. She felt a tug on her chest, a mixture of intuition and inspiration.

"You fancy yourself in love with her."

Rich's eyes flew wide, and he looked over at Penny for the first time.

Penny barked out a laugh. "You think that if you can at least get her to look at you, in whatever light, that you'll gain her approval, her admiration." The absurdity of it pulled another laugh from her chest. "I became the cursed High Queen of Faerie, and she still treats me like a child. Why on Gaia's green earth would you ever believe that joining a group of people that want to kill her would ever garner her affection?"

His cheeks mottled with red, and his eyes blazed with more emotion than Penny had ever seen from the man. "I'm the only one who can save you," he said to Mother. "You'll understand soon enough that there's nowhere else for you to go. If you want to live, you'll have to choose me."

Mother surged forward, but the guards pulled her back. "I would rather eat my own liver, carved out with a spoon and served up with fried onions, than *ever* go anywhere with you *ever* again!" She spat on the ground in front of her. "You're *dead* to me, Richard Alden, and soon you'll be dead to everyone else too."

Rich took a deep breath. "I know you don't understand yet, but in time you'll see all that I've done for you." His eyes returned to Penny. "Starting with killing your rebellious daughter."

The guard behind Penny drew a knife and settled it against her throat.

"No!" Mother screamed, lunging at Rich still seated at his desk. "I'll kill you! I'll kill *all* of you!"

Penny turned her head and bit down on the grimy arm holding the blade. The man cried out, dropping the knife point first into the grass between Penny's knees.

Where was the rest of their group? Mother's scream would have reached them for sure.

Rich stood and walked around the desk toward her. "Savage child. Can't even die without causing everyone around her grief."

Penny bared her teeth and rolled away from the guard behind her, grabbing the knife with her knees. She dropped the knife, but moved her body so she could grab it with her hands tied behind her back. Thaen's training really had done wonders for her skills.

"Give me your sword," Rich ordered, holding his hand out to one of the guards.

The rebel handed Rich the blade, and the old steward pointed it at Penny's chest. "If you think you can trick your way out of this, you're wrong."

"No, you're wrong," Mother spat. "My daughter is clever, far cleverer than anyone gives her credit for." Mother straightened, the air in the room seeming too thin as she glared at the man. "And she has a mother who will do anything to make sure she never falls at the hands of sniveling cowards like you."

The air around them seemed to pull towards Mother, making Penny's ears pop. With a roar, Mother strained against the manacles behind her back until a green glow burst out between her fingers. In a torrent of power, the trees around them bent down and grabbed the rebel guards, hoisting them into the air and wrapping thick branches around them. The rebels still left guarding the fae prisoners ran in their direction. Creeping vines and thick bushes dragged them down to the ground and pulled them out of sight.

Mother stood, hands glowing and eyes alight with holy fire. "I curse you, Rich Alden. I curse you to never know peace in this life and to never know what it is to touch another human ever again. Your name will be forgotten, all traces of you erased from the face of this earth. You will receive nothing, and it will be left to the Goddess to decide which place in her realm of darkness to shove you into."

"You have no power to curse—"

Thick roots wrapped around his legs and pulled him straight into the ground. He hadn't even had time to cry out before the earth swallowed him whole.

Mother watched the spot of ground with unnerving dedication until she deemed he would not resurface. She turned to Penny, the green glow of her hands flickering erratically.

"Penny," Mother said with relief, taking a staggering step toward her.

Penny rushed toward her, tears breaking over her lashes. With her hands cuffed behind her back, she couldn't hug Mother the way she wanted to, so she stopped before they both ended up on the ground.

She sent a smile to Mother, but Mother's face was scrunched in confusion and possibly pain.

"What's wrong?" Fear trickled down Penny's spine. "Are you hurt?"

Mother frowned, looking over her shoulder at the strange flash of her tell. Turning back to Penny, she said, "I think I may have broken something."

Mother's eyes rolled back in her head, and Penny had no way to catch her as she fell.

"Mother!" Penny called, going to her knees beside her. Penny looked around until she spotted a set of keys sitting on the desk. She got to her feet, but with her hands at her back, she couldn't figure out which key would work. Pulling the manacles apart, she curled her legs in and tried to pull her arms under her, but she couldn't.

Blast it all!

With a growl, she grabbed the keys and ran over to where Mother still lay. Her breaths came in and out deeply, but Penny didn't know when the price of using so much magic would let her wake up.

Where the blizzards is Dair when I need him?

As if summoned by her thoughts, Dair, Jolly, and Farrah burst through the foliage, their clothing torn and bloodstained.

Penny stood. "What happened to you three?"

Jolly scratched the back of his neck. "Got a bit hairy back there when the new shift o' guards walked through the door and the other set din't get taken out by you and 'er Grace."

Farrah knelt by Mother. "What happened?"

"We met an old friend, but we took care of it. Dair, I think she could use a bit of help getting out of her slumber so we can get out of here."

Dair went to Mother's side, shadow swirling in his palm.

Penny spun around and jangled the keys in her hand at Jolly. "Would you mind unlocking these blasted manacles?"

43
SEPARATED

Aiden raked a hand through his hair, once again disheveling it in the mirror. He grumbled and set to fixing it again before he met with the remaining members of the Council in the war room.

How was Penelope?

When would the rebels reach Eagallach?

Had the families of the fallen fae been contacted?

Would they have enough soldiers for the coming battle?

Who would attack first: the Aigeans or the rebels?

Where was Penelope now?

"Stop fussing," Thaen said, materializing behind Aiden. "That is Rìgh's job."

"I have every reason to fuss, and you know it," he threw back, though he tried his best to take the bite out of it. Thaen had been nothing but patient with him since their return to Winter. Aiden wasn't sure he deserved such forbearance but was grateful for it all the same.

"Today is going to be long." Thaen stepped around until he faced Aiden fully. "Are you sure you are up for it?"

Aiden quirked an eyebrow. "Now who's fussing?"

Thaen grumbled but followed behind as Aiden left the room.

When they reached the hall leading out of the family wing, Farrah peeled away from the wall.

"Farrah," Aiden greeted her. Something in his very core eased seeing her alive and well, especially there. It meant Penelope was somewhere safe.

"Hello, My Sovereign." She fell into step beside him. "I've just returned from the palace."

Farrah had been back and forth for the last few weeks, exchanging messages from the Hermens and Penelope. Her last letter had come just before they'd gone to Olympia to take back the palace.

"Any news?" Aiden said, anxiety twisting his gut. He didn't know if he could take any more bad news at the moment, but it wasn't really his decision.

Farrah beamed. "They've taken back the capital. King Dion and Queen Carnation were able to take down the shield and reclaim their palace."

"And Penelope?"

Farrah smirked, obviously having kept the information from him just to drive him mad. "Penny and Dair freed the fae slaves being kept there. Their entire retinue will arrive at the border in no more than four days."

Four days. Only four more days would Aiden have to endure the torture of not seeing Penelope. So many emotions had come through the bond connecting them. Without anything to do but go sick with worry, Aiden was more than ready to see his wife again.

"Stay until after the meeting," Aiden told Farrah. "Then you can send word back to Penelope about our finalized plans to meet at the border."

"Of course, My Sovereign."

The three of them strode through the palace. It felt as if the very walls were holding their breath.

When they reached the Great Hall, Thaen broke away from them. Aiden slowed to watch as his cousin approached none other than Sissy, who for some reason had apparently taken it upon herself to polish the entire black granite floor.

Thaen stopped behind her, standing where she had not yet polished. "What are you doing?"

"Shining the floor," she answered cheerily without looking up at him. "What does it look like I'm doing?"

"But you are not a servant."

Sissy did look up then. "Am I not? While my father likes to claim he's king of his house and my mother is a magic caster with a loom,

I'm afraid they are still a farmer and a farmer's wife—making me part of the servant class."

Thaen crouched down at her side. "But you are not only a farmer's daughter anymore. You are a child of Danu, a Tuatha Dé Dannan. You were chosen to be the first of Her new creations, and I do not think it fitting that you are scrubbing a floor."

Sissy gave him a perturbed look. "Listen here, Your Highness. Yes, the Goddess in all of Her merciful goodness chose me—*me*—to be the first to return to this world. Trust me, I know what an honor it is, and I'm humbled beyond measure, but that privilege does not give me any right to any other kind of privileges. I will still work for my food. I will still scrub floors so I can ensure that I'm not a burden on those that have so kindly taken me in. There's work to be done, and I won't be one to shy away from hard things simply because I've been blessed." She turned back to the half-polished floor. "If anything, I should be working twice as hard in order to prove I'm worth such a gift."

Aiden decided to cut into the conversation. "I promise, Sissy, you're worth more than the gift Danu has bestowed upon you. You are Her child and there's nothing She wouldn't do for you." He crouched beside Thaen. "I don't think my cousin meant to cause any offense when he said you shouldn't be scrubbing floors. As my High Queen's lady-in-waiting, I would not ask you to do such a job."

Sissy's mouth dropped open in surprise. "Penny's lady-in-waiting? *Me?*"

Aiden smiled. "Of course. Do you think there's anyone better qualified to put up with my wife or even anyone else she would allow to do so?" Aiden didn't know why Penny hadn't spoken with the girl about it before. They'd discussed it before she left as it only made sense that she would serve in that capacity. None of the other fae nobles would take to the job as quickly, and honestly, he didn't trust any of them to. After what happened with the Spring Court, he would be wary to let anyone into Penelope's inner circle anytime soon.

Sissy dropped the rag and flung herself at Aiden. "Oh, thank you, My Sovereign! I promise, I won't let you down. I'll be the most dedicated lady you've ever seen."

Aiden patted her back lightly. "I know you will."

She squeezed him one more time and pulled away. "Now, since

my queen isn't here at the moment, I'll just finish shining up this floor and then ask the brownies what they need help with next. I saw them trying to clean one of the chandeliers earlier and their tiny arms just can't reach high enough to get some of the cobwebs."

They left Sissy to finish her task, Thaen surreptitiously glancing behind them a few times before they reached the hallway leading to the map room.

"What does she look like to you?" Aiden asked his cousin.

Thaen thought on it for a moment. "Like you and Penelope and moonlight."

When they reached the war room, Aiden took a deep breath before stepping through the threshold. It almost felt empty now. With Shirina taken and Chieftess Sgrios dead alongside Commander Fàil, their numbers were dwindling.

Rìgh, Sgiath, and Deireadh stood to one side of the table, chittering back and forth like birds. Stallion Mealladh stood at the end of the table, repositioning the small pieces they used to differentiate the armies on either side of this war.

Wind and snow, the pieces had moved so much since the battle at the mounds. Almost every blue piece on the board had been moved within the confines of Winter, leaving a handful of scouts and a few groups of fighters sprinkled in Spring and Autumn. The red pieces were not so bare. They almost covered the entire map, nearly triple the number of blue pieces now.

Aiden blew out a breath. "Report." The command almost came out as a question, as if somewhere inside of him he hoped there wasn't anything to report. He found a chair at the head of the table and sank into it. Praise the Goddess his wounds from the afanc had finally healed after many ministrations from Annalysa. She was a blessing from the Goddess for certain.

"My Sovereign," Mealladh said, "I have received word of movement by the rebels." He pointed down at the map. "They are coming to Winter."

"We have been expecting them to," Thaen said, taking a place beside Aiden's chair. "We are the last city standing and the first snows will be on us within a month."

They may have been expecting it, but that didn't mean Aiden hadn't hoped it wouldn't happen. "Where's The Cartographer?"

Mealladh pointed at the large piece near the Spring and Summer border. "They are coming around the mountain, avoiding the worst of the terrain while they have a small host going through the pass here." His finger indicated a set of mountains near the Autumn and Winter border. "They will corner us within days."

Aiden straightened. "How many days?" Penelope was set to meet him at the border in four.

"Three days," Sgiath answered, looking to Aiden with knowing in his eyes. Farrah had probably already told him about Penelope's imminent arrival.

Aiden stood and began to pace. "Then we have much planning to do before then."

Three days flew by in a flurry of preparations, planning, and worry.

Durant made her move.

She arrived at the edges of Lake Truaighe at dawn.

Aiden had known she would be there when he woke that morning. He had felt it in his bones when he'd laid down to rest the night before, and he felt it now, staring at the portrait of Queen Morana in the gallery. Had she felt as he did when she fought in the Faerie Wars? Had her stomach felt empty, yet any food offered made her sick? Aiden stared, comparing their lives alongside each other. He had also been the younger sibling, the assassin led by the older, golden-haired hero. Both of them had held magic that scared people, that made them think too much about their sin and their regrets.

There were so many similarities, so many reflections of himself in her. She was known for being one of the mightiest warriors of her time. How would she have handled today?

Footsteps sounded and Aiden turned toward the entrance as the last of the war council stepped inside. Their faces were grave.

"News?" Aiden asked.

Sgiath held up a sealed letter. "They've sent a request to parlay," he said, handing Aiden the missive.

Aiden cracked the wax seal and opened it. Durant's familiar scrawl took up half the page.

Little Aiden,

It is time to end this charade.

We invite you to parlay with us at the center of Lake Truaighe at exactly noon. Failure to meet will be taken as an invitation to meet with you in the palace proper. I would so hate to ruin that shiny jewel atop the mountain, but we will meet, or you and your little friends will face the consequences.

Well done with Olympia, by the way. Your darling wife has so much spine to her. I should have guessed she would be such a little nuisance since I liked her so much. I will have to take care of her soon, or she will grow into more than a simple thorn in my side, don't you agree? Her head would make a lovely addition to my collection. I think I'll put it up right beside your cousin's wife.

I hope to see you at noon.

The Future Empress of Faerie,

Adira Durant

"What does it say?" Thaen asked. He stood with his arms crossed over his chest, looking down at the pieces on the map in front of them. He couldn't see the drawing of the map, but he could see the figurines and guess the distances based on that. Praise the Goddess he couldn't read. He'd likely have gone straight to Durant's camp on his own.

Aiden waved the letter in his hand. "She wants to meet on the lake at noon to parlay."

"An intimidation tactic to be certain," Mealladh said. "'Come, look at your destruction!' it says."

Thaen's face turned dark. "I do not think that is her intention at all."

"She'll use my name," Aiden said.

Thaen nodded. "The moment you are within hearing. This letter was intended to rile you into fighting her, not an actual message to parlay."

"So, what do we do?" Rìgh asked.

"We ignore it," Sgiath answered. "It does not matter if we meet with her. She intends to attack the mountain no matter what. Better to stay and face the coming fight than lose our king before the battle begins."

"I agree with Councilor Sgiath," Mealladh said. "We cannot face such dire consequences. We meet them on the battlefield."

Aiden's eyes found Farrah across the room, tucked into a corner with a tray of sandwiches.

"It's time to meet my wife. If Durant plans to attack quickly, we'll need to get all the help we can here as fast as we can." He turned back to the rest of the room. "Prepare the city for an attack. Get our soldiers at the base of the mountain in formation and don't wait for me. I'll be back to join the fight as soon as I retrieve High Queen Penelope and bring her back here."

"Of course, My Sovereign," Sgiath said, going to his daughter. "Be safe."

Farrah brushed off her fingers on her tunic, leaving a smear of purple jelly on the red linen. "Don't worry about me, Papa. I'll be back in a flash." She began waving her hands at the air against the wall. A portal grew in moments.

Thaen took Aiden by the shoulders. "You too, cousin. Be safe. Bring our queen home."

Aiden nodded, slapping a hand on Thaen's shoulder. "You're in charge until I get back. Don't let the rebels take the palace before we've played another round of *glam agus lorg*."

Thaen's mouth twitched as he let Aiden go.

Aiden stepped to the portal, not looking back as he leapt through the shadows. The magic within Farrah's portal was different than her father's. His was shapes in the shadows, while hers were sounds. He could feel the magic push him from one place to another.

I'm coming, Penelope.

A jarring shake inside the darkness rattled Aiden's skull. The portal sucked him out instead of spitting him out as it normally did. He landed on his knees in snow.

"Farrah? What—"

He looked up, his body freezing as stiffly as the ground beneath his fingers.

Farrah had a blade to her throat, blood trickling down her neck as the iron blistered the skin around the cut. An entire mob of rebels, dressed in thick coats and fur-lined hoods, surrounded them.

One of the rebels walked forward, drawing their hood back to reveal silver hair and green eyes.

Aiden slowly got to his feet, a dozen swords pointed in his direction. Swords he would not survive a stab from.

Durant's smile stretched across her face in unreserved glee. She tossed a crystal box up and down in the air.

"Fae shields truly are a marvel, wouldn't you say, *Agesilaos*?"

44
COMMAND AND CONTROL

"So, this is what Faerie looks like across the border?" Dion asked, setting his hands on his hips. "Not much to look at."

Shaunie smacked his arm.

Penny fought a grin as the two of them began whispering back and forth to one another. Since they'd taken back the palace, Shaunie and Dion had almost regained a little more comradery with one another. They worked well as a team—they always had—but watching them now brought a smile to her lips. Hopefully, Dion could regain Shaunie's trust one day, and Shaunie would find that freedom she longed for.

"Has Aedon's brother always been such a brat?" Dair asked, eyes narrowed at Dion's back.

"Some days are better than—"

Hot, searing agony pierced Penny's chest, and she crashed into the sandy grass on her knees. The bond connecting her to Aiden shuddered within her, his side crying out to hers. She gasped, taking in short breaths. Her ears rang as she barely took in the white grains of sand and blades of grass beneath her fingers. Her hands glowed, the green and black only reaching to the crook of her elbow.

"Penny?" Mother said, kneeling on the ground in front of her. "What's wrong?"

"She has him," Penny choked. She still couldn't take a full breath.

Dair came into her line of sight. "*What?*"

Penny got to her feet and staggered a few more steps into the dune rising up in front of her. The screaming in her head was worse than the last time, her bond to Aiden having grown as they'd been married longer. She closed her eyes when she fully crossed the border, tugging on the connection with the Land beneath her.

Magic rushed through her. She allowed the Land to carry her across Faerie, the golden sands giving way to vibrant greens in moments.

When she reached the border to Winter, she wanted to weep. Thousands of men and women skittered about on the edge of Lake Truaighe. Banners waving the points of a compass snapped in the Winter winds and iron clanked together as hammers met anvils and chains met manacles. The rebel host stretched over the frozen ground, but she was pulled into the middle of the camp, to the austere tent centered in the middle of it all.

Her heart caught in her throat as she stopped inside. Aiden sat trapped in a chair, thick iron chains wrapped around his forearms and around his ankles. His hands shook as the metal burned into his skin; head slumped on the back of the chair as he fought to keep his Lord of the Underworld mask in place.

"My Little Aiden," a voice said from the other side of the room. Penny turned and found Adira, legs propped up on her desk and a devilish smile creasing her mouth. "I'm so glad we get this chance to catch up. I'll admit, I'm very impressed with how you've handled yourself. I know I wasn't around to see all your accomplishments, having only returned last fall from the continent, but I can't tell you how proud I was of you."

"Don't do this to yourself, Durant." Aiden's head lifted. The expression he threw at Adira said unrestrained boredom, but Penny saw the blazing fire in his eyes. "Debasing yourself to try to get me to have some sympathy for you may have worked when I was a child, but now it's simply unflattering."

The effort to speak with such calm cost him. Penny could see it in the way his breathing hitched just the tiniest bit. She walked to him, standing at his side. She reached out to brush his hair from his forehead but drew back before her fingers simply went straight through the dark strands.

"I don't remember you having such a mouth on you," Adira responded. "Did you pick that up from your brothers or from Penny?"

Aiden's spine went rigid, and he bared his teeth. "Don't you dare ever speak her name."

Adira's expression brightened. "Ah, at least I know the feelings aren't one sided. It was always difficult to know, when you were a child, if you would find someone. As your mother, I wanted you to have at least something of what I felt for your father."

"You have no right to call yourself my mother," Aiden said. "My mother was Queen Morana of Winter, someone you murdered in cold blood."

"And do you know how many people *she* murdered?" Adira stood coming around the desk. "Your so-called mother was a killer as well. She was paramount in the fight against the fae at the end of the Faerie Wars. Do you want to know how she accomplished her tasks? She would steal time from the folk around her, aging them until they were nothing but dust and bones. It was torture for those who went through it, their bones turning brittle and breaking apart before the organs in their bodies began to shut down. That's how the High King's consort died, her body falling apart right in front of her husband. Your aunt killed him right after, cutting him in half, head to toe."

"And you think what you're doing is better?" Aiden snapped.

"Of course not." Adira circled Aiden's chair. Penny held her breath as Adira passed right through her. "I am much worse."

Penny's consciousness returned to her body with a start.

Dair stood over her, his brows furrowed. "What did you see?"

She pushed herself up, her glowing hands finding greenery underneath her. Plants shimmied in the light, morning breeze—plants that had not existed when she'd gone with the Land.

"He's been taken by Adira and is being held in the enemy camp on the fringes of Lake Truaighe."

Dair's mouth fell open. "She is going to attack Eagallach?"

Penny nodded grimly and brushed the grains of sand from her trousers. "I don't know when or how, but it looks like the entire host of rebels waits at the eastern side of the lake."

"It will only take them a day or two to cross it and find our forces at the base of the mountain."

"I'm sure she's well aware," Mother said, joining them in Penny's patch of greenery, "which is probably why she hasn't moved to take the city. I imagine she'll wait for the fae to come for their High King. It will put them on a level playing field."

Penny rubbed her hands down her face. "It wouldn't even matter if she walked into the very city itself! We don't have enough fighters to take her on. Even if every Tuatha in Eagallach held up a sword, they'd be overrun by the rebels."

"Wait." Mother took Penny's shoulders in her hands. "Are you telling me Faerie doesn't have any army to defend it?"

Penny shook her head. "That's why we're here, to bring him an army."

Mother's face fell in shock. "Penny, not even the small host we brought from Olympia will match The Cartographer's force."

Penny drew back. "I know, which is why we're here. Didn't I—" She stopped. No, she hadn't explained what happened, what she and Aiden were planning to do. There hadn't been a good time to talk about Sissy's return. She took a deep breath. "Mother, Aiden and I were planning on raising an army. Right here, on the border."

Now it was Mother's turn to be surprised. "What kind of magic could make an army out of dirt?"

Penny smiled. "The magic of the Goddess and those willing to do as She bids." Penny opened her arms, the spot of new vegetation growing until it spread across the ground into a full oasis. When she stopped, she explained to Mother what happened. She told her about the ribbon, about the magic not working without the tree. Everything. "But without Aiden, I can't access the souls of the dead."

Black flashed over Mother's shoulder.

Sgiath stumbled out of the portal, fiery long hair whipping about his face. The small crowd around them went silent as he scanned every face. His eyes landed on Penny, and he sagged with relief.

"My Sovereign," he said, stumbling forward to try to get to her faster than his slow pace allowed him.

Penny went to him. "How, Sgiath? How did they get him?"

"Farrah." Sgiath's eyes limned with silver tears. "They had a shield, more powerful than anything I've seen. They used it like a wall instead of a bubble, blocking any portals out of Eagallach. When the portal ejected them out on the edges of the shield, the rebels caught them."

Penny set a hand on his arm. "They have Farrah too?"

Sgiath nodded, his face falling.

"What are we going to do?" Dair asked.

Sgiath took Penny's hand, and he fell to his knees before her. "Please, My Sovereign. Please save my daughter."

45
STRANDED

AIDEN HUNG BETWEEN TWO OF THE BURLIEST HUMANS HE'D EVER SEEN. Their hands probably could have wrapped around Aiden's head and crushed it with the slightest pressure, but right now, each of them had a hold on one of his arms as they dragged him along the frost-covered ground. Aiden's blood dripped from his nose and his left eye swelled shut.

"Since misery so loves company," Durant said from ahead of them, "I decided you needed a roommate."

Aiden wanted to roll his eyes but was too tired to do more than stare straight ahead. The iron around his wrists burned into his exposed skin. The charmed iron cut off his magic, preventing his rapid healing from doing its job. He could feel his magic bubbling under the surface of his skin. The inky black of his tell had started up on his hands no less than an hour ago. His heart throbbed with the strain of it.

"Since I know you can be quite surly, I figured you'd need someone who could... *dampen* that bite in you." She stopped at one of the tents covered in anti-magic charms. "Perhaps a little motivation to behave might be in order."

When she opened the flap, Aiden had to blink to see into the dim light. A pair of dark, sad eyes shimmered from the shadows within the tent.

Shirina.

Aiden yanked himself from the thugs, his training with Thaen kicking in as he lost control over his emotions.

"Stop, *Agesilaos*."

Aiden's body immediately froze.

Durant stepped in front of him. "If you would like me to give her time to recharge between our little get togethers, I recommend you behave. I would hate to see her waste away all because you couldn't keep yourself in check. Do not try to escape, *Agesilaos*, and I will not touch her."

As if he could even try to escape.

The thugs that had regained hold on him practically tossed him into the tent. His body landed in a heap at the opening to the tent and the flap fell into place as Durant laughed and walked away.

Aiden groaned as he tried to sit up. He looked around the cramped tent, finding a pole in the center and a long chain stretching across the room from it.

"Little Shadow?"

Aiden followed the chain to where Shirina huddled in the corner. When their eyes met, Shirina gasped and scrambled on her hands and knees toward him.

"Blizzards, what has that cursed woman done to you?" Shirina grabbed his shoulders to try to help him sit up. He tried not to hiss as he moved his arms. The burns deepened as the charms on the tent suppressed his magic—though the very same charms were keeping him from damaging his heart at that moment.

"Here," Shirina said, holding a cup of water. He reached for it, but Shirina brought it to his lips herself. He guzzled down the liquid.

When he finished, Shirina set the cup to the side and took his face in her hands. Her skin was chapped and stretched over the bones of her fingers. Wrinkles of pain and heartache creased her face in permanent lines. Rings of scars encircled her wrists from where manacles had wrapped around them and the skin had healed. Aiden's own wrists would likely look like that at the end of all of this.

"Aedon, what has happened? How are you here?"

He took a deep breath, trying to find some sort of equilibrium. "Durant caught Farrah and I as we tried to leave Eagallach. I don't exactly know how she did it, but she's getting ready to march onto Eagallach and no one will know what happened."

"We cannot lose hope," Shirina said. "The twins and Penelope are still out there."

Aiden's heart seized with a different pain than what his magic created. "Penelope is out there. What is she going to do when I don't show up at the border? She'll come here anyway. She'll walk right into a massacre."

"Breathe, Aedon." Shirina's words soothed him, but only a bit. "Start at the beginning. What has happened since I left?"

He took a deep breath and began his tale, revealing what had happened since the wedding: the rebels taking Olympia's palace, Penelope's going to find her mother, the battle at the mounds. He talked about how much Dair and Thaen had done and the efforts of the war council as well. Keeping his voice lower than a whisper, he revealed his plans to build a new army.

"With our combined magic, Penelope and I can allow for spirits in the Goddess's realm to return to ours. They're given new forms, attached to plant life, but only the spirits of bronties are able to come back. We figured it out after some trial and error." He felt tears gather at the corners of his eyes and blinked them back. "We tried to bring Fiadh back to you."

Shirina shook her head, her own tears breaking over her lashes. "It was not meant to happen. I will meet him in the next life, after I have fulfilled my measure in this one."

Aiden wiped his face on the sleeve at his shoulder. "We planned to go to the border. With Penelope able to stand on Olympian soil without repercussion and I at least able to walk outside of Faerie for a few days, we should've been able to create enough of these new creatures to fight against the rebels."

"But now you are trapped and cannot get to her."

Something in Aiden's chest cracked. "What are we going to do?"

Shirina reached out and held him as he tried to keep the tears clinging to the corners of his eyes from falling. His whole body felt heavy and empty at the same time.

"I don't understand why Danu would give me this curse—why she gave all the fae this curse. I thought She wanted us to be able to choose our own paths, to want fate to work its course but also to let us choose out own fate. I thought she loved us."

"She does, Aedon. Trust me, Danu loves us—loves *you*."

"Then why did She allow all of this to happen?" He lifted his chained arms. "I'm going to be used as a weapon against those I love, and I'll have no control. I'll have to watch my family and my kingdom die all because I told Durant my name, because of a mistake I made when I was a child. You were made to suffer because of my mistake. I can't even imagine what that devil woman has done to you. This should have never happened."

Shirina ran her fingers through his hair. "You were only a *child*, Aedon. The mistake was not yours in trusting the only parent that ever showed you any amount of kindness. The mistake lies with Adira Durant for taking advantage of you, and I promise, the Goddess will ensure that woman pays for her crimes, but we cannot say when that will happen. Danu has Her own plan, Her own time-line, and we are but the passengers in the boat. We can always choose to fight the current, but the river will still run its course. Peace, Little Shadow," Shirina said, laying her hands atop his shaking ones. "We have not lost yet."

Aiden closed his eyes, that word haunting him like nothing he'd ever experienced.

Yet.

Durant hadn't been able to use his name to make him harm anyone he loved... yet.

The rebels hadn't attacked Eagallach... yet.

Not all the residents of Faerie had become slaves... yet.

Penelope hadn't returned from Olympia to see the destruction of their kingdom... yet.

The waiting was sure to kill him.

"I don't know if I can do this," Aiden whispered, a sort of prayer and a confession at the same time.

"You *can* do this, Aedon," Shirina said, her sharp ears having caught his words. "You are one of the strongest Tuatha I know. Do not let someone like Adira Durant take that strength and use it against you."

Aiden couldn't stop the dark chuckle that rumbled in his throat. "But that's exactly what she's going to do. She's going to take every part of me and use it against those I love no matter what I do."

Shirina's face fell. "I am sorry this has happened, and I am sorry you believe that."

"What is that supposed to mean?"

Shirina shrugged. "I do not think the Goddess—the creator of our souls and the only being in the entire universe that knows us better than ourselves—would ever truly allow someone to have complete control over us."

"But there's a way nonetheless," he insisted.

Shirina raised a hand. "But is that true? Yes, Adira Durant may be able to control your body, but she cannot control your heart or your soul. You can still choose to fight, and I think you are strong enough to fight her, Aedon."

Aiden shook his head. "She knows me like no one else does. She's my cursed mother." Durant's words from the tent still echoed in his ears. It was true. Even if Aiden didn't want her to be, Adira Durant was the woman who raised him. She'd created a hole by killing his mother and fit herself into it.

"Do not give that vile woman that title, Aedon." Shirina's face darkened. "That creature does not even come close to comparing to your mother."

"She created me, Shirina, to be exactly what I am."

"No, she did not. That is the Goddess's power. Only Her will can create us."

"*Then why?*" he cried. "Why did She let all of this happen? Why am I even here?"

Shirina stilled.

Aiden's breathing was ragged in his chest, his heart bleeding as hope seeped out from the gaping hole where he thought it should have been safe.

"Little Shadow," Shirina said quietly. She crawled up to him and cradled his face in her hands. Her large onyx eyes captured his in a firm gaze. "Listen to me. The Goddess has a plan for each of us. We will not always understand it, but I know with a surety that trumps all other thoughts, that She has the best interest of Her children at heart in everything She does. It is our job to trust Her, to do Her will, even in spite of others who are working against that plan."

Her hands slid from his face to his shoulders, her eyes glimmering with tears. "I know it is hard. I know the pain and the grief overtakes the hope as clouds block the moon at night, but we have to have hope. Even if we lose this war, even if our people are enslaved and we lose our lives, I know that it is all part of something bigger than we can even imagine... and I know you know it too."

"What do I do, Shirina?" Aiden sagged against her. "What does the Goddess want me to do?"

"Pray, Little Shadow. Turn your will to Her, and fight for every inch She gives you."

So, Aiden did. He closed his eyes, reached for the traces of the bonds he still felt within him, and held them with everything he had.

And he prayed.

He prayed for Penelope to learn what happened so she wouldn't be left without answers.

He prayed that Thaen be wise about how to guide the forces in Eagallach.

He prayed the High Council and the few generals left after the battles would be guided to make the best decisions.

He prayed for Dair to find his inner strength and see what a fine king he would make.

He prayed for Danu's will to be made apparent. If Faerie's fall was part of Her greater plan, he only asked that its demise would be as painless as it could be made to be. That the folk wouldn't suffer under whatever path lay ahead.

And he prayed that his loved ones found the answers to their own prayers.

46

SOLDIERS AND SAVIORS

PENNY KNELT IN THE SAND FOR WHAT FELT LIKE THE HUNDREDTH TIME THAT day and prayed to the stars above her for the millionth.

Please. Please protect Aiden. Please help our kingdom not fall under into the hands of a tyrant and a murderer. Please keep my loved ones from harm. Please help Aiden find peace in that horrible place. I don't know what I'm going to do without him, but please help us figure out how to do all of this. I can't—

"Penny."

She opened her eyes and found Mother crouched in front of her. Penny wiped the trail of tears from her face and tried to smile. "I'm sorry. I didn't hear you. Did you need something?"

"Sweeting, it's nearly midnight. You need to get some rest before we start out in the morning."

Penny got to her feet, wobbling on exhausted legs. While the well of her magic had gone back to overflowing since she'd crossed the boundary into Faerie, fear and hopelessness were taking large bites out of her. "You're right."

Mother guided her down the dune, their feet sinking into the soft sand. The stuff was everywhere and somehow kept making its way to Penny's skin, which was not at all comfortable. She could understand why some might view the beautiful sea of sand as the worst kind of curse. Mother led her back to the tent they shared with Adele, who had come with the rest of the Underworld crew to get the soldiers organized before returning to Olympia. Dion had brought his full force of guards and Paulo had sent his best men to the border, but some of them would be returning to Olympia with their king in the morning. Rissa, Heff, and Adele would go back to Olympia, but Harper and Jolly had volunteered to go with Penny and the rest of the soldiers.

That is, if they didn't abandon Penny when they heard she couldn't summon more soldiers to their cause. She wouldn't hold it against them. No one wanted to die for a lost cause. At least they were able to take the palace back out of Adira's clutches.

Penny practically flopped down onto her bedroll, sand and all. Mother tied the tent flap closed and shucked the outer layer of her clothing.

"I'm sorry, Penny, about Aiden," Mother said.

"You didn't kidnap him, Mother."

"Not just about that."

Penny opened her eyes and turned her body so she faced Mother's bedroll. "What do you mean?"

"I'm sorry that you couldn't trust me with your relationship with him." Mother fidgeted with the hem of her gown. "While I'd like to think I would have been understanding, I couldn't honestly say. I only ever talked about him like some sort of fiend, and I realize now that was unfair. I wish I proved to you that you could have trusted me."

"He's truly not a fiend," Penny said.

"And I know that now. I would at least trust you enough not to get married to such a man. I taught you better than my parents taught me. You've got more spine than I think even I do, and you would never do something you didn't want to."

Tears began pooling at the corners of Penny's eyes. "Why are you bringing this up now?"

Mother scooted closer on her bedroll. "I just wanted you to know that I'm proud of you and that I'm sorry you couldn't trust me when it mattered."

Penny sat up and reached for her. Mother folded Penny in her arms and Penny realized just how small her domineering duchess of a mother truly was. She was only human, the same as Penny. Both of them had made mistakes, but they would see each other through the difficult things. Together.

They spent another half hour talking about their plan for tomorrow. When Penny's eyes couldn't stay open any longer, Mother dimmed the magelight and sleep overtook them both.

But it didn't last long.

The Land's magic seized Penny the moment her consciousness faded and zipped her across Faerie. The Courts whipped by them in a miasma of color and sounds. Gold, orange, white, green. Breaking rock, hammers on iron, voices, silence.

"Whoa! Slow down." Penny pleaded. She'd connected with the Land after Crann Mòr fell, but was this caused by more destruction of her kingdom?

Everything finally stopped.

Penny found herself floating above a house in the art district in Eagallach. The flicker of a candle swayed in an open window. Soft voices grew more distinct as Penny lowered herself closer.

When Penny floated into the house, her eyes widened. The entire place glimmered with metal. Metal sconces, metal wainscoting, metal tables and picture frames. The very walls were coated in swirls of copper, gold, and silver. A sleeping chandelier hung from the ceiling where steel vines looked like they'd grown over the exposed wood beams holding up the roof. The entire room looked like a work of art.

Two ellyllon, a male and a female, sat in front of the open window. Crates of broad-headed arrow points lined the walls opposite to stacks of steel ingots. As Penny drew closer, she realized the couple in front of her were making the arrowheads, their hands manipulating the metal in front of them and sending the finished product into the crates.

"Stop showing off, Labhrais," the female said, giving the male a tiny shove. "This is not supposed to be a race."

Labhrais laughed. "Just because you cannot keep up with your own gift does not mean I have to slow down, Flùr. I have had half the time as you to learn how to do it, so that leaves you little excuse."

Penny came around to face them. Both fae were summoning little bits of the steel to them and using their gifts—or gift since it seemed to be the same—to shape the arrowheads right in front of them. Candlelight glinted off the sharp edges of the points as they flew into a half-filled crate.

"I still do not understand," Flùr said, "how Danu gave you the ability to use my gift, and yet I have no access to yours. Even after nearly two hundred years of being married, I still have not been able to change the metal."

Labhrais shrugged, the bundles of heavy clothing he wore in front of the open window lifting almost comically. "Maybe I am simply her favorite."

Flùr rolled her eyes, but Penny could somehow tell the female was slightly pleased. "Maybe you are just a better flatterer than me."

Penny took a turn about the room, looking for any clue as to why the Land had brought her to this couple. "Why am I here?"

Something nudged her toward the ellyllon, and she drew closer to them.

Smiling, Labhrais molded his piece of metal into a solid heart instead of an arrowhead. As he worked with it, the shiny, gray steel changed to glittering gold. Penny gaped. He'd not only manipulated the metal but also changed what kind of metal it was. Labhrais twirled the now golden heart in the air and sent it toward his wife. Her hands reached up to grab the heart and Penny noticed the blue band around her finger. The couple was *taghadh*.

Flùr held the heart out in front of her. The heart expanded, hollowing as she stretched the metal into a filigreed heart, the design similar to the art around the room. A smile stretched over Labhrais's face. The heart crumpled and reformed into an arrowhead, but the golden color did not change. Flùr let out a huff. "I still cannot get the metal to switch."

Labhrais plucked the broadhead from her hand and it instantly turned back to steel. He sent it to join its replicas in an open crate. "I may be able to access your power, but I will never be able to access your creative mind. You are an artist, my love, and I merely your most devoted admirer."

Flùr's cheeks pinked. "Like I said. Flatterer."

Penny fell away.

She woke up with a gasp.

"Penny?" Mother woke next to her with a start. "What is it? What's happened?"

She stood up, glad she had fallen asleep fully clothed. "I know what we have to do, but I need your help."

Penny watched as the Olympian company followed their king out of the dunes. Dion and Shaunie had given their heartfelt goodbyes to Penny after breakfast and were now on their way back to fix the ruin the rebels had left of their kingdom. Penny wished them all the best as the two heads of golden hair faded out of view.

Now, it was time to get to work.

"This is absolutely mad," Dair said, plopping himself down in the sand next to Penny.

Penny leaned back in the cool sand. The sun had yet to hit that part of the dune. "Do you know folk in the art district well?"

"Some, but I cannot claim to know all of them."

"Do you know a couple by the names of Labhrais and Flùr?"

Dair sat silent beside her for a moment, seeming to mull it over. "I want to say either the metal workers or the painters."

"Metal workers."

"What about them?"

"Do you know that they're *taghadh* and can use one another's gifts?"

"You know, I think I did hear something of the sort, but I have never really investigated it. Married couples, especially *taghadh*, use their magic together in interesting ways."

Penny opened her eyes and turned to him. "Dair, these two didn't even have to be touching. He was able to access her gift as naturally as his own." She looked out toward the border separating Faerie from Olympia. "The Land took me to them the night before last and showed me how they worked with one another. I think the Goddess wanted to show me so I could know it was possible."

"Wait." Dair stood up. "You think you can do what you what you and Aedon planned? *On your own?*"

"I think I have to try."

Mother arrived not a moment later, carrying two buckets brimming with acorns. "I got what we're going to need. I've plotted each group stretching every five miles and the High Councilor has already begun portalling them. If we hurry, we might actually get this done today."

When the sun had fully risen yesterday morning, Penny had

instantly set Mother to the task of delegating the work. Penny had reached out to Dion and asked about acorns, knowing the royal family used the tree in their regalia. Dion informed them that the acorns were harvested in the garden every year and the palace had a store of them for the gardeners. Sgiath had gone with Mother to collect the acorns throughout the day yesterday while Penny and Dair stayed behind to plot the soldiers into groups. With the thousand men and women Dion had brought with them, they were able to stretch out the span of the border. It would provide a natural defense and give a dedicated place to the creatures Penny would summon.

"Excellent," Penny said, approaching the supplies. "Let's get to work."

It took the entire day to plant the acorns in the soil between Faerie and Olympia.

And it was one of the longest days of Penny's life.

Every few hours, a rush of pain would halt her steps or set her hands shaking. Adira was merciless in her commands to Aiden using his name. Penny could only guess what she was making him do. Her heart broke a little bit more every time that fresh wave of pain swept through her. They slowed as the day waned but sweat slicked the fabric of her shirt by the end of it.

But even with Penny's moments of distress, they finished sowing the acorns.

The Mist had been only one hundred feet thick and stretched miles and miles—nearly as far as Eleusia was from Olympia. Penny wanted this new border to be twice as thick. Sgiath had been hard at work, taking small groups and spreading them out as Mother had said. He bounced back and forth between the crews, returning the soldiers turned farmhands as soon as their task was complete.

Penny watched the sun give its last beam of light and fade beneath the horizon. The stars glimmered above them, seeming to watch as Penny gathered her courage and her magic. She knelt on the Olympian soil under her feet, her boots laid aside and her gloves lying next to them. Eyes closed, she reached for the bonds inside of her. The *taghadh* connection she shared with Aiden was weak, bringing a fresh wave of distress through Penny, though she couldn't tell if it was her emotions or his. She grabbed hold of it and tried to send comfort and confidence to him, though she still wasn't sure if it worked that way.

She focused on the Land's connection next. It took a moment, as she was on the Olympian side of the border, but once she found it, the magic jumped at her touch, like a pleased puppy ready to be played with. Penny smiled—at least, she thought she smiled—and grabbed hold of that as well.

"Sweet Gaia, I really hope this works."

With every ounce of strength she possessed, she pulled.

The magic spread from her in a shockwave. Her consciousness connected with the thousands of acorns in the newly tilled earth. The planters had done their best, planting as many as they could as fast as possible. Some were in haphazard lines, others in circles, and even some planted in no kind of pattern at all. Penny connected to each one and poured magic into them.

They began to grow.

Slowly, the acorns split open, roots reaching out and into the sandy soil under them until the taproot reached the water beneath. The seedlings stretched toward the sky, leaves sprouting and searching for the sun already sleeping. Penny pushed the magic to give the trees more, more, more.

Voices broke out behind her, but she didn't allow the noise to distract her. All she could really pay attention to were the trees.

It took hours to get the entire border thick with foliage. Penny's hands began to shake, and weariness settled into her bones. She hadn't felt this tired since she was shot in the leg by Adira. Being this close to the border strengthened her gift, but the magic took its toll all the same.

"Penny." Mother's hand settled on her shoulder—Penny recognized it instantly. "You should probably rest."

Penny shook her head, eyes still closed. "We don't have time. Adira could already be taking Eagallach, and we can't send Sgiath back to check." It was a miracle he got out in the first place, after what happened to Farrah.

Mother's hand moved from her shoulder, and she knelt on the ground beside Penny, her warmth taking away some of Penny's shaking. "Then I'm going to help."

Penny opened her eyes then. Mother held out her hand, the green of her magic flickering faintly between them.

"Are you all right?"

Mother reached out and settled her hand over Penny's in the dirt. "I don't know, but I'll help you in whatever capacity I can."

Weariness held back any further argument Penny would have made, and she allowed her magic to connect with Mother's. There certainly was something wrong with it. Instead of the neat well of magic that Penny had become accustomed to seeing when connecting with Mother's magic, it resembled a ragged, gaping hole that stretched and thinned uncontrollably. Penny reared back, disconnecting from the magic and pulling her hand away.

"Mother, that doesn't look right."

"It isn't right." Determination mingled with fear on Mother's face. "Since I used my magic through the charmed cuffs, I haven't been able to sprout anything."

Penny's heart dropped to her stomach. "What?"

"I've been trying all day to get some of these oaks to wake, but I can't get any acorns to sprout." Her hands clenched in her lap. "I can manipulate the already-established foliage, and I can mature plants quickly, but I can't do anything until they've broken through the ground."

Penny placed her hand over Mother's. "It's going to be all right."

Mother pulled away. "No, it most certainly won't be all right." She stood and began pacing. "Penny, I can't use my magic to grow anything. We just ran the rebels out of Eleusia and are well on our way to getting our duchy back. How am I going to run the farm by myself when I can't sprout anything? Winter is coming shortly to Olympia, and I had been making plans for barley."

Of course Mother had already come up with a solution. Barley would grow within a month if Mother tweaked it the smallest bit. If they could get enough of it planted, it would get the kingdom through the winter. It would be difficult, but there would be grain along with any other root vegetables they could get planted.

But not if Mother couldn't help it along.

"How am I going to help our kingdom get back on its feet when I have to wait for the seed to sprout? Every day we have to wait is a day people go hungry. The first frosts will likely see them dead in the ground if I can't get them to grow faster." She stopped, her face falling into her hands. "The people are already starving, and I can't do anything to help them now."

Penny stood on shaking legs and wrapped her arms around Mother. "We'll figure it out. Together. Just like we always do." She pulled back to look Mother in the face and offered her hand out. "But right now, we need to save my kingdom."

Mother let out a shaky breath but gave one firm nod of her head and grasped Penny's hand.

Penny pushed the magic out.

The small saplings thickened, the trunks becoming firm and immovable as they gained height. The slight breeze only shook the leaves and Penny fed more and more magic into the trees.

She opened her eyes and found the scene around her completely changed. Young oak trees stretched out before her, like stripling warriors readying for battle.

"How are you going to do this, Penny?" Mother asked.

Penny took in a deep breath and let it out slowly. "I have absolutely no idea." She called her magic back, allowing Mother's well to continue to work on the trees as Penny dove into the connections within her heart.

Danu, please let this work.

Warmth blossomed in her chest, a kind of peace taking over her body as she connected with Aiden.

Then there were spirits.

Mother jerked beside her. "Penny?"

"Do you see them?"

"There are so many."

Thousands of spirits appeared before them, all human, all with a look of reverence and determination. Men and women all gathered closely, their eyes taking in the old world around them. Their forms were still transparent, but they were there. They looked ready to fight for their lives. They looked ready for war.

Penny's legs wobbled and Mother caught her before she could fall on her face in the sand. It didn't stop the smile from stretching across her face. They'd done it. They'd actually done it.

One of them approached, his head of brown hair bouncing as he wove through the souls around them. His tall frame stood out among his fellows, and he moved with an energy Penny hadn't seen in most others.

Tears pooled in Penny's eyes. "Hart."

Something in her chest snapped back into place, leaving a sore spot but also healing it at the same time. She hadn't even thought she'd see him there. He had at least a drop of fae blood, but it seemed his human side was just as important.

Hart's face split into a large grin. "Hello, Penelope. Have you come to save the day once again?"

Penny shook her head. "No. Just like last time, you'll be the one doing the saving."

She opened her connection to the Land once again, this time using the connection she shared with Aiden in tandem. She kept her eyes closed, concentrating on the souls and the growth of the trees around her, but even through her eyelids she could see the green of her magic growing brighter.

Penny.

She almost lost her tentative hold on everything at the sound of the familiar voice.

Penny, repeat the words that I give you.

"Praise the Goddess," Mother breathed.

Penny's hand tightened around Mother's as the Goddess gave her the words.

Child of Danu, do you swear to cherish this second chance...

She repeated all the words Danu gave her, her body and mind so overcome she couldn't even process what she was saying. With Sissy, it had been as simple as telling her to become whole, but this was different. This was true magic. Penny could feel it in the ground, in the touch of Mother's fingers on her arm, in the very air that stirred her hair and raised goose flesh on her arms.

... now, become one with this tree.

The mingling powers surged from Penny, a blast of magic so strong it made her knees buckle. Before she fell, a hand reached out and grabbed her. Penny opened her eyes to find a pair of dark brown ones staring back at her.

"Don't go collapsing on us now, Your Majesty." Hart's eyes twinkled. "We've got a kingdom to save."

Cheers of victory shook the ground beneath their feet, the old army roaring alongside the new.

47

SNOW

THE FERVOR OUTSIDE THE TENT HAD AIDEN'S WHOLE BODY SHAKING. IT HAD begun that morning and only grown throughout the day. As they approached noon, it had increased tenfold.

He glanced at Shirina's sleeping form across the tent from him. She slept much more than he remembered, sometimes even a short time into the night. He couldn't imagine what she'd been through in the weeks she'd been there. Her thin body was an outward testament of her suffering at Durant's hands, but he wasn't even sure if anyone would be able to see her heart under all the scars he knew she must carry with her now.

A cheer rang outside of the tent and Aiden's heart kicked.

Nothing that excited the rebels this much could be good for Faerie.

Aiden had been trapped in the camp for the entire week, his entrapment separated between this tent and Durant's. She'd haul him out of the tent and command him to do a ridiculous number of things.

Jump on one foot.

Cut down this tree with only your magic.

Hold your breath.

She would have him for minutes or hours. Whatever she deemed enough for him to return to the tent with Shirina. Time seemed to consist of only the rising and setting of the sun and the bowls of thin gruel that came with the changing light.

He clenched his hands and reached for the thin bonds he still held within him. Not two nights before, he had felt Penelope, felt her love and her confidence. It had sent shame and joy rattling through him all the next day. He should never have allowed despair to overtake him. The love of his life still had hope, and even if she didn't know what awaited her here, he could have hope for her as well.

Shirina turned over on her small bedroll, her dark eyes alert. "They are growing more restless."

Aiden nodded. "I still can't hear anything though."

Shirina scanned his face and sat up. "Anything you want to talk about? I cannot sleep with all this ruckus. I forgot how loud humans are. You and Penelope are practically silent compared to this."

Aiden's lips twitched, but he couldn't summon a full smile at the moment. "You should have heard her before she became a spy. She was like a troll stomping through Autumn's mounds of crunchy leaves."

Shirina chuckled, but it devolved into a coughing fit. He grabbed her a cup of water and she sipped at it as her hacking subsided. "You did mention you trained her when you told us how the two of you became connected. How did she manage to convince you?"

The story tumbled out between his lips. Him sneaking into Lady Barclay's study. Penelope nearly strangling him with the vines before he could get to the door. Sissy coming to check what was going on and Penelope trusting him. Shirina chuckled when he told her how seventeen-year-old Penelope had practically blackmailed him into letting her be involved.

"I knew I liked that girl," Shirina said. "Crafty as a pùca and quick as a pixie. She will be an amazing High Queen."

"I can't keep up with her half the time. She's a marvel."

Shirina's smile turned wistful. "I am so glad she came into our lives. I know I said it would be a mistake to allow her to stay in Faerie, but I have never been so glad to be wrong. Having a *taghadh* is one of the greatest gifts Danu has given Her children. I am happy to know you will share in that joy that so few of us ever get to experience."

Aiden looked at the amber ring around her finger and then

looked at the green one around his own. "I don't want to let her down."

"You will not. I have faith in you, Little Shadow."

The room darkened slightly, and Aiden turned toward the opening to the tent. The flap swung open. A biting Winter wind blew through, bringing snowflakes the size of pixies swirling in. The first snows of the season had arrived yesterday, only to melt into mud by the afternoon.

An ox of a man walked in, dark hair growing in a frizz on his head and face, making him look like a disgruntled bear. His dark eyes landed on Shirina, and he took a step toward her.

Aiden was on his feet before the man could take another. "You will not touch her."

The man stared down at him, a leer growing under his bushy beard. "I'll do whatever I please, fae filth. Move."

Aiden straightened his shoulders. "You'll have to make me."

The tent flap let in another flurry. "You're not in a position to make threats, my boy." Durant stepped out from behind the man, her green eyes glittering. "Though I shouldn't be surprised." She turned back to the man. "Grab the Councilor. His Majesty will follow without trouble if he doesn't wish for her to come to harm." The threat was evident. Aiden would have to let them take Shirina if he didn't want her death on his own hands. Durant didn't even need to use his name.

The man barreled past him and grabbed Shirina's arm in his rough grip. She stumbled as he dragged her out of the tent, but her eyes told Aiden not to do anything foolish.

"Come along, Aiden," Durant called over her shoulder. "We're expecting some company this afternoon."

Aiden followed her out into the cold wind. With the irons around his ankles, it was difficult to move in the rapidly growing snowdrifts, but he kept pace until they arrived at the main tent. One of the guards held open the flap as they stepped inside. Durant's crew of rebel leaders all stood around the table, looking over maps.

Durant grabbed a chain attached to one of the thick tent posts and gestured for Aiden to go to her. She attached the end of the chain to the links connecting Aiden's legs to one another.

Once that was done, she made her way to the table. "How are things coming along?"

A young man cleared his throat. "We've just received word that the Aigeans should pass through Spring tomorrow and join us the morning after."

"Excellent," Adira said. "Have we scouted out the path to the base of the mountain?"

Teagan, the continent man, trailed his finger along the map. "We've found three different ways to the fortress at the base. If we want to maintain a bit of the element of surprise, I recommend taking the western route around the lake where the foliage is thicker and sending another force over the ice after them to act as second infantry. The third route is longest but can be used if necessary."

Durant nodded, jotting down notes and measuring out how far each path was with the featherless quill in her hand. "I agree, Teagan. I think it's also wise to send the second force to stomp down some of this snow for the siege engines we need to get up the mountain that our portal-making friend can't manage."

Aiden's blood boiled, but he was relieved to find out Farrah was still alive.

Durant set down the quill she'd been using, and Aiden realized the cursed woman had *his* quill, the one Dion had gifted him for his birthday a few years ago. It was his favorite because it never ran out of ink, and it fit right in his pocket. *How the blizzards did she get my quill?*

"Has our guest arrived?" she asked.

The woman with the salt-and-pepper hair—whose name Aiden still couldn't remember—answered. "Should be here any second."

As if on cue, the tent flap opened once again, and Thaen walked through.

A storm of fury settled on his brow, and he took in the room. His anger only heightened when his eyes met Aiden's, and he looked downright murderous when he saw the way Shirina sagged in her captor's grip. Aiden couldn't begin to imagine what she looked like to Thaen.

"Ah," Durant said, "Prince Bàsthaen, I presume?"

Thaen's head snapped in the direction of Durant and the other leaders. His pale eyes took in the lot of them and ended on Durant. He blinked. Once. Twice. His brows furrowed once more before the storm on his expression broke and a smirk replaced the frown.

"Adira Durant, I presume?" he replied, in the same tone Durant had used. He pursed his lips, clearly not impressed. "I think I have seen all I need to see." He whirled and made his way back to the opening of the tent.

"Pardon?" the salt-and-pepper woman said, obviously shocked at Thaen's reception.

Aiden was feeling a little shocked himself.

Thaen turned back and gave the room a quirked eyebrow. "Was it something I said?"

"You demanded a meeting with us to offer ransom for the prisoners," one of the other rebels snapped.

Thaen gave them a look Aiden could only describe as his flat assassin face. "Were you actually going to consider a ransom?" His words were mild, but he showed too much teeth as he spoke for it to be interpreted as anything but annoyed.

Durant smiled. "No." The other leaders at the table looked to her in surprise and she shrugged. "Why lie? He obviously already knew and only came to make sure his family was still in one piece... for the time being."

Thaen gave a small bow of his head. "Glad we are on the same page." He took another step for the exit.

Durant walked back around the table. "Though perhaps a trade could be arranged. I'd give up the portal wench if you agreed to stay in her place."

Aiden silently fumed. For one, Farrah was one of the noblest females of his acquaintance and second, she was as old as Durant herself.

Thaen's eyes sparked at the insult to Farrah, but his facade stayed firmly in place. "And why would I do that?" He moved, only a blur of shadow indicating he'd gone from one place to another and was looming over Durant a second later. Those with swords in the room drew them, but Thaen didn't touch his and neither did Durant.

"I assume you would revel in the challenge of this coming fight, and I would hate to make it any less fun for you."

Durant laughed, delighted. "Oh, Your Highness, it's going to be quite a highlight to beat you."

Thaen bowed his head, not in deference but as one combatant to another. "I will see you on the field of battle then."

He made his way to the door.

"Tomorrow," Durant called behind him.

Thaen stopped at the threshold, his knuckles whitening as he clenched the fabric of the flap.

Durant's grin deepened, having caught the tension in him as quickly as Aiden had. "We move for Eagallach at dawn."

48
TREES AND THINGS

THESE NEW CREATURES HAD MORE THAN A FEW TRICKS UP THEIR SLEEVES.

It had taken them two days to collect everyone from the border and regroup in Spring.

Once they did, however, the moving went much faster.

The first night in Spring, one of the new soldiers had fallen into a tree.

Not like she landed against one, but her body went fully into it.

It had taken Hart hours to figure out how to get her out, but once he did, she told everyone about how the inside was like a house. Then, the rest of them had figured out how to step inside. It had made setting up camp much simpler and with much less clean up.

"Duck!" Hart said and Penny moved her head so they didn't crash into a low hanging tree branch. Now, they were two days into Spring, and if Penny's connection to the land was correct, they'd already made it more than half of the way through. They passed from one trunk to another and every time they did, Penny saw more and more of what the inside of the trees looked like.

She always knew they were solid wood, but the way the newly formed creatures saw them was nothing of the sort.

Each tree was different. Some had empty rooms as vast as the Grand Hall in the Winter Palace and others had rooms smaller than Aiden's office back in the Underworld. Some were dark wood and some light. Some were infested with living things, others empty. All of them connected to one another, a network of portals stretching for miles.

"I still think this is highly improper!" Mother said, her legs wrapped around the waist of one of the new soldiers as they disappeared into another tree.

Penny knew they came out somewhere ahead, but she didn't see them again before Hart had leapt into another trunk. This one had a skunk living beneath it, and both Penny and Hart came out of another trunk gasping for air. Hart stopped and grabbed the water skin hanging at his side. He needed more water than Penny did, but she took the chance to sip at hers as well.

A moment later, one of the creatures that had been sent out to scout ahead of the group burst out of one of the trunks. "Your Majesty," he said breathlessly, "there are water folk up ahead."

Hart disappeared a moment later, likely to check out the scene for himself.

Penny capped her water skin. "How far?"

"Maybe two miles?" said the scout.

Penny closed her eyes and propelled her consciousness forward. She saw Hart jump in one tree and out another nearly five hundred feet ahead. Even after they won this war, their ability to travel so quickly would be invaluable.

Hart stopped ahead of her consciousness, and she flew above the trees to get a better look. The scout was right. Two miles ahead, a force of about two thousand Aigeans were moving toward Winter. They coasted on the Spring's natural water sources, jumping from pond to pond with waves for their carts to ride on for short distances. They left the forest ragged behind them.

Penny returned to her body. Her mind whirled with ideas. "We need to gather our forces and meet the Aigeans."

"Now, Your Majesty?" the soldier asked.

"Yes. We can't allow them to join the force at Eagallach. If we can defeat them here, in the forest, we can use the trees to our advantage. They aren't used to fighting on land and will gain a greater advantage with the snow in Winter." With a force that big, they could probably thaw the eternally frozen lake and use it to drown the city.

Hart rejoined them. "Spread the word. Have them meet us in the clearing just on the other side of these trees."

The scout jumped into the closest tree and left them to walk to the clearing.

As they walked, Hart lifted a hand to one of the trees. A thin branch stretched out and fell into his waiting hand.

"What did you just do?" Penny asked, coming around him to stare at the straight piece of wood in his hands.

Hart smirked and pulled more elements from the tree. In seconds, he held a bow and a quiver of unfletched arrows. "While I'm finding I can't get things to grow the same way you can, I have apparently inherited the ability to manipulate the bits of the trees to fulfill my needs." He frowned at the ends of his arrows. "However, I don't think they can give me any feathers and these leaves will shred in seconds."

"I think I can help with that." Penny's arms took on their green-and-black tell, and a riot of orchids rose from the ground. She plucked a few of the leaves of and handed them to Hart. "Will these do?"

Hart ran his fingers over the edge of the leaf and nodded. "Much better."

As Hart plucked more leaves and began fletching his arrows, the others began to arrive. Dair hopped from the back of another young man, both of them laughing as if they were the best of friends. Sgiath came next, looking a little green—well, green for Sgiath. All the new members of their army all had the same green hue to their skin and hair that Sissy did, especially the ones that had obviously had lighter hair in their human forms.

Mother showed up last, her hair a tangle of auburn waves and her face flushed with embarrassment. She scrambled off the back of her burly companion and straightened her dress before coming up to Penny.

"Really, Penny, this is completely undignified."

"We're at war. The time for squeamishness passed long ago." Penny shrugged. "You should have taken me up on my offer to get you a pair of trousers."

Mother grumbled and Penny couldn't help but smile a bit.

"Gather around," Hart called. He'd taken the roll of general to their new people easily, and the others followed him almost instantly. He'd always had a natural charisma, and his time as Aiden's third had only encouraged his strategic prowess. He unrolled the map Penny had given him and pointed at a spot in the middle of Spring. "This is about where we are now. The Aigeans are two miles ahead and sweeping up toward Winter. Under the direction of our High Queen, we will be meeting them before they reach the border."

A murmur broke through the clearing, and it sounded as if the very trees around them had an opinion as well.

"Quiet, please," Penny called over the whispers and the sound settled. "I believe our best chance of defeating them will be here, in the forest, but we need to move quickly. We're faster than them, but they're closer to Winter than we are at this moment. We need to stop them before they reach the rebels on the lake."

"We'll separate into groups. Some will need to stay behind to treat wounded and act as second wave. This clearing will act as our point of return if we need a place to fall back to. I need a hundred of our best weapon experts to assist our brothers and sisters with crafting weapons while the Olympians gather whatever supplies will be needed for the fight and leave behind things to make camp."

When everyone broke to begin preparing, Hart turned to Penny. "I would ask that you remain here to lead the camp."

Penny put her hands on her hips. "You know I can kill you just as fast as I brought you back, right?"

Mother seemed to choke, but Hart laughed. "It was worth a try," he said, "but we'll need someone to take care of the camp."

"I can manage that," Mother said, regaining her composure. "I'll be no help in a fight, but I can certainly organize a camp."

"Thank you, Mother." Penny turned back to Hart. "It's settled. Let's get these fighters outfitted. I'd like to leave within the hour.

Penny leaned around the trunk, watching the Aigeans pass underneath the thick branches a dozen feet below. Hart crouched next to her, his newly grown bow hanging from his hands as he watched the water folk scurry by beneath them. It had taken the other new soldiers a bit to figure out how to manipulate the plants, but it hadn't taken long to outfit the entire army with enough weapons to take out this threat. Thick, bark armor also started popping up in the ranks. Five thousand soldiers decorated in steel and wood stretched out through the forest, another two thousand left behind at the camp. They'd left three thousand more to guard the border to Olympia, cutting the rebel forces off from one another.

Hart pulled back on the string of his bow, his arrow trained on the last cart crashing through the underbrush beneath them. A handful off fae huddled in the back, their faces drawn and wrists clamped in irons. With an exhale of his breath, Hart let the arrow fly.

It sank into the hind quarters of the kelpie pulling the cart. The water horse reared up and its webbed feet, where hooves would have been, flailed, hitting the Aigeans in the immediate vicinity. By the time the creature's front feet returned to the ground, Hart had shot four of the Aigeans around it and was nocking his fifth arrow.

The soldiers in the other trees jumped from the trunks, taking out three selkies underneath them. One swung his sword in great arcs, spraying blood and water as he went. Another snuck around the carts, crawling into the back and unhitching them from the beasts pulling them. The kelpies caught on to what she was doing after the second cart and began chasing after her, their sharp teeth snapping.

Hart's bow twanged over and over, the thunk of arrows meeting flesh growing indiscernible over the sounds of fighting below. When he loosed his last arrow, he slung the bow over his shoulder. "Time to join the fray."

Hart scaled the tree like a squirrel while Penny climbed down like a slug. He drew his sword and clashed with a group of merrows before Penny had even touched the ground.

She finally reached the forest floor and drew her own blade. The steel sang as she lunged at one of the merrows that had broken off from Hart's group of attackers. When he went down, Penny moved to the next one. She worked her way through the water folk like a plow in soft ground.

As they fought, more and more of Penny's army came into view. Tree-men—was that what Penny would call them?—and Olympians fought with dogged determination as they boxed the Aigeans in on all sides. Streaks of magic used by Olympian mages counteracted the water folk magic while the Green-men—*no that's not it either*—jumped from tree to tree, bringing an enemy with them and leaving them behind in the tree to grab another with brutal efficiency. The water folk fell as fast as they conjured waves to fight.

A blast of sound roared through the trees.

A male siren stood on one of the carts, his mouth open in a scream that brought everyone including his own comrades to their knees.

Penny remained standing, her connection to the Land pulsing inside of her, keeping her wits from being overrun.

She charged the cart. Her blade flashed in the golden light of the late afternoon, catching the siren's attention. He sucked in a breath and started a new tune, one to soothe and calm a person.

Penny heard right through it.

She swung at him, cutting off the sound as he jumped back to avoid her blade. He turned to the green fighter next to him and used his magic to turn the new soldier into a mindless shield. Penny dodged him, sliding past him toward the siren still blasting away on top of the cart.

The siren stabbed one of the green soldiers in the back.

The solider arched his back, but before he could cry out, he disappeared.

Penny stopped short, her heart racing.

The siren stumbled, the blade falling from where it had been held in the soldier's spine, and Penny took advantage of his distraction. The siren's eyes flared with alarm as Penny brought up her blade and cut him down.

The fighting didn't last long after that, and right before dusk, the last of the Aigeans surrendered.

Hart ordered their weapons taken and supplies distributed through Mother's camp. The water folk left standing—about a dozen or so—were bound and Sgiath set to the task of sending them to Olympia. A few of the new creatures offered to go with a small group of Olympians back to the border. The soldiers would take them to the dungeons in Olympia where Rissa could write their ransom notes to the Isles.

As the last of them went through the portal, Penny smiled. She looked about as the rest of the soldiers gathered the dead under the midnight sky. Some of the Olympian's had lost their lives in the fight and their comrades were busy burying them.

Hart passed by, having put a crew on gathering the Aigean bodies and returning them to the water where their kin could find them.

"Hart!" Penny called, grabbing him by the arm. "I saw one of yours disappear after he was injured, and I haven't seen any other of your kind dead on the ground. I don't fully understand what happened."

Hart pursed his lips. "There are many things our new forms allow for us, but I don't understand all of them. Perhaps we simply fade and return back to Danu."

"Actually," someone called out, "I know what happens."

Penny gasped when she saw the same man that had been stabbed in the back walk toward them.

"I saw you die," Penny said.

The man nodded. "Aye, but it seems these new bodies of ours bounce back pretty quickly." He turned to Hart. "When I was hurt, my body immediately went back to the tree that bound me to this earth. Once there, my injuries were gone, but I wasn't able to come back the same way. It took me a few hours, but I was able to use that handy trick with the trees to get back here."

Hart whistled. "Well, that's good news. I'll go see how the rest of the crew is doing."

Penny nodded, still shocked as Hart sauntered off. If this was true, the new soldiers were practically invincible. Yes, their return to their trees would render them useless from such a distance, but they wouldn't lose the lives they'd regained by agreeing to return here. It was an absolute miracle.

"That is quite a pleased look for a queen drenched in sweat and blood," Dair said coming up next to her. "What has elicited such a look?"

Penny felt hope bloom in her chest. "Today, we thwarted Adira's plans. Tomorrow, we save the rest of our people."

49
SUNRISE

Dawn came too quickly.

Aiden sat, watching the shadows grow lighter through the thin gap between the tent flaps. The rustling of the wind turned into the racket of a waking army. Full sunrise would happen within the hour.

Dread pooled in Aiden's limbs. Today would be the beginning of the end—whatever end the Goddess had in store.

Shirina shifted beside him, peeking out into the freshly fallen snow. Aiden had prayed for mounds to simply bury the encampment, but only a scant two inches had fallen overnight and would likely melt within the first few hours of sunlight.

"Have you felt anything else?" Shirina asked.

Aiden had told her about Penelope's surge of emotion from a few days ago, but he hadn't received anything since then. He shook his head.

"I believe in her, Aedon. No matter what, she will do what is best for this kingdom."

Aiden pushed down the despair bubbling up inside him and clung to the hope Shirina offered him.

She stood up. "Come. There is no use waiting by the door. They will come when they please, and we will not be sitting like eager pups waiting for the call of their master."

Aiden made his way back to his bedroll, Shirina's words sparking defiance under his ribcage. He would not look afraid. No matter what

Durant had in store for him today, he'd go down fighting for every inch he could gain.

The camp came to full life within the hour. The chink of armored soldiers accompanied the hiss of iron chains against the icy ground. Shadows danced on the thin tent walls, the shapes stretching into grotesque nightmares.

Aiden had to force himself to breathe calmly. He would be calm when Durant came for him. He would not allow her to use his fear when he had so much to hope for. He closed his eyes and reached for the two thin connections inside of him. They were still there, and they weren't going anywhere.

Voices grew close to the tent, but Aiden kept his eyes closed and his breathing slow. Best to look as if he'd been sleeping. If he could rile her enough, maybe she'd be angry enough to make a mistake.

Shirina must have had the same idea because when the tent flap opened, Durant huffed.

"Get up sleepy heads. It's a glorious morning, and I have plans to wreak some havoc before the day is through."

Aiden pretended to wake slowly, squinting up at her as if he had been deep in sleep. Shirina gave a loud yawn that had Durant frowning. With a roll of her eyes, she turned her full attention to Aiden. "Let's go, my boy. We have things to do."

He stood and the guard that had walked in with Durant unchained his hands and feet. He tried not to look at Shirina, but he could see her worry out of the corner of his eye as the iron fell. The charms around the tent kept his wounds from healing, but it was a relief to not have the iron burning his exposed skin.

Durant strode from the tent and the guard pushed Aiden after her. Aiden looked back at Shirina then, and she knelt on the ground, a fist over her heart as she met his eyes.

The tent flap fell between them.

The sun's crown rose over the horizon. Durant strode through the swarm of tents, a fist raised in the air, a call to arms. The crowd around her thundered with bloodlust. She collected an entourage as she walked back to the main tent and jumped on top of a cart, setting a stage for her legendary theatrics. If Aiden thought it would help him, he'd have rolled his eyes. She grabbed the charm at her throat.

"My friends," Durant began, her voice projecting out through the charm she held, "today is a glorious day to go to war."

The soldiers cheered; their swords raised high over their heads.

When they settled, Durant continued, "We have done much good since our taking of Eleusion last Autumn. In one year, we have seen two kingdoms brought to their knees under our power. While our brothers and sisters in Olympia were thwarted by that false king, we have continued to persevere and soon, we will deliver them from the hands of our enemies. But today, we will take what is rightfully ours. Today will be the day that magic will fall and the reign of bronties will begin!"

She gestured for Aiden to be brought forward as the cheers made it impossible to hear her again for a moment. She grabbed Aiden by the hair as if he were a pet.

"Today, the High King of Faerie will be made an instrument in our hands. A tool, just as the rest of the fae, in our new world. Today, we are The Cartographers of our own lands, the writers of our own destinies. So rise up, my friends, my brothers and my sisters! Rise up and make it *yours*!"

With screams of adoration, the soldiers ran through the camp, collecting their weapons and dragging fae through the frozen mud under their boots. Horns sounded within the camp, trumpeting the coming storm.

Durant pulled Aiden's hair back far enough to make him look up at her. A savage grin split her face in two. "Are you ready to lose everything, my boy?"

50
WAR AND WARNINGS

THE DISTANT SOUND OF HORNS HAD PENNY BOLTING UPRIGHT IN HER bedroll.

"Oh, by every blasted star in the cursed sky." She untangled herself from her bedroll and leapt from the tent without even putting her boots on.

Hart was sticking halfway out of a tree trunk, staring to the north. He met Penny's eye. "It's already begun." He disappeared back into the tree, likely using the forest network to travel to the border quickly.

Mother thrust her head out of the tent she shared with Penny. "What's going on?"

"The battle has already started," Penny said, jumping back through the opening and searching the pile of rumpled bedding for her things. "I thought we'd have another day at least. The Aigeans wouldn't have made it until tomorrow anyway."

"Perhaps the devil woman had planned on them as a second wave," Mother said.

"But why all the building supplies?" she asked.

Dair's head popped through the opening a second later, making Mother shriek and begin ranting about the bounds of propriety. "Siege engines," he said over Mother's tirade. "I have been thinking about it all night. Durant was going to use the Aigeans to siege the capital after they had taken out the encampment at the base of the mountain. With their affinity with water and their greater stamina, it would make sense for the humans to clear out the soldiers on the lake and then allow easy travel for the Aigeans to sweep in behind them."

"Get your tent packed, Dair," Penny ordered. His purple head disappeared as quickly as it came.

"Uncivilized ruffian," Mother grumbled. She began packing her things alongside Penny. "It was a good thing we stopped the water folk. We likely saved the city."

"Not quite yet," Penny said, buckling her scabbard to her waist. She grabbed her pack of maps and supplies and burst out of the tent. In the seconds she'd been inside, the camp was already awake, and the tents fell faster than they'd gone up.

"My Sovereign," Sgiath called, his languid walk preventing him from reaching her quickly. Penny bounded over to him instead, and he flashed her a grateful smile. "What would you have me do?"

Penny dropped the bag from her shoulder. "Can you watch this for a second?"

Sgiath nodded and she closed her eyes and connected with the Land. She found Hart jumping from tree to tree at the edge of the forest, taking in everything, but she focused on what was happening on the ice. The shield barring her entrance had gone down since they'd checked last night.

"I need you to go to the encampment and find Thaen." She ripped open her bag and found parchment and a stick of charcoal. She set the stick to the parchment and stilled.

Idiot. Thaen couldn't read.

She stuffed the supplies back in the pack and turned back to Sgiath. "I need you to make sure he's completely alone and report our numbers. Tell him we'll be there at dawn tomorrow and he only needs to hold them off until then. If he knows that the rebels were planning on a second wave, it could help him react accordingly to whatever strategy they were going to use. Spare no detail and let him know I'm coming."

Hart shot out of a tree, eyes wild and breathing ragged. "They've got two forces headed for the base of the mountain. One is headed straight over the ice, but another has made its way around the forest on the west side and will likely work to flush the fae out onto the ice and into the arms of the other half of the army."

Penny met Sgiath's eye, and he nodded, adding the information to the list to tell Thaen.

"Can I go with you?" Dair asked Sgiath, appearing once again where he wasn't supposed to be.

They both turned to Penny, awaiting her orders.

She automatically opened her mouth to object but stopped. "Actually, yes. It would be good to send you back to help Thaen. You'll be more help to him there than you will be to me here."

Dair let out a breath as Sgiath summoned a portal in the air behind them. As the portal grew taller, Dair grabbed Penny in a big hug. "Please, do not die."

Penny squeezed him back with just as much ferocity. "Same to you."

He let go, and without a backward glance, jumped through the portal and disappeared.

"Oh, praise the Goddess," Mother said, standing outside the tent. "That boy was a menace."

Penny went to her and the two of them tore down their tent as fast as they could.

It took two more hours before the rest of the army was ready to leave and Penny had practically wrung her fingers to the bone. After the battle with the Aigeans, their company's supplies had become too much for the Tree-jumpers—*nope, not that either*—to carry everything on their backs. If they pushed, however, they could reach the border by nightfall.

"Let's move," Hart bellowed over the crowd, and the soldiers fell into line behind them. The force of new magic pushed the trees back, clearing a path straight through to the border and keeping their force together rather than making them weave through the trees.

While it would cut down travel time, it still wasn't fast enough for Penny.

With the last rays of sunlight, Penny's patience dwindled. As the rest of the army began readying for camp, Penny threw down her pack and stomped toward the trees.

"Penny?" Mother called after her. "Where are you going?"

Penny searched in her mind for some excuse, anything to make Mother stay with the rest of the camp. "High Queen business. I'm going to commune with the Goddess." That should keep anyone from bothering her.

"Well, don't go too far. We don't know what's out there."

Penny grumbled under her breath. She could literally connect with every living thing within miles around her. She knew *exactly* what was out there.

They'd been moving the entire day and still they were too far from the battlefront. Adira was moving on the folk, and Penny was too far to do anything about it. The cursed woman had hundreds of fae in chains, the last soldiers in the kingdom under siege, and thousands of men at her beck and call. Penny might have been able to stop the Aigeans from joining the rebels, but it still wouldn't stop Adira from taking Eagallach if she couldn't get there in time.

And Aiden.

Penny wanted to scream into the blanket of silence the forest created.

Adira had taken him, chained him, cut off his magic. Even now, Penny could feel the dulled connection to him, the charms weighing him down. Her soul still ached from Adira's use of his name. The cursed woman would be using it more and more the closer they got to the battle. She'd probably make him fight most of her battles in the skirmish. By the Goddess, she'd probably keep a chant of his name going all day.

Penny gasped and crashed down to the soft ground beneath her. How would she lead everyone while Aiden suffered through that? How would Penny win this fight, even as her *taghadh* writhed under the demands of that cruel creature?

"Penelope?" Penny's head snapped in the direction of Hart's voice. He stood at the base of one of the trees. "Are you all right?"

Penny tried to smile, but when she did, she felt the stream of tears still trailing down her face. She scrubbed at them with the sleeve of her jacket, but they kept coming.

Hart crouched next to her. "That was a stupid question. Let me try again. What do you need?"

The question released the sob she had trapped in her chest. "I need Aiden. I need him to be free from Adira's blasted influence. I don't want to fight him on that battlefield. I don't want—" She couldn't even say the words.

"You don't want to have to kill him." Hart blew out a breath, and he let himself fall back to sit in the loam around them. "I can't tell you what to do, Penelope, and I can't promise you won't have to kill him to free him from Adira's influence. He's the one that must overcome that particular struggle."

Penny swiped at her nose. "What do you mean? He can't do anything."

The corner of Hart's mouth quirked up. "I hope that's not true. By the Goddess, that curse is a blasted scourge."

"How did she even get his true name?"

"I don't know that it's really my story to tell, Penelope."

Penny wiped her face again. "I just don't understand how he would have let her in like that. I've read about the sacredness of those names. Aiden would have had this innate desire to keep it hidden, to keep it from the knowledge of those who would use it against him."

"The relationship Durant had with Aiden. That's going to take some getting used to." Hart blew out a breath. "Anyways, what she had with him was different than what she shared with others. She didn't lord over him the way we've all seen her do. While the woman is a sociopath, she really did treat him like her son. They did everything together. When she had to leave the capital to attend to the king's wishes, he went with her. They broke bread and made jokes. The only other people he did that with were his brothers and me."

"So, she tricked him into giving her his name?"

"I don't even know if it was a trick," Hart admitted. "I think they really did love each other at one point. I think they grew close enough in whatever twisted way they could to trust one another. If things had gone differently—if Aiden hadn't had his brothers or if he'd been just slightly less morally sound than he is—I think none of this would have ever happened. I think the Tyrant King would still be alive, and Olympia would be all the worse for it."

Penny rubbed her forehead. "And here I thought she abused him as a child."

"Oh, she certainly did, but how does a child understand such abuse when it's all they've known? He was a weapon in his own right, and his father treated him as one from the get-go."

"So, it was simply a mistake?"

"It wasn't a mistake at the time, I think. I remember they'd just returned from a mission in the city. I'd been part of the spy network for a little over a year. I'd started out as a runner for the first few months, but Durant learned of my skill with a bow pretty quick after and I was brought into the palace before I turned eight. Aiden had been eleven, I think. There was a big riot on the docks, though I can't remember exactly what about. The two of them had been in a rough spot during it and had almost died. Durant had saved Aiden when he froze up during the fight."

Realization took hold of Penny. "He gave her his name so he wouldn't be a liability to her."

Hart nodded. "Exactly. He never did freeze up again, but she still had his name, and she used it as soon as she got it, but only for one thing."

Penny leaned in. "What was it?"

Hart dug a finger into the ground in front of him. "She commanded him to never do her harm. His magic couldn't touch her, and he would never be able to raise a sword against her."

Penny's shoulders sagged. "So, there's no way he could ever win in a fight against her?"

Hart looked out over the small clearing. "I have a suspicion, Penelope, but I'm not sure if divulging it will help you or hurt."

"And why not?" Penny asked. "If this is something that could help—"

Hart held up a hand. "That's just it. I don't know if it's a reality or a fantasy, but I want to find out. However, I need you to do something for me."

Penny pursed her lips. "What?"

"When we do face Aiden on the battlefield, I need to be at your side."

"Won't you want to be with the others?" A thought popped into her mind. "Did he or Adira share the name with you?"

"Aiden never shared his name with me, and the magic surrounding such a sacred thing prevents anyone from hearing it uttered from Adira's lips." Hart got to his knees in front of her and took her hand in his firmly. "Please, Penelope. I just need you to trust me. I wouldn't ask this if it wasn't important. I want to see all of us make it through to the other side of this."

Penny reached out and clasped his arm. "All right, but I expect a full explanation in the future."

"And I'll give it as soon as I'm sure. I swear on Adele's life, I will."

Penny let go of his arm. "I'm sorry she wasn't there to see you."

He shook his head. "It's for the best. I don't know what will happen after this. It's better that I stay dead for her than give her a hope only to cut her open if this ends poorly. I love her too much for that."

"I can understand that." She squeezed his arm. "But I also know that chasing that love will also be worth it. Don't let the unknowns keep you from her if you have the chance to see her again."

Hart patted her hand on his arm. "Let's not keep dwelling on my love life when yours is much more important at the moment. How else can we prepare to help Aiden get out of Durant's claws?"

Penny stood and dusted the soil from her trousers. "I don't completely know yet, but whatever we do, we're going to free him no matter the cost."

51

SHIVER

Without a cloak, the cold ripped through Aiden's clothing even as he sat atop the steaming horse. He was certainly more attuned to the cold, but he was only half fae and every so often that small part of his humanity reminded him of its existence. The only warmth he received was the comfort of having his connections to Penny and the Land restored to full strength outside the charms, not that they would protect him from the cold, but they helped buoy him, nonetheless.

He shivered as his horse trailed behind Durant's across the lake. Two guards rode on either side of him, and an entire army walked at his back. While his shadows flickered around his mount's ankles, making the others around him twitch, they didn't dare touch Durant.

It took most of the day, but they made it halfway across the lake when he saw the smoke streaming out from between the mountains.

"No," he whispered.

"Oh, yes," Durant said over the wind, bundled in thick furs and covered in heating charms. "I suspect the fae will be running this way within the next half hour."

But they didn't.

One hour turned to two, then three, then four. Durant continued to lead the charge forward, but her countenance grew darker and darker the further they went. The sun set over the horizon before they could reach the base of the mountain.

"Your Grace," one of the generals rode up to them. "We should break for camp. This wind will turn deadly if we don't get under cover before the temperature drops."

Durant glared at the back of her horse's neck as if she could summon the fae army to her and slaughter them with her bare hands. "Fine," she snapped. "Break for camp. What's one more day to wait for victory?"

Aiden tried to hide his relief, but Durant saw right through it.

"That's right, my boy. Your Faerie friends have bought you one more day, but mark my words, they'll only live to regret it."

The soldiers made camp right there on the ice, driving iron stakes deep into the ice to hold down the thick canvas. Aiden was led from his horse to the main tent where Durant was holding court with her generals.

"We've no news from the Aigeans since this morning," one of the rebels reported.

Durant rubbed at her brow. "I imagine we won't hear from them until they arrive. We—"

A messenger from the other battalion arrived, his face streaked with ash and blood. "Your Grace, General Nedra has fallen."

Aiden looked about for the missing faces at the table. Two of the leaders were missing, including the salt-and-pepper-haired general. She was the one who had fallen, praise Danu.

Durant didn't look up from the map on the table. "That is a shame." She didn't even take a second to mourn the loss of her general. "What's the report on the attack? Were we able to take the encampment before they retreated to the ice?"

The rebel hesitated. "No, Your Grace. The fair folk were ready for our attack and kept us from taking the encampment. We were able to take everything outside of the fortress, but most of the host retreated inside the walls."

Durant's fingers curled around the edge of the desk. "You mean we didn't even make it inside the fortress?"

The messenger began to shake. "I'm sorry, Your—"

A knife lodged itself in his throat, cutting off his unnecessary apology. Durant hated those almost as much as she did bad news— he'd learned that in his earliest years the hard way. The messenger had signed his own death sentence the moment he walked in.

The light faded from the young man's eyes and Aiden said a silent prayer for him.

Durant waved a hand and the guard at the door dragged the body out.

"Now that all of that unpleasantness is out of the way—"

The tent flap opened and the guard remaining at the door stuck his head in. "Your Grace—"

"*What on Gaia's green earth do you blasted want?*" Her chest heaved. "Am I to be interrupted every five minutes?"

Every pair of eyes in the room found something to look at besides Durant and the guard.

The guard's throat bobbed as his eyes flicked from Durant's furious expression to the trail of blood leading out the door. "A fae portal appeared on the outskirts of camp."

Durant stilled, then grinned like a cat that had finally caught her mouse. "Excellent." She turned to the rebel next to her. "Gather the men."

Everyone in the tent rushed out, Durant's volatile moods urging them on. When they all left, Durant unlocked the chain attaching Aiden to the post and grabbed him by the arm. "Let's go see what your little family has been up to, shall we?"

Durant hauled him through the camp, following the crowd. Aiden's hobbled ankles kept him from running but also kept Durant from moving too fast. Aiden held back a smirk when she glared at the chains she'd put between his feet. Around them, the rebels hooted and hollered over one another, a pack of yapping wolves gathering around their alpha. When they reached the edge of the camp, Aiden saw the looming portal and the three males lined up in front of it, waiting. Durant shoved Aiden into the arms of another rebel, almost making him slip on the ice under their feet.

"Well, this is a surprise," Durant said, her voice as smooth as the draw of a blade. "To what do we owe the pleasure?"

Thaen's sharp glare would have cut through anyone else. "We have come to give you one final warning. You will not win this fight, Adira Durant."

Durant's hand clenched the grip of her sword. "Oh? Unfortunately, my men say differently."

The crowd screamed at her prompt; bloodlust clear on every face.

Thaen's expression remained unimpressed, and the crowd's voices died down.

Sgiath stepped forward. "You have lost your hold on Olympia and her palace. You have not been able to kill her king. The battle today was thwarted. What other signs do you need of your folly?"

"Folly?" Durant chuckled. "Just because we have lost a little ground does not mean we will surrender. This is more than just a fight. It's a revolution."

Dair glared. "It is a vendetta. You have dragged all these people through blood and pain simply because you believe yourself a victim of something no one living on this earth has done to you. You blame children for the vices of their fathers and the gifted for the frugality of our Goddess."

Durant's nostrils flared, but she schooled her expression. "Perhaps you're right. That's what this started out as." She turned her back to them, facing her army, and raised her voice. "But how many of us can claim the same? How many of us have been left in the dirt and the filth because those tainted with magic stepped on us to get ahead? How many of us were discarded, thrown to the wayside because someone with *a gift* came in and took what we had worked to gain for ourselves? How many of us are tired of standing aside while the chosen and the blessed take from us?"

A cheer thundered over the ice, shaking the slick surface under Aiden's boots.

Durant grabbed him again, shoving him to his knees on the sharp ice. She clawed her fingers into the hairs of his scalp and pulled his head back, baring his throat and setting an iron dagger against the artery jumping against the skin of his neck.

"Your time is up, Faerie Prince," Durant hissed. "Tomorrow, when the sun crests your beloved mountains, this will end. We have come to take what is ours and give nothing back!"

The army behind them roared their approval.

Sgiath summoned a portal behind them. "If you will not cease, then we will leave you to your delusions." He looked to Aiden and mouthed *I am sorry* before stepping through.

Me too.

Dair met Aiden's eyes with his own warm, honey ones. "Hold fast, cousin. She is coming."

Aiden's spine wanted to straighten, but the hold Durant had on his hair stopped him from moving. Dair couldn't mean Penelope. Without the army they were going to create, she needed to stay as far from here as she could.

Durant snorted. "And who do you think is going to save you?"

Thaen's mouth stretched into a full smile, and he threw back his head. A laugh the sound of thunder and as dark as shadow roared out from his chest. The entire army grew silent at the sound. Thaen spread his arms. "Death, Adira Durant. Death the likes of which your mortal eyes have never beheld."

Dair looked at his brother, mouth gaping. "Whoa, brother." He rubbed his arms. "I just got chills."

52
AIM AND FIRE

PENNY HOVERED ATOP THE TREE, HER EYES TRAINED ON THE FLICKERING lights of the fires on the frozen lake. The echo of nickering horses and jostling men could be heard in the dream even from that distance. There had to be ten thousand soldiers spanning the ice, keeping her from her new family.

From her husband.

"I saw him today," Dair said, coming to sit, or rather float, next to her on the bed of broad leaves. "She has him chained up like an animal, but he is alive."

Penny blew out a breath, rubbing the golden tattoo around her finger. "I know he's alive."

Dair snorted. "Right. Forgot about that bit." He drew his knees up, letting his arms dangle over them. "I told him you are on your way, though I do not know if he was relieved or frightened. The dagger at his throat was a tad distracting."

"The dagger?" Penny swallowed. "Never mind. I can probably guess." Of course Adira paraded Aiden out in front of his family like that, dangling him like bait.

"The fortress is still holding. The rebels made camp at the base under A'bagairt."

Penny looked toward the mountains making up Eagallach. "Which peak is that again?"

"The westernmost one." He pointed in that direction, but Penny still couldn't see the city from that distance. At the moment, she didn't care to.

Her attention went back to the lake. "How long until this group hits the training grounds?"

"If they move as slowly as they did today, they'll reach it before nightfall tomorrow."

Penny tugged at the end of her braid. "We won't be able to reach them before the sunrise the following day." She looked over the edges of the lake. "We'll split the forces, following the same path the rebels did. The Olympians will come across the ice, pushing the rebels over the lake and boxing them in. The rest of us will go through the trees, and we'll push everyone out onto the ice, just like Adira had planned for the Winter encampment. Once the rebels are out, Thaen can lead from the rear and the fae can make a defense for the capital."

"And what about the prisoners in The Cartographer's camp?" Dair asked.

Penny wrapped her arms around her middle as her soul caressed the bond tying her to her husband huddled in a tent below them. "I have a plan for them as well, but you're going to have to do everything I tell you, no matter how much you don't want to."

"What do you mean?"

Penny took a deep breath. "I need you and Thaen to find your mother and Farrah and leave Aiden in Adira's clutches."

Dair stood, nearly plummeting through the leaves before he caught himself. "You cannot be serious."

Penny stared out at the lake, the light from the coming dawn graying the horizon and giving edges to the shadows around them. She would need to wake soon to get the soldiers moving.

She turned back to Dair. "With the power Adira has over him, she won't allow him to be far from her side. If we want to get both of them out, I need you two to sneak through their forces and grab Shirina. We need her out, so Aiden doesn't feel like he needs to stay to help her."

"She will not let us take her without him."

Penny stood, feet hovering over the branches. "After this fight, he'll be free whether if it's by his own will"—she took a deep breath —"or by his death."

Dair stared at her, wide eyed. "You would kill him?"

A lump formed in her throat. "By the Goddess, I don't want to, but we can't let Adira win. If she has him, she has the upper hand."

"But are you even capable of ending your husband's life? Could you truly do it?"

Penny closed her eyes. A few moments passed and she felt Dair leave. It was then that she finally opened her eyes and stared once again down at the rebel camp, at the small tent near the middle that stood covered in charms. Where her heart reached out.

Tears fell onto her cheeks, though she couldn't tell if she was actually crying in her sleep or if it was simply in this form. Dair's questions echoed in her mind, and she finally allowed herself to answer into the silence around her.

"I don't know."

Green light flashed as Penny wove the vines around the axle of the cart. It was their third break that day and Penny had gotten good at repairing them quickly.

"Good to go!" She shouted up to the driver. The Olympian soldier tipped his head and urged the horses forward. It was one of the few carts not being pulled by men.

Penny followed behind. Moving an army was a battle in and of itself.

"I pray that's the last one you have to fix," Mother said, coming up beside her. "I worry about you straining yourself before the fighting even starts."

"I actually don't have too many limits here in Faerie. The Land charges my magic before I have to, though I don't know what it would look like if I used it up faster than it could be replenished. I haven't had a chance to try that out yet."

"So, in Olympia, you have a certain amount of magic left to you without a way to refill it, but here you're practically limitless?"

Penny shrugged. "I wouldn't say I'm limitless. I still get tired, but my magic is replenished before my energy is."

Mother's expression remained intrigued, though Penny swore she saw something like sadness linger behind her eyes. "So, you're powerless in Olympia."

"I wouldn't say that either." She stopped walking. "We saw how much I could do with the power I had there and if we go by the level of my tell, I hadn't even reached halfway."

"But you were still tired more and your energy levels didn't replenish like they should with sleep. If you used your magic in Olympia, you would have to return to Faerie eventually."

"And why wouldn't I return? I'm High Queen now. I have a responsibility to these folk."

Mother pulled her off the path. "Penny, the fae aren't just going to start playing nice simply because you're their queen. You've already been a target for them."

"Mother, they can't harm me. The Land won't allow it."

"But others can. The girl in the MacGregor's house is proof that not all threats come from within either."

Penny pulled her arm from Mother's firm grasp. "And if I'm threatened, what do you expect me to do?"

Mother groaned, rubbing at the skin between her brows. "Perhaps this wasn't the best route to convince you."

"Convince me of what?"

Mother turned away, her hand dropping to her side. Penny couldn't see her face, but she could see how uncomfortable she was by the set of her shoulders. "I need you to come home after this, Penny, no matter who wins this battle. My magic..." She took a deep breath. "I can't do everything by myself anymore."

Penny set a hand on Mother's shoulder and went to face her. Tears fell down Mother's face and she hastily wiped them away. Penny had never seen Mother cry, not like this.

"Do you think I won't help you? Do you really believe I'll just leave you after all of this is done?"

Mother gestured to the trees around them. "Do you blame me? Look at this place. Look what you can do here. Coming home to Olympia would be like asking a phoenix to live in a birdcage, but I don't know what else to do."

A twig snapped and Penny looked over Mother's shoulder and found Hart standing at the edge of the road.

"Sorry to interrupt, but we need you at the front, Penelope."

She nodded and turned back to Mother. "I can't promise you anything today. Right now, I need to focus on saving my kingdom and getting my husband back. If we don't win this fight, there might not even be an Eleusion to return to. I'm sorry the future is so uncertain right now, but I know we'll get it figured out." She reached out and took Mother's hand in hers. "Together."

"You're right." One last tear trickled down Mother's face, but she lifted her head. "Let's go take down that vile creature once and for all."

"That's the spirit!" Hart cheered. "Now, Your Majesty, you're going to want to put your big girl crown on."

"Why?" Penny asked.

"Because there are some folk stopping our progression into Winter."

"Get us up there." Penny pulled Mother toward the road and allowed Hart to pull them through the trees.

Within a few minutes, they had traveled the length of their army, stretched out behind them for miles. Penny stopped at the line of brownies, trow, redcaps, and other bwbachod lined up in front of them.

One of the brownies shoved her way forward, her mop of brown hair bobbing as she skipped to Penny.

"Fee!" Penny called, laughing as she leaned down to scoop the Winter Palace's brownie up in a hug.

"My Sovereign, we have come to aid you."

Penny set the brownie down and looked over the group gathered behind her. "How did you know where we would be?"

"Prince Dair sent us from the palace. He said you would need help getting to the battle quickly."

"You're right, but I don't know what he thought would be helpful."

Fee smiled and let out a sharp whistle. The pùca standing in their humanoid forms quickly shifted into the black, majestic horse form they sometimes took.

"Have you ever seen a pùca pull a cart before?"

Penny stood, her own smile blooming on her face. "No, but I can imagine it's quite the sight to behold."

Fee turned back to the group. "You heard her! Get those pùca strapped into the harnesses, quick as you can." She began calling for the others to help in other ways, easing the burdens of those that would be fighting this war for their kingdom.

All the bwbachod passed Penny, their fists at their chests and their heads bowed. Penny returned the greeting, tears pooling at the corners of her eyes.

"Oh, do not cry, My Sovereign," Fee chided, taking Penny's hand and leading her back toward the waiting army. "I know we are not many, but we will do in a pinch."

Penny stopped the brownie and knelt next to her. "Fee, I'm not crying because of how little you all are, but because of how magnificent."

Fee's large, brown eyes lined with her own tears. "And this is why we brownies do not show our faces very often. We sure are ugly criers."

Penny laughed and led the small brownie toward the waiting army, hope blossoming in her chest and a new plan taking root in her mind.

53
SNAP

AIDEN'S HEART DROPPED TO HIS STOMACH AS HIS HORSE CARRIED HIM farther into the fray. The crash of terrible magic and the screams of dying souls rang in his ears. Light and shadow flew through the air from both sides, the slaves Durant had captured fighting against those that had not fallen to iron.

A spiked battering ram slammed into the thick wooden gate of the fortress. The rebels drew it back, the thick log swinging back on thick chains before the shackled fae shoved it forward again, using their supernatural strength to push the spike deeper into the wood.

"Glorious, isn't it?" Durant said, riding beside him, the sun shining directly over her silver hair making it shimmer. "Your father wasn't a king made for war. He didn't think he needed anything more than what he had. It was a topic of contention between us, him being happy to settle for what the Goddess gave him and me not wanting to give up even an inch of everything I gained."

Aiden blew a piece of his dark hair from his eyes. "Queen Rhea must have been a real treat if you despised her enough to do this to a kingdom she never even stepped foot in. Murdering her after Dion was born wasn't enough for you?"

Durant slapped him across the face hard enough to make him sway in his saddle. "You know this isn't about Rhea anymore. This is about *you* and what you did. Your father was the only thing keeping me from war. Do you understand that? If you hadn't killed him, we wouldn't be here, now, watching your kingdom crumble into nothing."

"And if I hadn't killed him? You'd have been happy watching Olympia die under his reign?"

"I would never have let that happen."

"It was happening," Aiden hissed. "Every moment that my father sat on that throne someone died. He glutted himself while babes perished in their mothers' arms. He picked up and tossed away women like they were nothing but a handkerchief to wipe his sweaty face with. For even a whisper of the smallest infraction, he killed noble and peasant alike."

"He was a king," Durant said plainly.

"He was a *monster*! He had no soul left within him, and even if he did, I'm glad I hid his ashes away so he would never see the Goddess's face." Father had burned on a pyre, the same as the lowest of criminals in Olympia. He'd deserved it a thousand times over. Only Aiden and his brothers knew where the ashes were hidden, and Aiden prayed that knowledge would end with them.

Durant grabbed him by the collar, pulling him forward so he hung between their two horses. "Your father deserved a king's burial. After this is over, you and I will be taking a little trip to where you hid him. Mark my words, Aiden, you will pay for that disrespect in full."

Aiden yanked his shirt from her grasp. "You'll have to make me."

A vicious grin crawled across her face. "Trust me, I will."

Durant pulled her horse to a stop in front of his, drawing her sword and lifting it in the air. The soldiers behind her did the same, and with a flick of her wrist, she sent the entire company flying forward. Horseshoes and boots pounded the icy ground into slush as they ran toward the fortress, the only thing keeping Winter from falling into her hands.

The battering ram pulled back once more and with a great scream of its chains, it tore apart the front gates of the fortress.

54
TUCK AND ROLL

"Can't they go any faster?" Penny said in Hart's ear, once again hanging from his back like a deranged monkey.

She watched behind them, their group of tree folk—by the Goddess, she was never going to come up with a good name—trying to catch up.

"We can only go as far as we can see the tree. Our spirits have to call to it and the tree must let us in."

"And you can see farther than everyone else I take it?"

Hart turned his face and winked. "I was the Lord of the Underworld's best sharpshooter for a reason."

Penny rolled her eyes as they disappeared into another tree. When they came out the other side, they were halfway around the lake. The autumn sun sneaked closer to the horizon, preparing to hide from the horrors it had seen that day. The smell of smoke choked Penny as Hart leaped into another tree.

It had taken the entire day to get everyone split up and moving toward Eagallach. The Olympians were only a third of the way over the ice, the pùca hauling the carts faster than the normal horses would have been able to. But it still wasn't fast enough. Dark clouds of smoke billowed out from the base of the mountain. The snow glistened gold and pink at the base of the mountain where the grounds around the fortress burned.

"We'll make it by full sundown, Penelope, just as you planned.

The others will be there in the morning. Somethings you simply can't rush."

No matter that she had prayed to exceed all of those plans. She took a deep breath but coughed at the bitter smoke.

She still hated fire.

55
STILL

Aiden trailed behind Durant as she charged through the front gates. It had taken hours for the men to clear the gates enough to get horses through. The fighting had already made it through the inner bailey and into the main hall.

Aiden's heart tripped as a streak of purple-tinted shadow flew past them. Praise the Goddess, Thaen was still up and fighting.

Durant dismounted and spoke to her squad. "Take as many prisoners as you're able. We'll need them to take the mountain."

Chains unraveled at the rebels' feet as they rushed about, taking any lingering fae in the courtyard and trapping them in iron shackles. The bodies of the fallen were piled in the center of the fortress, human and fae alike. There was no dignity with these rebels. Everyone was simply fodder for their hatred.

A young boy ran past, and Durant grabbed him by the collar. "Find out where the Aigeans are."

The boy ran off and Durant shook her head. "Cursed water folk. They were supposed to have caught up with us two days ago. They're supposed to be here to help take the mountain."

Aiden's hands were untied from the pommel of his saddle, and he jumped down from the horse. "Are you such a coward, Durant? Letting others fight for you just to sweep in after and take what you want?"

Durant shrugged. "Someone has to do it, and I don't trust anyone to get this part done. Anyone can pick up a sword."

"You really haven't changed," Aiden spat. "Even when you were spymaster, you had Nox do all of the dirty work."

Durant spun on him, a blade flashing in her hand. "Don't ever talk about that man in my presence."

"You mean your *husband*?" Aiden hissed. "The man you married and used like a dog? The man you murdered in cold blood so you could escape Olympia without anyone the wiser?"

Durant's knife was against his cheek, the cold steel doing nothing to his face, but the threat there all the same. "I was the best thing that ever happened to Nox. He was nothing without me."

Aiden leaned into the knife, breaking the skin over his cheekbone. "You're right. He was *less* than that with you."

Durant drew back, her face filled with disgust. "All of that is in the past, Aiden."

"Yet you are the one who continues to define the future of your rebellion by those pains of the past. Don't be a hypocrite."

"Oh?" Durant said haughtily. "And I'm supposed to be taking your advice now?"

Aiden glowered at her.

"Your Grace!" A trio of rebels ran towards them, wide eyed and trembling.

"What?" Durant barked.

The three of them exchanged nervous glances. The two larger ones pushed the smaller man forward.

"The Aigeans, Your Grace. They never arrived at the camp."

Durant narrowed her eyes. "What do you mean they never arrived? They should have crossed into Winter already."

"Of course, Your Grace, only..." The man ducked his head. "They never showed up. There hasn't been sign of them. Scouts came back with reports about seeing strange things in the trees."

The other two rebels paled behind him.

"So, what you're telling me is that the Aigeans never arrived, and we have no idea where they are." She took another step forward. "You're telling me that the wave of water folk I was expecting to help take the mountain is nowhere in sight, and my carefully laid-out plans to take the city up those mountains has been for naught."

"I'm sorry, Your—"

With a scream, Durant drew her sword and separated the man's head from his shoulders. Both thumped into the mud at Aiden's feet.

The remaining two jumped back, scrambling away from their dead comrade and raging warlord. Durant stared at the body, chest heaving as she watched his blood fill the boot prints in the mud. Aiden watched her, wariness seeping through every bone in his body. He'd only seen Durant so still when something did not go her way. When she was backed into a corner.

A cheer rang in the fortress behind her, but she didn't turn. Only when one of the captains arrived did she finally look up.

"We've taken the fortress, Your Grace. The fair folk are retreating up the mountain."

Durant wiped the drying blood from her sword and sheathed it. Slowly, she drew a set of keys from her belt and turned to Aiden, a feral, crazed grin on her face.

All the heat in Aiden's body fled.

Durant's grin deepened until he was looking into the face of a devil. "Come now. It's time to put your mettle to the test. Our glory or our doom awaits us on the other side of this fortress and I'm willing to kill every fae on that rock to get what I want." The iron bracelets fell to the earth. "*Agesilaos*, follow me."

56
SEEK AND FIND

PENNY DROPPED DOWN FROM HART'S BACK, HER BOOTS SQUELCHING IN THE slush of melted snow and fresh blood glittering in the moonlight under her feet. They had reached the outlying fields of the training grounds outside the fortress, but only the wounded dead were there to greet them.

She gasped as the tether to Aiden cried out for the third time in the last half hour.

Hart pointed up the mountain. "They pushed the fighting up there. The rebels must have made it through the fortress and forced the fae up the side."

"But that means we can't draw them back out onto the lake." The rebels would have the higher ground, making the battle up the mountain that much more difficult.

"Yes, but we can still box them in and turn their focus away from the city. It would possibly give Prince Thaen time to rally his troops back to him as well and allow anyone coming from the city down to defend it. We would be taking the worst of the attack, but we'll also have the larger force to counteract it."

The other members of their company began appearing at the edges of the trees, green-tinted skin turning ghastly in the firelight. A loud *boom* swept over the field and a huge cloud of shadow went up into the sky on the other side of the fortress.

Penny gritted her teeth, another wave of pain rippling from within her. "How long until the rest get here?"

"They were an hour behind us last I checked."

Another shudder rippled over the ground.

Penny took a deep breath. "We can't wait for them."

Hart met her eyes. He grabbed the bow from his back and nocked an arrow.

Penny drew her sword and stabbed a rebel through the back.

He hadn't seen her or the five thousand green skinned warriors creeping through the camp behind him.

The rebel's body fell, his comrade looking over at the sound and whirling straight into Penny's already bloodied sword. His shout was cut off, but it still alerted the rest of his friends to Penny's arrival.

The small squad all turned their way, their team having been left at the outer gate of the fortress. Penny and Hart had already taken out the others left to defend the training grounds. Adira hadn't left a large force, likely believing the Aigeans would arrive soon to take up the task.

Sweet Gaia, she would be in for a surprise.

Penny's men took down the rebels with ease, only subjecting themselves to a few cuts and bruises. Hart found the captured fae within the main fortress, and he and a few of the others set to work freeing them. Two hundred ellyllon and bwbachod joined their ranks, the rest of their kin still fighting up the mountain.

Penny knelt at the open gate of the fortress and called on the Land. Thick vines shot up from the ground, filling the hole left by the broken gate. If the rebels had any plans to retreat to the encampment, they would find themselves blocked from the outside and would have no choice but to flee to the ice where the Olympians awaited them.

"Keep moving!" Hart hollered from ahead, calling on his new kin and the freed fae as they raced up the mountain.

Penny lifted her sword and chased after them.

57
SWORD

ANOTHER BODY FELL INTO THE SNOW AT AIDEN'S FEET.

Then another.

And another.

His sword dripped with Tuatha blood.

A pair of boots stepped into view, purple and black shadows swirling around them.

Aiden looked up, his body shaking from the strain of holding himself still.

Please. Please, Danu, don't make me do this.

Thaen grinned down at him.

"Hello, cousin."

Durant laughed from behind him.

Aiden's screams rattled his own mind, never breaking past his lips.

58
UP AND UP

P<small>ENNY TRUDGED UP THE HILL, THE SNOW REDUCED TO NOTHING BUT BROWN</small> sludge after the armies had already trekked through it.

The clash of swords and the cries of the dying could be heard over the wind.

Penny pushed past the bodies of the dead lying around her.

Faster.

Faster.

Faster.

Hart kept the grueling pace with her, his determined expression likely mirroring hers.

They hit the rearguard, steel weapons flashing against iron ones. The steel held under the onslaught, but the sheer force of the rebels bore down on them. Cries sounded from before and behind Penny, but she watched, waiting for the flash of black or gold.

They pushed through the rebels, the point of an arrow driving through the flesh of a body.

Closer.

Closer.

Closer.

A flash of black skittered past her. Following the direction it had come from, she saw shadows shoot in every direction from the western front of the rebels, slamming into fae and human with abandon.

Penny called at Hart ahead of her and pointed her sword in the direction of the blasts.

"That way."

59
STAB

AIDEN YELLED AT THAEN FROM THE RECESSES OF HIS MIND, TRYING TO TELL him which way his sword would go and where his guard would open.

Nothing came out.

Would their new bond allow Thaen to feel what he felt? Would being his guardian help Thaen defeat him?

Aiden's body was a whirl of flesh and magic. With only the command from Durant driving him, he had no qualms about Thaen maiming him.

Thaen, on the other hand, avoided it at all costs.

"Aedon, I know you are in there."

Aiden swerved and jabbed at Thaen's exposed side. Thaen dodged the blade by a hair.

"I know this is not you."

Aiden called on his magic and formed a volley of shadow darts and sent them zipping toward Thaen. Thaen called up a shield to block them.

Durant laughed from somewhere behind him.

"You are a king of kings, a leader of magic and a servant of the Goddess."

Aiden sliced at his head and Thaen ducked. Aiden's borrowed sword lodged itself into the tree. He tried to pull it out, but Thaen batted him away from it.

"I am your *claidheamh spìoraid*. I will not abandon you."

Without his sword, Aiden summoned more of his magic and flung shadow after shadow in Thaen's direction.

Thaen's shield repelled them as if they were nothing but dandelion fluff. Thaen closed the distance between them. Aiden summoned his own shield, and the two barriers clashed against one another.

Thaen's pale eyes flashed. "You are stronger than that creature, Aedon."

Aiden dropped the shield and leaned forward, ready to fall on the blade Thaen had poised between them.

Thaen dropped his guard to protect Aiden from getting hurt.

Magic pooled in Aiden's hand, and he screamed, this time the sound rushing from his mouth, as the shadow blade sliced Thaen all the way through his chest.

60

VIOLET AND GOLD

She broke through the battle in time to watch Thaen fall to the ground, blood pouring out from a wound in his chest.

Another scream rang through the air, and Dair sent what had to be a hundred of his slivers of shadow into the rebels between him and his brother. Rebels and fae alike slumped to the ground, and Dair ran toward the clearing where Aiden and Adira stood. Adira turned toward him, bloodlust shimmering in her wild, green eyes.

With a flick of her finger, Penny summoned a root to wrap itself around Dair's legs.

He fell to the ground with a scream of rage. He set his sword to sawing through the vines.

With a nod, she sent Hart his way. Hart would tell Dair what he needed to do.

Adira's face lightened and she glanced around until she found where Penny was standing. "Penny!"

Aiden swung around; his eyes wide with horror.

"Hello, Adira." Penny stepped out into the clearing, allowing her magic to light the skin of her arms. Trees sprouted up at her beckoning, blocking the rest of the armies from their little circle.

Durant laughed, manic glee plain on every line of her face. "I was beginning to wonder if you would be joining us, but now that you're here, I shouldn't be surprised. You were the one who stopped my friends from joining in on the fun, weren't you?"

Penny held up her sword, keeping the point between her and Adira. "Unfortunately for you, that reunion was cancelled."

Adira threw back her head and laughed. "Oh, but this is going to be so much more fun! All of us here, ready to rip each other to shreds." She looked to where Dair had been a moment ago and found Hart standing in his place.

Adira frowned. "Hart, my boy, I thought I killed you."

"You did." Hart unsheathed the sword at his waist and swung it playfully. "Lucky for me, the Goddess has seen to gift me the opportunity to return the favor."

"Well, it will certainly make this all more exciting." She turned to Aiden, her lips moving, but the beginning of the sentence silenced by the magic of true names. "... kill him."

61

SEE

AIDEN'S JOY AT SEEING HIS FRIEND ALIVE IN FRONT OF HIM WAS QUICKLY eclipsed by the sensation of his magic hurtling toward Hart. They were completely boxed in by the trees, and Hart had nowhere to run.

Hart smiled and took a step backward.

The magic crashed against the bark of the tree Hart disappeared into.

Hart reappeared a moment later, emerging a few trees down the line.

"Nice shot. Would you like to try again?"

62

OLD AND NEW

"Well, that's certainly a fun little surprise," Adira cooed, watching as Hart popped back into being on the other side of their little clearing. She turned to face Penny. "I assume you and your gift had something to do with this development."

Penny allowed her magic to flare, driving grass and blossoms up through the snow at their feet. "You would assume correctly."

Adira smiled, that feline grin stretching out under her mossy-green eyes. "I knew not killing you would come back to bite me. All my plans scrapped because the Domineering Duchess's daughter couldn't keep to her little farm. It really is a shame Hart was the one that died instead of you."

"I'm sure Hart will appreciate the sentiment, but unfortunately you now have to come to terms with your mistakes." Penny widened her feet and held up her sword. "All of them."

63

SLICE

A<small>IDEN STOOD STILL, EYES SCANNING THE TREES.</small>

One moment there was a trunk. The next, Hart was running toward him, sword raised overhead.

Aiden brought his shadow sword up to meet it, the blades sparking by whatever magic made the shadows keep his opponent's blade from going through them.

Hart was fast. Much faster than he'd been before.

"Aiden, listen to me."

Aiden shoved him off and sent a spear of shadow in his direction.

Hart dodged it, leaping to the side and disappearing once again.

Aiden whirled as Hart's blade slashed the air where he'd just been standing.

"You don't have to listen to Durant, Aiden. I know you're stronger than her."

Aiden's blade shot out toward him, and Hart used the opportunity to sneak in on his open side. Aiden felt the cut, but it didn't stop him from whirling around and dealing Hart his own.

The brown sleeve of Hart's shirt split, and amber liquid spilled from the slash. Hart brought his fingers to the cut, his eyes wide. "That's not something you see every day."

He transferred his sword to his other hand and came toward Aiden.

"Now listen, Aiden, I know you can fight off Adira's hold on you. You can hurt her. You've done it before, and you and I are going to figure out how to do it again so you can save your kingdom, and I can say I at least had a part in it. I've got that whole hero complex to satisfy you know."

64
BARKS AND BITES

PENNY'S WOODEN SHIELD DEFLECTED ADIRA'S SWORD JUST IN TIME.

"I must say, I'm impressed with your skill," Adira said, pulling her blade from where it had stuck between the wooden slats of Penny's shield. "I thought you've only been part of Aiden's little operation since last year."

Penny struck with her sword, Adira's snaking out to keep her head from being detached from her shoulders. "I trained under the Lord of the Underworld himself as well as the infamous Lòchran. I suspect there aren't many that will match what I've been taught in the short time I've been under their tutelage."

Adira's blade swatted Penny's, and the shield cracked with the hit Adira dealt it in the next moment.

"Well, we'll certainly see how well you retained their lessons."

Adira's blade was a steel viper, striking again and again at Penny.

Penny's wooden shield shattered, and she shook the remnants from her arm, backing up against the wall of trees. She brought up her sword just in time to stop Adira from stabbing her in the chest.

Adira laughed, the veins in her throat bulging with the action. "You may have been taught by the two best warriors this kingdom's got, but I'm the woman that trained one and killed the other."

65
SHOVE

HART PUSHED THE CROSS GUARD OF HIS SWORD INTO AIDEN'S SHADOWED one.

"Fight her, Aiden. Just like that night when we went to the bakery, shake her off and fight for your queen."

Aiden shoved him away, shaking his head.

"I've known you for most of my life, Aiden. I watched you with Adira Durant. I know what you can and can't do. I know you haven't been able to touch her with a single shadow since you gave her your name. But you did that night."

Aiden's sword went a bit wide. Had it actually missed because he'd willed it to or was he just seeing things?

"I know my tiny bit of fae blood doesn't help with much, but I still heard her. I heard Durant order you not to protect Penny. I heard her tell you to watch as she killed her. It's how I knew to shoot the crossbow bolt."

The small bit of control Aiden had on his body slipped as he tried to focus on Hart's words and his sword nearly took off Hart's leg.

"But you moved. You called the shadows to you and made a shield. It wasn't quick enough to keep Penny from harm, but you shouldn't have been able to do it. I know Durant wasn't specific enough for you to have been able to go to Penny after. You broke the command to watch Adira kill her. And that wasn't the only time."

Aiden swung his sword again, aiming for Hart's head. He almost wished his friend would cease talking so he could focus on not killing him before Hart got to the blasted point.

Hart ducked away. "You didn't see it, but I did. As Durant held me by the throat and blood filled my lungs, I watched as your shadows flew from you and one sliced her cheek. By the Goddess, you even blew up the alley, but I watched that spot on her cheek bleed.

The night came back to him as clear as if it had been yesterday. Durant, crouched down by Hart, her arms over her head, protecting herself. He hadn't even realized it. All he could think about in that moment was getting Penelope to safety.

Aiden stared at Hart standing at the other end of his shadow sword.

Hart gave him a sad smile. "It was the last thing I saw before I left this world. I died knowing you could destroy her, but I couldn't tell you. That was one of my biggest regrets in dying. That, and not having told Adele goodbye."

He squared his shoulders. "Don't let that demon woman win. Don't let her take the love of your life away from you too."

Penelope screamed behind him.

66

PLEASURE AND PAIN

ADIRA'S DAGGER PLUNGED DEEPER INTO PENNY'S THIGH, THE PAIN SENDING her knees quaking. She gritted her teeth and shoved Adira away from her.

Adira cackled. The crazed fire in her eyes only heightened as she stepped back, smearing blood on her cheek as she brushed her hair away from her face. "You should have known to wear more armor than that measly chest plate."

Penny's hands shook as she looked down at the blade sticking out of her leg. Adira had left it in which would keep Penny from bleeding out, but it would make it nearly impossible for her to move. She kept her knees locked and raised her sword.

"You should have known better than to make me bleed."

67
STOP

AIDEN ROARED INSIDE HIS OWN HEAD.

The dagger stuck out from Penelope's leg, but she kept her gaze and her sword on Durant.

He still saw her hands shaking.

"You can save her," Hart said from in front of him.

Aiden's gaze slowly shifted from Penelope to Hart. The shadow sword in front of him flickered once. Twice.

"She believes in you, Aiden. Find whatever thing that binds you together and hold tight to that."

Aiden searched deep down within himself for that bond, that Goddess-given connection he had to his wife. He searched, pushing and pulling his very soul this way and that. Durant's influence smothered everything within him.

"Adira Durant has no power over you, brother, so don't let her believe that she does."

The faint throb of his heart beat out Penelope's name and he found it. He found his *taghadh* and he grabbed on with both hands.

68

CHECK AND MATE

Penny faltered and Adira used the opportunity to grab hold of the dagger in her leg and yank it out. Penny screamed and her leg fell out from under her.

Adira swung her sword, driving Penny down to both knees. Penny had to use both hands to keep the blade from cutting into her neck as Adira bore down on her.

"You see, Penny? You can't fight the inevitable. No matter what, this battle was always going to end with you dead. Even if you could have almost beat me, even if you'd gained the upper hand, I still would've summoned our little Aiden to cut off your pretty head. But I think this victory will be all the sweeter simply because I beat you in every possible way."

Penny's fingers began to slip as the blade drove into her hand, cutting into her palms and slicking with her blood.

"You may have thought you won this and maybe, at the end of this war my men will be defeated. But the real war, the one between the big players, that will have already been won, and your body will have been left here on this cursed hill to rot until the carrion come to pick at your bones."

Was Adira right? Would she be simply another body to litter this ground? Could the rebels be vanquished and Faerie saved, but the fight here, in this small circle lost? Her gaze left Adira's taunting leer and found Aiden, her husband, standing opposite one of his best friends. One that had been dead but had miraculously been brought back. Would Hart simply fade away as all the other spirits if she died? If Aiden's magic...

Penny's hand finally slipped, and Adira's blade almost cut off her head, but she caught it before the blade could sink into her neck. She gritted her teeth, an idea beginning to take form.

"But that's where you're wrong," she said.

Her arms flared black and green.

69
STARS

Green light flared over their clearing. The very mountain under their feet shook, and thick roots broke from the ground, exploding through the frozen ground. One speared through Durant's leg, making her scream as Penelope had.

Penelope's magic flickered, then faltered. The roots around them seemed to sway as she lost control of them until they finally fell limp to the ground.

Durant's breaths came in heaving gasps, eyes wide as Penelope's concentration over her magic wavered. "It's too bad, Penny. You almost had me." Durant turned toward him, her eyes sparkling with rage and victory. "*Agesilaos*, kill your wife."

Penelope looked up at him, dark lashes fluttering with pain and fatigue.

Aiden staggered toward them.

Durant began to laugh. The sound wasn't that of someone who was reveling in victory, but that of a creature watching the world crumble around them.

Aiden's limbs shook as he neared them, his heart straining at the sight of his wife.

"The perfect ending," Durant declared. "Don't you think? A full circle. I was the one that created him, and now I will be the one who destroys him piece by beloved piece! I'll break him down until he's nothing but an empty husk, and only then will I end his miserable life and take his crown!"

Aiden's entire soul revolted as he reached for his wife. His trembling fingers encircled her neck, lifting her from the ground. But she didn't cry out. She didn't squirm. Even as his fingers tightened, she only held his gaze.

Her flickering fingers, the only sign of her distress, grasped his wrists. "It's all right, my love," she rasped. "We've got this."

Aiden felt a single tear run down the side of his face. Her pulse pounded against his pinky. He raged, grabbing onto the bond as tightly as he could and holding fast to the connection he had to Penelope. It couldn't end like this. Not after everything they'd been through together.

Penelope held his gaze. "I just need you to touch her, Aiden. You're strong enough to push that much. All you have to do is touch her."

Durant groaned, holding her leg where the root still protruded. "What are you whispering about, Penny? Aiden, just kill her already."

The fingers around Penelope's throat tightened, and her eyes bulged. Her nails dug into the skin of his wrists, but she didn't writhe. Why wasn't she fighting? Why wasn't she at least trying to get away from him?

Durant pointed a finger in Penelope's direction. "Kill her now, *Ages*—"

Penelope's hand shot out and grabbed Durant's finger. The green and black of her gift burst out from her hands, nearly blinding Aiden.

But he wasn't blind enough not to see the souls.

Dozens of souls surrounded them. Men, women, children, all circled Durant, their forms growing more solid by the second. Mage and bronty alike stood shoulder to shoulder, their attention trained on their killer. Dion's mother, Queen Rhea, stood at Durant's left, her violet eyes flashing with anger.

Durant tried to yank her hand from Penelope. "Let me go!"

Penelope held on, but Aiden could feel her strength waning, could feel her pulse flagging.

She was going to die.

With a roar that made it past his lips, he reached out and grabbed Durant's wrist, right under where Penelope held her hand. His fingers remained at Penelope's neck, but with a force he couldn't name, he loosened his fingers just enough for her to breathe.

She gasped, gulping in as much air as she could. And then she smiled.

If Aiden could have laughed, he would have. But it took every ounce of his will to keep from snapping his genius wife's neck. She'd figured this out. She'd told him to touch Durant. She'd summoned these souls.

Durant's head whipped in his direction. "What are you doing? How are you—"

Her words halted as a soul step forward.

Aiden recognized him instantly.

"No," Durant breathed.

Nox Durant took another step forward, his shoulder-length, brown hair falling to the side as he tilted his head. "Hello, wife."

"No!" Durant screamed. "You're dead! You're all dead!"

Nox shook his head, continuing toward them. "You and I have much to discuss."

Durant howled, trying to break from Aiden and Penelope's grasp. Blood oozed from where the root kept her tied to the ground, but it was as if every thought in Durant's head only revolved around getting as far away as she could.

Aiden's grip on her wrist tightened further as Nox made his way across the small circle of trees.

"I'll kill you!" Durant screeched. "Do hear me? You're *dead*!"

"Yes, my dear." Nox stopped and placed each of his hands on either side of Durant's head, his long fingers forming the only crown she would ever wear. "And so are you."

With a twist of his hands, her spinal column snapped, her neck broken, her life ended in an instant.

And with it, Aiden's last remaining link to her. The tight bounds across his chest evaporated as the bond between him and Penelope hummed. Aiden's consciousness resumed control of his body. He instantly removed his hands from Penelope's neck and Durant's lifeless wrist, holding them tightly to his chest. With their connection broken, the spirits faded, and Durant's body fell to the ground in a heap.

"Oh, that works," Penelope said, right before her eyes rolled back into her head.

Hart reached Penelope as she slumped to the ground.

Then, as if with her own strength she had been holding it aloft, the night sky began to fall as well. Darkness covered everything around them, smothering the light from the rebels' flames and the beams of magic. Not even the Day Court's flickers of light could penetrate the black surrounding them.

Shirina.

Aiden knelt beside them as silver-streaked darkness surrounded them, blocking out anything further than five feet away. It was only because he was fae he could see anything at all. The screams of dying men rang through the darkness. The earth shook around them, and he felt the magic of the Land guide each and every Tuatha through the dark.

"What's happening?" Hart yelled.

Aiden closed his eyes, relief filling him as he took Penelope fully into his arms.

"We're ending a war."

70
ENDINGS AND BEGINNINGS

"My Sovereign…" The voice faded for a moment, as if it had gone underwater before pushing back toward the surface again. "… put her down and let me examine her injuries."

A low rumble against Penny's ear answered, but she couldn't make out the words. A small drum beat next to her ear, matching the beating of her own heart.

Thump.

Thu-thump.

The voices continued and she felt the warm cocoon around her start to retreat. She whimpered and the cocoon stopped.

"Penelope? Love? Can you hear me?"

The beat of the tiny drum at her ear sped up and Penny realized it was not a drum, but a heart. Aiden's heart. Penny shoved her eyelids open, not caring one bit that they wanted to be closed right then.

Blood and ash streaked the lines of his face, but Aiden's golden eyes were clear and bright.

"Aiden?"

Aiden blew out a breath as if the entire world had been taken off his shoulders. "Skies, Penelope." His lips skittered across her forehead, her nose, her cheeks, until claiming her lips.

Something inside of her clicked into place. It felt like years since she'd been in his arms, their hearts pressed together with the same rhythm. Penny sighed and reached up to deepen the kiss, but when she moved, a searing pain shot down her leg. She cried out and Aiden drew back.

"Now will you let me look at you?"

Penny looked over and found a very displeased Annalysa standing at the edge of a curtained-off pallet where Aiden sat, cradling her. Why were they on a pallet?

"What?" Fog still muddled Penny's brain. Where were they? She reached up to rub her head but winced when her palm stung at the movement. She opened her fingers and found them caked in blood.

Annalysa huffed. "High King Aedon brought you into this fortress no less than five minutes ago, but you have been stuck to him like a spider to her prey since you walked in here, and I do not appreciate being prevented from treating my patients."

"Prevented?"

Annalysa pointed above them. Three thick vines of poison ivy swayed above their heads, ready to strike at anyone who got too close.

"Sweet Gaia," Penny said, sending the ivy away. "I didn't mean to—"

Annalysa waved off her apology. She settled herself on the edge of the pallet and took Penny's injured hand. "This will heal up before the end of the night, but the leg will take longer."

Penny watched as the flesh of her hand began to knit itself back together. "What happened?"

"We defeated her, that's what happened," Aiden said.

When Annalysa asked for her leg, Aiden adjusted her in his arms so he could still hold her in his lap, but her legs were stretched out in front of them. Blood still oozed from the wound. Penny bit back some choice words as Annalysa probed at the edges. *Curse Adira and her obsession with damaging my thighs.*

Oh, right.

Adira had stabbed her in the thigh.

And Penny had passed out.

Again.

Annalysa finished by wrapping a thick layer of gauze over the wound. It would take a few days to fully heal, the blade having gone through most of the muscles in Penny's leg.

Tears distorted Penny's vision. By the Goddess, they'd actually made it out. Penny grabbed hold of Aiden's arms around her as she allowed the sobs to wrack her chest. Hart hadn't told her what he knew, and when Aiden had put his hand around her throat, there had been a moment—a single, tiny moment—where Penny hadn't been sure Aiden wouldn't kill her. The relief at being in his arms, having defeated the vile woman that had plagued them for so long brought on a fresh batch of tears.

"By the Goddess," she said, wiping tears from her cheeks, "I really need to stop doing the swooning maiden thing."

Aiden's chest rumbled with soft laughter against her back. "Swooning maiden? My love, you were a warrior goddess out there. You were the one that figured out how to beat her. If you hadn't grabbed her when you had, you would be dead." He tightened his hold on her. "You're a hero, Penelope. You saved all of us."

Between him and Annalysa, the rest of the story unfolded. Adira's fall was the first of many victories. Without the Aigeans to bring in their second wave of attack, the rebels were already falling to the fae. The arrival of Penny's army turned the fighting on two fronts, splitting the rebels' attack and making it easier for the fae on the frontlines to go on the offensive. With Shirina's magic, the rebels were cast into complete darkness. Being in the Night Court, the fae fighting on the mountain were more than happy to dive headfirst into the darkness and bring down the fighters.

"Now do not get too excited," Annalysa said. "We are still fighting a battle on the mountain, but the wind has certainly turned in our direction and it will not be long before news comes of a victory."

"I think it'll come in less than a day," Aiden added, "and all we'll have left is to clean up what rebels are left over. There were a few faces from Adira's camp that I didn't see in the fray, but I'm sure they'll poke their heads out of whatever hole they've hidden in sooner or later."

More tears prickled at Penny's eyelids, and she blinked to keep them back. "We really did it though? It's over?"

Aiden's face split into a wide grin. "Yes, it's over."

Penny wrapped her arms around his neck, the fresh tears falling and landing in Aiden's soft hair under her cheek. "I'm so proud of you," she whispered. She kissed his neck, then his ear. "I knew you could do it. I knew you were stronger than that stupid name."

Aiden's arms wrapped around her middle, and he nestled his face against her neck. "Only because of you, love. I couldn't have done it without you."

Shirina arrived a few hours later.

A team of fae and the newly created soldiers brought her in on a stretcher of tent canvas and rope. Penny pushed Aiden up out of the bed, and he helped settle Shirina in the empty pallet across from them.

"Ah, Little Shadow." The voice did not at all match the strong, noble woman Penny knew.

Penny got to her feet and hobbled to Aiden's side. He wrapped an arm around her waist to steady her as she took in Shirina's emaciated form. All Penny saw was skin, bones, and dark, tired eyes.

"Shirina," Aiden choked out. He settled Penny on a stool at the end of the bed and knelt at Shirina's side. He took her small hand in his. Her fingers looked like brittle branches in his palm.

Shirina hadn't aged since Penny last saw her, but it looked as if every ounce of life and been sucked from her body. All that was left was a tiny husk of the woman that had welcomed Penny into this kingdom, that had fought so hard for Aiden's cause and sacrificed herself for their happiness.

"Do not cry, My Sovereigns," Shirina rasped. "This is a happy thing."

"Not you too," Aiden whispered, blinking back tears. Penny felt her own cheeks grow wet yet again.

Shirina's dark brows furrowed. "Me too?"

A ruckus started at the door, and Dair stumbled in with Farrah leaning on his shoulder. Farrah had a large swath of fabric wrapped around her torso and a swollen eye, but she grinned when she saw her mother headed her way.

Annalysa took Farrah and Dair hurried to his mother's side.

"*Màthair*," he said in a hushed voice.

"My son, my little dreamer." She looked around at them. "Where is Bàsthaen?"

"I—I killed him." Aiden shuddered. "When I was under Durant's sway. He tried"—his words caught, and he cleared his throat—"he tried to stop me. He died protecting me from myself."

Shirina slowly moved her hand over to Aiden's. "It was not your fault."

Annalysa arrived at the edge of the bed, having placed Farrah in a seat a little way's down. "How are you feeling, my lady?"

Shirina smiled. "Like death has finally come for me and I am ready to greet it."

A sob broke from Dair's chest.

"Do not cry, Little Shadow. This is Danu's plan. Once your *athair* left us, I knew it wouldn't be long before I followed after. I am just grateful I was able to do it on my own terms." She looked up at Penny. "Come closer, My Sovereign."

Penny stood, with the help of Aiden and Dair, and moved to sit beside Shirina's thin form on the bed.

Shirina patted her hand. "Listen to me. You have performed miracles in the name of the Goddess and this kingdom. Do not forget it and do not allow the rest of the fair folk to forget it either. I do not expect your coming reign to be easy, but what you have done will create the bridge to earn the folks' trust. Keep them in line. Do not let them push you around and prove to them, as you proved to me, that you have every right to be here as much as they do."

Tears fell onto the bed and Penny gave her a watery smile. "Thank you."

"Now, Aedon." Shirina squinted at him. "You will not allow any regret about what happened during this war to seep into your life. Adira Durant is the one who will pay for the sins committed on that battlefield, not you. You are High King. Do not let fear and guilt cloud your judgement. Believe in what the Goddess has planned for you."

"Please, don't say goodbye," Aiden whispered.

"I wish I could be here for you, but I am not sorry the Goddess is calling me home. Fiadh is waiting for me, and I will not prolong our separation any more than I have to." She turned and looked at Dair. "Now, my son, be a good king."

Dair's eyes snapped to Aiden. "You told her?"

Aiden shook his head. "I didn't say anything."

"He did not need to," Shirina's voice grew fainter. "I know a future king... when I see one. Your *athair* always had the same look about him. Danu has prepared you to take his place. You will do well and... we will be watching over you on the other side."

Penny shifted where she sat next to Shirina on the pallet and looked up at Annalysa. "Has anyone found Prince Thaen's body?"

"His body, My Sovereign?" Annalysa wiped a bead of sweat from her brow. "Well, I suppose the big hunk has been sleeping an awful long time."

"*Sleeping?*" Penny and Aiden parroted.

Annalysa frowned. "Why of course, My Sovereigns. He's just on the other side of that curtain there."

Aiden was on his feet, thrusting aside the curtained off space next to them.

Thaen lay on the pallet, his chest bare and torso wrapped in white linen. His pale eyes were hidden behind closed eyelids, but the rise and fall of his chest told Penny he was most certainly alive.

Aiden tensed, every muscle in his body going rigid. He stood there for a few painful seconds.

"Praise the Goddess," he gasped, falling to his knees beside his cousin's bed. "Her command is actually gone. I don't have to kill him. I don't have to kill any of them."

Penny's eyes welled up again and she smiled. Adira's power over him truly was gone.

Annalysa looked back at Penny. "Did he not know?" she whispered.

Penny shook her head, more tears falling from her cheeks. "No, but it was a very good surprise."

When Mother's domineering form filled the doorway, Penny cried anew.

Mother swept across the room and wrapped her arms around Penny. "By the Goddess, I'm so happy you're alive."

Penny pulled back from her, smiling. Mother brushed the tears from her cheeks and the soft touch made more fall. "I didn't know what would happen to you after I left. I'm so glad you made it here."

It was Mother's turn to fill her in on her side of the story. The rebels had fully been pushed out of Winter, most of them running for the forests of Spring. Hart arrived at the Olympian camp with news of Adira's death and the army's retreat. He had rounded up more of his people to chase after the fleeing rebels. It seemed he'd taken to his new role as guardian of Faerie with fervor. That ambition would be important in the coming days, as they continued to purge Adira's men from their lands. Once they had left, Mother had asked one of the remaining Tree-folk—*maybe*—to bring her to Penny.

Mother looked over Penny's shoulder at where Aiden slept soundly on the pallet. "Is he injured?" she whispered.

Penny shook her head.

"So, you saved him?"

Penny nodded, another round of fresh tears bursting out. "Yes, and he saved me right back."

Mother looked between the two of them. What a sight they must have been to her. The sleeping High King and her daughter, the High Queen, both lying on the same pallet in borrowed clothes, still cleaning blood and ash from their bodies. "I can't tell you how proud I am of you, Penny. You have found a calling that far surpasses anything I could have ever imagined for you."

"Mother," Penny began.

Mother held up a hand. "You don't need to explain. Just know that after watching you these past few weeks, I've come to realize that I raised a smart, capable woman that has made her own choices. I'm only sorry I can't be here to watch you grow into the queen I know you will be."

Penny clasped Mother's hands in hers. "I've thought about what you said, in the forest in Spring. You were right. Without the ability to sprout new plants, it'll take ages to get Eleusion going again. Dion and Shaunie are already worried about feeding the people, when they learn about your broken magic, they'll be devastated."

Mother shrugged. "I don't know how I'll fix it, but I'm sure we'll come up with something."

Penny pulled Mother in closer. "I think I've come up with something that will be good for the both of us."

Shirina's last hours were difficult for everyone.

Penny, Aiden, Dair, Farrah, and now a fully woken Thaen all sat around her bedside, tears streaming down their cheeks.

Shirina slept through most of it, but watching her body shut down was agonizing.

Not a single one of them left the room.

And none of them slept until she finally did too.

71
STRONG

A KNOCK SOUNDED ON THE BEDROOM DOOR. "ARE YOU READY YET?" DAIR asked.

Aiden adjusted the knot on his neckcloth one more time.

Penelope appeared in the mirror behind him and stilled his fingers. "You look wonderful, love. Stop fretting."

Aiden dropped his hands and turned to face her. "*You* look wonderful."

Penelope stepped back and gave a short twirl; the skirt of her sapphire dress flared out, the crystals embroidered in the fabric sparkling in the light coming through the window. "I can't believe the brownies were able to put this together in only three days."

Aiden's heartrate picked up. Stars, she looked like an angel.

They'd returned to the Winter Palace two days after the battle had ended and began to rebuild in the aftermath. The rebels were still in the process of being rounded up, having broken off into smaller groups to try to get back across the border. Hart and his men had made it their duty to make sure not one rebel made it through the freshly grown forest now marking the border between Faerie and Olympia. Those that were caught were kept in the trees along the border, the magic of Faerie's newest folk creating inescapable dungeons in the trunks of the oak trees. The aftermath of the battle had been difficult for everyone. They buried fae for an entire week, and no one had any time to do anything else. Shirina's funeral had been saved for last, and Aiden felt not as if it were an end to a story, but only the very beginning.

Aiden caught Penelope's waist and drew her closer. "You know, when we get back, I would very much like to see you spin in that dress again."

"Oh?" Penelope tried to pull away, but he held her to him. She laughed. "I thought you wanted to watch me spin."

"Love, if you spin again, we won't make it out of this room."

Another knock broke through the room. "Stop flirting with your wife and get out here," Dair said through the door.

Penelope's face flushed a delicious shade of pink, and she pulled away from him.

Aiden groaned and followed her toward the door. Before she could open it, he grabbed the handle. "I will save my flirtatious remarks for later tonight, when we don't have any perturbed cousins eavesdropping."

Penelope stood on tiptoe and planted a kiss on his cheek. "I'm looking forward to it."

Dair made gagging sounds on the other side of the door.

Aiden rolled his eyes and pushed it open.

Dair stood in the hall, black and silver covering him from head to toe. His lavender hair was pulled back in a tight braid and kohl lined his amber eyes. He looked every bit the Faerie King.

"Come on, you two. We do not have all day." Dair strode toward the end of the hall.

"Almost a king and he still plays errand boy," Penelope said, smiling as she curved her fingers over the crook of Aiden's elbow.

"I think it makes him feel needed," Aiden said.

"I heard that."

Aiden stepped out of the portal to the cheers of thousands of voices.

All of Faerie gathered at the base of Crann Mòr. In the days following the battle, the citizens of Crann Mòr had returned to the capital, using their magic to restore the city. The Great Tree's trunk had been cleaned of all soot, and the Green Man himself—who had in fact not perished in the fire—led a team to heal what they could of the base of the burned husk.

Penelope came out of the portal followed by Farrah who closed it behind them. Everyone else that had arrived before them spread out into a line on the small hill they'd portalled to.

Aiden raised his hands, and the cheers quieted.

"Tuatha Dé Dannan, all of Faerie is in the hands of her Goddess's chosen rulers once more."

Cheers erupted, sending heat to the tips of Aiden's ears.

Why everyone insisted he speak was still beyond him.

"We have gathered today to mourn together, to remember the fallen and to bear one another up in the coming days. We have much to be grateful for, but we have loved ones still left to bury and prayers left to be said."

The procession began and Aiden grabbed Penelope's hand as they followed the small group to where the Tuatha were buried. The twins stopped at the still-blackened roots of the Great Tree and approached the freshly dug hole in the ground, Shirina's linen-wrapped body floating on the magic they stretched between them. They laid her to rest atop where they had buried their father.

Sissy walked down the row of attendants, passing out lilies and enchanted snowflakes. As more and more folk passed by, they also dropped flowers into the grave. Not only lilies, but crocus, tulips, and roses filled the grave.

A young fae stopped at the edge of the grave, his palms empty. "I am sorry, My Sovereign," he said to Aiden with wet eyes, "but I do not have anything to offer the queen."

Penelope knelt beside him, not for a moment noticing that her new blue skirt was soaking up the wet earth beneath her. She pressed her hand to the ground and between her fingers sprouted a single white daffodil. She plucked it from the ground and handed it to him.

"Here, now you may offer her something."

With a small smile, the child gently took it from her hand and laid it atop the rest of the blooms covering the grave.

Then more ellyllon children stepped forward to ask Penelope for a token.

Then bwbachod.

Then even ellyllon adults.

Penelope gave each one of them a white daffodil to place on the grave and not a single fae told her what she was doing was blasphemy. In fact, more than a few placed a fist over their hearts and bowed low to her.

When the last had come and gone, Penelope met Aiden's gaze, her eyes filled with unshed tears. *Finally*, they seemed to say. *Finally, they see me.*

Aiden took her hand and helped her stand from the ground. Her skirts were caked with mud and leaves, but her smile shone so brightly it obviously didn't matter. Aiden kissed her hand and pulled her toward the trunk of the tree.

He set a hand on the trunk of Crann Mór, feeling the magic gathered under the ground. He looked out over the crowd, the fae that had come to mourn the loss of their queen, but to also witness the new dawn of their kingdom.

A small nudge formed under his ribcage, and he found Penelope watching him. He pulled away from her as she drew closer to the Tree.

Words settled on the edge of his tongue, and he did not know if they were his or Hers, but he gave them all the same. "Do not allow the hurts of yesterday to weaken the bonds we've created today. There are blessings to be seen in destruction, and I believe Faerie will be all the stronger for them. We will wear our scars with pride and make a new Faerie, one where we all remember the Goddess we serve and always strive to help one another."

The crowd cheered once again; the Night Court mingled in with the Day Court.

Aiden smiled, stepping fully away from the trunk. "But there are some scars that can be healed, some magic strong enough to erase the horrors of yesterday."

The throng quieted as Penelope's hands glowed green and black. Without a word, she closed her eyes and sent her magic into the Tree.

EPILOGUE
THERE AND GONE

SIX MONTHS LATER...

Penny folded a nightdress over her arm before setting it next to the other clothes to go into her pack. The Aunties were supplying her with an enchanted sack, one that would be able to fit her entire wardrobe if she so desired. How she wished she could have had such a thing when she'd been trekking through the Day Court a little over a year ago.

"I cannot believe you are actually leaving." Fee flopped onto her back on the coverlet of the bed. The small brownie barely took up any space on the mattress now piled with clothing and supplies Penny would need to go into Olympia. "I feel like you were finally making some headway with the Spring Court."

Penny's eyebrows lifted. "And how would you know such a thing?"

Fee smirked. "We brownies know everything. Why, just yesterday I heard your name being passed about by the Spring Courtiers after you sent those rebels that tried to light the border on fire running with their tails tucked."

Though it had been a few months, Faerie was still dealing with the aftermath of the war. Fae from Olympia and the Day Court were still missing, some having been taken to the Continent and others likely still trapped somewhere in Olympia. The Autumn and Spring forests were in tatters after the Aigeans traveled through them. The Council was working with the few fae gifted with plant magic to restore what had been lost. Flùranach was completely destroyed and would likely never again reflect the beautiful city it had once been. The Hunt was put in charge of rounding up the rest of the rebels and bringing them to Hart and his men. After creating the new forest at the border, the rebels had been trapped on the Faerie side and rooting them out had become quite a task. Penny had even been roped in to help on a couple occasions.

"I didn't realize everyone knew about that."

Fee blew out a breath, her lips flapping. "It is all everyone has been talking about. You have become the talk of the town."

Penny laughed. "Perhaps, but I'm willing to bet most of the Tuatha still don't want to get too close to the mage they all were jeering at only last year." She grabbed an extra cloak from the hook in the wardrobe, her hand brushing against one of Aiden's jackets. While most of the fae had come to accept her, the noble fae were still dragging their heels. "But that's just fine. Everyone can talk about how much they miss me, and you can report on how many admirers I still have when I get back."

Fee sighed. She opened her mouth to speak when another brownie popped up onto the bed, practically appearing from thin air, and whispered in Fee's ear before vanishing once again.

"Your dryad is on the way," Fee said.

Penny stopped, the cloak in her hand hovering over her pile. "My what?"

A knock sounded on the door, and Fee disappeared as well. Penny set the cloak down and went to open it. Sissy stood on the other side, her arms filled with bags of food and packets of seeds.

"What on Gaia's green earth is all this?" Penny asked, letting Sissy into the room before shutting the door behind her.

"More supplies. The Andàn insisted you take it as a gift to the king and queen," Sissy answered, her voice straining as she lugged the items into the room. She dropped them onto the sofa close to the fireplace and stretched her arms. "I wish I could have inherited a bit more of that fae strength with this new body of mine."

Penny closed the door and came to her side. "Sissy, do you know what a 'dryad' is?"

Sissy tilted her head, her greenish-blonde braid slipping over her shoulder. "I've never heard of such a thing. What is it?"

Penny looked back to the bed where Fee had just been. "I just heard it somewhere. I kind of like the name though." *Dryad.* She'd have to ask Fee about it later.

Sissy shrugged and dove into the pile that only added to the chaos of the rooms. When it wasn't covered in supplies, the royal suite Penny shared with Aiden in Crann Mòr was a dream. Light filtered in through the open windows stretching along one side of the room. Soft, white curtains hung from the top of the four-poster bed. The sitting room was lined with shelves of books lit in the evenings by magelights dangling from the ceiling. They were still working on getting a few more pieces of furniture, but Penny's return at the end of the summer would solve that.

Sissy swept through the sitting room toward the bedroom. "My Sovereign told me to tell you he expects everything to be ready within the hour."

Penny looked out the window and saw the day fading into night. The nights were still long, but the dawn would be there quicker than she wanted.

Her hand caressed the glass where she could see the edge of Lake Truaighe and the tops of the forests in Spring. The view held two of her favorite places, the green of Spring and the familiarity of Winter.

Sissy looked up and stopped at the expression on Penny's face. "What's the matter?"

Penny pulled away from the window. "I thought I would be happy to go back, but now that I'm actually going, I find myself rather torn."

Sissy wove through the furniture and stopped next to Penny. "Well, you are leaving your very handsome and broody king behind. I can imagine you'd feel a bit torn."

Penny smiled at Sissy's description of Aiden as she fiddled with the edge of the curtain hanging to the side of the window. "I feel like I've finally started to find my way here. Now, I have to leave, and I fear this very fragile beginning is going to crumble without me to nurture it."

Sissy set a hand on her arm. "I don't think there's anything to worry about. While I agree you've progressed in even the short time

I've been here to watch, I don't think the Goddess would allow all your work to go to waste."

Penny straightened and turned from the window. "You're absolutely right. The sprouts have already started growing, and I should trust nature to take its course."

"Plant mages." Sissy snorted, grabbing another item off the chair. "Oh, I nearly forgot. There's a package here for you as well. Came in just as I was passing the front door."

In Sissy's hand was a thick, paper-wrapped parcel. Penny took it from her and turned it over, finding a circle of indigo wax stamped into the folds to keep it all together.

"It's from Paulo," she said, breaking the seal.

As she pulled the first page from the package, the door to the room opened and Aiden slipped in. His golden eyes glimmered in the light of the fading sun behind her.

"I guess I'll just slip out for moment," Sissy said, setting down the books she'd been gathering and sneaking out of the room.

Penny set down Paulo's package when Aiden reached her. Even though they'd blocked out as much time as they could to be together for the past week, she still felt like there hadn't been enough.

"Do you have everything packed?" he asked, wrapping his arms around her.

"Nearly." Penny looked over at the giant pile sitting on the bed. "Do you think you'll fit in there with all of the things the Aunties are making me take?"

Aiden chuckled and rubbed his hand up and down her back. "I wish I could go with you."

"But you promise to come get me, right?" Aiden had been adamant about being the first fae she saw when her time in Olympia was up. He would be there, with Farrah, to bring her back to Faerie. "You can't leave me with my mother for too long, or I'll start getting crazy ideas."

"Oh? And what crazy ideas do you think you're going to come back with?"

Penny scrunched her nose. "I don't know, but I'm sure they will be dastardly."

Aiden leaned forward and kissed the tip of her nose. "Don't make that face. I can't resist it."

Penny scrunched her nose again and this time Aiden's kiss found her lips. Penny grabbed the lapels of his dark jacket and pulled him closer. His kiss still shot lightning down her spine and sent tingles all the way to her toes.

He pulled away, kissing her forehead before settling his own against it.

"Can't I just go tomorrow?" she whispered. It wouldn't be such a wait for Mother. Yes, Penny had been putting it off as long as she could, but one more day wouldn't be that much more to ask.

"I'd give you a thousand tomorrows if I thought it would do us any good. But don't worry, I'll be there in the cottonwoods the moment harvest begins."

Penny pulled the collar of his jacket, bringing his lips to meet hers once again. She held him there, praying he felt the love and wonder she felt at having him be hers. She broke from the kiss and opened her eyes to meet his bright, amber gaze. "You better be."

"You know I would keep you here if I thought that was what you truly needed, but I know you, Penelope Barclay." He pressed a gentle, quick kiss to her lips once more. "It's time for you to return home, love."

Penny wrapped her arms around his neck, stretching up on her toes to press her beating heart, the heart that beat only for him, against his chest. She felt his heart answer hers.

"Aiden," she whispered, "I am home."

Penny and Aiden's battle may be won, but there's still one more story
to finish telling.

Turn the page for a sneak peek of
The Fated Mage

PROLOGUE: AN
UNEXPECTED PACKAGE

Paulo pressed his seal gently into the hot wax. The indigo wax curled up around the metal seal, hugging it tightly. Paulo sat back in his chair to wait for it to set, but his eyes didn't move from the small package. He touched his breast pocket where he had carried that weight with him for months.

He'd wanted to send it before they'd even put Laurel's body in the ground. Before she even had the chance to draw her last breath.

But that hadn't been in the lines of Fate.

He'd watched a hundred different packages be stolen, destroyed, lost, and even misplaced. In one of his visions, a cursed dog grabbed it and ran off with it. The Goddess could be awfully callous when She wanted to, and it seemed She wanted Paulo to feel every bit of this pain. To leave the nightmares plaguing his sleep only to keep waking to this one.

The wax set and he pulled the seal away with a *pop*. The twisted lines around the symbol of the sun in the center were slightly crooked, but he didn't care. Penny would know who it was from.

He took the already sealed letter he'd written and set it on top of the palm-sized package. Digging around in his drawer, he found less than three inches of twine. *Curses.* He pushed himself away from his desk and stood, the crumpled-up remains of his previous drafts crinkling under his boots. Jenkins would be a muttering mess when he saw the state of Paulo's room.

Though, maybe not.

The castle had been much quieter of late.

It wasn't the quiet of bated breath or the hush of isolation. No, it was the suffocating silence of heartbreak and mourning. Paulo wasn't the only one who faced every morning with an empty chest. He'd thought he knew what true heartbreak was after Father had died, but this... this devastation had not let up. Paulo understood now why Mater had never relinquished her full mourning black even after so many years. Paulo likely wouldn't give up the color either if this package didn't make it into Penny's hands. If this one last spark of hope was finally put out.

He stepped into his study and found Mater shuffling through some papers. She looked up when he closed the door behind him.

"Were you able to finish?" she asked. She didn't know the chain of events that would begin to roll today, but she knew Paulo harbored that last spark and that was enough for her.

Paulo crouched down next to her, pulling open the bottom drawer of his desk and grabbing a fresh roll of twine. "This is the last thing I need."

Mater ran a hand over his hair. She hadn't done that since he'd been a lad, when she'd actually been able to reach the top of his head. She gave him a whisper of a smile. No more words passed between them. None needed to.

He stood and marched back toward his room. The postman would arrive in two short hours.

By the Goddess, if the border wasn't still closed, he would march all the way to Faerie on his own two feet. But he'd already gone to the border and not even his connection to Faerie's High Queen could gain him access to the magical land. To the place of impossible miracles and second chances.

So, he found a seat at the window in the front parlor and watched the driveway, doing his best to breathe life into that infinitesimal spark sitting where his heart used to be.

AUTHOR'S NOTE

Persephone's abduction by Hades led her to find love, power, and a kingdom to call her own. When I was figuring out Penny's character, I really thought about how Persephone embraced her role in the Underworld. How she not only became a wife but a queen as well. I wanted to emulate this. I wanted to show a character that grew into a role she never expected to be given, but also one that made her into a new creature. One that gave her a new name.

If you look up the etymology of Persephone's name, you're given several interpretations. There were two that really stood out to me: *to bring death* and *she who brings light through.*

I saw Penny in both of these names.

When I started writing this series, I had no idea how Penny and Aiden were going to defeat Adira. Like Aiden, I felt hopeless against her. She was too cunning. Too wily. How was I going to put her down? I'm a major critic when it comes to young adult books where the teenagers outsmart the very mature and wise villain that has an entire army at their disposal. I love the "love can conquer all" idea of it, but love, more often than not, won't stop a bad guy from cutting off someone's head. They're a bad guy for a reason.

But what could Penny and Aiden's marriage, their bond, do that they wouldn't be able to do without it?

It wasn't until I was researching dryads for the fae lore in The Unseen King that I realized what Penny and Aiden would discover.

That it wasn't just love that would get them through to the end but working together to create something new. That when we combined Aiden's gift over the dead and Penny's gift over life, the dryads were born—or rather *re*born.

Now, you might be asking, "What's next? Is this the end of the line for our heroes? What about Dair being king? What about Evan being trapped by the Aigeans? What about Hart becoming the leader of the dryads? What about whatever is going on with Sissy?"

Well, like any good story, it doesn't end on the last page.

Like any good ending, this is only the beginning.

ACKNOWLEDGEMENTS

Holy. Freaking. Cow.

We made it you guys! We've finally reached the conclusion of Penny and Aiden's story. It went by so quickly and there are so many people that I need to thank for it.

First, my family. Eric, you are a freaking superhero. You've jumped, feet first, into this crazy author world with me, and I seriously couldn't be more grateful. I would never have gotten this far without you—I also certainly wouldn't be this exhausted either, but that's not the point. Thank you for coming with me as I've chased this dream and for never letting me give up even when it's been hard.

My kiddos also need my thanks. Girls, I know your mom is seriously crazy. Thank you for being such good kids and for going on so many adventures with me. All of this is as much for you as it is for me.

As always, I need to thank my dad. I would never have sat down to write all of these books if you hadn't told me I could. Thank you for reading every single thing that I write and for always bringing magic into my life. We're magic makers, you and I, and I can't be more glad to have you along for the ride.

Thank you to my publisher, Oliver-Heber Books, to Tanya, and to the team. You guys are all crazy and I am here for it. Thank you for making my dreams a reality. Thank you, Kate Ward, for always reading my books and making them make sense. I love you. Please never leave me. Thank you, Sally O'Keef, for your magic machete. I don't know how you catch so many typos. I'm pretty sure you're some kind of wizard.

Thanks go to Jeff Wheeler for his continued support. None of this would be possible without your kindness. Thank you for being my friend and mentor. I know I have a lot to learn, but I'm so glad I have you in my corner.

A huge truckload of thanks goes to Tyleah Merino—one of the best freaking women on the planet. Thank you for always being my first reader, for reading my stories at their worst and finding the beauty in them. I love you so much and I'm so glad I get to do this with you.

And now for the long list of writers I need to thank. To my OSAWG group: Dad, Robbie of the Beams of Stuffle, David Haynie, Ben Bailey, Tracy Tyler, Aimee Hall, Marci Johnson, and Jared Jensen. I really can't imagine why you all still let me come to the meetings. To my Third Thursday group: Bonnie Jo Pierson, HR Boyd, Amber Marcusen, Kayla Tillotson, KayLynn Flanders, Tarry Perry, Natalie Kraus, Sally O'Keef, Marci Johnson, Lindsay Hiller, and Kelsey Larson. You guys make this job worth it.

I need to thank my audiobook team as well—especially on behalf of my mom who only listens to my books. Thanks to everyone at Podium for taking a chance on my books. Thank you to Caitlin Kelly and Michael David Axtell for bringing Penny and Aiden's voices to life. You guys seriously nailed it.

Thank you, Cauldron Press Designs, for the stunning cover. I can't even count the number of times I've heard the words "Your books are so sparkly!" You seriously nailed it on these covers.

And last, but definitely not least, thanks need to go to the Big Man upstairs. Thank You for telling me I'm supposed to do this and for the miracles you daily bring into my life.

DEDICATION: CHASE AIDEN MANZO

I would like to take a moment to address my dedication at the front of this book.

Chase Aiden Manzo was the nephew of a girl I went to most of my years of school with and we all attended church together. When Disney's *Tangled* came out in 2015, I cut my hair like Rapunzel's at the very end of the movie. Chase and his older brother Trent noticed and asked their family if I was the real Rapunzel. They were no older than eight at the time, so of course their family didn't want to ruin the magic. They all said yes. From then on, I was no longer Alli, their aunt's friend, but Rapunzel, the *real* princess that lived in the house behind the church instead of the tower. I remember anytime I came across Trent and Chase at church or the store or sports games, they would always wave and call out, "Rapunzel!" There was even one Halloween that I convinced a friend of mine to dress up like Flynn Rider and we went to visit the boys. It was probably one of my favorite Halloween memories of all time.

A few years later, Chase was diagnosed with Ewing Sarcoma. For over two years, Chase battled against this terminal disease until it finally took him from his family much too soon. While I had moved away by this time, I watched the community I'd grown up in rally around this sweet boy and his family. It was inspiring to watch videos of him laugh and live his life to the fullest in the short amount of time that he had. He inspired me with his strength of character and his love of his family and community. His loss is still one that weighs heavy on the hearts of so many people, and I don't imagine any of us will ever forget him.

Thank you, Chase, for being such a big piece of this story and for continuing to inspire all of us.

ALSO BY ALLISON ANDERSON

ABOUT THE AUTHOR

Allison Anderson lives her best life as a wife, a mom, a dedicated member of The Church of Jesus Christ of Latter-Day Saints, and a fantasy writer. As a lifelong fantasy nerd, she finds it natural to create stories of her own and you can often find her jotting down new story ideas or talking about dragons. She's spent most of her life across the southwestern United States.

https://www.allisonandersonauthor.com/